John Case is the pseudonym of an award-winning investigative reporter and the author of two non-fiction books about the US intelligence community. He is also the best-selling author of *The Genesis Code*. He is a resident of Washington, D.C.

Praise for *The First Horseman*

'Superchilling tale . . . Mind-blowing Arctic amazement and an unholy crew of fanatics combine lethally to destroy the reader's sleep . . . Far more realistic than Stephen King's superflu in *The Stand.*' *Kirkus*

'Gripping . . .[A] tense thriller . . . Case breathes excitement into his topical story.' *Publishers Weekly*

'An excellent thriller' *Chicago Tribune*

Praise for *The Genesis Code*

'*The Genesis Code* rattles you to the bone . . . I woke up at three in the morning wondering: What if . . . ?' Stanley Pottinger, author of *The Fourth Procedure*

'Impeccable in plot, immaculate in story resolution, moves with high skill from locale to locale and from suspense to suspense' Norman Mailer

'A sizzling thriller . . . Well-written and extremely gripping' *Daily Mail*

'*The Genesis Code* cracks along . . . more than enough murder, mayhem, and scientific mystery to keep the reader entertained' *Sunday Telegraph*

THE
FIRST HORSEMAN

John Case

ARROW

Published in the United Kingdom in 1999 by
Arrow Books

3 5 7 9 10 8 6 4 2

Copyright © John Case, 1998

The right of John Case to be identified as the author of this
work has been asserted by him in accordance with the
Copyright, Designs and Patents Act, 1988

First published in the United Kingdom in 1998 by Century

Arrow Books Limited
Random House UK Limited
20 Vauxhall Bridge Road, London SW1V 2SA

Random House New Zealand Limited
18 Poland Road, Glenfield, Auckland 10, New Zealand

Random House South Africa (Pty) Limited
Endulini, 5a Jubilee Road, Parktown 2193, South Africa

Random House UK Limited Reg. No. 954009

A CIP catalogue record for this book is available from the
British Library

Papers used by Random House UK Limited are natural,
recyclable products made from wood grown in sustainable
forests. The manufacturing processes conform to the
environmental regulations of the country of origin

ISBN 0 09 918402 8

Typeset by SX Composing DTP, Rayleigh, Essex
Printed and bound in Germany by Elsnerdruck, Berlin

PLEDGE OF THE GERMAN GUNNERS

'. . . and most of all, they shall not construct any poisoned globes, nor other sorts of pyrobolic inventions, in which he shall introduce no poison whatsoever, besides which, they shall never employ them for the ruin and destruction of men, because the first inventors of our art thought such actions as unjust among themselves as unworthy of a man of heart and a real soldier.'

From: Siemienowicz, C., *Grand Art d'Artillerie* (1650),
as quoted by Appfel, J.
'Les projectiles toxiques en 1650,'
March 1929, p. 234.

THE
FIRST HORSEMAN

PROLOGUE

THE HUDSON VALLEY
NOVEMBER 11, 1997

Tommy was nervous. Susannah could tell, because she knew he liked to talk, and yet, he hadn't said a word for fifty miles. Not that she could blame him. She was nervous, too. And excited. And scared.

It was dusk when they got off the Taconic Parkway, switching on the headlights as they traveled through rolling farmland, a Ralph Lauren landscape where the houses were so perfect, you just knew they were owned by doctors and lawyers. They were 'mini-estates,' or enclaves with names like 'Foxfield Meadows,' and they didn't really grow anything except, maybe, sun-dried tomatoes and arugula.

As they passed the Omega Institute, Susannah wondered aloud – what's *that?* And the driver, Tommy, made a sound like a duck – *kwak-kwak-kwak!* So both of them laughed (a little too loud), and Susannah thought, Some kind of New Age thingie.

The thing was – what made her nervous was: the whole deal about the teeth, about *pulling out* the teeth. No matter how you looked at it, pulling out the teeth was creepy. It was like Nuremberg or something. So if they got caught, it wouldn't just be murder, it would be . . . what? Charles Manson, or something.

Not that she'd be the one to do it – she couldn't hurt

a fly. That was Vaughn's job, the teeth and the fingers. And giving the injections. He had to do that, too, because he was the doctor. (And a good one, Tommy said. 'Vaughn's an "Old Blue," aren't ya, Vaughn?' Whatever that was.)

Still, you had to wonder why it was necessary to do the teeth. And the fingers. Why not just . . . *dump* them? Or, better yet, leave 'em where they lay.

Susannah thought about it for a while, then shrugged to herself. Solange moves in strange ways, she thought, smiling at the in-joke. Sometimes he did things just to be theatrical. Make a splash. Shake 'em up.

Not that it made any difference. They weren't going to get caught. Everything had been rehearsed, from the knock on the door to the handcuffs, and there wasn't anything they hadn't thought through.

Like the U-Haul. The U-Haul was Solange's idea, and it was brilliant because, once they'd fixed it up, it gave Vaughn a sort of operating room in the back. So he could do what he had to do even while they were driving away.

And it was inconspicuous, too. Because U-Hauls were everywhere. There wasn't anywhere in America they didn't belong. Not even *here*. Everybody used them,

Her job was to get inside the house and, once there, make sure the Bergmans couldn't get to their gun. So it was two jobs, really, and what made everyone think she could bring it off was the fact – she wasn't bragging, really, it was just a fact of life – the fact that she was 'cute.' Cheerleader cute. And pregnant. Which made her kind of vulnerable-looking.

And that made people trust her. Which was important. Because the Bergmans were totally paranoid – like someone was out to kill them. Susannah smiled at the thought. Talk about irony – *hello*?

But mostly it was scary and horrible, and she wished that she wasn't a part of it, except: it had to be done. She knew it had to be done because Solange said so, and Solange never lied. Ever.

And it wasn't going to be painful. Vaughn said they wouldn't feel a thing. Just 'a bee sting' from the needle. And that would be that.

Unless, of course, something went wrong. Like, if they had a Doberman or something. But, no: they didn't have a dog, because if they did, Lenny would have mentioned it. Lenny was their son, and if there was a Doberman walking around, he'd have told them about it,

Like Marty did with the gun. Not that Marty was related to them, but he was close. He'd said, *I don't think the old fuck knows how to use it, but he's got a .38 Special that he keeps in the vestibule – in a little table, just under the telephone. I used to kid him about being 'strapped,' and he'd say, 'What are you talking about, what strap? I don't see any strap.' And the thing is, he wasn't kidding. I mean, like this guy is livin' in another century.*

Even so . . . what if the needle broke off, or the woman started screaming? Everything would go real bad, fast. Like with Riff – when she was a kid, and the car hit him. And her father tried to put him down with the .22, but he was so nervous, he couldn't find the heart. So . . . he just kept shooting.

If that happened, or something like that, there'd be blood all over the place – and all over *them*. And the thing is, *legally*, what they were doing was murder. Which, for someone who'd been brought up Catholic, even if she didn't *practice* anymore, was about as bad as it gets.

3

Because killing was wrong. She knew that. No ifs, ands, or buts. Killing someone was dead wrong –

Unless . . .

Unless you were a soldier. And that's exactly what they were – she and Tommy and Vaughn, and the French guy in the back of the truck. They were soldiers. Knights, even. Just like in the Crusades.

Susannah was thinking about the Secret War, Solange's war, *her* war, when the turn signal began to click, and the truck turned down a two-lane country road, scattering a clutch of deer that were feeding on the verge.

A battered U-Haul with Arizona tags, the truck trembled and shook as it rattled over the washboarded lane, slowing down at every letter box, then speeding up, then slowing down again as the driver hunted for the right address. Finally, the truck came to a stop beside a rusting mailbox:

BERGMAN

For a long moment Tommy stared at the silvery, stick-on letters, muttering to himself. Then he killed the headlights, backed up, shifted into Drive and, holding his breath, entered the long driveway.

Susannah squirmed in her seat and took a deep breath. Exhaling, she made a sort of stuttering sound, then wet her lips with her tongue.

The truck crunched slowly over the gravel toward the front porch of a white farmhouse. There, beneath a bower of old walnut trees, Tommy killed the engine, the passenger door opened, and Susannah climbed out.

She was, as anyone could see, pretty, young, and pregnant, with huge brown eyes and ash-blond hair.

4

She wore a yellow sun dress under a tattered, gray cardigan that was much too big, and which might well have been her father's. With a *Here goes* glance at the driver, she took a deep breath and mounted the steps to the porch, glancing at the pots of mums on either side.

Reaching the top of the steps, she hesitated, suddenly queasy and weak. For a long moment she swayed in front of the door. Finally, she knocked – ever so softly, secretly hoping that no one was home.

There was no answer at first, but she could hear the television inside, and so she knocked again. Louder this time. And then again, almost banging on the screen door,

Eventually, the inner door swung open, and a woman in her fifties peered out from behind the latched screen door. 'Hello?' She pronounced the word as if it were a question.

'Hi!' Susannah said, looking sheepish and beautiful.

Martha Bergman's eyes took in the pregnancy, then drifted to the U-Haul, where a wiry young man (the girl's husband, she supposed) gave a little wave. The side of the truck was painted with the image of a senorita, a Spanish lady peering coyly over the top of her fan. U-Haul liked to do that, painting the trucks with scenes that suggested where they were from: cowboys and lobsters and skyscrapers. Martha figured that this truck must be from New Mexico, or someplace in the Southwest.

'Can I help you?' Martha asked.

'I hope so,' Susannah replied, shifting her weight from one foot to the other. 'We're really lost.'

Martha's face softened. 'Where are you looking for?'

The girl shook her head and shrugged. 'That's the

problem. We lost the number. But I know it's one of these houses – one of the houses on Boice Road.'

Martha winced. 'It's a long road, dear.'

'I was hoping – if I could use your phone . . . I could call my brother. He's at the house now.'

Martha's face settled into a frown. Then her eyes fell to Susannah's stomach and, suddenly reassured, she smiled, unhooked the latch to the screen door, and held it open. 'Of course,' she said. 'Come on in. The telephone's over there, on the little table.'

'That's *so* nice of you,' Susannah said as she stepped into the vestibule. 'And, wow – what a beautiful house!' In fact, it was a lot like her parents' house, with fake Bokharas on the hardwood floors and over-stuffed furniture from the Pottery Barn.

From the next room a man's voice boomed out above the noise of the television. 'Martha! What are you doing? You're *missing* it!'

'I'll be right there.'

'Who are you talking to?' the man asked.

'I'm letting a young woman use the phone,' Martha answered, and, turning to Susannah, sighed hugely. 'The Jets are playing,' she explained.

Susannah smiled knowingly and shook her head, as if to say, *Men!* – then crossed the room to the table where the phone was. 'I'll just be a second,' she said, and picked up the receiver. Turning away from the older woman, she dialed the cell phone in the back of the truck and waited. There was a ticking noise for several seconds, a warbling sound, and –

Cliiick! Yeah. It was Vaughn.

'Hiiii!' Susannah gushed, emoting for Mrs. Bergman's benefit.

You're inside?

'Yup!' And then, just as they rehearsed, she

6

launched into a spiel about how she was just around the corner, or thought she was, but they'd lost the number to the new house – and what was it, anyway?

What about the gun?

Susannah threw a smile over her shoulder as she talked and, almost idly, cracked open the drawer to the end table. Seeing the .38, she said, 'Got it! No problem.'

You're sure?

'Absolutely.'

Be right in.

She kept talking for a few seconds after Vaughn hung up, then replaced the receiver in its cradle, turned and leaned against the end table.

'Well, that was easy,' Mrs. Bergman remarked, though she felt a bit awkward that the girl remained where she was, standing in front of the telephone. 'Which house is it?' she asked.

Susannah shrugged and, turning, opened the drawer and removed the .38. Seeing the older woman's reaction, she put the gun behind her back and smiled. 'It's going to be okay,' she said. 'Really.' She was thinking about Solange, and what he'd told them the night before: *Try not to scare them too much. There's no point in starting a panic. Not yet, anyway.*

It was then that Harry Bergman came in, scowling, a glass of wine in one hand and a newspaper in the other. A pair of reading glasses hung from his neck by a black cord. 'There's *a truck* in the yard,' he announced, as if it were the most astonishing thing in the world. And then, double-taking on Susannah, 'Hello?'

'That's just us,' Susannah mumbled.

Harry looked from the girl to his wife and back again. 'What's going on?' he asked, tensing at the look

7

on his wife's face. No one said anything for a moment, and then a screech tore through the yard-like nails on a blackboard, followed by a crash of metal.

Martha jumped.

'What the hell –' Harry said,

'That's just the truck,' Susannah replied, trying to be reassuring. 'It's just the back door going up. It needs grease or something.'

'Right,' Harry said and, pivoting, took a step toward the little table next to Susannah.

'Uh-uh,' she muttered, and waved the Browning at him. 'Better not.'

Harry didn't quite freeze – he more or less *subsided* into himself, and as he did, his wife stepped in front of him. 'Just leave him alone. He's not –'

'Martha –' Harry protested.

'Take whatever you want.'

'Well, thanks,' Susannah said, 'but . . . that's not the point.'

The Bergmans gave her a blank look, and she could have kicked herself. But then the screen door opened and Vaughn came in, carrying a sawed-off shotgun as if it were a briefcase – never pointing it, never needing to. The French dude was right behind him with a set of plastic restraints, the kind the police use when they're making lots of arrests at the same time. Tommy was on the porch outside, keeping watch.

'Okay, everybody listen up,' Vaughn said. 'You do what we tell you, we'll be out of your hair in ten minutes. That's a promise, okay?'

Harry Bergman put his arm around his wife and nodded, not so much because he agreed, but because he was too frightened to say anything.

Then the guy with the cuffs stepped behind them, and with an improbable *S'il vous plaît,* gently removed

Harry's arm from his wife's shoulders. Bringing the older man's arms behind his back, the Frenchman looped the plastic cord around Harry's wrists and pulled it tight. This done, he turned to the woman and did the same.

'Great,' Vaughn said, and turned to Susannah. 'You know what to do, right?'

Susannah nodded – quick little jerks of her head – and watched as the Bergmans were led outside. As they went through the door she heard Vaughn say, 'By the way, I spoke to your son the other day. He sends his love.'

You could hear them gasp.

Then the screen door slammed and Mr. Bergman's voice was in the air, scared and growling, like a small dog protecting his patch from a rottweiler: 'What is this? Where are you taking us?' And Vaughn's voice, laid-back and matter-of-fact: 'We're just going to the truck. . . .'

Well, yeah, Susannah thought and, with a shudder, took a handkerchief from her pocket and wiped the .38 clean. Then she put the gun back in the drawer and erased her fingerprints from the wood and the phone. What else? She was supposed to turn off the TV, and the lights, too, and close the front door behind her. It was supposed to look like they just –

Suddenly, the air was split by a frightened, almost feral bark, a prehistoric gasp of unadulterated terror. Hearing it, the night fell silent and Susannah, shaken, found herself running from the house, pulled by the sheer, centripetal force of someone else's fear.

As she came off the porch, she saw Tommy. He was coming around from the back of the truck, walking fast, head down, mouth open, blinking wildly. 'What happened?'

Tommy just shook his head and got behind the wheel. 'Don't go back there,' he said.

But how could she not?

Turning the corner, she saw the man – Mr. Bergman – on the ground, his body trembling as if it were in the grip of an unseen and powerful amperage. A few feet away the woman was on her stomach in the driveway, pinioned by the Frenchman, who had his hand on the back of her neck and his knee in the small of her back. For a second Susannah's eyes locked with the woman's, and it seemed as if the night shivered in the space between them. Then Vaughn stepped over the husband's still twitching body and, squatting beside the wife, administered an injection to the back of her shoulder, piercing the thin cotton dress that she wore.

Immediately, the woman's eyes widened, rolled, and went white. The connection between her and Susannah, a duplex of hatred and pity, was shattered as 10 cc of pharmaceutical morphine slammed into her heart. She stiffened for a long moment, then just as suddenly softened. Finally, the tension drained from her body and she was dead.

It took a moment for Susannah to realize that she'd been holding her breath forever. Letting it out, she felt a need to explain why she was standing there. 'I heard a sound,' she said.

Vaughn got to his feet and nodded. 'That was the guy. The guy freaked when he saw the needle.'

The Frenchman climbed into the back of the truck, where a pair of 55-gallon drums waited beside a white metal table. The floor was covered with sheets of black polyethylene. A string of lights hung from the ceiling, and the Frenchman switched them on. Then he jumped back down to the ground and shook his head. 'No,' he said. 'It wasn't the needle. It was the truck. He saw the

10

plastic, and it scared him.'

Vaughn shrugged. 'Whatever. Help me get her in the back.'

The Frenchman took the woman's body by the arms, while Vaughn took hold of her feet. As they lifted her, Vaughn glanced at Susannah. 'You saw the light go out, right?'

Susannah looked puzzled. 'What light?'

'The light in her eyes,' Vaughn said. 'You were looking at each other when it hit her.'

Susannah nodded slowly. Yeah, she'd seen it. The eyes went . . . *slack*. The two men heaved the woman's body into the back of the truck.

Turning to Susannah, Vaughn threw her a sympathetic look. 'I could tell,' he said. 'I could see it in your face.'

'See what?' Susannah asked.

'The way you reacted. It was like . . .' His voice trailed off.

'*What?*' Susannah asked, almost as if Vaughn were flirting with her.

Vaughn thought for a moment, shook his head, and laughed. 'It was . . . complicated,' he said. 'It was *way* complicated.' Then, stooping, he seized the dead man by the arms and pulled him toward the truck.

Susannah couldn't believe it – the way the feet made little furrows in the ground, so perfectly parallel they seemed, almost, like lines on a page.

11

I

THE DIAMOND MOUNTAINS
JANUARY 26, 1998

At first he didn't hear it. The noise was a long way off
and hundreds of meters below, a distant growl gusting
on the wind. Trudging slowly up the hillside, Kang
kept his head down, ignoring both the wind's moan
and the sound that it carried in its jaws.

The cold made him clumsy. Twice he'd slipped on
the ice, and twice he'd broken the fall with his hands,
plunging his fingers into the crusted snow. With the
holes in his gloves, it was like grabbing broken glass.

Even so, he'd surprised himself by coming as far as
he had – and in the dead of winter. He was, after all, a
cripple. But tough. *Korean* tough. And though others
had come this way before – he'd climbed through a
ghost forest in which a thousand pines had been
reduced to stumps – they'd had two good legs to carry
them.

While he had only one.

Most of the trees had been cut years ago, for
firewood. But as he climbed higher, Kang saw pines
that had been flayed alive, the bark stripped from their
trunks for food. Or what passed for food in the famine
years.

The soft wood, just beneath the bark, filled the
stomach. And while it was barely digestible, it was

pleasant to chew. It took away the hunger pains – at least for a while – and the bark itself could be used to make a weak tea.

Still, taking the bark killed the trees, and wounded the land.

It was the women, mostly, who climbed the hills to look for wild grasses, bark, and firewood. Until the sickness had taken her, as it had taken so many others, Kang's wife had climbed this very hill, armed with the same folding saw that he now carried, and the same length of rope.

It was she who'd told him to go in this direction. And though the way was impossibly steep, he'd kept his promise and done as she'd suggested. Since her death, he'd made the trek a dozen times, trading the wood that he'd gathered for herbs, rice, and a pair of old boots. By now he knew the hills above Tasi-ko as well as he knew the cracks in the ceiling above his bed.

He paused for a moment to catch his breath, and gazed at the uphill terrain, calculating the most efficient way over the rocks, deciding ahead of time where to set each foot. This was more complicated than it might otherwise have been because one of his legs was made of wood below the knee and was insensitive to differences in footing.

An open area stretched ahead of him, and he picked his way carefully across the snowfield, wary of crevasses. Finally, he crested a ridge and came upon the place that he was looking for, a grove of sturdy pines, bristling with green needles above the snow.

As always happened when he came here, his wife's face flashed before him and his eyes brimmed with tears. Then he lurched toward the wood and, finding a sapling, broke a twig from its trunk and sucked at the resin. As he did, he glanced around for a suitable tree,

13

one that he could cut with his saw and drag to the village.

And that's when he heard it, heard it for the first time in the silence of the pines: riding on the back of the wind was a separate and distinct noise, a mechanical whine that he recognized in an instant.

It was the sound of deliverance, the clamor of rescue.

Hobbling back to the ridge, Kang squinted down the hillside to the road, where a convoy of trucks rolled toward Tasi-ko, miniaturized by distance.

All in all there were six troop transports, a jeep, and a couple of flatbed trailers with orange bulldozers strapped to their backs. Watching them, as Kang did, it was possible to trace the path that the convoy had taken, winding its way through the valley. The chained tires, chewing into the snow and ice, churned up the earth so that it seemed, almost, as if the trucks had drawn a line across the jagged contours of the land.

For the first time in weeks the corners of his mouth lifted and Kang smiled. With a grunt of relief he sat down heavily in the snow and, using a small tool he carried for the purpose, adjusted the screws in his artificial leg. Things would be better now.

Not that they could have gotten worse. This was the most monstrous winter in anyone's memory, a season of paralyzing cold in which hunger had turned into famine, and famine to plague. Even now, thirty-one people – a fourth of the village – lay on the floor of the factory, their bodies stacked like cordwood. (This building, shaped like a coffin and made of cement, was a place where brooms – *good* brooms – had been made for more than twenty years. Now, Kang thought, the building was as dead as its inhabitants. Without fuel, the lathes had fallen silent even as the air grew still and cold.)

Daunting from the outside, the building's interior was terrifying – a makeshift morgue paved with the cadavers of men, women, and children whose blistered limbs had turned a startling blue in the days before their deaths. As the only medical worker in Tasi-ko, it had been Kang's responsibility to carry the bodies to where they now lay, awaiting burial in the spring.

Until he'd seen the trucks winding toward the village, Kang had begun to doubt that, by spring, anyone would be left to bury the dead. And if by chance someone was, it seemed unlikely that it would be him or, if it was, that he'd have the strength to wield a pick and shovel.

Now he felt ashamed, ashamed of the bitterness in his thoughts. At some point, perhaps when his wife had died, he'd surrendered to pessimism. He'd begun to think that the suffering in Tasi-ko had gone unnoticed, or that it was being ignored because the village was remote and insignificant. These were subversive thoughts, as Kang well knew. If shared, they might weaken the resistance of all citizens. And they were wrong, as well as subversive. Clearly, the life of a farmer in Tasi-ko was worth as much as that of an engineer in Pyongyang. The proof was there, on the road below. It had simply been a question of time, and the allocation of scarce resources.

The army's presence was a rebuke to his negative thinking. The trucks would have food and medicine in them – and doctors, *real* doctors, not medical workers like himself. These were people who had gone to the university in Pyongyang. They'd know what to do.

Whereas he could do nothing. In less than a month he'd seen the village decimated by an illness whose symptoms were so violent and strange that, on hearing of them, a doctor had been sent to Tasi-ko from the Institute for Infectious Diseases in the capital.

The doctor had been very short and very old – a compact little nut of a man with large, yellow incisors. He chain-smoked imported cigarettes and talked in short bursts, punctuated by long silences. Kang knew that to smoke so much, the man must be important. But even so, Kang didn't like him.

In the end the doctor examined a dozen patients, four of whom had since died. He made notes of their symptoms and questioned Kang about the progress of the disease. He took blood samples from four of the villagers, and arranged for two of the dead to be wrapped in sheets and taken to the capital for autopsies.

As the doctor was leaving, Kang asked what he should do in his absence, but the old man didn't answer him. He lit another cigarette and, leaning out the window of his car, pointed toward the building where the dead were kept. 'All this,' he said, 'Spanish Lady. Spanish Lady did this!'

Though it wasn't Kang's place to contradict a senior physician from Pyongyang, he couldn't help himself. As the car began to pull away he jogged beside it. 'But, Doctor – this is not correct! We haven't had any visitors. No foreigners –' Suddenly, the car began to pull away, and Kang shouted out: 'What can I do?'

The old man turned in his seat for a last look, and shook his head, leaving Kang in the road, thinking he was mad.

But that didn't matter now. The old man was back. He'd come with medicine – and bulldozers to bury the dead.

Kang knew that he should hurry down the hill to

help the soldiers. But the cold made him hesitate. Whatever cures the army might bring, whatever food they might bring, firewood was nearly impossible to come by, and it would be a waste to have climbed so far, in such cold, only to return empty-handed.

Leaving the ridge for the wooded hillside a hundred yards away, he pounced on a small tree and, kneeling in the snow, sawed furiously at its trunk with his little folding saw. The pitch was sticky and gummed the teeth of the blade, but in the end the tree keeled over, and Kang scrambled to his feet. Knotting his rope around the branches at the base of the pine, he turned and hurried back up to the ridge, dragging the tree behind him on its leash.

At the crest of the ridge he stopped to catch his breath, and what he saw puzzled him. About a kilometer south of town half of the convoy – three trucks and a flatbed – pulled to a halt in the middle of the road and waited. Meanwhile, the other trucks continued on their way, rumbling into and ... *through* the village.

Except for the jeep. The jeep pulled into the little square that, in better days, had served as a marketplace for local farmers. Idling in the cold, it drew the villagers like iron filings to a magnet, though Kang knew what the real attraction was: the promise of medicine, food, and news.

He started moving again, but then he hesitated. The convoy south of town had not moved. Its trucks sat in the middle of the road, their engines stilled, while soldiers stood around, smoking cigarettes and slinging their Kalashnikovs.

And there, to the north, the scene was being repeated. The second half of the convoy rolled to a stop about a kilometer past Tasi-ko. Soldiers jumped from the backs of the trucks, then stood and waited.

It was a disquieting sight, even from so far above. The village was being quarantined. And though it disturbed Kang to see Tasi-ko isolated in this way, he began to see the wisdom of it. Whatever the pestilence might be, it would have to be contained. Betrayed by China, battered by floods, and beset by famine, his country would be hard put to withstand yet another disaster.

Once again he was thinking dangerously, seditiously. But what he thought was the truth. And a second truth was that he was very tired and, being tired, he lacked the energy to 'weed the garden of his mind.'

This was the metaphor that Kang had been taught in the army, when he'd served for six years as a medical officer in a reconnaissance unit at the DMZ. Some thoughts were flowers; others were weeds. Still others were vipers. Constant vigilance was needed to correctly identify each.

But 'constant vigilance' required more energy than Kang could spare. Over the years, he'd lost too much – his leg to a land mine, his wife to sickness. For the past week he'd eaten little more than wild grass, and now – now, his mind was anything but a garden. It was a ruin, and he just didn't care. What more could the world do to him?

Suddenly, an electric bullhorn crackled and whined in the square. Kang strained to hear what was being said, but as the words floated up the hillside, they softened in a way that made them impossible to understand. But he could see their effect: repelled now, the people withdrew from the jeep and, one by one, disappeared into their homes. Before long the village – a cluster of decrepit wooden houses surrounded by fallow fields and an abandoned factory – looked eerily empty. Only then did the jeep pull away from the marketplace, trailing a plume of white exhaust as it rolled north to rendezvous at the second roadblock.

First a quarantine, Kang thought, and now a curfew. But in the middle of the day? Why? And what about the doctors? Where were they? Kang's face, impassive for so long, crumpled into a frown. What he was seeing did not make sense, and his instincts told him to be wary. And though it seemed unlikely that anyone would notice him from so far below, he removed the red muffler that his wife had made with the yarn from an unraveled sweater. He tucked the muffler inside his jacket and sat down on the tree that he'd been dragging. Then he snapped a twig from one of its branches and began to chew it as he watched the road.

Over the course of the next hour nothing much happened. Except for soldiers and the barricades, the Pyongyang road remained empty. Too empty. Never busy, it was now entirely deserted. Not a single car, truck, or pedestrian arrived at either barricade. Which could only mean there were other barricades, farther from town, and that the ones he saw served a purpose far different than he'd imagined. They weren't there to keep the traffic *out*. They were there to keep the people *in*.

Kang's heart wobbled in his chest.

And then, abruptly, there was movement. As if on cue, soldiers at both ends of the village scrambled to the side of the road, where they hunkered down in ditches. Kang didn't know what to make of it – even when he saw the plane, coming over the mountains.

Like every other plane he'd ever seen, this was a military aircraft. Its aluminum skin was a dull brown

19

that seemed, almost, to absorb the sunlight. Kang watched the plane as it drew closer to Tasi-ko, its engines rumbling in the frigid air. Suddenly, a piece of the fuselage detached and fell, tumbling, toward the village. Kang didn't believe what he was seeing. The plane banked to the east, leveled out, and accelerated toward the horizon as Kang, unthinking, jumped to his feet.

He opened his mouth to shout or to scream – at the plane, at the village, at the soldiers – but it was too late. The world *pulsed*. There was a flash of light, and a low *whummmmp* that sucked the air out of the sky. For an instant Kang saw an incinerating wave of light roll outward in every direction from Tasi-ko. Then a tidal wave of heat smashed against the ridge, bowling him over. He gasped to breathe, gasped again, then panicked with the realization that there was no *air* in the air – only heat, and the smell of burning hair,

They're killing everyone, he thought. Frantic, he slipped on the ice and landed hard, flat on his back. A shower of light went off behind his eyes and something cracked, deep inside his head. Kang's vision shuddered and the last thing he saw, before his senses shut down, was Tasi-ko, shuddering in a sea of flames.

When he woke, it was dark, and the air was sharp with the smell of smoke. His face felt as if the skin had been peeled from his cheeks, and the back of his head was pounding as rhythmically as a drum. With the fingers of his right hand he touched the place where the pain was, just behind his ear, and instantly drew back, shocked by the lump that was bleeding there. For a moment his stomach swayed, and it seemed as if his chest was about to turn inside out. But nothing happened.

Machines growled in the distance, off to the left and far below.

Below. Where was he?

Slowly, Kang sat up and looked around. He was on a ridge, just like the one above Tasi-ko. The ground was slick with ice, and here and there tree stumps poked from the snow. Turning toward the noise, he saw bulldozers moving back and forth across a field of rubble, lit by the headlamps of half a dozen trucks.

He was on an overlook, above a construction site. But how had he gotten there? He'd been gathering wood and . . . The pain in his head made it impossible to think. A stream of broken images meandered around the inside of his skull: a brown plane; a jeep; his wife's face-fire.

He needed a doctor, and instinctively he called out to the men below. But, of course, they couldn't hear him. Struggling to his feet, he made his way down the hillside, calling out against the bulldozers' rumbling noise. A spray of small stones and rocks preceded him in a little avalanche and, as he drew closer, he saw for the first time that the construction crew consisted entirely of soldiers, and that the soldiers were wearing gas masks.

Strange.

He was halfway down the ridge when one of the soldiers saw him and began to shout. Relieved, Kang paused to catch his breath and, standing amid a clutch of boulders, waved and shouted back. Then a peculiar thing happened. The soldier raised his Kalashnikov to his chest and began to fire in the disciplined way that soldiers do, peppering the air between them with short bursts of gunfire that sounded, almost, like the telegraphic code that ships use at sea.

And as that happened, the moment expanded.

Suddenly, Kang knew where he was – which was just where he seemed to be: on the ridge above Tasi-ko. And then he remembered:

they're killing everyone.

The boulder beside him was spitting stones as 9mm slugs slapped into it. Even so, Kang didn't move. His eyes were in the distance, ignoring the soldiers as they ran toward him, staring instead at the cratered wasteland that lay, smoking, in the headlights of the trucks. Tasi-ko was gone.

The realization frightened him even more than the guns, frightened him in a way that he had never felt before. Because this was a fear that had no point of origin or focus. It came from within and without at the same time. It was terror, pure and oceanic, and it radiated from him like heat from a fire.

Jolted, Kang turned and began to run, scrambling up the hillside from rock to rock, moving from one shadow to another. Behind him, his pursuers gave ground as they moved deeper into the cold, dark, and unfamiliar hills, swinging their flashlights in great, useless arcs. Soon it was obvious that they had no idea which way he'd gone and that, in fact, they were beginning to worry about their own whereabouts.

Still, Kang kept moving. Far from feeling the usual clumsiness of his wooden leg, he covered the ground with immaculate economy, invisible as a shadow in the night. And though his lungs were on fire and his quadriceps were drained, he moved higher and higher into the mountains until the soldiers' voices dwindled to nothing and the bulldozers fell silent.

After four or five hours in the freezing cold, his shirt was soaked with sweat and his stump was a bloody mess. His fingers were frozen, his skull was fractured, and his face was a blister. The parts of him that didn't hurt were dead. It was as simple as that.

But he kept on moving, and eventually he found a sort of track that led downhill. Following it, he emerged from the mountains just as the night grayed toward dawn. Finding himself beside the Victory Road, he followed the highway without thinking or caring where it went. The truth was: he had nowhere to go and, clearly, he was dying. The likelihood was that whatever energy he had left would soon disappear. He'd sit down for a rest, and that would be that. If he was lucky, there would be a tree, and he could lean back against it . . . close his eyes . . . and just let go.

He looked forward to dying that way, like an old monk, dreaming the world. Indeed, the image lifted his spirits and, as he walked beside the road, he kept his eyes open for the perfect tree. The death-tree. *His* tree.

But it was nowhere to be found. Morning molted into afternoon, the air warmed and, step by step, the day dissolved into evening. Night fell, the temperature dropped, and still Kang kept walking.

So it went for a second day, and then a third. Instinctively, and without thinking, Kang trudged toward the one place he knew as well as the environs of Tasi-ko. This was Korea's Demilitarized Zone. A closely watched no-man's-land that runs for more than a hundred miles, stretching from the Yellow Sea to the Sea of Japan, the DMZ was at once a nature preserve and a killing floor. Honeycombed with tunnels and bristling with land mines, it was a ribbon of green in a sea of mud and ice – tranquil, forested, and dangerous. Gateway to the Vampire South.

Perhaps he would find his tree there.

FLASH

TEXT OF TELEGRAM 98 SEOUL 008070
SECRET
INFO CIAE-04 DODE-01 INR-02
PAGE 01
FROM AMERICAN EMBASSY SEOUL
TO CIA LANGLEYVA IMMEDIATE 8030
DIA WASHDC PRIORITY
TAGS: PINS, CHIEF, N.ASIA/ROK
SUBJ: (K) DEFECTION – KANG YONG-PU
REF: SEOUL
1. SECRET ENTIRE TEXT.
2. ROK ANSP REPORTS US/ROK FORCES DETAINED
DPRK-CIT KANG YONG-PU ON 01-29-98 AT 0400.
KANG CLAIMS ENTRY DMZ SAME NITE VIA
'INFILTRATION TUBE' APPROX 27 MILES WEST OF
SEHYON-NI.
3. KANG DISABLED VET AND 'MEDICAL WORKER'.
SAYS DEFECTION FOLLOWED MILITARY INCIDENT TASI-
KO.
4. ANSP ASSIGNS ZERO-RELIABILITY TO KANG'S CLAIM.
SOURCE 'VELOCIPEDE' (PYONGYANG) REPORTS NO
MILITARY ACTIVITY IN II CORPS.
5. KANG CONSIDERED 'UNSTABLE.' DEFECTION
OPPORTUNISTIC.
6. ACTION: NO ACTION RECOMMENDED. (SUBJECT TO

Taylor Fitch loosened the tie at his throat, leaned
back in his chair and, with a sigh, read the cable for the
third time that afternoon. A former newspaper
reporter (well, okay, even if it *was* a cover, he'd *still*
written stories), he grimaced at the use of unexplained
acronyms. How many people knew that the ANSP was
'the South Korean CIA' – the so-called Agency for
National Security Planning? How many people could
tell you that DPRK stood for Democratic Peoples
Republic of Korea (a.k.a. the Commies)?

The answer was: hardly anyone, that's who. And
Fitch wasn't talking about the public. He was talking
about the Agency.

The CIA man rubbed his jaw and wondered idly if
he ought to dye his beard. He'd had it since college,
and it was going gray, like the hair at his temples. He
didn't like it. In fact, he hated it (though not, he had to
admit, as much as he hated the recent expansion of his
waistline). Maybe he should join a club. Maybe –
Maybe he should pay attention to what he was
supposed to be doing. He could lose fifty pounds, and
the cable would still be there. He had to do something
with it,

Like . . . file it. Just get it off his desk and punch out.
It wasn't as if what's-his-name was part of anyone's
inner circle. He wasn't a member of the People's
Assembly – not even close. In fact, unless the station in
Seoul had completely fucked up, this guy Kang wasn't
even a member of the Korean Workers Party. All he
was, was some kind of nurse – and a rural one at that.

Tasi-ko. Where the fuck . . . ?

Fitch swiveled in his chair and looked up at the large

map on the wall behind him. It was an ordnance map of North Korea, with an alphabetized list of cities, towns, and villages at the bottom. Next to each entry was a set of coordinates, giving the longitude and latitude in degrees, minutes, and seconds.

The map itself was rooted in the DMZ – a thick green line that ran east to west, following the 38th Parallel. North of the line, little red pins marked the whereabouts of DPRK infantry and artillery units, while naval stations and airfields were flagged with blue and white thumbtacks.

Tasi-ko was in the K-7 sector. That was II Corps, in the foothills of the Diamond Mountains, about eighty miles north of the DMZ. Middle of nowhere. Except . . .

Something had happened there. Or maybe not. The source in Pyongyang didn't know of any 'incident,' and neither did Fitch. But that didn't mean much. North Korea was a mysterious place. Lots of things happened that didn't get reported inside *or* outside of the country. So the only thing you could really say was that this guy Kang had taken his life in his hands to defect. And while it was possible that famine had driven him to do it, why would he lie about it? Why would he manufacture some kind of 'incident' when all he had to say was, 'I was hungry'?

So maybe something *had* happened. But *what*? The cable didn't offer a clue, and Fitch thought he knew why: Seoul hadn't asked – because Seoul was lazy.

It was supposed to be an elite posting, but the reality was that, half the time, the station took what the Koreans gave them, typed it up, and sent it back to Langley. They didn't *process* it. They didn't question it. They just passed it on, and adjourned to the nearest whorehouse.

Fitch muttered to himself and turned back to his desk. Pulling his keyboard closer, he drafted a cable that, stripped of its headers, read:

WHAT 'INCIDENT'?

Then he hit the Encryption button in his word-processing program, printed the results, and sent it on its way to Seoul over the big, red fax phone that sat, like a bust of Nathan Hale, on a pedestal next to the window.

The decoded reply was on his desk in the morning. According to MOTOWN (which was the way 'Seoul' liked to refer to itself), Kang claimed that Tasi-ko had been completely destroyed about ten days earlier: This, he said, was accomplished by what sounded like a fuel-air explosive dropped on the village a few hours after it had been cordoned off by soldiers. There were no survivors other than Kang, and the village itself had been bulldozed into the ground. Nothing remained.

SOURCE CLAIMS TASI-KO SITE OF EPIDEMIC STARTED BY (UNIDENTIFIED) SPANISH WOMAN. CLAIMS DPRK ACTION FOLLOWED INSPECTION BY SENIOR PHYSICIAN, PYONGYANG INSTITUTE FOR INFECTIOUS DISEASES.

What *Spanish* woman? Fitch thought. There aren't any Spanish women in North Korea. Or, if there are, there's about as many as there are banjos in Timor. And anyway, how would they know who started it?

The message ended with a short disclaimer in which MOTOWN emphasized that it had no way of verifying the story – which, it reminded him, was on offer from a source that could in no way be considered reliable.

They were right, of course, and Fitch had to admit,

this guy Kang was looking crazier and crazier. Still . . . it wouldn't hurt to make a couple of calls. Because you never knew. You just never knew,

What he needed was pictures, pictures of Tasi-ko (or what was left of it). And there were a couple of places that just might have them,

The first was the National Reconnaissance Office, or NRO. This was the $6 billion a year CIA 'subsidiary' that specialized in high resolution photographs taken by spy satellites. Unfortunately, the NRO required that every request for imagery had to be cleared by the Agency's liaison office – which meant that the requester needed to provide a crypto unique to one of the Agency's Special Access Programs.

In this case, though, there wasn't any program, and hence no crypto. Fitch was simply following a hunch, and the liaison office frowned on that.

Fortunately, the Pentagon was more cooperative than the NRO, and Fitch felt sure that he could get what he needed from the National Imagery & Mapping Agency. This was the military's sole provider of space-based imagery, and in many ways its archive was more comprehensive than the NRO's. While the latter concentrated on ultrasensitive targets such as troop deployments and nuclear reactors, NIMA's mission was a lot broader.

In addition to an array of conventional military assignments, NIMA was tasked with the massive responsibility of mapping the world – the *entire* world – in three dimensions, while at the same time keeping track of shifting coastlines, changes in climate, and agricultural developments on every continent.

It was with this last responsibility in mind that Fitch contacted the liaison officer at NIMA and told her what he was looking for: 'Pix.'

'Well, you've come to the right place. What kind of "pix"?'

'North Korea.'

The woman made a noncommittal sound, a sort of half grunt smothered by a moue.

'Is that a yes?'

'Well, that depends. It's a big place.'

Fitch spun round in his chair and searched the map's index for Tasi-ko. 'I've got the coordinates right here.'

'Give 'em to me.'

He did.

'Do you have a time frame?'

'Yeah. In fact, I have two. I need something that was taken in the past week, and something a month or so earlier.'

'Before and after,' the woman said.

'Exactly.'

'Well . . . I'll see what I can find, but if it's in the boonies – what sort of resolution do you need?'

'That's the good news,' Fitch said. 'Nothing much. Terrain shots, is all. So long as I can tell the difference between a parking lot and a rice paddy.'

'Oh, well,' the woman said, perking up. 'I don't think that should be a problem. Though if you want to know the truth, I think you could probably get what you want off the Internet.'

'I'm not *on* the Internet,' Fitch said.

'Well, you should be!'

'Not really: if I was, they'd have to kill me.'

'What do you mean?'

'It's a security thing. None of the computers here are hooked up to phones.'

'Well, just in case: we're at dubba-ya dubba-ya dubba-ya dot nima dot com.' There was a pause. 'Did you get that?' she asked.

'Yeah,' Fitch replied. 'I got it. But until I get hooked up, y'know, it's moot.'

The photos arrived late that same afternoon, hand-delivered by a Pentagon courier just as Fitch was putting on his coat to go home. Standing in the doorway, he pried open the envelope and removed a pair of 11 × 14 images. The first was a false-color Landsat photo that covered a ninety-second arc – about three kilometers in width. It showed a cluster of what appeared to be concrete huts, surrounded by fallow fields in the foothills of the Diamond Mountains. A notation on the back gave the time, the date, and the coordinates:

13:07:23Z
1-13-97
38°41'16"N, 126°54'08"E

The second picture was black and white, and bore a stamp on the back, indicating that it was the product of an Air Force reconnaissance program whose cryptonym had been blacked out. The photo was dated January 28, 1998, and gave the same coordinates as the first picture. And though the arc was different – only thirty degrees – the image itself was in no way ambiguous.

It showed a field. With snow all around.

Fitch's heart beat faster as his eyes moved from one photo to the other and back again. He checked the coordinates a second time, but there wasn't any need to do that, really. The same two-lane road that ran through the village in the Landsat picture ran through the 'parking lot' as well. Jesus, he thought, it's like a magic trick. Now you see it, now you don't.

And though he knew what the pictures represented – a massacre – he also knew that because he was the first to notice it, he'd get a lot of credit. A medal, maybe, or at least a commendation. Which was why, standing there in the doorway to his office, with the certainty of so much death in his hands, a small grin lifted the corners of his mouth.

It took almost forty-eight hours to obtain a copy of Kang's interview, and when it arrived, the text was still in Korean: twenty-six pages of hangul, accompanied by a knee-jerk apology from MOTOWN (whose translators were said to be 'all backed up'). Fitch had hoped to hand out translations to everyone in (what he had to admit was the somewhat pretentiously named) 'Tasi-ko Working Group.' But since that wasn't possible, he settled instead for inviting Harry Inoue. A Japanese-American, Harry was fluent in Korean and four other languages as well.

The group consisted of five people. In addition to Fitch and Inoue, there was Janine Wasserman, a veteran case officer who'd just returned to headquarters from a tour of duty in Seoul; Allen Voorhis, a gifted analyst who'd spent most of his career at the National Photo Interpretation Center; and Dr. George Karalekis, a physician in the Directorate of Science & Technology.

Fitch welcomed each of them to the little conference room that he'd reserved that Friday morning, and handed out copies of the pictures he'd received from NIMA. Then he asked Harry Inoue how soon he could get the debriefing translated.

'That depends,' Inoue said. 'Can I take it home?' Fitch shook his head, and the linguist shrugged. 'Tuesday, then.'

'Okay,' Fitch replied. 'Meanwhile, why don't you take a look at it? See what it says.'

Inoue nodded and began reading.

When everyone had taken a seat, Fitch explained why they were there. He told them how a medical worker named Kang had crossed the DMZ at night, bringing with him a story that might have been unbelievable – if the photographs in front of them hadn't confirmed it. For some reason, the North Korean Army had used what sounded like fuel-air explosives to destroy an entire village. And a friendly one at that. If a thirty-year-old census could be relied on, more than a hundred people had been killed.

'I don't see any bodies,' Voorhis said, peering at the photographs through the bottom of his bifocals. 'All I see is a lot of rubble.'

Fitch nodded. 'You're right,' he said. 'Kang could be wrong. Someone else might have gotten away.'

'Maybe they all did,' Wasserman suggested.

Fitch looked at her. She was a tall, heavy woman in her late thirties, with a gravelly voice and piercing blue eyes. She was dressed, ever so elegantly, in what Fitch supposed were designer clothes. (Someone said she had a lot of her own money, and that she was related to the Guggenheims, or maybe it was the Rothschilds. Old money, in any case, and lots of it.) 'What do you mean?' he asked.

Wasserman shrugged. 'It wouldn't be the first time the North Koreans relocated people. And it wouldn't be the first time they staged something, either.'

Fitch thought about it, then said, 'Good point. Maybe they moved them. Maybe they want the site for something else.' He paused. 'But that's not what Kang says. And Kang's our only source.'

Karalekis broke in with the obvious question: 'Well,

now that you mention it, what *does* Mr. Kang says? What was the motive for all this destruction?'

Fitch turned to Inoue and raised his eyebrows.

Inoue cleared his throat and leaned forward, keeping his eyes on the report in front of him. 'He says – and I'm paraphrasing – that the village was in the midst of an epidemic. A lot of people were dying.'

'Doe he tell us what they were dying *of*?' Karalekis asked.

Inoue shook his head and turned a page. 'No. He says he'd never seen anything like it. Fevers of a hundred and six. Gangrenous genitalia.' He looked questioningly at Karalekis, whose face betrayed nothing.

Inoue turned another page. 'Projectile vomiting, explosive hemorrhaging – mouth, nose, eyes . . . good lord, listen to this! Some of them turned blue. "Bright blue."'

Karalekis nodded, as much to himself as anyone else.

'That doesn't surprise you?' Inoue asked. 'People turning blue?'

Karalekis shrugged. 'It happens. It's called "cyanosis."'

Fitch turned to the doctor. 'You know what this guy's talking about? Any of this ring a bell for you?'

Karalekis rolled his eyes. 'It could be anything.'

Fitch and Inoue stared at him. Finally, Fitch said, 'No. It couldn't be "anything." It couldn't be the common cold, for instance. It couldn't be hemorrhoids.'

Karalekis chuckled. 'That's not what I meant. I meant that I don't know how reliable an observer Mr. Kang is. I don't know how much training he's had or –'

Wasserman leaned forward. 'Could we . . . *please*? I don't see what this has got to do with the North

33

Korean Army destroying a village. So some people were sick –'

'Apparently, they were very sick.'

'So what?'

Inoue held a finger in the air and waggled it from side to side. 'Hang on a minute,' he said, and turned a couple of pages. 'It says here, 'They wanted to' . . . the nearest word in English would be "cauterize." They wanted to cauterize the place.'

'And how would Mr. Kang know what the army's motive was? Did they tell him?' Wasserman asked.

Inoue looked abashed. 'No,' he answered. 'You're right. It's just his guess. But he says he was losing one out of three, one out of four, patients, when a doctor came from Pyongyang. And it was right after that, a week or so later, that the town was . . . destroyed.'

'So he figures they "cauterized" it.'

Inoue nodded. 'Like a wound.'

'What if they weren't trying to control the disease?' Wasserman asked. 'What if they were just trying to hide it?'

'Why would they want to hide it?' Fitch asked.

'Because the economy's a wreck, the factories are shut, the people are starving, nothing works,' Wasserman replied. 'The last thing they need is more bad publicity.'

'And you think they'd kill a hundred people for that?'

Wasserman thought about it. Finally, she said, 'Sure.'

Karalekis turned to Fitch, who let out an exasperated sigh: 'What about the doctor,' Karalekis asked, 'the one from Pyongyang? What'd he say about the epidemic?'

'He said –' Fitch glanced at Wasserman and, seeing

the skeptical look on her face, corrected himself. 'Excuse me. We don't know *what* the doctor said. But *according to Mr. Kang,* the doctor blamed the whole thing on a, uh . . . a Spanish woman.'

Wasserman guffawed, and Fitch ground his teeth together.

'Hey! I'm telling you what the guy *said!*'

The room became quiet. Voorhis blew his nose and Karalekis coughed, but no one knew what to say. Finally, Inoue broke the silence. 'Actually,' he said, 'it's not.'

Fitch looked perplexed and annoyed, all at once. 'What's not?'

'It's not what he said.' Inoue tapped the transcript in front of him. 'He didn't say "a Spanish woman." He said "the Spanish *lady.*" He said "the doctor blamed it all on the Spanish lady."'

'Oh, well – in that *case – excuse me,*' Fitch said.

Inoue made a hapless gesture, as if to explain that he was only trying to help, when he suddenly realized that Karalekis was staring at him. 'What's the matter?' he asked.

'What'd you say – exactly?'

Inoue looked embarrassed. 'You mean, about the transcript?'

Karalekis nodded.

'Well, it was just a detail, but . . . according to Mr. Kang, the doctor said . . .' He looked at the debriefing page. '"The doctor blamed it all on the Spanish lady."'

' "The Spanish lady," ' Karalekis repeated.

'Yes. That's what it says he said.'

'*Not* – "a Spanish woman."'

Inoue shook his head. 'No.'

Karalekis held the translator's eyes for a long moment. Then he swallowed hard and turned to Fitch.

'I think you better call Atlanta,' he said.

'"Atlanta"?' What's "Atlanta"?' Fitch asked.

'CDC,' Karalekis said. 'If your guy's right, this thing could kill more people than the Second World War.'

3

In the weeks that followed, the Tasi-ko Working Group was anointed with its own cryptonym (BLINDSIDE) and 'augmented' by two members.

The first was Dr. Irving Epstein, an influenza specialist with the National Institutes of Health (NIH). The second was Neal Gleason, a lanky FBI agent with liaison responsibilities to the CIA.

To Fitch, Gleason's appointment rankled as much as Epstein's was welcome, but there was nothing he could do about the G-man's presence. Gleason's job was to work with the Agency on matters relating to chemical and biological weapons. This was (in theory, at least) an extension of the Bureau's mission to protect the country against acts of domestic terrorism. In reality (or, at least, in Fitch's *opinion)*, Gleason's inclusion was another example of the Bureau's relentless efforts to expand its authority in the aftermath of the cold war.

Not that Gleason was particularly interested in Fitch's little group. He had bigger fish to fry, shuttling twice a month between Washington and Amman, where he met regularly with American monitors assigned to the United Nations inspection teams in nearby Iraq. Predictably, this left him in a near permanent state of jet lag – a condition that he hid behind a wall of nonchalance and Maui Jim sunglasses.

For the FBI agent the Tasi-ko Working Group was only a sideline, one of a dozen groups whose deliberations he 'audited' (when he was not on his way to one departure lounge or another). 'Just think of me as a fly on the wall,' he told Fitch 'I won't make a peep.' And, for the most part, he didn't.

Epstein was another kettle of fish entirely. A short, fat, talkative man in his early sixties, he affected the raiment of a New Dealer, replete with bow tie, suspenders, and a seersucker suit. Secretly thrilled to be part of 'the secret world,' (if only on loan), he delighted in explaining the nuances of influenza in general, and the Spanish flu in particular. 'Spanish lady,' he noted, 'was a nickname for the malady, derived from its particularly heavy toll in Spain. Cartoons of the era often showed a slinky woman in a come hither posture – whose lace mantilla hid a grinning skull.

Armed with maps of Asia and a laser pointer, the epidemiologist was delighted to explain that influenza is a fragile virus that exists in a state of constant mutation. Depending upon its antigenic makeup –

'Its *what?*' The voice was Fitch's, but the question belonged to everyone – or almost everyone.

'He's talking about the protein coat,' Karalekis explained. 'The surface characteristics of the virus.'

Fitch grunted.

'Depending on its protein coat,' Epstein continued, 'the virus is classified as one of three general types: H-1, H-2, and H-3. There are others, but those are the biggies.'

Fitch's brow furrowed – he didn't like being lectured to – but Janine Wasserman restrained him with a soft touch on his arm.

'Within each of these types,' Epstein went on, 'you

38

have what amounts to an infinite number of strains –'

'So when we talk about the flu,' Voorhis interjected, 'we're actually talking about a *class* of diseases.'

Epstein shrugged. 'I wouldn't put it that way, but you can, if you want. The important thing is, we have to produce a new vaccine each year because, as the virus mutates, last year's pandemic strain gives way to its successor.'

Epstein bathed his audience in a benign smile, but Fitch wasn't having any of it. 'Doc, you keep using words –'

'He means the dominant strain, worldwide,' Karalekis said.

'Like an epidemic,' Voorhis suggested.

Epstein shook his head. 'No, a pandemic is *not* "like an epidemic." A "pandemic" is global. An "epidemic" – like the one in Tasi-ko – is a localized outbreak.'

'Which would make it – strictly – a North Korean problem,' Gleason pointed out.

Karalekis furrowed his brow. 'Well,' he said, 'it *would* . . . unless –'

'Unless it spreads,' Epstein concluded. For a moment the two doctors basked in one another's smiles.

Voorhis shifted uncomfortably in his chair. 'But some epidemics are worse than others, right? Depending on the . . . *strain.*'

'Exactly,' Epstein replied. 'Some strains are a lot more virulent than others, and sometimes they attack different populations. The Spanish flu went after the young. Children. Kids. People under thirty.'

'Why was that?' Wasserman asked.

Epstein shook his head. 'I don't know.'

Fitch frowned, and Karalekis turned to him. 'No one does,' he said.

'Why not?' Fitch asked.

Karalekis shrugged. 'Because no one's ever studied it.'

'The *flu?*' Fitch asked.

'No. We're talking about this particular virus,' Epstein said. 'No one's ever seen it under a microscope.'

'Why not?'

'Because viruses are submicroscopic. You need an electron microscope to see them, and they didn't invent it until 'thirty-seven, which was – what? – almost twenty years after the disease had come and gone.'

'So no one's ever really seen it?' Fitch asked.

Karalekis nodded.

'Including the Koreans?' Fitch added.

Karalekis and Epstein looked at one another. After a moment, Epstein said, 'Yes . . . including the North Koreans.'

'Which *means,*' Fitch went on, 'that the guy from Pyongyang –'

'The doctor,' Wasserman supplied.

'*Whatever*. It means the guy was guessing – when he said it was 'the Spanish Lady,' he was *guessing*.'

'Well . . .' Karalekis thought about it.

'He had to be,' Fitch insisted. 'You just said –'

Epstein shook his head. 'It's not as simple as that.'

Fitch looked puzzled. 'Why not?'

'Because he saw patients. He treated symptoms. He observed the course of the disease.'

'And on that basis,' Karalekis said, concurring, 'he compared it to the Spanish flu.'

No one said anything for a long moment, then Janine Wasserman spoke. 'Not really,' she said. 'He didn't *compare* it to anything. He said it *was* the Spanish flu. Period.'

Voorhis rolled his eyes. 'According to the translator ... according to the doctor. According to the defector.' He paused and looked around the room. 'Is it just me, or –'

Neal Gleason snorted derisively, then glanced at his watch and scraped back his chair. Getting to his feet with a wince of phony remorse, he announced, 'This is all very interesting, but I've got a two o'clock at the Navy Yard, so, uh ... keep me posted, okay?' And with that he grabbed his coat and left the room.

Wasserman seemed not to notice. Leaning forward, she rested her elbows on the conference table and tapped her fingertips together. Once, twice. Three times. Then she turned to Karalekis with a frown and said, 'The thing I'm wondering about, George, is ... well, I guess what all of us are wondering about: the way the Koreans reacted.'

'Of course.'

'Because, unless I'm mistaken, you can't stop an influenza epidemic by killing the people who have the illness –'

'Why not?' Voorhis asked.

'Because,' Epstein replied.

'There's more than a single vector,' Karalekis explained.

'Exactly.'

Voorhis looked from one physician to another, as if he were following a tennis match. Finally, he asked, 'What's "a vector"?'

'A means of transmission,' Epstein said.

'Like what?' Fitch asked.

'People. Rodents. Ducks,' Karalekis replied. 'With influenza, wild ducks are huge,' he said, warming to the theme.

'The migration of waterfowl –' Epstein began.

41

'It's the name of the game,' Karalekis said.

'The herald wave – which is the first wave of people afflicted by a new strain – almost always begins in China,' Epstein added.

'Why is that?' Voorhis asked.

'They've got the waterfowl, they've got the population densities you need to get the wave started –'

'There are lots of reasons,' Karalekis remarked, 'but it's lucky for us because it takes about a year for a new strain to hit the States. Which gives us time to make a vaccine and get it distributed.'

Janine Wasserman cleared her throat. 'If we could just . . . stay on the point . . . we were *talking* about the Koreans' reaction. And how illogical it was.' For a moment the doctors' faces fell: they'd been enjoying their lecture, or repartee, or whatever it was. 'And I was thinking,' Wasserman went on, 'about their certainty – or their apparent certainty – that it was the Spanish flu – rather than something "like" it.'

Epstein and Karalekis opened their mouths, but Fitch cut them off with the slightest gesture of his right hand.

'And it occurred to me,' Wasserman went on, 'that the North Koreans must have known that killing people in Tasi-ko would be very unlikely to affect an outbreak of this kind. Because the disease would continue to spread in other ways.'

The doctors glanced at one another. Finally, Epstein conceded the point with a tilt of his head.

'So what they did was entirely irrational *unless* . . . they somehow *knew* . . . that there *were* no other vectors for this particular outbreak. That it was somehow . . . a one-off proposition. A fluke.'

Karalekis pursed his lips and made a sucking sound.

'Mmmm,' he said. 'I see your point.'

Epstein frowned, genuinely baffled. For a moment he looked like a little boy whose mother had dressed him in his father's clothes. Turning from Wasserman to Karalekis, he asked, 'What point?'

Karalekis kept his eyes on the table in front of him. 'Ms. Wasserman is suggesting that an accident may have occurred, and that what happened at Tasi-ko was . . . an attempt to contain that accident.'

'You mean, a *laboratory* accident?' Epstein asked.

Karalekis looked up. 'Exactly. Otherwise –'

'They'd have known there was nothing they could do about the outbreak,' Fitch said, finishing the sentence for him. 'They'd have sucked it up. They'd have had to.'

A worried look came over Epstein. 'But is that realistic? I mean, do we know if the North Koreans are experimenting with this sort of thing?'

Karalekis huffed. 'Yes,' he said. 'We do know. They've got one of the most intensive bio-weaponeering programs in the world. Now, having said that, we don't have inspection teams in the country, so I can't tell you where all the labs are. But we know they've got a program – and for a country like North Korea, it makes sense.'

'Why do you say that?' Epstein asked.

'Because,' Karalekis said, 'biological weapons are the most cost-effective weapons in the world. Look at it this way: a nuclear weapons program costs a couple of hundred million – just for starters. But you can make anthrax, cholera, and typhoid in a garage – using home brewery equipment. And you don't need missiles to deliver it: an off-the-shelf aerosolizer works fine.'

'I'll give Dr. Epstein a book about it,' Fitch said impatiently. 'What I want to know is, if there's a weapons lab near Tasi-ko, how would something like this get out?'

Karalekis shrugged. 'Accident. Leaky pipe. It doesn't happen a lot, but it happens.'

'Third world,' Voorhis remarked. 'I'll bet it happens all the time.'

'Of course,' Karalekis said, 'if it *was* an accident . . . and if it *was* the Spanish flu . . .'

'Yeah?' Fitch asked.

'Well it raises rather a large question, doesn't it?'

Epstein snorted. 'I'll say!'

Fitch looked from one doctor to the other. 'And what question is that?'

Karalekis raised his eyebrows. 'Well . . . I mean, where'd they *get* it?'

The question hung in the air for a long while. Finally, Voorhis chuckled. 'You're putting us on, right?'

'What do you mean?' Karalekis asked.

'You're pulling our legs.'

It was Karalekis's turn to look puzzled. 'No,' he said. 'I'm not. Why would you think that?'

'Well, because . . .' Voorhis broke into a broad grin. 'It's *the flu,* for chrissake! Everybody gets it. It's not *Ebola.* It's not *Q fever!* Why would the Koreans play around with something like *influenza,* when they've got – what? Anthrax! Sarin! There must be a million things more dangerous.'

Epstein and Karalekis looked at one another. After a moment Epstein turned back to Voorhis. 'I don't think you quite understand,' he said. 'The mortality rate of the Spanish flu –'

Voorhis looked skeptical. 'I know what you're saying. It's a monster. But it's not *poisonous.* You wouldn't use it to attack an army.'

'That's true,' Karalekis remarked. 'You probably wouldn't. But if your intention was to debilitate the enemy – to attack the civilian population in a systemic way – the Spanish Lady would be a very effective instrument.'

Epstein picked up the theme. 'I was just going over the numbers last week,' he said. 'Look at New York: they've got fifty-six 911 receiving hospitals – eight thousand beds. That's it! Or almost it: they've also got a couple of decon vans – *two* – each of which can handle – what? Maybe three people an hour.' He paused. 'A biological attack on New York, or any city, would be . . . unrecoverable.'

'The other thing about the flu, of course, is that it's self-sustaining,' Karalekis said. 'Once you get it started, there's a kind of chain reaction that takes place: the virus, or bacterium, produces more and more of itself. So it's like a fusion reactor. But in another way, it's like a neutron bomb, because it doesn't do any damage to the enemy's infrastructure. It kills the people, and leaves the buildings intact.'

Voorhis grunted. 'So just how deadly *is* this stuff?'

'Well,' Karalekis replied, 'if you had the right bug . . . theoretically, you could start a kind of biological *crown fire* that would kill everyone on the planet – unless they'd been immunized.'

'I understand,' Voorhis replied. 'But we're not talking "theoretically." We're talking about this bug in North Korea. And what I'm wondering is: just how deadly is it?'

'Okay. Let me put it this way,' Karalekis said. 'In the fall of 1918 the Spanish flu killed more than half a million Americans. That's more than died in the two world wars, Korea, and Vietnam put together. *And it happened in four months.*'

'What about the plague?' Fitch asked. 'That had to be worse.'

Karalekis rocked from side to side, weighing the proposition. 'Maybe. But the plague took twenty years to do what it did. The Spanish flu killed twenty or thirty million people in twelve months.'

'Jesus,' Fitch whispered.

Epstein turned to Voorhis. 'You mentioned Ebola,' he said. 'Well, it's a terrible microbe, of course, but . . . it's stable. And the truth is, it's really quite difficult to contract.'

'It's as hard to get as AIDS,' Karalekis said.

'There has to be an exchange of fluids – and I don't mean a sneeze,' Epstein continued. 'But, influenza . . . well! It's just as you said: "Everybody gets it."'

'And it's anything but stable,' Karalekis added. 'We don't have a vaccine for next year's flu –'

'Even more to the point,' Epstein said, 'we don't have a vaccine for yesteryear's flu. And the simple truth is, the Spanish Lady was the most lethal medical event in history.'

'And that was in its natural state,' Karalekis added.

'What do you mean, it's "natural state"?' Fitch asked.

'Well, I'm just speculating, but . . . if the Koreans started playing with the bug, tweaking the genes . . . they could create a chimera virus that had an even greater lethality.'

'A "chimera virus"!' Voorhis exclaimed.

'He's talking about gene-splicing – creating a monster by melding one bug to another,' Epstein said.

'Yeah, but – you'd have to have a pretty sophisticated lab to do something like that, wouldn't you?' Voorhis asked.

Epstein shook his head. 'Genentech sends kits to

magnet schools. Or you can buy them for about forty bucks.'

No one said anything for a moment. Then Fitch broke the silence. 'So what you're saying is, we're up Shit Creek.'

'In layman's terms,' Epstein replied, 'yes, that's quite possible.'

As they thought about that, Janine Wasserman got to her feet and, ever so languidly, walked around the table. Finally, she stopped beside the map of North Korea that was hanging from the wall and studied it for a moment. 'There are two problems,' she mused. 'The first is to locate where the accident occurred.'

'DOD can help with that,' Fitch said.

'I'm sure we can get some overflights,' Voorhis suggested. 'U-2s, at least.'

Fitch nodded. 'And ECHELON.'

Everyone murmured agreement, except Epstein. 'What's "echelon"?' he asked, looking from one CIA employee to another.

Fitch squirmed in his seat, chagrined by the mistake he'd made with an outsider in the room. Finally, he said, 'It's a . . . uh, classified program,' he explained. 'I shouldn't have mentioned it.'

In fact, the ECHELON dictionary program was one of the intelligence community's most sensitive and secret operations, a worldwide, electronic eaves-dropping network of astounding proportions. Linking satellites and 'listening posts' to a series of massively parallel computers, the U.S. intelligence community and its allies were able to intercept and decode virtually every electronic communication in the world – in real time, as they were being transmitted. Then, searching for key words, the same program identified and segregated messages of particular interest.

'So, what words do we use?' Voorhis asked, pen at the ready.

Fitch shrugged. 'There's not much we *can* use. 'Influenza' won't get us anywhere. . .'

'Yeah, but . . . "influenza" and "North Korea," or "influenza" and "Tasi-ko" . . . in fact, anything with Tasi-ko in it would probably be of interest.'

Fitch nodded. 'That ought to do it.'

'Even if we do find the lab,' Voorhis said, 'what are we going to do about it? I mean, it *is* North Korea.'

'If we get to that point, it's a diplomatic issue. State can handle it,' Fitch said.

'What about a vaccine?' Wasserman asked. 'How long would it take to develop one?'

Epstein's answer was unhesitating. 'Six months. Soup to nuts.'

'Could you do it any faster if you had to?'

Epstein looked at Karalekis, who raised his eyebrows. Finally, Epstein said, 'If we could make it at all, we might be able to knock a month off. But it's hypothetical in any case. You can't make a vaccine without the virus, and –'

Karalekis finished the sentence for him. 'We don't *have* the virus.'

Wasserman leaned forward and squeezed Karalekis's shoulders so hard that he almost winced. 'Well,' she whispered, 'that's the second problem. I think we'd better find it.'

If the virus was to be found anywhere, Karalekis thought, the most likely place was a windowless building on the grounds of the Walter Reed Army Medical Center in Bethesda, Maryland. This was the National Tissue Repository – or as the tabloids sometimes called it, 'the library of death.' A warehouselike structure, it was packed with row upon row of metal shelves piled high with cardboard boxes. Inside each of the boxes were bits of human tissue that had been preserved in formaldehyde and encased in little blocks of paraffin wax. All in all, the building held more than 2.5 million pieces of diseased but dormant flesh, most of which had been culled from soldiers who'd fallen in their country's wars.

Karalekis suspected that in one block of wax or another, traces of the virus could be found. And the most likely place was among the lung tissues. These were paper-thin slices of flesh harvested from soldiers who'd died of respiratory ailments in the fall of 1918. Even there, however, the likelihood of finding a useful sample was negligible. Because the influenza virus begins to decompose within twenty-four hours of its host's death, the probability was great that, even if it were found, it would be useless for making a vaccine.

Still, the effort had to be made, and so it was. Backed by a National Security Research Priority Directive, Karalekis initiated a tedious and time-consuming search that threatened to take years. It was all that he could do. He had little confidence that the U-2s would find anything: bio labs were easily disguised. And the ECHELON program, however massive, was only as effective as the enemy was indiscreet. If North Korean communications failed to mention Tasi-ko, ECHELON would come up empty. And the CIA would be fucked.

Or maybe not.

On a brilliant February afternoon, while seated at his desk in the Directorate of Science & Technology, Karalekis was startled by Fitch's sudden appearance in his doorway.

'I think Epstein may have solved our little problem,' Fitch said.

Karalekis looked skeptical. 'Reeee-ally?!' He drew the word out, as if he were pronouncing it on a water slide.

'Yes, *really*.' Fitch dropped into a chair and tossed a file onto Karalekis's desk.

The physician regarded it mistrustfully. 'And this would be . . . what?'

'It's a grant proposal,' Fitch replied. 'An old one. Epstein told me about it, and I got a copy from the NSF.'

Karalekis glanced at the cover page:

'In Search of "A/Kopervik/10/18"'
Submitted by
Benton Kicklighter, M.D., Ph.D. (NIH)
Anne Adair, Ph.D. (Georgetown University)

'"A-Kopervik, ten-eighteen"' he said. 'What the hell is that?'

Fitch grinned. 'Well,' he said, *'that*, my friend, is the Big Kahuna.'

'Is it?'

'You bet it is,' Fitch said. 'Whatever you want to call it, the Spanish flu is the Spanish flu.'

Karalekis frowned. 'I don't get it.'

'Look, this is a grant proposal, a *rejected* grant proposal, from a doctor at the NIH. Guy named Kicklighter, somebody named Adair. Turns out, there's these dead Norwegian miners –'

'Great.'

'– and they want to dig 'em up. They're in a graveyard way the hell up in the Arctic Circle.'

'And this is going to hell us . . . *how?*' Karalekis asked.

'They died in 1918. And according to this, it's pretty obvious what killed them: the symptoms are classic. High fever, cyanosis, projectile-everything . . . And from what this says –' Fitch tapped the proposal with his forefinger, once, twice, three times. '– they've been buried in the permafrost ever since.'

Karalekis leaned forward in his chair. 'Reeeally?!' he said. 'In the *permafrost* . . .' He repeated the word as if he were pronouncing it for the first time. 'And . . . they think . . . ?'

Fitch shrugged. 'They don't know. No one knows. Until an expedition gets there, there's no way to tell. But what it looks like, this whole area around Kopervik – which I guess is some kinda ghost town – is crawling with polar bears. Polar bears, right?'

'Yeah. So what?'

'So they buried 'em deep,' Fitch said. 'They buried 'em cold.'

4

MURMANSK
MARCH 23, 1998

'Item four,' the tall, gangly man in the front of the room was saying, 'arctic goggles.' Hand aloft, he dangled a pair from one finger. 'Don't under any circumstances go out during daylight hours without them, not even for a minute.'

Annie Adair glanced down at the long equipment list with alarm. If, as it seemed, each piece of gear was going to require its own fifteen minute lecture, they'd be sitting in this cramped and stuffy cabin for *hours*.

The tall man bent forward from the waist to demonstrate the preferred procedure for putting the goggles on, jiggling his head in an exaggerated way to set the eyepieces firmly against his face. When he straightened up, with the black and bulbous goggles on, his head resembled that of a large insect. 'The fit should be snug – like swimming goggles,' he elaborated. 'The gaskets at the temples should not admit any light *whatsoever*.'

Annie stifled a yawn and glanced at Dr. Kicklighter. He was famously impatient, and from the signs – tapping his foot in irritation, gnawing on a knuckle – she could tell that he was going to blow. And she couldn't let that happen. Doctor K had zero people skills and no concept of professional courtesy. He just didn't seem to get it – that it was better to endure a couple of hours of tedium than to antagonize people you were depending on.

And who, after all, were *doing you a favor*.

Icebreakers were routinely booked years in advance. So finding one that was flying the right flag in the right place at the right time, and which, moreover, was willing to accommodate the Kopervik expedition was . . . well, it was asking a lot. And yet, somehow, it had all fallen into place. The grant proposal she'd given up on more than a year ago had been suddenly and finally funded – and space had somehow been found aboard the *Rex Mundi,* a vintage icebreaker leased to the National Oceanic and Atmospheric Administration (NOAA).

How Doctor K had arranged this was baffling, though she had no intention of looking a gift horse in the mouth. The one time she asked him about it, he grinned a cryptic little grin and said, 'Well, Annie, it turns out we have friends in high places.' And so they must have: among other things, Annie's piggyback ride on the *Rex Mundi* meant that the Snowmen – NOAA's team of snow and ice physicists – would have to give up five days of shore leave in Oslo.

The last thing they needed, then, was friction with either the physicists or the crew. The latter, of course, were a problem in their own right. Despite the promise of a generous bonus, a number of the crew had left the ship on learning that the Kopervik leg of the trip would involve the exhumation of bodies. Replacements had been found, but not without difficulty. There were sailors' superstitions, she'd been told, about transporting a cargo of corpses.

The man in the goggles was droning on about angles of refraction and solar intensities in the Arctic. On her own, she would have sat there patiently all day long, but one of her jobs as a protégé was running inter-ference for her mentor. Doctor K could be truly offensive, and seeing the tempo of his foot accelerat-ing, she suddenly plunged in. 'I think we get the picture,' she said in what she hoped was a bright and conciliatory voice – Katie Couric breaking for a commercial.

'Excuse me?' The Snowman couldn't quite believe that she'd interrupted him.

'I . . . we . . . I mean we understand that we should wear the goggles whenever we go outside.' Annie clumsily faked a yawn, hoping he'd get it: *These people are tired. They just got off a transatlantic flight.*

Instead, he looked as if she'd slapped him in the face. She knew she'd violated an unwritten rule – when experts briefed 'civilians,' even when those civilians were scientists themselves, the expected behavior was polite attention, if not obeisance. It was a turf thing. If Doctor K were to host strangers in the lab and instruct them on the proper way to handle a viral smear, he'd expect rapt attention. A little nervous laugh escaped her, but she pushed on. 'Look, I'm the last person you have to lecture about going snow-blind,' she said breathlessly. 'It actually happened to me once.'

'Oh *really*.'

'Uh-huh. At Vail. I dropped my goggles off the lift.' God, now she sounded like an airhead. 'There was a moment, up above the treeline, when I couldn't see a thing.'

There was a pause and then the physicist's voice took on an acid tone. 'Well, real snow-blindness is a whole different magnitude. We're not talking about disorientation. We're talking about pain, intense pain – as if your eyes were filled with ground glass. It can disable you for days, even weeks, if your exposure is

54

severe enough.'

For a moment there was silence, and then the foot-tapping started again – albeit in a slower cadence.

'No-ted,' Doctor K said in a cold voice.

'Excellent.' The NOAA physicist tore off the goggles – which left red welts around his eyes – and picked up a neoprene face mask. 'Item five. When the temperature falls below –'

'Excuse me,' Dr. Kicklighter interrupted, 'it's your business, I suppose, but – just . . . by the by, won't you have to repeat all this for our *scribe* when he arrives? Wouldn't it make more sense to wait? I mean, he'll need to preserve his vision and so on every bit as much as *we* do.'

'What "scribe"?' The physicist glared at them, and Annie thought, That's it. We're done. He hates us.

'A man named Daly –'

There was a sharp rap on the door and a thin, blond man stepped into the room, not waiting for a reply. Annie recognized him as the senior physicist.

'You're gonna have to finish the briefing on board, Mark. There's a *mother* of a storm heading this way, and the captain says either we get out of here in a couple of hours – or we'll be in port for three or four *days.*'

'We're *leaving?*' Doctor K asked. 'But –'

The blond man shrugged. 'We do what the captain says,' he said.

'And anyway, he's doing us a favor. If he wanted, he could make us sit. And then where would we be? You'd lose your slot.' He paused a moment to let the words sink in, and then, with a grin, said, 'Twenty minutes! We'll have the van in front of your hotel.'

And with that, the blond man left, the way he'd come.

Mark the Physicist was already stuffing the equipment into a large, blue duffel bag.

'But . . . what about Frank Daly?' Annie asked.

'Who's Frank Daly?' Mark asked.

'Our scribe,' Kicklighter replied.

'We had an arrangement,' Annie said. 'I mean . . . God, he's come a million miles!'

Mark looked up with a smile, shrugged, and, straightening, hitched the duffel bag onto his shoulder. 'Offhand, I'd say Mr. Daly's gonna miss the boat.'

'Blessing in disguise,' Kicklighter muttered as he got to his feet. 'We need him like we need an abscessed tooth.'

Mark chuckled and slipped out the door, leaving Annie to ponder the irony of Frank Daly being left behind. After all the agonizing about the desirability (or maybe it was the *inevitability)* of a reporter on the expedition, now he'd arrive in Murmansk – only to find the *Rex Mundi* gone.

Half an hour later Annie stood outside her hotel waiting for the van that would take them to the ship. The air was heavy, warm, and still, filled with a hushed malevolence that painted her frustration with fear.

She'd tried to reach Daly, to get a message to him, tell him not to come. But the connections were horrible, and now . . .

The temperature was rising, from twelve to twenty-two, and by the time they arrived at the docks, snowflakes were shooting back and forth in a damp and gusty wind.

She was a little afraid as she stepped onto the swaying walkway that led to the ship's deck. The thick swags of rope that served as handrails were slick with ice, and when she looked down (big mistake), there was nothing but black water. For a moment she hesitated, and Dr. Kicklighter clasped her elbow and propelled her forward.

Then she was safely on the deck, and the two of them stood for a moment, hands on the railing, watching a litter of plastic cups rise and fall against the seawall.

'We're on the edge of the world,' Kicklighter said, nodding toward the city. 'That's what the Saamis call it.'

Annie nodded politely, but she didn't know what he was talking about. 'Call what?' she asked.

'"Murmansk." It means "the edge of the world."' His brow wrinkled and he paused. 'Or maybe it's "the end of the world." I'm not really sure.'

Annie looked at him. 'Well, it's a big difference,' she said, and flushed to see the doctor smile.

Slowly, he raised his arm and waved, the wind plucking at the fabric of his parka. 'So it is,' he said to no one particular, and added, 'Bon voyage.'

5

MARCH 23, 1998

Frank Daly was halfway into the three-hour flight from Moscow to Murmansk when the plane – an Ilyushin-86 – began to tremble. Distracted, he looked up from his laptop and glanced out the pitted window to see that the aircraft had entered a cloud. The air was nearly opaque – though he could make out the dark contour of the wing as the jet ghosted through the whiteout.

And then the tremble intensified, becoming a heavy vibration that escalated into a shudder. Daly closed his computer, zipped it into its padded case, put the case in his backpack, and wedged the backpack under the seat in front of him. Then he sat back, thinking, *It's my fault. If we go down, it's because I was playing Doom when I should have been working on the Spanish Lady.* The Air god didn't like slackers, and now it was he who was Doomed. Except . . .

He didn't believe in God. Except . . . well, under the circumstances. Being in a hurricane at thirty thousand feet – what the hell was *that*?

The jet yawed to the west, shivered violently, bounced and moaned. *Never play Doom in an airplane,* Daly told himself, gripping the sides of his seat. *What was I thinking of? How could it possibly be good luck?* Thoughtlessly, he tapped the seat rest with his knuckles, three times, and again. It was a ritual he had, whose origins were long forgotten. But it seemed to keep black cats at bay. And broken mirrors, too.

And crashing planes. At least, he'd never been in one.

Even so, he recognized the practice for what it was, an abbreviated form of prayer, the last remnant of an early Catholic upbringing.

From the aisle seat a powerful man with a bushy mustache produced a surprisingly feminine 'Ooooh!', tossed Daly a look of pure terror, then buried his face in his hands. Moments later the sky was dark, the carry-on bins were rattling open, and the overhead lights popped on and off: *No smoking! Fasten seat belts! Prepare to die!* A tray of drinks crashed, a man cried out, and the plane dropped, wobbled, and plunged, fighting the turbulent air around it.

And so it went for another ten minutes, as the passenger cabin grew dense with the smell of vomit. Bottles of vodka and cans of beer and soda rolled down the aisles and under the seats, as an overhead bin popped open and suitcases tumbled out, provoking yelps of pain and surprise.

Finally, Flight 16 banked to the east, turned tail, and headed south. People were sobbing on both sides of the aisle, while a man in the back of the plane chanted at the top of his lungs in a language that Daly couldn't place. The smell of alcohol combined with the reek of vomit, creating a woozy miasma. After a while, the stewards gamely set about restoring order, attending to the injured, replacing errant baggage, soothing the hysterical.

There was never any announcement. Just a ragged round of applause when, half an hour later, the aircraft slammed onto the tarmac, bounced, slammed down again, and coasted with a roar. Through the window the snow could be seen blowing sideways past a low gray terminal, stenciled with Cyrillic characters.

'Where are we?' Daly asked of no one in particular.

The answer floated back from several seats ahead, where a florid Australian shouted over the wailing of a furious infant: 'We're in Archangel, mate. We're in bloody, fuckin' Archangel.'

Daly spent a frustrating hour trying to find out about the next flight to Murmansk – which turned out to be anybody's guess. The Aeroflot rep spent ten minutes on hold, only to report that the runways at Murmansk were closed. 'Is storm,' she explained, as if Daly could not have figured it out for himself.

'So how do I get to Murmansk?' he asked. 'It's really important that I get to Murmansk.'

The agent shrugged, then wrote down the telephone numbers and addresses of two travel agencies in town – Intourist and Sputnik. They could advise him, she said, about 'rail travel and motor coach.'

The pay phone in the lobby was five deep with waiting customers, so Daly went outside to look for a taxi. Surprisingly, he found one almost immediately. It was a black ZIL with crumpled fenders and a heater that blew cool air at his knees. Tiny pellets of snow bounced off the windshield like BBs.

'You speak English, right?'

The driver glanced at him in the rearview mirror. 'Sure,' he said. 'Am speaking everything.'

'How far to Murmansk?'

The driver shrugged. 'Maybe five hundred,' he replied.

'Miles?'

'Dollars. Rubles. Kilometers. Is same thing. Because you can't get there.'

'I *have* to get there!'

The driver chuckled. 'Someday, sure. Not today.'

'But –'

The driver's smile was as wide as the road, and his eyes twinkled in the rearview mirror. 'Welcome to Archangel,' he said. 'Is gateway to North Pole.'

By the time they reached the center of town and the offices of the Sputnik Travel Agency, it was four-thirty in the afternoon and pitch-dark – not surprising, given their latitude. According to Daly's guidebook, Archangel was only thirty miles south of the Arctic Circle.

For a while, as he stood in front of the desk of the Sputnik travel agent, there was hope. The Sputnik agent was tossing him one hopeful grin after another as she worked the phones, trying to find a way – any way – to get him from Archangel to Murmansk. There was a moment when she seemed excited. Her professional smile softened into a grin, and it was clear that she was rooting for him, holding the fingers of her left hand aloft in a sort of twisted Boy Scout salute.

But then the animation faded, the fingers uncurled, and her lips sagged. She made a disgusted *tsk* and replaced the telephone receiver in its cradle. 'The rail is closed. Between here and Murmansk, also here and Moscow, also everywhere to east. Is –'

'I know: big storm'

'Yes. There is too much snow.' She shrugged. 'So I think, maybe, you are staying here one or two days.'

Daly groaned, but there was nothing to be done about it. 'What about a hotel reservation? Can you – ?'

The woman shook her head. 'Only transport.' Daly

must have looked crestfallen because the woman took pity on him. She looked him up and down, trying to reconcile the expensive boots and parka that he wore with the ratty backpack that he carried. This last was a khaki-colored object made of canvas. It had plastic snaps that were supposed to look like leather but didn't, and a crude peace symbol had been painstakingly drawn in ballpoint on its flap.

She gestured at the peace symbol. 'Is for Chechnya?' she asked.

Daly thought about it. 'Yeah,' he said. 'Probably.'

The woman smiled. 'Try Excelsior,' she said. 'Is nice – around corner. You'll like.'

The Excelsior *was* nice, but it was also booked solid, so he sat in its comfortable lobby and consulted *Russia, Ukraine & Belarus*. As far as hotel rooms were concerned, the publishers were blunt. Accommodations in Archangel were either 'cheap and nasty,' or 'acceptable and expensive.' For Daly, whose expenses were covered by a foundation, this was a no-brainer, or ought to have been.

But as he found out, the A&E hotels (which was how he thought of them) were crammed with oilmen and diamond dealers, commodity brokers and white-collar hustlers from every corner of the globe. Archangel, it seemed, was the jumping-off point for a vanguard of venture capitalists intent on 'developing' Siberia. He visited three A&E's, each of which was fully booked, lugging his suitcase through the snow. Finally, he slipped a few bucks to the desk clerk at the Pushkin and asked him to find a room – anywhere.

It took almost an hour, but in the end he emerged from the lobby with a scrap of paper in his hand: *Chernomorskaya – ulitsa Ya Temme, 3.*

The doorman looked doubtful when Daly asked for a taxi, gesturing vaguely at the weather and shaking his head morosely. 'Bus is better,' he said, and pointed toward the stop, half a block away, where a couple of very cold-looking types stood under a flickering street lamp, stamping their frozen feet. Daly started to insist, but the doorman looked so puzzled – almost *hurt* – that he gave it up.

He trudged toward the bus stop, thinking: wouldn't Dad be proud? The Old Man never tired of cautioning him that he'd never really get anywhere or 'make something' of himself if he didn't learn how to 'face facts' and keep his temper. *You got to keep your Irish down, Frankie. Look at me.* He'd thump himself on the chest. *My whole life I'm working for chump change, and why? Because I always have to be right. Because I can't keep my smartass mouth shut. Because I never figured out sometimes it isn't worth it to make a federal case out of something. It's like that gambling song, where the guy says, 'You gotta know when to fold 'em.'* Daly shook his head at the memory of his father's reverence for the wit and wisdom of Kenny Rogers.

Meanwhile, he was freezing, slowly, in all his extremities: toes, feet, and face. Stamping on the ground did no good at all. The only thing that could help was the bus itself, so that when it arrived, he hurled himself on board as soon as the mechanical doors lurched open. The driver glanced at the paper in his hand and, pointing to his watch, made a semicircle with his forefinger. Half an hour to the Chernomorskaya.

Daly found a seat as close to one of the heating vents as he could and settled in. Rattling through Archangel in the rickety bus, its windows so fogged and frosted that he might as well have been in the clouds, Daly grimaced at his inability to suppress the song in his head.

Like a roach in a sugar bowl, it went round and round.

You played the hand you were dealt, which meant that you could hold 'em, fold 'em, walk away or . . .

What? He thought for a moment, and then he remembered, *Oh, yeah: you could run.* That was the part he always forgot. *You could run.*

By the time he got to the hotel, suitcase in hand, the snow was blowing sideways and the electricity was out. Or mostly out. A generator pounded away in the basement, providing just enough juice to see by, but not much else. The few lights that burned were supplemented by candles, which dimmed the seediness of the lobby to a sinister yellow gloom that smelled of wax.

Daly entered with a wary look and glanced around. In a corner of the lobby a jaundiced prostitute, shrink-wrapped in polyester, perched on a red plastic couch, painting her nails. Nearby, a Japanese businessman sat in a tattered easy chair, reading a comic book, while three young men in black leather jackets argued across a bottle of vodka.

Daly filled out a reservation card at the front desk and paid the clerk in dollars. As the Russian counted the money, Daly read the hand-lettered sign that hung on the wall behind him:

NEED MONEY? YOU CAN SELL
YOUR BELONGINGS TO OUR SHOP
ON THE SECOND FLOOR. FAIR
PRICES PAID!

Daly was amazed by the Russian kleptocracy in which everything that wasn't bolted down was up for grabs, or up for sale. In Moscow two people had tried to buy his sunglasses, and a kid on a moped had grabbed for his watch. Drivers took their windshield wipers with them into restaurants, laying them on the table like so much extra cutlery. After two days in the Russian capital, Daly had realized that it was only a matter of time before someone tried to kill him for his computer, so he traded its expensive, leather carrying case for a ratty-looking backpack. The laptop – a $4,000 ThinkPad – fitted easily in the canvas bag, which in an earlier life had no doubt been the repository of crayons and peanut butter sandwiches (or whatever it was that Russian children ate for lunch. Beets, maybe).

After a while he gave up waiting for the elevator and, key in hand, headed up the stairs, which were dark enough to make him nervous. Somewhere between the second and third floors he heard shouting. The noise was muffled and panicky, distant and near at the same time. After a moment he realized that it was coming from inside the walls, and the realization made the hair at the back of his neck stand up. Then it hit him: nothing supernatural; someone was trapped in the elevator. With a sigh, he went back the way he'd come and told the clerk who, with a shrug, turned his palms toward the ceiling. 'Every night, this is problem,' he said in a low, gravelly voice. 'I tell guests about conservation policy. But . . .' He shrugged again. 'One hour – maybe two.'

Sucks to be them, Daly thought, resolving to stay out of elevators. His room was on the fourth floor, and it took him a while to figure out how to open the door in the gloomy corridor.

Once inside, he tossed his suitcase on the bed and, with a sinking feeling, surveyed the stained wallpaper, cracked sconces, and scabrous ceiling tiles. A radiator rattled next to the wall, but remained cool to the touch. Nearby, the room's only window opened onto an airshaft, which meant that the room was darker, and probably warmer, than many of the others in the hotel. Even so, the wind had muscled its way into the crack where the sill met the sash, and a little pyramid of granular snow sat on the threadbare carpet. Daly watched it for a moment, hoping for a telltale sign of moisture, but in the end decided that the snow wasn't melting.

Crossing his arms, he jammed his fists into his armpits and sat on the edge of the bed. Exhaling mightily, he watched his breath tumble through the air, and shivered.

Still, he thought, however cold and uncomfortable he was, there was one consoling fact: at least, with a storm like this, the *Rex Mundi* wouldn't be going anywhere.

6

Annie stood on the catwalk, staring nervously ahead at the pack ice. *Fast* ice, she reminded herself. As in landfast. Which meant that it was connected to the land.

Keep it straight, she told herself.

She didn't like to make mistakes. It gave the Snowmen a chance to make fun of her. Or, if not to make fun, then to patronize her with amused glances and helpful corrections. She didn't handle that kind of thing well. It made her feel stupid, she blushed and got defensive. She couldn't help it. She was always told 'it ran in the family.' *Thin skin.*

And until she was old enough to understand that this was only a metaphor, she thought of it as a kind of disease, an illness that she'd inherited along with her mother's cheekbones. *Thin skin.* It sounded like something that was waiting to break. Like ice on a pond.

Fast ice. Everywhere.

They'd outrun the storm and it was a brilliant day, with blue skies and temperatures just above zero. The *Rex Mundi* was grinding through the ice at a crawl, its deck and fixtures coated with frost. The ship was heading for the Storfjorden, a passage of water and ice that flowed between the glaciated east coast of Spitsbergen and the west coast of Edgeoya, a smaller island in the Norwegian Sea.

Annie was staring at the crumpled carpet of ice that stretched ahead of the bow as far as she could see. She was looking for a dark speck, the first hint of what the Snowmen called 'a lead' – a break in the ice that would take them into the inky blackness of open water.

And then they'd be able to go faster.

Despite the extra days afforded by their hasty departure, she was worried about the time and the logistics. The first part of the voyage – north by northwest through the Barents Sea – had gone quickly. Murmansk itself remained ice-free all winter, licked by the same branch of the warm Atlantic current that kept the route to the west coast of Spitsbergen accessible by sea much of the year.

But nearly as soon as they veered east, heading toward the Storfjorden passage, they found themselves surrounded by pack ice. And once inside the fjord, the ice was even thicker, which meant that for hours it had been fast ice and slow going. The helicopter had gone out repeatedly in search of leads that would guide them to the channels of water that ran through the ice like streams through snowy fields.

But now the Snowmen had put an end to that. The physicist who served also as the expedition's helicopter pilot decided they had better conserve fuel for hauling supplies to and from the site at Kopervik. Now there was nothing to do but plow through the ice, and hope.

Apart from the 'leads,' there were also patches of open water, lakes of a sort, in the midst of the 'permanent ice.' The lakes appeared more or less regularly, she was told, in the same locations each year. Charts with multilayered silhouettes recorded their size and position. She'd looked at one that morning. One of the crewmen had shown her exactly where they expected to find open water. It appeared on the chart as a long, feathery shape that curled inland toward one of the only black dots on Edgeoya – the Kopervik mining camp.

The problem was that the charts had not been kept for very many years and there was no telling when one of the 'lakes' might disappear and revert to ice. Crunching through fast ice cut the speed of the *Rex* to a fraction of what it could do at full throttle. So if they had to go through ice all the way . . . *well,* it would take a long time.

Then again, if they came to the open area within the next couple of hours, with a little luck they'd reach their anchorage by evening and be ashore by morning.

She couldn't help her impatience. The grant proposal had been her idea, and she'd been crushed when the National Science Foundation had rejected it, despite Doctor K's support. Now that the project had actually been approved, she wanted to do the science – and she wanted to do it *now.*

The idea was to extract viral isolates from the lung tissues of the miners. She and Doctor K would use a state-of-the-art technique called polymerase chain restructuring, or PCR, to re-create the virus in the lab. If they were lucky, and were able to generate enough product to culture the strain that had killed the miners, they could of course create a vaccine (in case one should ever be needed). But even more important (to Annie's way of thinking), they'd be able to test Doctor K's theory about the relationship of certain kinds of protein coats to the virulence of different strains of influenza. This was cutting edge stuff . . .

It had surprised Annie to learn that at the turn of the century there were still bits and pieces of this earth so inhospitable that they were not a part of any sovereign nation. The Svalbard archipelago, which included the island of Spitsbergen, was (until 1939) one of those places. Until then, when the archipelago became a part of Norway, the islands were up for grabs. Its resources were available to anyone and everyone, providing only that they were willing to endure months of darkness and isolation, foul weather, and the constant threat of polar bear attacks. (Even now, visitors to Svalbard tended to be armed – and not with .22s. They favored high-powered rifles and .45 caliber handguns, weapons that could be counted on to drop a six-hundred-pound bear dead in its tracks.)

Not that Svalbard was bristling with natural resources. Basically, there were seams of coal. An American businessman named John Longyear was the first to exploit the archipelago's resources, establishing the Arctic Coal Company in 1906. It was under the auspices of Arctic Coal that a mine was opened on the island of Spitsbergen, an event that sparked what amounted to a 'coal rush,' with adventurous Brits, Danes, and Russians staking out mines up and down the archipelago.

Profitable at first, the coal became increasingly expensive to mine. But that was hardly the point. The real prize was the archipelago itself, which sat strategically on the roof of the Atlantic, guarding the entrance to the Barents Sea. The Russians and Brits, Norwegians and Danes, were staking claims to a lot more than the coal in the ground.

In the end it was the Norwegians who prevailed, and they did so by continuing to operate mines like the one at Kopervik – a nearly inaccessible outpost that eventually produced the most expensive coal in the world. Or it did until the question of sovereignty was finally settled in Norway's favor, whereupon the mine was immediately shut down.

Now, almost sixty years later, Annie and Doctor K were after a different kind of buried treasure: a virus so virulent and contagious that it might serve as a standard against which all others should be measured. It lay, or so they hoped, three feet under the permafrost, deep in the lungs of five Norwegian miners who'd drowned in their own sputum eighty years before. According to the meticulously kept records of the Lutheran minister who'd lived in Kopervik at the time, the miners' bodies were in the westernmost corner of the graveyard, just behind the chapel.

Of course, the NOAA team would have to take ice-core samples from the permafrost before any exhumation would proceed. If the ice patterns within the cores revealed melt-and-thaw cycles, a decision would have to be made as to whether or not to go forward. Since the influenza virus deteriorates so quickly after its host's death, it would be pointless to disinter the dead if the cadavers had thawed at any time since 1918.

Which, when you thought of it, seemed likely.

This damned ice, Annie thought, gazing ahead at the rumpled white ocean, hoping for a glimpse of black water. But there was none to be seen, only the crystalline blue sky and mounded waves, white as sheets and just as dazzling.

The thing was . . . this was her baby. No wonder she was impatient.

She was the one who, with Doctor K's encouragement, had spent nearly all of her spare time researching high altitude settlements in places as remote as Chile, Siberia, and Tibet – looking for what

71

Doctor K called 'viable victims.'

Eventually, she'd read about Spitsbergen in a back issue of the *New York Times*. The article was about Russian and Norwegian claims to the Svalbard archipelago. Almost in passing, it mentioned the region's coal mines, and how, in 1918, those who'd worked them had been hard hit by the Spanish flu. It didn't surprise her to learn of the miners' deaths. What did surprise her was that the miners had been buried in situ, rather than taken to the mainland. Intrigued by this, she'd delved further into the story, and soon learned more than she'd ever expected to know about burial practices in the frozen North.

Most often, among the natives, the dead were laid to rest above the ground and covered with a cairn of rocks and stones. Digging was impossible. The ground was frozen solid to a depth of several feet. Better to let nature take its course, and so they did. In the end the bears always had their way with the dead.

But the mining companies had an alternative, and that was dynamite. Drilling into the frozen earth, they'd stuff the holes with explosives, and blast the graves out of the ground to a depth of about three feet. Which was more than enough: neither heat nor bears would ever get so far.

Or so Annie hoped. And, with Doctor K's permission, she had written to the mining company about the burials. The company went out of business in the Second World War, but the law firm that represented its interests put her in touch with the church whose minister had served the camps at Kopervik and Longyearbyen. Church records identified the miners and their next of kin, whose descendants had then been contacted for permission to exhume (and subsequently to reinter) their relatives.

Through all of this, Doctor K had played a passive but encouraging role. And in the end, when the groundwork had been laid, he applied for a grant in both their names – only to be turned down.

Everyone agreed that the proposal was promising. Interesting. Deserving. And timely: it was common knowledge that a major mutation of the influenza virus would soon occur. It happened every thirty years or so, and the world was 'overdue.' There was also agreement that 'if past was prologue,' the coming shift would be to an H-1 strain – like the Spanish flu. There was general accord as well that Doctor K's theory held promise and that valuable data about the relationship between virulence and antigenic structure might be gleaned from a sample of the 1918 strain – if one could be found.

If Doctor K was right, the more virulent strains of influenza could be identified by the relative prominence of a hooklike protuberance on the protein coat of the antigen. Among virologists this was known (half jokingly) as 'Kicklighter's Horn.'

Even now, H-1 strains could be found in one part of the world and another – and those infected with them weren't dying en masse. Doctor K's studies of these strains tended to support his theory: they lacked the more prominent hook and, as he'd predicted, the virulence that went with it. It was fair to say, then, that apart from everything else that might be learned, a look at the 1918 strain would go a long way toward proving or disproving his theory.

And, though it sounded selfish, Annie couldn't help but think that if the expedition were successful, she'd be well on her way toward tenure at Georgetown.

Indeed, she'd be even further along if the grant had not fallen victim to what amounted to bad timing.

Only a month before the application was submitted to the National Science Foundation, there was a highly publicized accident at the National Arbovirus Research Laboratory in Cambridge, Massachusetts. When a test tube shattered in one of the lab's centrifuges, two doctors and a lab technician had been infected with Sabia, an often lethal hemorrhagic fever that had previously been seen only in Brazil. Though the incident was immediately contained, the tabloids had gotten wind of it, and the result was an afternoon of congressional hearings that had a distinctively chilling effect on the NSF. Fearful of further criticism, the foundation declined to fund an expedition that in essence promised to rescue from oblivion one of the most dangerous viruses in history.

And then, when a year had passed and she'd nearly forgotten about the proposal, the funding came through – not from the NSF, but from a small foundation that operated out of a town house behind the Supreme Court.

Annie had never heard of it, and what's more, hadn't even known that Doctor K was submitting the proposal to funding sources outside the NSF. But Doctor K was like that. He kept things to himself – probably to shield her from further disappointments. Which was okay with her.

Annie lowered her binoculars, even as she stared ahead, trying to coax a lead into existence by sheer force of will. But there was nothing. Just the ice and the snow, and . . .

A swirling patter, like fractals forming and reforming in her field of vision. She'd read about this. It was a common hallucination, and Annie knew, from the reading she'd done the week before, that the first person to report it had been a nineteenth century explorer who'd walked halfway across Baffin Island with his crew – after their ship froze in and was crushed 'like a walnut' by the ice.

At least *that* wasn't going to happen; there was no chance of getting frozen in. The *Rex* was built for the Arctic, and with its steel-strengthened hull and powerful engines, it was capable of plowing through ice as thick as fifteen or twenty feet.

She just wished it would go faster.

Annie squeezed her eyes shut for a moment, as she'd been told to do when she began to hallucinate. The thought of the polar explorer and his crew made her feel cold. First, they'd eaten their dogs, then pieces of canvas, then parts of their clothes. The last thing they ate were their boots, and by then most of their teeth had fallen out. Eventually, the leader's diary was recovered by a subsequent expedition. It had been preserved in oiled paper and stored within a tobacco tin. In the diary, the expedition's leader wrote about the succulence of boot leather on the tongue, and the way he held it motionless in his mouth until it dissolved like a communion wafer.

And then, apparently, he died.

A change in the air caught Annie's eye, and she squinted into the distance. There were rain clouds on the horizon, or so it seemed. She took a closer look with the glasses, and her mood sank. Thunderheads thrust into the blue sky. That's all they needed. Another storm.

Despite the layers of clothes she was wearing – starting with thermal underwear and working up to the puffy, red, Michelin-man parka issued by the *Rex* – a shiver rattled through her. She *was* cold, but she didn't want to go back to her cabin, or even retreat to the warmth of the bridge. She had a superstitious feeling that if she didn't keep staring ahead, the open water would never appear. And it must appear. *Soon.*

Her eyes drifted to the catwalk below, where Doctor K was standing with his arms folded, jaw set, watching the horizon. He was probably nervous – he *had* to be nervous. There was a lot riding on the next few days. But, of course, he wouldn't show it. Unlike her, he kept his feelings inside.

Except for his acid intolerance of other people's mistakes. Around Georgetown and the NIH, Kicklighter's brilliance was taken for granted. As a virologist, he was one of the world's foremost experts on RNA viruses. There was talk of a Nobel – there was *always* 'talk of a Nobel' – but he himself dismissed the idea. 'I'm not interested in trophies,' he lied.

As an emeritus professor at Georgetown, he was famously unpopular. When people learned that she was one of his postdoc assistants, they raved: 'You work with *Dickbiter*? How can you *stand* it?'

He's shy, she'd say. He lives inside his head. And . . . he just doesn't have good people skills.

That was one way of putting it. And, really, Doctor K was never mean. He didn't get angry. And he never held a grudge. It was just that if you were working with him and you couldn't follow the leaps that he took (and, let's face it, a lot of students couldn't), then he had to stop and explain. And sometimes this meant that he lost something, and sometimes what was lost was valuable.

And if a question was particularly ill-timed, he got the look that his grad students loved to mimic. His shoulders would sag, his head would list to the side, and slowly, patiently, he'd begin to explain, talking in a voice so remote that it seemed at times almost like a recording – a recording that dissected the question as if it were a frog, laying bare the false assumptions that were its skeleton.

It was a crushing experience, yes, but she could see that behind it all he was bereft, mourning the rush of insight that had been lost to a dumb-ass question.

Not that she would ever *say* anything like that – because, she knew if she did, it would sound as if she were bragging, implying that *she,* at least, was brilliant enough to follow Doctor K's careening mind. Though now that you mention it . . . she thought. Sometimes she could stay with him all the way, and spiral right up to wherever he was going – and then, when he lost momentum, *she'd* be the one to push him on. And that was very exhilarating. Anyway –

'You'd better go inside, sweetheart.'

She jumped. The voice was right in her ear, and it sent her heart crashing against her chest.

This was something she'd never get used to – the bizarre intimacy forced upon them by the *Rex*'s noise. The ship's din was amazing as it crunched through the ice 'like a giant chewing boulders' – she'd read that somewhere. And that was only the noise from the bow. The engine was aft, a constant, blasting racket that pulsed through the decks even as the ice ground along the ship's sides.

Obviously, the crewmen were used to the decibel level, and so were the Snowmen, who'd spent enough time on icebreakers that they, too, had adapted. There were eight of them on the *Rex*, and they all seemed to use a kind of sign language, so that when they wanted to communicate by speaking aloud, they didn't bother with preliminaries: they just lowered their heads and shouted into your ear.

It was a weird intimacy, feeling the man's breath

against her skin. Obviously, she was not used to it. Even when she saw it coming, when one of them began to duck his head, she jerked backward, as if dodging a kiss. And then she felt stupid. And blushed, just as she was doing now.

It was Mark, the senior ice physicist. He ducked his head again, and this time she barely flinched. 'You've got a patch of frostbite starting on your cheek.'

He straightened up and touched his own cheek with his gloved finger. She motioned for him to lower his head so she could tell him something, but he shook his head impatiently and made a shooing motion that told her to get inside. She pointed to Doctor K, but Mark grabbed her arm and pushed her toward the door.

After a minute he came in after her. In the warm air, wisps of vapor came off their clothing like smoke,

'What are you,' he said, with a nod of his head toward the outside, 'his baby-sitter?'

'He'd never notice if he was getting frostbite. I was just –'

'*You* didn't notice you were getting frostbite.' He took his goggles off and bent to look at her cheek. 'Superficial. And you can relax – the professor is fine, I checked him out. What were you doing out there anyway? Someone said you've been out there for more than an hour.'

'I was looking for water,' she said.

'Well, don't worry about it. We'll get to water in half an hour – maybe less.'

She gave him a skeptical look.

'There's a blink,' he said.

She just looked at him, not sure if he was teasing. 'A blink,' she repeated.

'You're so suspicious! C'mere,' he said, and taking her arm, guided her to a porthole. 'Look at the sky, just above the horizon. You see those dark shapes?'

Annie nodded. 'There's going to be a storm,' she said.

Mark shook his head. 'There's not going to be a storm. And those aren't clouds. Like I keep trying to tell you, we don't get a lot of snow up here. In fact, we get more in Atlanta. The Arctic is a desert.'

Annie squinted through the glass, which had a layer of film on it to cut the glare. 'Why do you say those aren't clouds? Look at them! They're *clouds*.'

'It's a reflection. With ice and snow, you get temperature layers in the air – and it makes for some crazy refractions. A lot of times you can see over the horizon.'

'Right,' she said. 'And on a clear day, you can see the future – or is it "forever"?'

'I'm serious. When you're surrounded by ice, and the conditions are right, you see the water up ahead, just beyond the horizon, reflected in the sky. If you're in water, you can see ice – which used to be the more important use of the phenomenon. In the old days, ships posted somebody on bow watch to study the sky for early warnings about icebergs.' He gestured ahead. 'They call it "blink." Water blink. Ice blink. Snow blink. Up there – that's a water blink. We'll be in the open sea inside an hour. You'll see.'

She didn't really believe it until it happened. She was in her cabin, changing into dry clothes, when her heart was slammed by a sudden silence. Without warning the ice gave way, the boulder crunching ceased, and the world – the entire world – surged smoothly ahead, like a drill bit that has just broken through a thick board.

With a smile, she fell back on her bunk and closed her eyes. It was almost as if she could see it: the clean sharp line of the raked prow as it knifed through the open water, the dark sea parting in furls of phosphorescent foam.

And just ahead, almost within reach: Kopervik. The virus. And her future.

7

ARCHANGEL
MARCH 24, 1998

'Is gone.'

'No,' Daly said, 'that's gotta be a mistake.' The blizzard hadn't even slowed down yet, so the clerk at the Polarsk Shipping Agency had to be wrong. 'It was *scheduled* to depart yesterday, but, look – I couldn't even *get* to Murmansk.'

The young man listened patiently, twisting a long lock of greasy hair around his forefinger. Then he repeated what he'd said: 'Is gone.'

'But – there's a storm. There's a fucking hurricane! Nobody's going out in that!'

The clerk sighed, flattened a sheet of thermal fax on the desk in front of him and put his finger next to a line in the middle of the page. 'I hear you, man, but this ship, she's an icebreaker – she's leaving *ahead* of the storm.'

'What?' Daly was taken aback as much by the clerk's use of slang as by what he'd said. For the first time, he focused on the fact that the kid was wearing an AC/DC earring.

'Yeah,' he said. 'She goes out at 1100 yesterday.'

Daly ran his hand through his hair and sat back in the chair. He had a feeling the kid knew what he was talking about. And then it hit him: not only had he missed the boat, but it had left *even before he himself was scheduled to arrive.*

Which pissed him off. Here, he'd been feeling guilty about holding up Kicklighter and Adair – they'd be wondering where he was, and so on – only to find out that they'd blown him off, just like that. As if he'd been standing outside a movie theater in Washington rather than sitting in the Chernomorskaya the *fucking* Chernomorskaya – in Archangel!

'You know where I can send a fax?'

'Not to the *Rex Mundi*.' The kid shook his head. 'It's not possible.'

'Why not?'

'Because . . . It's a ship.' He shrugged. 'So, you must send telex.'

'Telex?' Daly wasn't even sure what a telex was. Some kind of telegram or something. But he said: 'Okay, so I'll send a telex. Where do I do that?'

The main post office was just around the corner on ulitsa Voskresinia. And a good thing, too. As Daly stepped out of the shipping office, the cold surged at him like a dog on a chain. For a moment it was as if he was – literally – frozen in his tracks. This wasn't the kind of cold you had in the States, he thought. It wasn't the kind of cold you had *anywhere*. It was straight out of hell, and even as he stood there, paralyzed, it sucked at his heart.

A stiff wind was blowing out of the north, straight from Murmansk, needling his face with a pebbly snow that felt like a mixture of ice and sand. With a shudder, he hunched his shoulders, pulled his parka closer to his throat, and staggered forward. Taking one tentative step after another, he navigated the ice floe that passed for a sidewalk, and headed downhill toward the frozen river.

It was twilight and he couldn't see much. The street was to his left, but it was more notional than real. With his chin on his chest, he found himself in a monochrome world, following the street lamps toward the Dvina. Beneath the lamps the metal posts were flocked with snow and nearly invisible; their lights hung in the air as if by magic, pale and blurry, rocking in a gray wind.

Nearby, a snowplow bulldozed its way back and forth in the square, the ploshchad Lenina, banking the snow into berms on every corner. I could be here for a while, Daly thought, gritting his teeth against the cold.

Arriving at the post office, he climbed the icy steps to the door, yanked it open, and stepped into a warm cocoon that smelled of wet wool, sweat, and cheap tobacco. Red-faced men and women milled around in bulky clothing, queuing in front of numbered windows. Daly went from one person to the next, asking, 'Telex? Telex?' But no one seemed to understand. Finally, a man in a fur hat took him by the sleeve and explained, in perfect and accentless English, how to send a telex.

Daly went to a counter in the rear and composed a message on the back of an envelope from the New World Aster Hotel in Shanghai.

> DR. BENTON F. KICKLIGHTER
> KOPERVIK EXPEDITION
> M/V REX MUNDI
> FREQ 333-80
>
> IT'S A DARK AND STORMY DAY.
> STRANDED ARCHANGEL.
> MEET YOU HAMMERFEST
> ON 28TH.
>
> FRANK DALY

He read the message over, and wanted badly to add something more, something nasty and vituperative about being left in the lurch. But even though he was capable of carrying a grudge into the afterlife, within his professional life he'd disciplined himself not to whine. At least when it would do no good.

He read the message again, frowned, and crumpled it up. First of all, the charge was by the word, and the rate was high enough to discourage anything but nouns and verbs. More to the point, Kicklighter didn't seem like the kind of guy who was easily amused. He wouldn't appreciate: 'It's a dark and stormy day.' On the contrary, in the few conversations they'd had, the professor had impressed him as a condescending sonofabitch who was suffering from a terminal case of GMS – the Great Man Syndrome. What was it that he'd said?

To tell you the truth, Mr. Daly, I'm not much impressed by journalists. You tend to have short attention spans.

And then he'd made that little clicking noise, dismissing Daly and the world of journalism with a single click of the tongue. It had taken an act of considerable will for Daly to keep his mouth shut. There was a time, not so long ago, when he'd have replied that he himself was not much impressed by virologists – who were said to have short dicks. Instead, he'd shrugged and, looking abashed, expressed the hope that the doctor would give him a chance to prove himself.

Looking for another piece of paper, and finding none, Daly flattened out the envelope from the Chinese hotel and edited the message on its back:

STRANDED ARCHANGEL.
MEET HAMMERFEST. DALY

That's better, he thought. Four words, and just the last name. *Daly*. Like Charlemagne, except Irish.

It occurred to him that he ought to add Anne Adair's name to the heading on the telex . . . but no. Though the expedition had been her idea (according to the *NIH Record*), she was still only Kicklighter's assistant. Great Men tended to be sticklers for protocol – even, or especially, where a protégé was concerned. Better, then, to leave her off.

Envelope in hand, Daly joined the end of a long line that led to the telex window. Steam rose off the back of the pear-shaped woman in front of him, and the air was acrid with the stench of Turkish cigarettes. Boots shuffled and squeaked on the wet wooden floor. Occasionally, he heard American and English voices in the din, but he could never place them. The line moved in lurches of one or two feet at a time, punctuated by long periods of restless waiting. Not that it mattered. There wasn't anywhere to go, and there wouldn't be for days.

After he finally got the telex off, he stopped in to see the Sputnik clerk and make a reservation for a flight to Hammerfest, Norway. Giving the storm a chance to blow itself out, and the Archangel airport plenty of time to scrape off its runways, de-ice its Ilyushins, and reopen for business, he picked a flight in three days time – which would still put him in Hammerfest before the *Rex* was scheduled to return.

That done, there wasn't much else to do but make his way back to the Chernomorskaya – and work.

Returning to his room, he pulled the laptop out of his backpack, and hesitated. He had the transformer that he needed, and the converter for the plug, but he didn't want to use them. Not with the power the way it was: every so often the overhead light pulsed like a star that was getting ready to go nova. If he worked off the hotel's power supply, he might wind up with a scrambled disk. Better to use the batteries. With his coat on, he could work until his fingers froze or the juice gave out. Whichever came first.

Pulling up a chair, he sat down at the desk and switched on the computer. When the command line finally appeared, he went into the /FLU directory and called up the interview notes that he'd written in Shanghai the week before.

> Lu Shin-Li – M.D., Univ. Beijing. Ph.D., Johns Hopkins. Head, Infl. Brnch., Shanghai Inst. of Allerg. & Infect. Diseases. Author, 'The Spanish Lady in China: an Historical Overview' (East-West Journal of Epidemiology). 1918: 10 million killed (India alone!). WWI. Russian rev. 'Drift' v. 'Shift.' Epidemic, pandemic. H-1 shift 'way overdue.' Next year? S-L: 'I don't want to spec. Intrstg. bug.'

Daly had gone to Shanghai to interview Shin-Li because he was the number one epidemiologist in China – and China was the epicenter of every influenza pandemic in history.

His interview went on for about five pages, and there were another ten pages of miscellany: a brief account of a visit that Daly had made to a Chinese farm, abstracts from various technical articles that he'd scanned into the laptop, quotes from Shin-Li's piece about the 1918 pandemic, and, finally, the article that had tipped him to the Kopervik expedition in the first place.

This last was a two-paragraph notice in the *Record,* the biweekly newsletter published for employees of the NIH:

Daly tapped the page down key with his finger as he tilted back in his chair, flipping through the notes a screen at a time. He saw it as a three-part series. He'd begin with a couple of thousand words, basic stuff about influenza viruses and, in particular, the 'Spanish Lady' – then go to part two, the expedition to Edgeoya. He'd call it 'Funeral in Reverse.' Then he'd finish with an account of Kicklighter's work at the NIH and his theory about protein coats.

If everything went brilliantly, he might be able to place the piece with *Harper's* or the *Smithsonian,* then use the published article to get a book contract. Which was the basic idea: to graduate from being a reporter on leave from the *Post* to being a *writer*. To work for himself, in other words, instead of someone else.

The only problem being that he'd missed the boat in Murmansk, and now he was going to miss the 'funeral in reverse.' Which meant that he'd lose a lot of the color he was counting on, unless he could find a way to tell the story through someone else's eyes.

Anne Adair was one possibility. Or maybe one of the crew, or the NOAA scientists. They could talk about the cold, the machines and the permafrost, the terrible loneliness of an island in the northernmost reaches of the Norwegian Sea.

But it would have been better – who was he kidding? it would have been a *lot* better – if he'd been there himself when the graves were opened. With a low growl, Daly leaned forward and typed *Part I*. Then he hit the carriage return and began to work on the lead. Half an hour later he finally had something he liked:

(Shanghai) They called her the 'Spanish Lady,'

though she was anything but that. Her roots were in China, not in Spain, and, far from being a lady, she was a killer. Indeed, within a few months of coming to the States, she'd killed more Americans than all of those who'd died in World War I.

And the bitch was just getting started.

Daly crossed his arms and leaned back in his chair. With a smile, he read what he'd written, and thought, Not bad. Good hook. Except they wouldn't let him use it. He'd never get away with a line like that. It was too interesting. With a grimace, he replaced 'the bitch' with 'she' and continued typing.

Dr. Liu Shin-Li, chief of the Influenza Branch of the Shanghai Institute of Allergies and Infectious Diseases, says that 'the Spanish flu was one of the most deadly pandemics in world history, killing as many as thirty million people around the world.'

Daly frowned, and thought, *As if.* Shin-Li's English wasn't nearly as good as he was making it sound. Still . . . that's what he'd *said*.

The speed with which the illness killed was as startling as the virus was deadly. In Westport, Connecticut, a woman playing bridge bid three hearts – and fell over dead. In Chicago, a man hailed a taxi – and died before he could open the door. in London, a soccer goalie leaped to make a save – and was dead when he hit the ground.

By all accounts, each of these people appeared to be in good health – until they died. But millions of others were less fortunate, suffering an array of symptoms so various that it seemed as if a dozen diseases were at work.

A physician in New York City reported that his patients were 'blue as huckleberries, and spitting blood.' Fevers of 106 were commonplace, as were projectile nosebleeds and endless bouts of vomiting and diarrhea. Genital gangrene was widely reported, as were instances of leucopenia (a sort of leukemia in reverse), sudden blindness, and complete loss of hearing.

Patients wept at the slightest touch, and physicians were mystified by a disease whose symptoms mimicked those of so many terrible illnesses. On one military base, hundreds of soldiers were treated for what doctors thought was a chlorine gas attack. Elsewhere, victims were given appendectomies, or treated for pneumonia, cholera, dysentery, typhoid, or sandfly fever.

In the end, most of the dead were found to have coughed their lives away, drowning in a slurry of blood and mucus, even as their lungs dissolved to the texture of 'red currant jelly.'

The battery light blinked on the computer, and Daly checked his watch. It was just past seven, and he was getting hungry. But the story was going well, and besides, it was freezing outside. He kept on typing.

According to Dr. Shin-Li, 'Wild ducks are the main reservoir of the virus, and we have more of them than any other country in the world. Not only that – because we raise chickens, ducks, and pigs together, the virus is able to move back and forth among them, from one species to another, changing as it goes.'

Because influenza is a shapeshifter, and animals

are constantly swapping viruses, mutations are frequent. While microbes like smallpox and polio are extremely stable, influenza is an RNA virus with a segmented chemical structure that is held together by only the weakest bonds. Lacking the DNA function that guards against mutation, the virus is constantly 'reassorting' itself in its animal hosts. This means that segments break off only to recombine with other segments, generating new strains of the flu.

It is this characteristic that forces scientists to develop a new vaccine each year.

The battery light was glowing steadily now, a soft yellow blip on the matte surface of the laptop. Daly figured he had about ten minutes left before it died.

Why the Spanish flu should have been the most deadly of all influenzas is the subject of a study by Dr. Benton Kicklighter.

The battery light flared, the computer beeped, and Daly jumped. He had about a minute left before the laptop crashed, but he didn't want to quit. He was getting to a part of the story that bothered him, the part that didn't make sense. It was the part about the expedition, and the reason it was mounted. If he stayed at the computer and wrote about it, or tried to, he might be able to figure it out. At a minimum, he should be able to articulate his own confusion – which was the first step to getting the story right.

But not this time. The laptop beeped again and, with a sigh, Daly saved the file to disk and shut the computer off. Then he pushed it into his backpack and shoved the backpack under the bed. His fingers were stiff and his stomach was rumbling, although after looking at the size of the pile of snow near his window and noting the ongoing blizzard in the airshaft, his appetite faded. It looked like he was going to have to take his meals in the basement of the Chernomorskaya.

Why did his heart not sing?

8

78°20′N, 220°14′E

Annie woke from her nap all at once, bursting into consciousness from a sleep so deep that, when her eyes opened, she gasped to find herself in the world. Jumping to her feet, she made her way down the corridor to the main deck, goggles in hand. Eager to see where they were, she leaned into the metal door that led to the deck, then pushed it open and stepped outside – where the cold air went off in her face like a paparazzo's flashbulb. Suddenly, she was more awake than she had ever been in her life, and utterly transfixed – as mind-blown as a dandelion in a gust of wind, her thoughts gone in an explosive scatter.

Icebergs! But what a bland word for what amounted to floating palaces of ice. The *Rex* was sailing through a flotilla of drifting blue mountains. And they were nothing like she expected, not big ice cubes bobbing on the dark water, but architectural wonders, carved by wind and water into complex and convoluted shapes. There were parabolic curves, Gothic spires, columns turned on a lathe, shimmering ridges and rippled slopes, cantilevered mountains of ice. And all of it was fashioned of a translucent material that had nothing in common with the ice she knew, but pulsed with a pure blue, heavenly light, as if lit from within.

This was the blue of Montego Bay, and of the robes

the Virgin Mary wore in statues found in little gardens in the Boston suburbs. It was the pure, inviting aqua chosen for the walls of swimming pools. And it was the radiant, unearthly blue that converged on the scene of the crime, whirling on the roofs of police cars.

Near dusk, they reached their anchorage, and Annie could see the coast of Edgeoya – a rumpled island hunkering in the sea, its bleak shores defined by a ragged line of black rocks. An hour after the anchor dropped, she and Dr. K, the Snowmen and the captain, took dinner together in the captain's mess.

The captain himself was a big Latvian with a florid face and thinning blond hair that he combed in strands across the top of his head. Annie liked him, but sitting at the table, she was in a subdued mood. Her delight and amazement at the Arctic had given way to a sense that *we shouldn't be here, we don't belong, it's too beautiful.* The empty perfection of the landscape, with its limited palette, the clarity of the air, the piercing silence – all of this was shattered by the primary colors of their parkas, the cloud of diesel fumes that hung above the ship, the trivial din of their presence.

'What's wrong?' the captain asked, his beefy face flushed with wine.

Annie shook her head. 'I don't know. Nothing. It's just – I feel like we're trespassing.'

Doctor K chuckled. 'And the miners? I suppose they were trespassing, as well.'

'Them, too,' she said, then shook her head as a burly waiter came to her side with a serving dish of liver and onions. 'I'm not hungry. Thanks.'

'You gotta feel sorry for the miners,' one of the physicists remarked. 'I mean, it's not like those guys were *explorers*. There wasn't any glory in it. They were

93

miners. Which meant that they spent all day in a hole, and when they came up – they were *here*.'

The captain nodded. He'd brought a few bottles of Spanish champagne to toast their arrival on Edgeoya. Uncorking one, he leaned across the table and began to fill people's glasses. 'This place is hell,' he said matter-of-factly.

The physicist, a weight lifter named Brian who doubled as the ship's helicopter pilot, laughed and tasted the champagne. 'Well,' he interjected, 'I don't know about that. It may be a little *chilly* for hell.'

The captain shook his head. 'No, I disagree,' he said. 'The temperature is perfect.'

'And how do you figure that?'

'Dante,' Annie said.

Everyone at the table looked at her. The captain smiled and gave her a deferential nod as he set the bottle down on the table.

Brian frowned. 'I don't get it.'

'The young lady is correct,' the captain said. 'Dante – he is the expert on hell.'

'Oh, you mean the *poet*,' Brian said.

Mark, who'd warned Annie about frostbite earlier that day, joined in the conversation: 'I thought that was Milton.'

The captain shook his head. 'No. Milton is expert on devil. Dante is expert on hell.'

'So . . . what's the *point*?' Brian asked.

'Simple point. But . . . maybe the young lady puts it better?'

Annie felt ambushed, but there was nothing she could do: she'd opened her big, fat mouth, and now she was on stage. 'Well . . . in the *Inferno* – which is the ninth circle of hell, which is the worst place – it's a palace of ice. Not fire, but – the opposite, a place

94

where it is always cold. Like here. My classics teacher,' she said, feeling the blood rush to her face, 'thought the idea – that hell was cold – was very old . . . a remnant of the Ice Age – when fire meant life, and death came from the cold.'

The captain nodded. 'I come to Spitsbergen three, four times a year, though never to Edgeoya,' he said, pouring himself a second glass of cheap champagne. And every time, I think, "We have no business here." The human beings are not meant to be here. No one is.'

Mark laughed. 'Well, let's hope NOAA doesn't find out, or we'll *all* be out of a job.'

'And I tell you,' the captain continued, 'when I have this feeling, I stay on my toes.'

'And why is that, Captain?' Doctor K looked genuinely curious.

'Because – this is like an alarm in my blood. Like ice or water is going to punch ship around, maybe. And I feel this – strong – when we come to the settlements.'

'Jeez, Captain, maybe you're not the right guy for this kinda work,' Brian joked, glancing slyly in Annie's direction. 'Maybe you should be on the Love Boat or something.'

The captain looked puzzled for a moment, and then his face became solemn again. 'This is hard place. Your miners found that out.'

'They certainly did,' Kicklighter said, 'but it wasn't the Arctic that killed them. It was a pathogen. And it would have killed them no matter where they were. They would have died in Paris, Oslo, anywhere. A lot of people did.'

Mark turned to Doctor K. 'You're talking about the Spanish flu, right?' Kicklighter nodded. 'My great-grandfather died of it. And one of his brothers. My grandmother said they couldn't do a thing.'

'They didn't even know what it was,' Annie said. 'They couldn't see it under the microscope. And even if they could –'

'They would have had a better chance with a lion at their throats than with this in their lungs,' Kicklighter said.

Brian leaned back in his chair. 'Ooooh,' he said. 'Lions and tigers and bears – oh my!'

Mark chuckled and Annie blushed. The professor blinked several times, rapidly, as if he'd lost the conversation's thread. Finally, he offered a weak smile. 'Indeed,' he said.

They were making fun of him, Annie thought, and by extension they were making fun of her as well. Not that it ever affected Doctor K. The professor was immune to ridicule, so secure in his own identity that he didn't really care what other people thought. And now, having finished his dinner, he folded his napkin, scraped back his chair, and got to his feet. With a nod to the captain, he said, 'Well . . . we have a big day tomorrow.'

He was halfway out the door when he paused and, turning, reached into the pocket of his jacket. 'I almost forgot,' he said. 'This came yesterday.' Taking a sheet of paper from his pocket, he handed it to Annie. 'I suppose it was the storm,' he added. And then, with a little wave, he was gone.

Annie unfolded the paper and glanced at the message:

STRANDED ARCHANGEL.
MEET HAMMERFEST. DALY

'I guess the lion tamer needs his rest,' Brian said.

Annie's face was suddenly warm. 'You can laugh,' she said, 'but he's the best in the world at what he does. And if you don't think it takes courage, you don't know anything about the pathogens he handles.' She pushed the telex into her pocket.

'Oh?'

Her face was burning now, and she knew that the wine had gone to her head. 'I just wouldn't be so blasé,' she said, 'especially if you don't know what you're getting into.'

' "Getting *into*"?' Brian frowned, and Mark gave her a quizzical look.

Annie fumbled with her napkin. 'That's not what I meant,' she said. 'I meant, if you don't know what you're talking about.' *God, that sounded even worse.* Flustered, she turned to the waiter, who was standing beside her with a pot of coffee, waiting to serve. 'Please,' she said, in a voice that was much too loud and bright.

Brian kept his eyes on her. 'I didn't know we were getting "into" anything,' he said.

'We aren't.'

'I mean, I thought we were just moving some body bags around.'

'That's right,' Annie replied, much too quickly. She took a couple of sips of coffee, noting how Mark and Brian exchanged glances. Then she folded her napkin and pushed her chair back. 'I thought I'd take a look at the Northern Lights,' she said, grabbing her parka.

'Good idea,' the captain remarked, and getting to his feet with a small bow, opened the door and held it for her.

Annie's heart was beating like a drum as she made her way down the corridor to the outside. Lying didn't come easily to her. In fact, it almost never came at all.

And when it did, she walked away, just as she was doing now.

The truth was, the expedition was not without its risks. Though they'd taken every precaution imaginable, there was always a possibility, however remote, that the virus remained viable, and that somehow it would get loose. And if it did, everyone aboard the ship would be in danger. So, in that sense, they *were* 'getting into' something, though it was unlikely that anything would actually happen.

Annie stood by the railing of the ship, her eyes fixed on the Northern Lights as they pulsed behind the horizon, a rippling curtain of green that rose toward the stars.

She was having second thoughts. Though Doctor K's name was first on the grant proposal, the expedition had been her idea. Admittedly, nothing could have been done without Doctor K's endorsement. But without *her,* the expedition would never have been imagined.

So if anything went wrong, and half the people on earth died . . . it would be her fault.

Annie made an exasperated sound. There wasn't a chance of the virus getting loose. Even if the *Rex* lost power and the generators failed in the Cold Room, the body-transfer cases were hermetically sealed; and the cadavers themselves would be wrapped in formalin-soaked sheets. Even if they hit an iceberg, *and sank,* the bodies wouldn't *go* anywhere. Even if the fish didn't get them, the *Rex* was smack in the midst of the Arctic gyre, a clockwise current that circled the North Pole: anything that went overboard would move around the top of the earth forever, and do so in water temperatures that were actually below freezing.

So there really wasn't anything to worry about. *She*

knew that, and so did the foundation. Otherwise, they wouldn't have changed their minds about the grant proposal.

The real worry, then, was that the expedition would turn out to be a waste of time. Suppose the bodies were too close to the surface? Suppose they got back to Washington and there wasn't enough virus to work with? She'd have wasted everyone's time, and a whole lot of grant money.

Her mind was at the races, and it stayed that way. Later that night, as she lay in her bunk with her eyes shut, trying to sleep, she found herself thinking of Frank Daly. In a way, Daly was her fault. In her enthusiasm, she'd encouraged him to come on the expedition, only to learn that Doctor K was aghast at the idea. She'd have rescinded the offer, but Doctor K wouldn't hear of it: 'It would just make him suspicious,' he'd said. As if they'd had something to hide.

And now, to have set sail without him, after he'd come so far – well, it was a disaster.

Somehow, they'd make it up to him. She'd see to that. But in the meantime there was so much to be done.

Rolling onto her side and pulling her pillow close to her cheek, she imagined the day that lay ahead of them. She'd climb out of bed at dawn, pull on her thermals and snowsuit, grab a cup of coffee from the mess, and help Doctor K organize the equipment. When that was done, she and the others would travel overland on Sno-Cats to the camp at Kopervik. The Snowmen thought the trip would take about an hour. Meanwhile, Brian and Doctor K would begin to move the gear by helicopter, ferrying it to the camp.

And there was a lot of equipment – the Jamesway

hut that would serve as their headquarters, a couple of field tents, two portable generators, three drums of diesel fuel. There were boxes of food and cooking equipment, rifles and ammunition to keep the bears at bay, masonry tools for digging. There were jackhammers and shovels, a palette of body-transfer cases, ropes, and a trunk full of formalin-drenched sheets.

If Doctor K was right, it would take about three days to excavate the coffins, assuming they weren't buried any deeper than three feet.

She didn't remember falling asleep, but she must have because, quite suddenly, it was morning. She was sitting in the chair next to her bunk, with a book in her lap – she remembered getting up in the middle of the night. There was a blanket over her knees and a light burning over her shoulder, but its illumination was entirely unnecessary: the cabin was suffused with daylight. Reflexively, she turned to the porthole and, seeing the sky, blinked twice, then scrambled to her feet like a six-year-old who's overslept on Christmas morning. She took the quickest shower of her life, being careful to keep her hair dry, then pulled her thermals on and dove into her snowsuit. Moments later she was standing on deck, adjusting her goggles.

'We've got problems, sleepyhead.'

'What?'

Brian brushed past her, hurrying toward the helicopter. 'Problems,' he said over his shoulder.

'With what?'

The physicist kept walking and, without turning, pointed wordlessly at the bridge. At first Annie didn't understand, but then she saw it: the ship's flag was standing at attention, snapping in the wind.

Striding toward the helicopter, Brian put his arms out like wings and rolled from side to side. 'Wind!' he shouted.

Annie's heart sank. She didn't know anything about helicopters. How much wind was too much?

'Don't worry about it,' Mark said, coming over to her with a mug of coffee. 'Here,' he said, 'I brought this for you.'

'Thanks.'

'It's going to get better, not worse.'

'Are you sure?' she asked, holding the mug in both hands, then sipping.

'I saw the weather report.'

'But –'

'Brian's a dramatist. He likes everyone to think he's pulling their chestnuts out of the fire, even when the fire's out.'

'So the wind –'

'Don't worry about the wind.'

An hour later they were on the ice, a caravan of bright red snowmobiles buzz-whining over the frozen ground, heading directly into the morning sun. There were two of them in each of the Sno-Cats, but the noise was overwhelming and conversation impossible. Annie didn't mind. It was the greatest day of her life. A polar bear paced them for a mile or more, staying a hundred yards to the west, white on white, galloping. And then, quite suddenly, it was gone, vanishing like smoke from a burnt match.

There was nothing to see. There was everything to see.

Midway to Kopervik the ship's helicopter passed slowly overhead, its rotors thumping the air. Annie waved, and for a moment it seemed to her as if the helicopter replied, yawing on its path to the abandoned settlement.

Soon afterward, the snowmobiles found themselves in a field of crevasses, sinkholes, and pits that might easily have swallowed them whole. At Mark's direction, they backtracked to the west and made a long detour to the north, avoiding the field.

Finally, almost two hours after leaving the ship, the Sno-Cats growled into Kopervik.

It was, as she'd known it would be, a ghost camp. And not much to look at. There was a dark gray, windowless wooden church with a small spire, a tidy row of cabins, and a clutch of oil drums. Linking everything together, and connecting it to a mine shaft at the side of a featureless white hill was a frozen track of churned-up tundra.

Seeing it for the first time, Annie was thrilled by the bland emptiness of the camp, knowing the secrets it concealed. Getting to her feet, she cast her eyes around, and was surprised to see Brian's helicopter sitting on the ice, waiting to be unloaded.

Annie laughed. 'Let's get going,' she said to the Snowmen, and gestured to the chopper. 'We've got a lot to do!'

The graveyard was at the back of the church, and, eager to see it, she almost bumped into Doctor K as he came around the side of the building.

'Whoops!' she said, laughing with surprise. 'Sorry 'bout that! I was just –' The look on his face stopped her in her tracks, and for a long moment she wasn't even sure that he recognized her. Then: 'Annie,' he said, and reached out to take her by the arm.

His unhappiness was so complete, it frightened her, and she drew back. 'What's wrong?' she asked, not wanting to know.

Doctor K started to say something, then turned away in frustration. 'Something terrible has happened,' he said.

Annie's stomach fluttered. 'What?'

Doctor K turned toward the graveyard, then nodded over her shoulder at the side of the church.

Annie turned. For the first time, she saw that the dark gray, clapboard wall had been slathered in white paint. Graffiti? she thought. At this latitude? She blinked, nonplussed, and stepped away from the church to get a better look at the wall.

Raising her eyes, she saw that the crude slashes of white came together to form a single image, a primitive drawing that reminded her of Picasso's *Guernica*.

'It's a horse,' she said, pronouncing the obvious even as she frowned to see the animal's wild eyes, its bared teeth and flared nostrils.

Kicklighter nodded.

For a moment neither of them said anything. 'Someone's been here,' Annie said. 'Haven't they?'

Doctor K's shoulders slumped. 'Yes,' he said. 'Someone's been here.'

9

HAMMERFEST, NORWAY
MARCH 27, 1998

Although the flying time was only three and a half hours, it took Frank Daly more than a day and a half to make the trip from Archangel to Hammerfest. Except for the first leg to Murmansk, neither of the connecting flights ran on a daily basis. Murmansk to Tromso was a Tuesday-Friday run, but Tromso-Hammerfest was possible only on the weekend.

But it didn't matter. He had plenty of time to spare: the *Rex Mundi* wouldn't arrive in port for at least two days, by which time he'd be all settled in. Whatever else might happen (and even now a new storm was shouldering its way across the North Atlantic), he would not miss the boat a second time.

And neither would he miss the Chernomorskaya. By comparison, even the airport lounge in Murmansk had been an improvement. Though he'd spent nearly an entire day slumped in a hard plastic chair, buffeted by incomprehensible announcements, he'd been warm. And that was more than he could say for the days he'd spent in Archangel.

It was with a sense of elation, then, that he finally laid eyes on his destination, Hammerfest, as the Norsk Transport jet dropped through the clouds. From the air the town looked tidy and pristine, a collection of neat little buildings crouched at the edge of a flat gray sea. As the plane banked he could see that the harbor, fringed with small buildings, lay in the lee of a towering cliff, and that several ships were tethered to the docks. Three long wharves jutted out to sea, where trawlers and pleasure boats bobbed at their moorings.

From the air, at least, the town reminded Frank of his mother's Christmas village, an expanding collection of ceramic buildings, trees, and figurines lovingly arranged each year atop an expanse of immaculate cotton snow. No one – neither favorite nieces nor visiting cousins – was ever allowed to touch the village or any of its inhabitants. The tiny windows of each house and store twinkled with light; the mirrored surface of the pond was always shiny and unmarred. Places had been established for each figure and never varied – every year, the same characters sang Christmas carols in front of the same house, while a tall man with an armful of presents hurried up the walk to the pluperfect Georgian town house.

His mother dusted the houses daily, and even as a child, Frank came to understand that for her the village was a parallel universe. Instead of her life in a pinched duplex, barely a mile downwind from a refinery, his mother imagined herself in one of these tidy little buildings, baking cookies.

The village, then, was an ideal and ordered world where the snow was always white, and no one called on Saturdays to ask about the mortgage payment. It was the kind of town, a Christmas town, where dads came home with flowers, and no one ever drank too much or cheated on his wife.

Daly shifted uncomfortably in his seat as the village rose toward the plane. He didn't like to be reminded of his childhood. And, anyway, his mother was dead now, and the Christmas village stored away in Aunt Della's attic. It amazed him how his mother's sisters had descended on the house after her death. They'd handled all the arrangements when 'Frank Senior' couldn't be found. (And no wonder: he'd been shacked up with a dancer all the way over in Breezewood – how was he to know his wife was dead?) And then, when Himself had shown up for the funeral, stunned as much by guilt as grief, he'd been gripped by a sudden, and very uncharacteristic, generosity. 'Here,' he'd said, dispersing his wife's possessions, 'Dottie would want you to have this – me and Frank Junior, what are we going to do with a Christmas village?'

Later his father reverted to form, bitterly accusing 'the weird sisters' of looting 'Dottie's worldly goods.' Predictably, his mother's 'collectibles,' which everyone had always called 'that junk in the basement,' skyrocketed in value – but by then they were gone. 'Divvied up,' as Frank Senior liked to say.

As the plane banked closer, the impression of a Christmas idyll receded, and once he was on the ground, Frank saw that Hammerfest was far from perfect. The snow was mottled with soot and grit, and diesel fumes hung in the air. What had seemed a Christmas village at five thousand feet turned out to be a rather ordinary place, more remarkable for its modernity than anything else. Later, he learned that the town had been occupied by the Nazis during the Second World War, the port a staging ground for U-boat forays in the North Atlantic. When the Germans were finally driven away, they'd torched the place, so that today almost nothing remained from the prewar era.

Except, perhaps, for the desk clerk at the Hotel

Aurora, a pallid septuagenarian who insisted on carrying his bags to his room. There, Frank unpacked, and after enjoying a long hot shower, returned to the lobby.

According to the schedule Annie Adair had given him, the *Rex* was due back from Kopervik on Saturday at the earliest. That should have given him two free days, but after all that had happened, it seemed like a good idea to check on the ship's progress. Frank asked the desk clerk where the harbormaster's office was, and the old man gave him a crisp brochure that had a map on the back.

'It's just there,' he said, drawing a line from *You Are Here* to a street corner near the harbor.

Outside, it was forty degrees and overcast, with the sun reduced to a dull glow on the horizon. The air was damp, and a raw wind blew from the west, smelling of the sea. Though the Aurora was only ten minutes from the harbor, Frank was chilled to the bone by the time he got there.

And he was surprised. The harbor was bigger and busier than he'd expected. Surveying the scene, he watched a monster crane swivel and clank as it unloaded containerized cargo from the hold of a Croatian freighter. Warehouses abutted the street that ran along the quay, while purse seiners and trawlers rocked in the suddenly choppy water. Overhead, a flock of gulls cawed and wheeled in the heavy air, while nearby, a woman in foul-weather gear sluiced down the wharf with a high-powered hose, driving a glitter of fish scales into the sea.

Outside the harbormaster's building, a sheet of metal, not unlike a placard holding a restaurant menu, rattled in the wind. It displayed a printed sheet listing the day's arrivals and departures, the names of the vessels, their flags and home ports. He looked idly down it – the *Annelise,* the *Goran Kovasic,* the *Stella Norske* – never expecting to see a listing for the *Rex Mundi* since this seemed to be a daily schedule. But there it was:

Amkomft 1250 Skip *Klara*   Hammerfest
Amkomft 0240 Skip *Rex Mundi* Murmansk

He glanced at his watch. It was nearly one-thirty. Unless this was a mistake, the *Rex* was two days ahead of schedule and would arrive in about an hour and a half. He ducked into the harbormaster's office to ask if the schedule was correct and, if it was, where the ship would dock.

He'd expected an old salt with reading glasses and a ruddy complexion, but the harbormaster turned out to be a young man with long black hair tied so tightly into a ponytail that his eyes had an Oriental cast. He sat in front of a battered monitor with his feet on the desk, reading *Rolling Stone.* Recessed lighting illuminated the blond roots that lay next to his scalp.

'I was looking at the schedule,' Frank said.

The kid looked up. 'Yes?'

'And what it says, it says there's a ship, the *Rex Mundi* –'

The kid glanced at the monitor and nodded. 'Yeah, she's an ice-breaker. The pilot's already aboard.'

'So it's not a mistake . . .'

The ponytail swung left to right. 'She'll be at C Wharf in an hour. Out my door, right, then down to the end.'

Frank couldn't believe it. He could have missed them *again.* Who the *fuck* did they think they were? *Who?* How could they *not* tell him their schedule had changed again? What if he hadn't come to Hammerfest? What if he'd stayed in Archangel or Murmansk? What did they think he was? Some schmuck on a junket?

He'd been scrupulous about keeping people informed. He'd given the foundation his fax and phone numbers, arrival and departure times – everything and anything they could want. And then he'd seen to it that they forwarded the information to the ship, and copied everything to Kicklighter's office at the NIH. So there was no way they didn't know where he was, or how to reach him.

And now they were *dissing* him, treating him like a cub reporter for *News of the World* or something. What he oughta do, Frank thought, slamming his way out of the harbormaster's office, was pack up and go home. Just – forget about it – he needed this like a message from the Dog Planet.

Though, actually, the mistake was his. He should have kept his mouth shut, but instead he'd talked up the story. Told everyone (and, in particular, the foundation's director, Fletcher Harrison Coe) how interesting it was. How important. How *exciting*. And now, thanks to him, the foundation was looking forward to a three-part series with reprints in the *Post,* the *Times,* and God knew where else. Even now, Coe was probably taking managing editors to lunch at the Century or Cosmos Club and telling them just how terrific the piece was going to be (and by extension, what a wonderful reporter Frank Daly was). So that, if he should now come back to Washington with nothing in his briefcase but a swizzle stick from Aeroflot and a postcard from the Chernomorskaya, people were going to be disappointed.

In *him.*

And they wouldn't care, really, whose 'fault' it was.

Which is why it suddenly seemed terribly important for him to be there when the *Rex* tied up. He needed pictures. If he wasn't going to get pictures of the disinterment on Edgeoya, then he might at least get some shots of Kicklighter and Adair coming down the gangplank, and the body-transfer cases being off-loaded.

Returning to his hotel, he took the stairs two at a time to his room on the first floor. Yanking his suitcase out of the closet, he tossed it on the bed, got out the Nikon that he'd bought the month before, and rewound the film inside. He wanted a new roll in place when the ship docked because the pictures he'd taken over the past few weeks were mostly useless – snapshots of Shanghai and the like. The only ones that he knew he'd use were pictures of Shin-Li, holding forth in his office as plumes of cigarette smoke curled around his head.

When he thought of the pictures he'd *missed*, he felt sick: the *Rex Mundi* bashing through the Storfjorden, its deck glazed with ice; Adair standing next to the opened graves, looking beautiful –

No, that wasn't right.

Adair standing next to the opened graves, looking *intelligent* as the miners' coffins were winched out of the ground. Also, Kicklighter. Kopervik, Helicopter shots. And who knew what else? Polar bear attacks.

He'd have to make do with what he could get here. But whatever he got, the one shot he absolutely had to have was the body-transfer cases coming off the boat. They'd probably use a crane, lifting the cases out of the hold on a pallet. Then they'd load the pallet into the back of a Norwegian Army truck and take it to Tromso Air Force Base, where a C-131 would be waiting to fly them to the States. In the absence of pictures from Kopervik, *that* was the shot he needed.

But first he'd have to keep his temper. It wouldn't do any good to *go off* on Kicklighter, and besides, he'd spent too much money in the past month to indulge what he had to admit was a predilection for cutting off his own nose just to spite his face.

So he took a deep breath, forced an insane smile, and bounced down the steps to the lobby and into the street. A minute later he passed B Wharf, and then, turning a corner into the wind, he saw it – the *Rex Mundi,* following a fat tugboat as it glided into the harbor.

Once again Frank was surprised. Its name might mean 'King of the World,' or something like it, but this was the ugliest ship he'd ever seen. Its business end was a bulbous black prow, streaked with rust – the nautical equivalent of a blackjack. Near midships the superstructure looked like a cheap motel that someone had bolted to the deck.

It came to the dock with its engines growling and deckhands rushing this way and that. Frank began snapping pictures, then stopped to watch as the men on deck threw ropes as thick as his arm to workers standing on the dock. It was beautiful, really, the muscular precision of the sailors, the coiled lines unfurling in wobbly spirals –

'Hvor tror du du skal?'

The voice caught him by surprise, and so did the hand on his arm – which he shook off, jumping backward. 'Jesus Christ,' Frank said, 'you oughta wear a bell or something!'

There were two of them – young guys in khaki-colored uniforms with red armbands – and they were frowning.

'*Er du Engelsk?*'

Frank nodded. 'Close enough. American.'

The first guard deferred to the second, who stepped forward and apologized in a way that made it clear he wasn't sorry. 'I regret . . . you are not possible to proceed.'

Frank cocked his head. 'Really,' he said. They looked like military policemen: stupid, blond, burly, and buzz-cut. Each of them wore a Glock in a patent-leather holster that made it difficult for Frank to take them seriously. 'Why not?' he asked.

The cop frowned, took a deep breath, then wagged his forefinger like a kindergarten teacher scolding the class. 'Regret – we are having to close . . .' The frown grew deeper and his voice trailed away in frustration.

'The dock?' Frank suggested.

'Yes!' the guard said. 'Regret we are having to close the *dock* for the public. The public is not permitted to pass!'

Frank shrugged. 'I'm meeting someone,' he said, and added, 'and, anyway, I'm not the public. I'm a journalist.'

The guards whispered to one another in Norwegian, then the *Engelsk*-speaking cop turned back to him. 'You must wait,' he said, and turning on his heel, walked toward a waiting jeep.

'Daly!' Frank called. 'Frank Daly. Tell 'em I'm with Kicklighter. *Doctor* Kicklighter!'

Just as he said this, a BMW turned the corner, followed by a large Mercedes. The Beamer had a small American flag, like the kind children wave at parades, flying from its fender, and both cars had tinted windows. Slowly, they rolled toward the dock and stopped, looking very much out of place amid the forklifts, cranes, and service vehicles.

'Who's that?' Daly asked when no one got out.

The cop made a sort of moue and rocked on his heels. His colleague was talking animatedly on a cell phone he'd taken from the jeep. Finally, he tossed the phone into the car and returned.

'I'm sorry,' he said, 'but C Wharf is out of limits.'

' "Off-limits," ' Frank corrected.

'Excuse?'

'You mean 'off-limits.' You *said* –'

The cop shook his head and leaned toward him with a mean grin. 'Thank you,' he said, so close that Frank thought about handing him a breath mint.

'Anytime.' But why get into it? There was no point. The guy was just doing his job. Being a soldier.

Which, now that Frank thought about it, made him wonder: what's a soldier doing on the docks, which are public, and what's it got to do with the *Rex?* And why was a car from the embassy there?

'Hey, look,' he said in a conciliatory voice, 'you told them "Daly," right? You gave 'em my name?' He was just talking, more to hold his ground than anything else. If he saw Kicklighter or Adair, they might intervene.

'Yes,' the cop said. 'Nobody ever heard of you.'

'Oh.' They could show up any second now, Frank thought. The ropes had been secured to the dock's gigantic cleats, and a gangway carried to the side of the ship, where it was now being maneuvered into place. *Someone* had to come down it.

Or maybe not. Suddenly, the car doors swung open and half a dozen men stepped out into the blustery afternoon. To Daly's eye, the action had a choreographed look, as if they'd practiced it – an impression reinforced by the men's appearance.

Each of them wore a dark suit and topcoat. Frank

113

didn't need to look at their feet to know there were wing tips on the wharf: it was a given. And it was as faintly sinister as it was slightly comical. Appearing so suddenly – in broad daylight – you never saw guys in clothes like that, standing in the open air. Not in the boondocks, not in *Norway*. On Wall Street, yes. On K Street – at lunchtime – maybe. But here? In Hammerfest? Without a funeral? I don't think so, Daly thought, watching the men climb the gangplank en masse, talking to one another. In a flash they were gone, disappearing into the bowels of the ship.

'Please,' the cop said. 'You will be leaving now?'

Frank nodded, but he didn't move. 'Yeah, but . . . what's going on?' he asked. 'Who *was* that?'

The cop shook his head, and his partner said something to him in Norwegian. It sounded impatient, and Frank was pretty sure he could translate it: *Let's get this jerk out of here.*

'You must leave.'

'Was there an accident?' The idea hadn't occurred to him before, and when it did, something surged in his chest. To his alarm, it was the kind of low voltage worry that was all tied up with caring. Had something happened to Adair?

I don't need this, Frank thought. I have enough problems.

And then he saw her – or, rather, he saw a small figure with blond hair, sandwiched between two of the suits, heading down the gangplank. Kicklighter was right behind her, his silver hair and red parka conspicuous among so many Hickey-Freeman suits.

Annie was talking over her shoulder to a lanky American in a charcoal-gray topcoat and what looked like a pair of Maui Jims. Behind her, Kicklighter stumbled on the steps and was promptly righted by the two men flanking him.

Maui Jim looked familiar. He had the confident look of a man who was used to crossing police lines. Tall and trim, he had reddish hair, and Frank could swear he'd seen him before – but where?

They were down the gangplank now, and heading for the cars.

'Annie! Hey!' When she didn't seem to hear him, he started to walk after her, but was stopped, cold, by the English-speaking M.P., who stiff-armed him in the chest. 'Back!'

'Annie – for chrissake!' This time she looked up, and her eyes widened as she registered his presence. *Frank.* He saw the name form on her lips as Maui Jim opened the rear door of the Mercedes and, putting one hand on her shoulder and another on the top of her head, pushed her into the car. As if she were a perp.

Then he made his way around to the other side of the Mercedes. Pulling open the door, he was half into the car when he hesitated and looked directly at Frank. And in that moment Frank recognized him.

'Gleason!' *You fuck – what are* you *doing here?*

Suddenly, the cars were in reverse, and Frank saw Annie's face in the rear window just as it rolled past. There was a look on her face that he couldn't quite read. Alarm. Bewilderment. Some kind of mute appeal.

And then Frank was left standing there, staring at the departing BMWs as they curved onto the service road and accelerated.

He couldn't believe it. He'd flown all the way to hell and back, and now – no one would even talk to him. He'd spent nearly $4,000 on hotels and airfare, and –

Jesus Christ! There they go! With Gleason!

*

As he made his way back to the hotel, camera swinging at his side, he was too angry to notice anything. The cold, the gulls, the sharp light, everything disappeared. And then he was there, standing at the front desk.

'You got a list of the hotels in this town?'

The desk clerk looked up at him. 'You don't like your room?'

Frank bit his lip. The old man looked genuinely hurt. 'It's not that,' he said. 'The room's fine. I'm looking for a friend.'

The desk clerk's relief, and the smile that chased it, reminded Frank of an illustration in a children's book. Gepetto, he thought. I'm talking to Gepetto.

'I think the tourist office will have this,' the old man said, and gave him directions.

Once he'd gotten a list of hotels, he spent the next hour and a half on the telephone. Neither Kicklighter nor Adair was registered at any hotel or guest house in Hammerfest.

Calling Washington, he tried the National Science Foundation and NIH, but no one at those locations could tell him where Kicklighter was staying. 'I don't think he's *in* a hotel,' a colleague said. 'I think he's in a tent on Spitsbergen or some such place.'

Desperate now, he remembered something Adair had said about the icebreaker being chartered to NOAA. Calling Washington for the fifth time that afternoon (who cared about the money? he was already drowning), he badgered his way through the bureaucracy until he found someone who had spoken to an ice physicist named Mark that very afternoon. 'They're in a place called the Skandia. Or maybe it's the Sandia. Something like that.'

In fact, it was the Skandia, and as Frank rode to the hotel in a taxi, he realized a couple of things. First,

Annie was scared. That much, at least, was obvious, just from a look. Second, there was something going down, or they wouldn't be back already. The dock wouldn't have been shut down. And Neal Gleason wouldn't be in Hammerfest, pushing people into the backs of cars.

Frank had met Gleason three or four times, during a two-year stint that he'd done on the national security beat. Gleason was not a source – had never been a source – would never be a source. On the contrary, the one time Gleason told him something, it had been wrong – a lie, in fact, and one that nearly cost Frank his job. Which made Gleason a prick. And not just any prick, but the kind of prick who is very unlikely to know anything at all about epidemiology.

What Neal Gleason knew about was terrorism. As Frank recalled, he was some kind of liaison. He had an office in Buzzard's Point, in one of those funny little buildings with cameras in the eaves. FBI/CIA – something like that. He'd look it up when he got home, but just knowing that Gleason was here made him feel better. Because Gleason didn't go anywhere that there wasn't trouble, and trouble was news.

Once he reached the Skandia, it took him about a minute to locate two of the NOAA guys. They were in the hotel bar, eating gravlax and herring, and drinking beer. He played it more or less straight with them, told them who he was and what he was doing there. Ever affable, he bought a round and spooled out his story, going into some considerable detail about all that he'd been through, only to get 'stood up, not once, but twice. So what happened out there?'

The physicists exchanged glances. Finally, the one named Mark said, 'I'd like to help you, but . . .'

'We could get into trouble.'

'It's sensitive,' Mark explained.

Frank turned the word over in his mouth, as if he was tasting it. ' "Sensitive," ' he repeated.

'Yeah.' The scientists looked at each other and nodded: that was definitely the word. 'We're not supposed to talk about it,' Brian said.

'We're kind of "sworn to secrecy," ' Mark added.

Frank nodded in an understanding way. 'I guess that's why the FBI was there. They handle a lot of the sensitive stuff. In fact, me and Neal go back a long way.'

'Who's Neal?' Brian asked.

'Gleason,' Frank replied. 'The guy in the sunglasses.'

Brian nodded, remembering. 'He's with the FBI, huh?'

'Yeah,' Frank said. 'He didn't tell you?'

Mark shook his head. 'He didn't actually introduce himself. I sort of got the impression they were with the embassy.'

Frank shook his head. 'Uh-uh. Neal's FBI all the way.'

The idea was to schmooze them, just keeping buying rounds until the subject got back to Kopervik – as it would have to, even if it took all night. So he dropped names shamelessly and gossiped amusingly. 'At St. Albans they used to call him "Al God." '

'Who?' Brian asked.

'The vice president,' Mark said. 'He was talking about the vice president.'

'Of the *United States*!?'

'Yeah.'

'But what's St. Albans?' Brian asked, as he drained his third pint of the evening.

'A prep school,' Frank said. 'You want another beer?'

'No, I –'

'Waiter!'

Frank asked Mark how he ended up at NOAA, and listened attentively to a long and wandering answer which involved a girlfriend studying oceanography and an internship in Glacier Bay. They talked about global warming and the Ross ice shelf, which was apparently calving at an alarming rate. By nine o'clock he knew that Brian had a retarded brother, and by ten, that Mark had gotten the clap twice – once in college and once on a trip to India. 'At least it wasn't chancroid,' Brian said, slurring the word.

Listening was an art, and Frank was a genius at it. People told him things because he was totally simpatico – whatever they had to say, he *understood*. He got the text, *and* the subtext.

'So . . . Kopervik – what was that like?'

Mark chuckled. He could hold his liquor – unlike Brian.

'I don't mean any of the secret stuff,' Frank said, 'whatever *that's* all about. I mean, Kopervik. What's *Kopervik* like?'

Brian was feeling very little pain. 'It was snowy,' he said. 'Lotta snow on the ground.'

'Really!' Frank said.

'Thaaat's right!'

'Think of that,' Frank remarked, then paused, and jumped back in. 'So you got there, and it was snowy, and . . .' He didn't quite know how to go on. 'And – well, what did you find?'

Brian peered at him over his glass. 'You're a very persistent person, aren't you?' he asked.

Frank nodded. 'I am.'

'Well,' he said, pronouncing his words with exaggerated care, 'persistence is an important characteristic, and it deserves to be rewarded.'

'I'm glad you think so,' Frank said.

'So I'll tell you what we found,' Brian said, leaning into the table and waving off Mark's attempted remonstrance. 'We found –'

'Brian!' Mark said.

'A big . . . white . . . horse.'

'Jesus!' Mark complained, getting to his feet.

'A *what*?' Frank asked, holding Brian's eyes with his own.

'A horse,' Brian repeated.

'We've got to go,' Mark said, taking his friend by the arm. 'We've got to get up at six.'

'*I* don't have to get up at six,' Brian objected drunkenly.

Mark pulled him to his feet. 'Yes, you do,' he said. 'We all do.'

'What *kind* of horse?' Frank asked.

Mark shook his head forcefully and threw a handful of dollar bills on the table. Then he began to drag Brian toward the exit.

'A *big* one,' Brian called out as the door swung behind him, 'Big as a church!' Then he laughed.

And then they were gone.

WASHINGTON, D.C.
MARCH 31, 1998

The thing about Washington, Frank thought, is that it's a kind of political theme park. There were monuments everywhere, mansions, plaques, statues, and parks. 'History' was all around you, so that it was impossible to go anywhere without bumping up against the past.

That's where Reagan was shot, he thought for what must have been the hundredth time, right over there, just outside the Hilton (thinkathat). Or, That's where the Argentine firecracker went for a swim with what's-his-name, oh yeah, Wilbur Mills (thinkathat). Frank made a left onto Massachusetts Avenue, and soon afterward entered the rotary at Sheridan Circle. And right there, he thought, just ahead, that's where Orlando Letelier was blown away by a car bomb. Right there. Right . . . under . . . my . . . wheels.

Meanwhile, even as this cognitive jetsam washed up against his eyes, he maneuvered his car through the city's traffic, trawling for a parking space within walking distance of the Cosmos Club.

The car was a white Saab hatchback, a 1990 marketing mistake that he'd bought new, soon after he'd been hired by the *Post*. His girlfriend at the time – Monica Kingston – claimed that new cars made her amorous. It had to do, she'd said, with the 'pheromones of money,' an assertion that she then set out to illustrate, or prove, very nearly causing him to crash within minutes of the Saab's leaving the dealership.

Now, Monica had moved on, and so had he. The car was old and in need of frequent repairs. He would have gotten rid of it, but it had a history. And besides, it went like hell.

There were no parking spaces. FedEx trucks and cars with diplomatic plates had taken everything, and then some. Also, he was about four blocks from the Cosmos Club, and for some reason, though he ran five miles at a clip, five days a week, he never *walked* anywhere. Not if he could help it. (And he usually could, though it tended, as now, to make him late to meetings.)

Then he saw it.

A Lincoln Town Car, somewhat smaller than an aircraft carrier, launched itself from a parking space next to a decapitated meter about two blocks from the club. With the reflexes of a diving goalkeeper, Frank executed one U-turn after another, setting off a cacophony of curses and horns. Pulling into the space, he yanked the keys from the ignition, jumped from the car, slammed the door, and jogged gracefully toward the old mansion in which the club was housed. It took him less than a minute to reach the broad and graceful staircase that led to the club's mezzanine.

This was a large and pleasant anteroom in which guests were made to wait for their hosts, who were, of course, members of the club. Half a dozen couches were scattered about the room, as were an equal number of club chairs. Most of these were filled with men of a certain age, wearing a certain kind of suit.

Almost all of them were reading the *Times,* though one or two could be seen whispering into cell phones. The walls, Frank noticed, were lined with photographs of old Washington and old Washingtonians – distinguished men and women whose common bond was membership in the club.

As a rule, he disapproved of clubs, but the Cosmos was different. (Or a little different.) It was dedicated to the arts and sciences, and included almost as many biologists and writers in its ranks as it did lawyers and foreign service officers.

This ought to have put Frank at his ease, but the truth was, he was nervous. His host, Fletcher Harrison Coe, himself an Arabist and former ambassador to Yemen, had high expectations for the series Frank was working on – a circumstance that seemed likely to end in disappointment.

Because, of course, he'd struck out in Hammerfest.

After three days in Norway, he'd failed to buttonhole any of the crew from the *Rex.* Neither had he succeeded in getting aboard the ship. Nor had he been able to restart the one conversation that he'd actually had – the one with the NOAA physicists, both of whom had checked out of their hotel. With Kicklighter and Adair nowhere to be found, Frank had reconciled himself to doing his expenses while waiting for the plane to Tromso, Oslo, and the States.

And the expenses were ugly. Nineteen days on the road. Nearly $3,000 in airfare, a couple of grand on hotels, six hundred and change on meals and entertainment. Then there was laundry and local transportation, phone calls, and . . . the whole thing came to a bit more than $6,000.

He'd e-mailed the accounting to the foundation, hoping it would get lost in the ether. But it hadn't, and now he was here, maybe ten minutes late, at Coe's invitation.

'*There* you are!' Jennifer Hartwig glided through the room like a Valkyrie passing through a nursing home. One copy of the *Times,* and then another and another, were lowered around the room. 'You're late! Give us a kiss!' Pecks on the cheek, and that dazzling smile, so radiant with the hint of inherited money.

'Tell me something,' Frank whispered as she looped her arm in his, were you the only blonde at Stanford, or were there others?'

She laughed and gave his arm a squeeze.

'I mean, really,' he said, 'you're perfect.'

She laughed again, and said, 'Thank you, and you know what? You're in trouble. He's seen your expenses.'

'Oh.'

It was Jennifer who ran the foundation's day-to-day affairs. She saw to it that the fellows got their stipends and expense checks, wherever they happened to be, and that the newsletter came out on time – six times a year. She responded to requests for applications, co-ordinated among the judges of the annual competition, and served as hostess whenever the foundation's 'graduates' were brought together at the foundation's expense.

Suddenly, they were in the dining room, amid the genteel din, navigating past one table after another on their way to the one where Fletcher Harrison Coe was even now getting up to shake his hand.

'Welcome home, Frank!'

'Sorry I'm late,' Frank said. 'I couldn't find a parking space –'

'It's the dips,' Coe replied, collapsing into his chair. 'They're everywhere.' He paused and, taking a pen from his shirt pocket, began to fill out their luncheon chit. 'So! What are you having?'

Frank opened the menu and glanced at it. The strip steak was probably terrific. And the meat loaf *chasseur*. 'I'll have the vegetable medley,' he said, smiling at Coe (whom he knew to be a vegetarian).

'Excellent!' Coe said, scribbling rapidly. 'I didn't know you were a vegetarian, Frank.'

'Neither did I,' Jennifer said a bit skeptically.

Frank shrugged. 'Well, I'm just cutting back on red meat.'

'That's the way to start,' Coe remarked. 'No need to go cold turkey.' He paused for effect, then laughed at his own joke, and signaling an elderly waiter, handed him the chit.

An interlude of civilized banter followed, during which Frank told funny stories – about the hair-raising flight from Murmansk, the Hotel Chernomorskaya, and the 'ghosts' who turned out to be guests stranded in the elevator. Coe reciprocated with tales of his own, recounting his days as an ambassador and, later, as a columnist for the *Times* ('the one in London').

The vegetable plates arrived, followed by a strip steak for Jennifer, which she attacked with the ferocity of a dingo. By then more than twenty minutes had passed since Frank had arrived at the club, and he was surprised to find that he was enjoying the company. He told a funny story about a snake that had gotten loose in the kitchen of a Shanghai restaurant, and Coe reciprocated with what sounded like a tall tale about a rotten egg he'd been served in Qatar.

His assistant chuckled, and Coe leaned back with a satisfied smile. 'Soooo. . . .' he said, looking at Frank, 'when can we see this wonderful series of yours?'

Jennifer flashed a smile and batted her eyes. 'Yes,' she asked. 'When?'

The silence was so pregnant that it seemed about to give birth to an hour. Folding his napkin with unusual care, Frank cleared his throat and leaned forward. Then he took a deep breath, fell back in his seat and said, 'Well . . .'

Coe frowned, and Jennifer did a thing with her eyes, widening them in a way that was pure mischief.

'Is it done?' Coe asked. 'The *first* part?'

Frank looked at him for a long moment. Finally, he said, 'No.'

Coe rubbed his chin. 'Oh . . . oh, dear.'

'There were some problems,' Frank elaborated, stating the obvious. 'Mmm.' The foundation chief looked away, suddenly distracted. After a moment he glanced at Jennifer, and then turned back to Frank. 'Well, I suppose we could push it back a bit, but –'

'I think maybe we ought to put it on hold,' Frank said. Coe's frown deepened. 'The series, I mean.'

'Hmmm,' Coe said, and signaled for the waiter. 'I think we'd like some coffee, Franklin. Decaf for me. Cappuccino for Ms. Hartwig. Frank?'

'Regular's fine.'

When the waiter had gone, Coe turned back to him. 'Well, I have to say, this is . . . unsettling.'

Frank grimaced. 'I know.'

'We'd pretty much decided to use part one as our lead piece in the May issue. Now . . . well, I suppose we'll have to look elsewhere.'

Frank grimaced in a way that was meant to be commiserating.

'What else *do* we have, Jennifer?

She thought. 'It's a bit thin. There's Marquardt's piece on the Taliban. But I don't think he has any pictures, and anyway, it's not all that fresh. Then there's Corona's story about low-riders in East L.A. That's a pretty good one, but –'

'The thing that bothers me,' Coe interrupted, 'is that you spent so much *time* on the story. What was it? A month? Six weeks?'

'Two months,' Frank said. 'It was about two months.'

'Well, of course, these things *happen,* but – you spent a fortune on it, Frank.'

'I know.'

'*Well?*'

Over coffee, he explained about missing the boat from Murmansk to Kopervik, and then told them about Kicklighter and Adair's sudden unavailability in Hammerfest. 'So what I've got is a pretty good opener about the flu, but nothing about what they found.'

Coe took a last, delicate bite of a string bean, sipped his coffee, and shook his head. 'Well, it seems to me that they owe you an explanation – at least. What do they *say?*'

'They say they're 'away from their desks.'

'I see . . .'

'But they're not gonna get away with it. I'll doorstep Kicklighter until the Fourth of July if I have to.'

The older man nodded distractedly. 'That's all very well, of course, but . . . I'm not sure it's the best way to use your time.' Then he leaned forward, as if to share a confidence. 'The problem is, I'm afraid I've been a bit of a fan. . . .'

Frank winced. He knew what was coming. 'What kind of fan?' he asked.

'Well, actually, Frank – a fan of *yours.* And, I have to confess, I've been counting my chickens – our chickens – before they – well, before they've actually . . . *hatched.*'

Frank shot him a puzzled look.

'The point is: I'm afraid I tootled on about the series with one or two managing editors . . . who are *quite* interested –'

'Oh, Jesus,' Frank groaned. 'Who?'

'The *Atlantic,*' Coe replied, 'the *Times.* The *Post,* of course – but then, the *Post* is easy.'

Frank sighed.

'I even had lunch with that idiot at *Vanity Fair,* but – well, I'm afraid there's going to be a certain amount of . . . disappointment.' He pronounced the word as if it were a synonym for *malignant.*

This was about as close as Coe ever came to dressing someone down. Everything was an allusion, with the important bits buried in the subtext or hidden between the lines. Occasionally, his meaning was subtle, and difficult to suss out. In this instance, however, the exegesis was simple: Frank had committed the unforgivable sin of making Coe look foolish. He, Frank, was one of those chickens that hadn't hatched. Or, to put it differently, he was a dud. And not just any dud, but a Very Important Dud – a VID. The Johnson Foundation sifted through thousands of applications each year, selecting half a dozen fellows for journalism's fast track. By all accounts, Frank had been motoring along quite nicely, and then, on his way to Murmansk, he'd spun out.

'Look – we can still do it,' he said, surprising himself.

Coe looked skeptical.

'The first part's fine, really. I can finish it in a day or two.'

'And how will you do that?'

'It's mostly done. I worked on it in China, and then in Europe. It's a solid introductory piece that gets you right into the subject.'

'What's the lead?' Coe asked,

'Antigenic shift. It's way overdue, and when it hits, it's going to hit hard. Once that's established, I get into the background about the wild ducks, viruses in general, and the 1918 bug in particular. I get into the way vaccines are made, and that brings us back to the antigenic shift – and the search for the Spanish flu. Which is where Kicklighter and Adair come in and, well – we leave 'em hanging. Waiting for part two.'

Jennifer surprised him by chiming in. 'The thing I don't understand is: if the Spanish flu did come back, wouldn't it be kind of anticlimactic? I mean, it's not as if it would kill so many people this time. Medical care is so much better. Am I right? I mean, people used to die of scarlet fever . . .'

Frank shook his head. 'Actually,' he said, 'if a strain of influenza – like the Spanish flu – came along, we wouldn't be a lot better off than we were in 1918.'

'You're kidding – why not?'

'There's no vaccine. We're talking about something that's so contagious, they buried people in mass graves.

'What, like in India?' Jennifer asked.

'No,' Frank replied. 'I'm talking about Philadelphia.'

'Yes, but what you're suggesting,' Coe said, dismissing the idea with a flourish of his hand, 'is a one-part series. That's what it amounts to.'

Frank smiled wanly. 'No, I'll have two parts for you. But I don't know what the second part is. Not yet. But I will.'

Coe grunted. 'Or so we must hope.'

Frank shook his head. 'No, there's definitely something going on. Annie was unbelievably helpful –'

'Who's Annie?' Jennifer asked.

'Dr. Adair. She really went way out of her way. I mean, she put me in touch with Shin-Li, she helped me with appointments at the CDC. And there was a point – when there was some doubt about finding a slot for me on the icebreaker, she went to bat for me.'

'And then had a change of heart,' Coe said. 'Happens all the time.' The foundation director glanced at his watch, then raised a manicured hand and scribbled in the air to indicate that he wanted the check.

'I don't think she changed her mind,' Frank said. 'Something happened. In Kopervik. I know it.'

'Oh?' Coe extracted an ivory toothpick from a tiny leather key case that he carried. 'How can you be sure? You weren't there.' He began to chew on the toothpick.

'That's true, but I *was* in Hammerfest. And someone else was there, too – and that's interesting.'

'Who are you talking about?' Coe asked, his voice edged with skepticism. The waiter came to their table with the check, and Coe signed it.

'Neal Gleason,' Frank answered.

Coe blinked once or twice, thinking about it, and then gave up. He rotated his wrists so his palms were turned toward the ceiling. 'And who's that?' he asked.

'He's an FBI liaison to the CIA. He's with the Bureau's National Security Division – which is a very spooky shop. The job description's classified, but it looks like he's the point man for WMDs.'

'And what are those?' Jennifer asked.

'Weapons of Mass Destruction.'

Coe blanched. 'You mean, like . . . atom bombs?'

Frank nodded. 'Yes but – not just that. There's chemical and biological weapons, too.'

'And this man was in Hammerfest?' Coe asked.

'He was on the dock,' Frank replied. 'He was on the boat. He shoved Kicklighter and Adair into a car. And that's when they stopped talking to me. Right after Gleason showed up.'

'Interesting,' Coe said. 'But . . . it's just that I hate throwing good money after bad.'

Frank nodded in agreement. What else could he do?

'Still,' Coe said, 'you think we could have part one –'

'In two days. Three days, tops.'

'Mmmm.' Coe pulled a pocket watch from his vest, glanced at its face, and got to his feet. 'Meeting,' he said. On their way out, the foundation chief gave a little two-fingered waggle to a man who looked a lot like William Rehnquist, and a second waggle to a giant. Bill Bradley, Frank thought.

At the entrance to the lobby Coe shrugged into a somewhat tattered camel's hair coat, and carefully wrapped a chenille scarf around his throat, Nearby, Jennifer paced back and forth, speaking into a tiny cell phone that seemed to be made of burled walnut.

Coe cocked his head and looked up at Frank. 'You know, the more I think about it . . .' A long pause.

'Yes?'

A kindly smile. 'I think one part will probably be enough. You don't need all this hugger-mugger about the Arctic.'

'But –'

'It's a question of cutting one's losses, don't you think?'

'I think Gleason's involvement –'

'Well, that's the other shoe, isn't it?' Coe pulled on a pair of soft leather gloves.

'What do you mean?'

Coe looked pained. 'I mean that if you pursue this, you're going to have to commit investigative reporting.'

'That's *bad*?'

Coe looked away, then took a deep breath. 'Times have changed. We have to change with them.' Coe frowned for the appropriate part of a second, then clapped his hands together. '*Ciao*,' he said and, turning, walked toward the waiting limo, with Jennifer hard on his heels.

As Frank watched them go, a black doorman stood next to him, rocking back and forth on his heels, hands behind his back, eyes on the street. Finally, he turned to Frank and said, 'And how are we today, sir?'

For a long moment Frank didn't know what to say. So he followed the path of least resistance and told the truth. 'We're fucked,' he said,

The doorman's face lifted in a bright smile. 'Yes, sir! So we are, and so we have *been*!'

After Russia and Norway, Frank's Washington apartment seemed like a palace. It was on Mintwood Place in Adams-Morgan, a rich-and-poor, black-brown-and-yuppie neighborhood that the guidebooks called 'hip and lively' – which meant that it had a lot of good ethnic restaurants, some interesting bars, and virtually no parking.

Even during the day, the streets were packed with young professionals in search of *yebeg wat, pupusas,* and *nasi goreng.* Teenage Goths lounged on the sidewalks, raven-haired and pale, while groups of Salvadorans gathered in threes and fours to share a bottle or make a deal. Boom boxes vied.

The apartment was an almost spectacular space –

he'd rented it long before the neighborhood became chic. There were Palladian windows, lots of exposed brick, and a $2,000 sound system that had been stolen twice (but never in the last three years). The rooms were large, and had once been stylishly decorated. Now they seemed almost spare, a consequence of the very attractive Alice Holcombe having taken most of the furniture with her when she decamped. (That was six months ago, and all Frank could say was, *Oh, well . . .*)

He lit the flame under the teakettle, then picked up the phone and dialed his voice mail. There was nothing of importance, really – certainly nothing from Kicklighter or Adair. An invitation to dinner. An invitation to play poker. Calls from friends who were 'just checking in,' and calls from sources and would-be sources, including one who claimed to have solved the Kennedy assassination 'and *more*!' The most recent call was a reminder that he had an indoor soccer game on Monday night at nine.

Frank measured an ounce of coffee grounds into a paper cone, then sorted through a stack of mail as the kettle began to simmer.

There wasn't much: the *Journal of Scientific Exploration,* the *Economist,* a bill from Visa, a bank statement from Crestar, and a lot of junk that wasn't worth the paper.

When the kettle finally whistled, he wet the coffee grounds and waited for the water to drip through to the cup. Then he poured some more and waited a little longer. The thing was: he was onto a big story. He was absolutely certain of that. Even though he couldn't say exactly what the story was, it was out there, and there was no mistaking it. He could see it, obliquely, in the peripheral vision of his mind: it was like a black hole

133

that reveals itself, indirectly, by the behavior of objects that are drawn to it – objects that disappear.

Objects like Kicklighter and Adair.

That afternoon, he sat down at the long wooden table that he used for a desk and wrote a form letter on Washington *Post* stationery to an alphabet soup of agencies: FBI, CIA, NIH, CDC, NOAA, DOD, and State. Each of the letters was addressed to the agency's Director of Information and Privacy, and each began with the same words:

Dear Mr. _____
This is a request under the Freedom of Information Act (5 U.S.C., 552), as amended.
I am writing to request any information or documents you may have concerning the expedition of Drs. Benton Kicklighter and Anne Adair, who recently sailed from the Russian city of Murmansk to the Svalbard archipelago aboard the Rex Mundi, *a Norwegian icebreaker. It is my understanding that the expedition was mounted under the auspices of the National Science Foundation (NSF), and had the object of recovering the bodies of five miners buried in the village of Kopervik. The ship left Murmansk on or about March 23, 1998, and returned to Hammerfest (Norway) five days later.*

Elsewhere in the letter, he asked that his request be expedited, inasmuch as it was being made in the public interest. When the letter was finished, and almost as an afterthought, he appended the following notation to the letter's end:

c: Williams & Connolly

This was the law firm that represented the *Post*. Reference to it should not have been necessary, since the law required that government agencies reply to FOIA requests within ten days. In practice, however, many of the agencies subverted the law's intent by responding in a formulaic way, acknowledging the letter's receipt without ever actually acting upon it. This was most often done when the letter writers were ordinary citizens, acting on their own, and unknown for their litigiousness. Frank wanted the agencies to know that he (and the *Post*) were ready to go to court.

When the letters had been printed out, he took them to the post office on Columbia Road. It was a short walk, but a colorful one, that took him past a man selling inflatable animals, shops that specialized in retro toasters, lava lamps, and gargoyles, a new Ethiopian restaurant, a funky bar named Millie & Al's.

The postal clerk was a cheerful Jamaican whose head was covered in a blue bandanna, tied foursquare in precise little knots. 'What you got dere, mon?'

Frank handed him the letters.

'Official *biz*-ness!' the clerk called out as he cocked an eye at one address after another. 'Check it out! C-I-A! Eff-Bee-Aye! Pent-a-*gone*!' He looked up. 'Interesting life, mon!' With a chuckle, he took Frank's money, made change, and tossed the FOIA requests into the canvas mailbag behind him. 'We thank you for your biz-ness. Next customer, please!'

In the days that followed, Frank made telephone calls and worked on the influenza story – which he still thought of as 'Part One.'

The calls went to the same three people, and the result was always the same. Neal Gleason was out of

135

the office, and Kicklighter was away from his desk. Adair was simply nowhere to be found, though her answering machine recorded his messages. Gleason's home phone was unlisted and so, in the end, was Kicklighter's. Twice, Frank got through to the scientist late at night, but the old man never said anything other than 'Hello?' After which he hung up – after which he changed the number and went ex-directory.

When the influenza story was finished, he had a courier take it over to the foundation's offices on K Street. The next afternoon, Coe called to say that he liked the piece a lot and thought it would 'stand on its own.'

'Great,' Frank said. 'I think so, too.'

There was a pause, which Coe soon filled with a question. 'What's next? Nothing expensive, I hope.'

'I was thinking of going to New Mexico,' Frank replied. 'There's a piece to do about the *Sin Nombre* virus. I thought I'd visit Taos, talk to the public health people there. It's a good story.'

Coe sounded relieved. 'Excellent,' he said. 'I'll look forward to seeing it.'

'Yessir.'

But Frank didn't go right away. On Monday night he went out to Springfield, where he played indoor soccer with guys he'd known on and off ever since he'd come to Washington. It was a close game against a Peruvian team that was almost as violent as it was skilled. Frank scored two goals in what turned out to be a losing cause, and went home bruised and cheerful.

That night, he called Annie for about the tenth time in a week, and to his amazement, he got through. 'I've been trying to reach you,' he said.

'I know. I just got back. I was seeing my parents, and – there were eight calls on the machine.' There was no irritation in her voice, no impatience, just a kind of constrained regret.

'Were you going to return them?'

There was a long silence on the other end, and then: 'Well . . . I don't think . . . I don't think there's anything to say, really. Except – I'm sorry you went to so much trouble. But, really, there isn't any point in talking about it.'

'Well,' Frank said, 'yeah, there is. It's an important story.' She was silent for so long that he finally prompted her: 'Dr. Adair?'

'Yes . . .'

'I said it's an important story.'

'I know. I heard you. It's just that – I can't help you with it.'

'Well, actually – you *can*. But you *aren't*. And what I need to know is, why?'

'Well . . .' She was quiet so long that he thought, for a moment, she'd put the phone down. Then: 'I have to go.'

'But it's so rude!'

The accusation took her aback, and Frank had to admit it wasn't something he'd ever have said to Gleason. '*What*?' she asked.

'It's rude!' he answered. 'When you think about it . . . I mean, I went all the way to hell and back on this thing. I spent a fortune. And now you won't even *talk* to me.'

'I can't.'

'Why not?'

'I just *can't*.'

'Because of Gleason, right?'

It was the first time he'd mentioned Gleason's name, and it surprised her. '*What*?'

'I said it's because of Gleason, right? *Neal* Gleason.'

'I have to go.'

'That's it? That's all you've got to say – "I have to go"?'

'No, really –'

'Are you under some kind of . . . what?' He couldn't think of the word. 'A *secrecy* oath, or something?'

Once again she was silent.

'Look, Dr. Adair –'

'Annie.'

'Huh?'

'Everyone calls me Annie.'

'Okay. *Annie*. The thing is, I really thought we got along. I mean, before all this . . .' He paused. The word he was going to use was 'bullshit,' but he didn't want to swear at her. 'You were so helpful! So nice!'

'Thanks,' she said. And then, a moment later, 'I guess.'

Frank laughed. 'So how about dinner?'

'Dinner?'

'Forget about Spitsbergen. We'll go out to eat. You name the night. You pick the place. Except – no Canadian food.'

The phone was silent for a moment, and then: 'That's funny, but . . . I don't think so. I mean, under the circumstances, I don't think that's such a good idea.'

She sounded genuinely regretful, and her regret encouraged him to plunge on. 'What "circumstances"?' he asked. 'I don't know about any circumstances.'

It was her turn to laugh. 'Well, you want me to tell you something and – I can't.'

'"Can't." Which means you *did* sign something!'

An exasperated sigh blew through the phone. 'I've got to go,' she said. 'And anyway, this isn't going anywhere. It can't.'

'Don't hang up!' he said. 'Give me credit for trying.'

'You should talk to Dr. Kicklighter.'

'Well, now, there's an idea!' Frank replied. 'Dr. Kicklighter! Why didn't I think of that – except, I did. And the problem is, he seems to have blown up his telephone.'

'I'm sorry. He's very busy.'

'We're all busy. You're busy! I'm busy! Even Gleason's busy!'

'I know, but . . . I really have to go. Really!'

'*Why?*'

He could hear her take a deep breath. 'Because I have a chicken in the oven, and it's burning, and even while we're talking, my apartment's filling up with smoke, and if I don't go, the smoke alarm will go off, and the fire department will come, and then the police, and then I'll lose my lease, and then I'll become a bag lady and freeze to death – is that what you want?'

Frank thought about it. 'No,' he said. 'But I'll be back in a week – and I think we definitely ought to have dinner.'

LOS ANGELES
APRIL 11, 1998

Susannah adjusted the diaper bag, propped the baby on her hip, and collapsed the new stroller. She had the hang of it now. There was a lever you pushed with your foot and it folded right up, easy as pie. Behind her an elderly Asian lady held the stroller for her as she climbed onto the number 20 bus.

'I put it here,' the lady said as Susannah paid her fare. 'Okay?' She put the stroller in a corral just behind the driver.

'Thank you so *much*,' Susannah said, and tossed the woman a big, grateful smile.

'Your baby sure cute.' The woman handed the driver a transfer.

'Isn't he, though?' Susannah lowered her face to the baby's and rubbed noses. 'He's just a doll-baby,' she sang. 'He's just a sweet lil' ol' doll, is what he is!'

She asked the driver to tell her when they got to Wilshire Boulevard, and then she took an aisle seat near the front, putting the diaper bag on the seat next to her so she wouldn't have to share. Then she touched her finger to the little guy's button nose and pushed it very gently. This always made him laugh, and he gurgled and smiled and showed his dimples. 'How did you get so cute?' she asked, seesawing her head back and forth. 'Tell me that. How did you? Hmmmmm?'

She looked out the window, where L.A. was sliding by, jiggling Stephen up and down, just a little, so he wouldn't fuss. She couldn't get over how much of the city was paved! Or how itty-bitty most of the houses were. And the palm trees – what good were *they*, anyway? They were skinny and straight and they didn't really give you any shade. They just stood there, next to the street, like a row of disappointments.

Which was too bad because, when she thought of palm trees, she always imagined them in a romantic way – leaning into the wind on an ivory-colored beach, a few feet from the water. Blue water. And a cloudless sky. But here in L.A., in real life, stranded in the desert, surrounded by concrete, they were . . . *what*?

Butt-ugly. That's what they were, and that was the only word for it. Butt-ugly. And as a matter of fact, if you asked *her*, this whole landscape was a downer – even here, just a little ways from Beverly Hills, where everything was supposed to be perfect, but wasn't – it was a downer. Even if the bus wasn't on the prettiest street . . .

She'd been riding buses for a while. This was the fourth one she and Stephen had been on.

Now the little boy's face was puckering up and he was making that *uh-uh-uh* sound and she could tell it was about time to feed him anyway, because her breasts were getting that full feeling. She'd better feed him now because otherwise her milk might leak out and *that* would be bad because the clothes she was wearing were just for today (she had the tags and everything tucked in where you couldn't see them).

Adeline had taken them shopping at the Pentagon City Mall, not far from their safe house in the Potomac Towers. That's what Adeline called it – 'our safe house' – even though it was really only a two-bedroom apartment. No matter what you called it, though, the apartment was *way* cool. It came with a new car, a bank account, and, neatest of all, a new identity. Whenever Susannah stayed there (and after Rhinebeck, she'd been staying there a lot), she was 'Mrs. Elliott Ambrose.' Which she liked, because it sounded classy. Classier, at least, than Susannah Demjanuk.

Anyway, the apartment was convenient – close to the mall, and close to the airport. They'd changed clothes there, and when they got back, they'd change them again. And return them, only a little bit used.

The thing about clothes was: you are what you wear. That's what Solange said. He said that if you dressed well enough, it was like being invisible – at least as far as the cops were concerned – and security guards, and people like that. If you dressed right, you didn't get hassled. It was practically *a rule*.

Even so, these clothes were *way* expensive – the suit alone cost more than her *plane ticket* – and there just wasn't any point in buying them. Especially if you could borrow them.

Mostly, she got her clothes at thrift shops. Everyone did. That way, they were recycling, and they weren't using up resources that could be spent on more important things (like a good centrifuge). Even cotton – which was supposed to be such friendly, natural stuff – making cotton was, like . . . drilling for oil, or something. It was really! So, this way . . . Belinda or one of the other guys from the office of Special Affairs could take everything back, once she and Tommy returned from the Coast.

Susannah scrutinized the bus.

When you came right down to it, a bus wasn't such a bad place to breast-feed a baby. The seats were high

142

enough to kind of hide you, and it wasn't very crowded.

Stephen made little wet smacking noises as he latched on. After a few minutes she shifted him to the other breast as L.A. slid past the window. It sure went by slow. There was a lot of traffic, and sometimes they just sat through the light, waiting for someone to move: red green yellow red *hello?* Nobody beeped or honked, though; they must be used to it. No wonder the sky was that nasty gray color.

By the time the driver said 'Wilshire Boulevard coming up,' her blouse was buttoned and Stephen had been burped. She folded up the cloth diaper she used to burp him on and put it back in the diaper bag and then, from the little quilted section in the bottom – actually, it was a compartment to hold dinner rolls! – she took out a lightbulb and bent down and held it in place under the toe of her shoe.

Practically as soon as she stood up and let it go, the driver accelerated around a double-parked car, then cut in to the bus stop. She heard the lightbulb rolling along the floor as she walked to the door at the front of the bus.

Of course, there was no way to tell when it would break, or where. It might roll around all day, or it might break before she got off the bus. You couldn't predict it. Not really.

Which was one of the things Solange liked about the lightbulb method. It was random, he said, like Nature.

When she got off the bus, she was all turned around – north, south, east, west. She could be anywhere. So she went over to a redheaded woman who was sitting at a table at a sidewalk café, only a few steps from the bus stop.

'Excuse me?'

The woman looked up from a little leather notebook in which she'd been writing. Her face had a puzzled look.

'Do you know where Rodeo Drive is?' Susannah swung Stephen from one hip to the other.

The woman gave her the once-over – as if she was adding up how much Susannah had spent on her outfit or, worse, doubted that the clothes were her own. Then she sighed and swung her eyes to the corner. 'It's just to the right,' she said.

Susannah smiled her thanks.

'And by the way,' the woman added, her face creasing in a poisonous smile that made Susannah want to get out a lightbulb and throw it at the bitch, 'it's Roh-*day*-oh Drive. Not Roady-oh.'

'Thank you so much,' she said, and walked off in the direction the woman had indicated. How was *she* supposed to know it wasn't pronounced the way it looked. Rodeo. Like a *roh*-dee-oh. This *was* the West, right?

Women checked you out *way* more than men, although men checked you out in a different way. Except gay men, who checked you out the same way women did. In fact, having a baby didn't change a thing as far as guys hitting on you was concerned. The truth was, she was getting a kind of good feeling from all the admiring glances. She'd lost all the baby weight, and then, with this boss outfit on and all, she looked *good*. And the truth was she had an even better figure now, with her boobs so big from nursing. Better than breast implants. And Stephen was so adorable, people couldn't take their eyes off the two of them.

It felt so good, she almost wished this was her real life. Walking down Rodeo Drive, pushing the baby in his brand-new stroller, nothing better to do than window-shop and think about maybe stopping for a Smoothie or something. The windows were so clean, the glass was like – not just transparent, but really invisible. And the shops were so expensive, you needed appointments in half of them, just to get in. And everything was displayed as if it was something holy. There were eyeglasses in cases that revolved, so you could see them from every angle, just like precious jewels. And a window with a purse in it. One purse, that was it!

Everything gleamed and shone, even the people.

Susannah checked herself out, scanning her reflection in the window. And guess what? She fit right in, she really did – she looked like she was somebody's wife, a producer or somebody. Or maybe she was a producer herself, out with her baby, shopping for earrings and rugs.

It felt good.

In fact, it felt so good, just walking along, that she started to feel guilty. But Solange had mapped out her route personally, using those little maps that came off the computer. They told her which buses she should take and which neighborhoods she should walk through. But the rest was up to her. She could put the lightbulbs wherever she wanted – on a bus, in a trash can, in a parking space beside the curb – so long as it was in the right neighborhood.

It had to be that way if they were going to track the results. And besides, all the neighborhoods were fancy ones because, well . . . who used the most resources? Who did the most damage?

And this was the belly of the beast, right here – the pep center, Solange called it. Or maybe not. But something like that. The pep center of conspicuous consumption. Right here, sucking at her on Rodeo Drive.

Ro-*day*-oh Drive.

She was down to the last of the lightbulbs. Because they'd only made a dozen or so. Stopping on the sidewalk in front of 'Bijan's,' Susannah adjusted the little umbrella that kept the sun out of Stephen's eyes. Then she reached into the diaper bag and, taking out the lightbulb, carried it to the street and laid it gently beside the curb, where a car was certain to crush it.

There was a crowd of people coming the other way, laughing. They had big white teeth and a predatory look that made her want to step on the lightbulb right then and there. But she didn't-not because it would make her sick, but because she was wearing stacked heels that cost $192 at Joan & David, and they couldn't be taken back.

Which meant that she got to keep them.

Washington DC
APRIL 17, 1998

It was the middle of April, and the city was luminous with spring.

Returning home from Santa Fe, Frank found winter dismissed and the landscape transformed. The streets and parks and verges were ablaze with tulips and azaleas, and all the dogwoods seemed to be in bloom.

When he got to his apartment, he tossed his suitcase on the bed, stripped to a T-shirt and running shorts, and went out for a jog, looking to get the kinks out after the long flight. He ran through Rock Creek Park, sticking to the bike path. For a quarter mile, near the zoo, the black asphalt path was littered with fallen blossoms from a stand of cherry trees. Every now and then a gust of wind set loose a shower of petals that fell through the air like confetti. Forget Paris, he thought. For a few weeks in the spring, Washington was the most beautiful city in the world.

Or maybe it just seemed that way because he'd spent the last two weeks in pickup trucks, rocketing around the desert where there was nothing but dirt and rocks and scrub. A single lilac bush would have seemed a miracle.

He tagged along as health workers tried to head off an outbreak of Hanta virus in the Four Corners area.

So far there had been only two cases, and those geographically separated by more than a hundred miles, but with a virus that killed seventy percent of those it infected, no one wanted to take any chances.

Sometimes, the households surveyed were on reservation land, and sometimes not. In either case, getting permission to set traps, take a blood sample, or inspect homes was a tricky business.

– You want to check my house for mouse shit? Who the fuck are you?

– We're trying to prevent another outbreak – like you had in 'ninety-three.

– And the mice . . . they cause it?

– Yeah. Sort of. It's a virus. The mice *spread* it.

– Uh-huh. And what do they call that virus?

– *Sin Nombre.*

– And that's the name of it? The no-name virus?

– That's right.

– You're shitting me . . .

Some people remembered '93. The fevers. The panic. The dying. They knew more than they wanted to know about *Sin Nombre,* and the name didn't amuse them. But for those who hadn't been around, or who hadn't paid attention, the name put them over the top, eliciting a look that said, *Get outta here.* You *gotta do better than* that – *some disease you don't even* name?

Others reacted with suspicion.

– You want to test me for antibodies? You talking about Aitch-aye-vee, you come right out and say so, don't give me that *Sin Nombre* shit.

In the end, the public health people got what they wanted, and there was no real outbreak – just the two cases. Still, it was interesting stuff, and the story was an easy one to write. Most important, Frank thought, it would make Coe happy and give him enough breathing room to go after the story he was really interested in.

He took a shower, then sat down at his computer and caught up on his expenses. He typed out a sheet and stuffed it into a manila folder, along with the receipts. He'd send it to Jennifer in the morning.

He slid the floppy from his laptop into the B drive of his desktop computer and copied the files from his trip. He called up *Nombre 1* and read through his notes, then created a new file, *Nombre 2*. He worked on the story for about an hour, but that was all he could take: it was spring, and he really felt like going out.

So he copied the files to a floppy, shut down the computer, and went into the kitchen. Opening the refrigerator, he looked in the back for the diskette carrying case that he kept behind the milk. It was, he knew, a peculiar practice, storing his backups in this way – but it was an effective one. The refrigerator was cold, but not freezing, and what was more important: it was insulated. If there was a fire, his backups would be fine.

It was late in the afternoon, with shafts of light slanting through the windows, when he picked up the telephone and called Annie Adair.

'Hello?'

'It's Frank Daly.'

'Oh!' A pause. 'Hi.' Between the two syllables, between the 'oh' and the 'hi,' her voice changed, subsiding from enthusiasm to wariness.

They went back and forth for a minute. How he'd been. How she'd been. Did she get the piece he sent? On influenza?

'Oh, yeah! It was *good,*' she said. 'I was impressed.'

It took a while, but he got around to it: 'I was thinking . . . Y'know, maybe we could go out – get something to eat.'

'I don't know,' she said. 'It doesn't seem like such a good idea.'

'Why *not*?'

'Because . . . well, because I still can't *talk* to you.'

'But you are! We're talking right now.'

'You know what I mean. I mean . . . about Kopervik. Hammerfest. That stuff.'

'You think that's why I called you?'

'Umm-hmmm.'

'My God, talk about a suspicious mind! Kopervik! You think I want to talk about Kopervik?'

'Umm-hmmm.'

'Huh! Kopervik . . . I'll tell you what – what if I promised not to talk about *any* of that?'

'I don't think I'd believe you. You seem kind of. . . tenacious.'

'"Tenacious"? Me? Nah. Not "tenacious." Hungry. So what if I swear? Solemnly. What if I give you my *word*?'

An edgy laugh that told him she was thinking about it. 'Okay – tell you what! I'll swear on *a stack of Bibles.*'

A little giggle.

'How about that? Bibles!'

'You don't seem like the religious type.'

'Okay . . . you're right. I'm not. So how about *Gravity's Rainbow*? *Gray's Anatomy*! You name the books, I'll stack 'em and swear!'

Silence on the other end of the line. Then: 'But . . .' A sigh. 'I know that you still want to know about the expedition. If it was me – I'd want to know.'

'Trust me. I did the piece,' he said. 'You read it. Now I'm moving on to bigger and better infections.'

'Like what?'

'*Sin Nombre.* I just got back from New Mexico.'

'Really?'

Easing into his most unctuous newscaster's voice, he read from the screen in front of him. '"Even before winter set in, health experts in the Four Corners worried that *peromyscus maniculatus* was reproducing in dangerous numbers. More often known as the common deer mouse . . ."' He paused. 'You want me to go on?'

'No.'

'Okay, so how about dinner?'

'Well . . .'

He always took the words 'well' or 'maybe' as consent. *Don't say no,* he used to beg his mother, *say maybe.* 'Great!' he said. 'Is Friday okay? I know it's prime time, but . . . I'll pick you up at seventy-thirty!' Then, without giving her time to reply, he broke the connection, thinking, If she isn't up to it, she'll call me back. And if she can't find my number, she just won't be there.

Annie lived about a mile from his apartment, in a Mount Pleasant town house that she shared with a woman named Indu from Kansas and a freelance computer guru from Caracas. 'They're both working tonight,' she said, and laughed. 'We're a bunch of grinds.'

It had taken him longer to find a parking place than to drive over, and he said as much to her as he opened the door to the Saab.

'Well, why don't we walk?' she said.

And so they did.

It had been a warm, rainy day. The sidewalks were

wet and clean, the gutters empty of their usual trash. Together, they navigated the six or seven blocks that lay between Mount Pleasant and Adams-Morgan, passing claques of drunks and double-parked police cars, Kenny's Bar-B-Que and the Unification Church. The air was heavy with honeysuckle and booze, salsa and rap.

'So tell me about your trip,' she asked. 'How did you get interested in *Sin Nombre*?'

'The name. It sounded so spooky . . . like it was the opposite of what they say about New York.'

'Which is what?'

'You know – how it's 'so nice, they had to name it twice.' But this thing is so bad, they didn't even want to name it once.'

'I always wondered why they called it that,' Annie said.

'Well, I can tell you!'

'Great!'

'But it's kind of disappointing.'

'Why?'

'Because it's all about political correctness,' Frank replied. 'They used to call it the Muerto Canyon virus, after the place where it first occurred. But that didn't work because the canyon's on a Navajo reservation, and the Navajos went ballistic at the idea of naming a virus after the place.'

'Why?'

'Because it was the site of a massacre – white guys killing Indians, a hundred years ago. Now, the virus was killing them, and it didn't seem very sensitive to name it after this earlier disaster. I mean, it would be like calling Tay-Sachs "Auschwitz disease."'

'So what happened?'

'They called it the "Four Corners virus."'

'Makes sense,' Annie said. 'Diseases are often named after the place they're first seen.'

'Hong Kong flu, Marburg, Ebola –'

'Right.'

'They're all place names,' Frank said. 'Except, Ebola's a river – at least, I think it is. But anyway, what happened was, after they named it the Four Corners virus, the locals got upset. The chambers of commerce, the tourist boards – I mean, you can see their point. It would be like living in a place called "Polioville."'

Annie laughed. 'So they didn't have a name for it, and in the end that's what they called it: the No-Name virus.'

'Except they translated it.'

'Yeah. I think they were sensitive to language issues, too.'

They ended up at an Ethiopian restaurant called Meskerem. There were no knives or forks or chairs. They sat on stuffed leather cushions and ate a spicy stew with their hands, using a spongy, sour bread called *injera* to lift bits of meat and vegetables from the tray to their mouths. It was the kind of dinner that promoted a casual intimacy, and yet, across from him, Annie kept her reserve. She looked as if she was ready to bolt the moment he mentioned Kopervik.

So he didn't. He stayed away from it. They talked about the politics of disease, and after a while she warmed to the conversation.

'You wouldn't believe it,' she said. 'You get outbreaks of cholera, typhus, diphtheria – whatever. Even plague. And they get reported to WHO and the CDC and everyone else. But does the State Department tell anyone? Hardly ever. Because if you say Thailand's crawling with VD, or there's cholera in Bolivia, it's seen as a political act – an attack on the country you're talking about.'

'You'd think they'd be more worried about people's health.'

'And the other thing is: every disease has its own lobby. So funding research has less to do with the-greatest-good-for-the-greatest-number than it does with . . . I don't know . . . skill at working the P.R. angle.'

'You think that's bad?'

She shrugged. 'It's just the way it is. You can't blame people. They feel passionately when the people they love are hurting. And at the same time, there's only so much money to go around, so . . .'

She had thoroughbred lines, long legs, and a dancer's posture. She was pretty enough so that when she maneuvered past the crowded tables on her way to the ladies' room, Frank's eyes weren't the only ones that followed her progress. And yet, within fifteen minutes of meeting her for the first time at the NIH, he already knew that she didn't have a pretty woman's psyche. She was embarrassed by compliments, and incapable of flirtation, or so it seemed. She was skittish and shy, and drew back from the slightest physical contact.

There was a naiveté about her that was all the more surprising because it coexisted with what Frank knew was her brilliance. On the one hand, she was probably a genius, and on the other, she wasn't even as wised-up as the sixth graders he'd talked to at the Hine Middle School (this, as a part of the *Post*'s 'outreach' program).

But as uncomfortable as she was with small talk, she had a sense of humor and loved to talk about her work. And her laugh was promising: a reckless giggle that sometimes got away from her.

So he played to the things she was comfortable with,

listening attentively to what she said, and steered clear of everything else. And it worked. He could feel her relaxing toward him, softening as the tension disappeared. This was something that he shared with his father, the flexibility of character that enabled him to become the perfect foil for anyone he was with, whether his aim was to seduce or elicit information. It worried him sometimes. This 'gift' he had.

But not even the thought of his father – from whom he'd been trying to distance himself all his life – could deter him from working on Annie Adair. When she returned to the table, he leaned forward and took her hand in his. There was a moment of awkwardness in which she tried, reflexively, to pull away, but he held on.

'Wait a second,' he said. 'I'm not getting mushy. I just want to look at your palm.'

'Why?' she asked, radiant with the suspicion that he might be making fun of her.

'So I can read your future.'

'Don't be silly,' she said – but her hand relaxed in his.

He stroked her palm, and then each finger. 'So you don't think I can tell the future?'

'No.'

'Well, I can.'

She giggled. 'And how did you come by this ability? In palm school?'

'Please,' he said in an officious tone, 'we don't call it "palm school." It's the American School of Chiromancy. "Palm school" is where you learn to tell a coconut from a date.'

A giggle.

'And no, I didn't graduate. But I did write a magazine piece about a palmist.'

'Really?'

'Yeah. You've seen the signs, right? There's like a big red hand with numbers on it, and it's usually in the window of a little white house, right next to the highway, in between a place that does flag repair and another place that does fish grooming. And I thought, 'Who actually goes to these people?''

'People with fish, I should think. And flags.'

'And palms,' Frank agreed. 'Anyway, I approached a certain Madame Rurak – the Oracle of Hyattstown. And with her permission, I talked to some of her clients. And it turns out, the clientele is really diverse. They're the same people who go to chiropractors, only what she "adjusts" is their psyches, not their backs.'

'And was it all—you know – just a lot of baloney?'

He shrugged and continued to stroke her palm and stare at it. 'I don't know. It wasn't as if she was handing out lotto numbers. She was intense, you know, really focused, but everything she said was kind of general.'

'Like fortune cookies.'

Frank winced. 'Ouch.'

She laughed. 'Well, what do you think they got out of it? The people who went to see this woman?'

'They always seemed to leave in a good mood. I had the impression that she was providing some kind of solace for the way their lives had turned out. She was saying, you know, it's right there, it's in your palm, it's already written. No matter what you did, it wouldn't have made any difference. You could have bought Intel at ten, you could have learned to play the guitar, you could have asked Sherry Dudley to the prom – and none of it would have mattered. Because it was all laid down ahead of time: the life line, the love line. People liked that. It seemed to take the pressure off.'

She laughed. 'And who was Sherry Dudley?'

'I can't talk about that,' he muttered.

She giggled again. 'But you don't believe in it, do you?'

'In what?' He curled up her fingers one at a time and then stroked them back out again, flat. 'You mean fate?' He leaned over her hand and peered intently at it. 'Of course I do. I seeee . . . someone . . . *new*! Someone *new* in your life.'

'Really?' she said, her voice thick with skepticism.

'Yes. And it's going to be wonderful. You should do whatever this person says.

'And would this person be tall, dark, and handsome?'

He scrutinized further. 'Well, yes – he's definitely tall and – hmmm – not bad-looking! Not bad at all. But . . .' He shook his head and frowned. 'Not very dark. More . . . oh, I don't know – Irish, or something. Blue eyes. Heart of gold. Never mentions Kopervik. That sort of thing.'

'I see.'

'There's more. It's an incredibly detailed line. Turns out, this guy has a sentimental attachment to his car, which he should trade in.' He looked up at her.

'And would the car be a Saab?' She giggled. 'By any chance?'

He glanced at her palm. 'I think it *is* a Saab! Amazing. You should try this! I mean you don't even have a hand to work with – and, my God, you're a natural.'

They went to Bob's for ice cream. The talk turned to family. Hers couldn't have been more different from his, a sprawling back-to-the-Mayflower New England clan, heavy on academics and 'Wall Street.'

'They spend quite a bit of time arranging charity

balls. It gives my mother the chance to spend really a lot of money on clothes and still feel good about it.'

'This would be your legendary "old money"?'

'Kind of old. But not so legendary. Granddad made a killing on the Depression. Puts and calls. He "called." What about you?'

'Actually . . . I don't have a family I mean, not really.'

Annie frowned. 'Everybody has a family.'

He shrugged. 'I've got some aunts and cousins, but I don't see them. No brothers or sisters. Mom's dead. Dad and I had a falling out.'

'That's *sad*.'

'Not really,' he said. 'Not if you knew the Old Man.'

They walked back to her town house. It was cooler, and a thunderstorm was rumbling on the horizon. She was easier with him now, more relaxed, leaning into him on occasion, touching his arm to make a point.

Even he found his restraint amazing. Not a word about Kopervik, except once, and that was in fun, And then, when they reached her door and she stammered an invitation to come in – 'I could make some coffee' – he declined. If he went inside, he wouldn't be able to keep his hands off her. And that could be wonderful, or that could be trouble.

So they stood in the doorway, a little awkwardly, until he said, 'Well, it was great, I'll give you a call' – and with a little wave, turned and went down the front steps to the Saab.

As he drove back to Adams-Morgan he listened to jazz on WPFW and thought about his evening with Annie Adair. He knew that restraint would pay off with her, but what he didn't know was what the payoff *was*. Was it Annie he wanted – or Kopervik? He couldn't be sure. He was attracted to her, but then again, he was attracted to lots of women. And then again – again – he wasn't just *attracted* to her. He liked her. She was sweet and smart and funny . . .

He wanted it both ways: Annie and Kopervik. Kopervik and Annie. In no particular order.

In the week that followed, Frank received form letters from half a dozen agencies, acknowledging receipt of the FOIA requests that he'd made. Soon afterward he received yet another reply, and this one had heft.

The packet, which came from the NSF, was about half an inch thick, and Frank knew, even without opening it, that the material inside would be a disappointment. Otherwise, it would not have been processed and mailed so quickly.

Still, it was his to read, and as the blues man said, *One never knows, do one?*

Seating himself at the kitchen table, he opened the envelope and found sixty pages of documents. The first of these was a cover letter that said the enclosed should be considered a complete response to his request, and that there would be no follow-up. Attached to this was a two-page sheet explaining the various exemptions to the Freedom of Information Act.

The remaining fifty-seven pages consisted, mosily, of the original grant proposal that Kicklighter and Adair had made to the NSF some two years earlier. Frank scanned the proposal from its title page to its end-notes, but there was nothing in it that he hadn't seen before.

That left three pages.

The first was a rejection letter, written under the letterhead of the National Science Foundation. Addressed to Dr. Kicklighter, it was dated January 11, 1997, and began:

> We regret that the Foundation is unable to extend support for your recent grant application (Ref. #96-14739). Should research priorities change, or additional funds become availabile . . .

Nothing new there.

The next page in the packet was also a letter, albeit a more recent one. Dated February 17, 1998, it was addressed to the Director of the NSF, and was signed 'Cordially.' But that was it. Nothing else could be read because every line of text – and the letterhead on which it was written – had been blacked out with a felt-tipped marker. In the margin, the redactor had written B(*1*).

Bingo.

Even without looking at the explanatory sheet, Frank knew that the B(1) exemption was reserved for matters of national security. Which confirmed what Neal Gleason's presence in Hammerfest had suggested – that there was more to the Kopervik expedition than 'pure science.'

And that, in turn, suggested a reason for Kicklighter's sudden unavailability, and Annie's unwillingness to discuss Kopervik or what had happened there. If this was a national security matter, they'd probably been made to take an oath of secrecy.

But why? The grant proposal was right in front of him, released in full, without a word redacted. The proposal described every aspect and goal of the expedition. It was what the expedition was all *about*. So what was the point of a secrecy oath – unless there was something else involved, something that was not in the proposal?

Frank stared at the blacked-out letter. It might have come from anywhere: FBI, CIA, the Pentagon – there was no way to know.

Frustrated, he turned to the last page in the packet, which was also a letter. Dated February 23, 1998, it, too, was addressed to the Director of the NSF

In three short sentences the writer thanked the director for his help and announced that the foundation was 'happy to report that it had decided to underwrite the Kicklighter-Adair expedition to Kopervik.' The letter was signed:

> Very truly yours,
> A. Lloyd Kolp
> Exec. Dir.

Frank glanced at the letterhead:

THE COMPASS TRUST

Its offices were in McLean, about three traffic lights from the CIA. Which didn't mean anything, of course. Or at least, it didn't mean anything – *necessarily*.

But A. Lloyd Kolp? Who was he when he wasn't running the Compass Trust?

Frank leaned back in his chair, with the letters on the table in front of him, arranged chronologically from left to right. First, the NSF rejects Kicklighter's proposal. Then, a year and a half goes by and, suddenly, someone from the intelligence community gets involved. *How,* we don't know. *To what end,* we don't know. But he gets *involved.* And a week later a letter arrives at the NSF thanking the director for his help (*what help?*), while announcing the foundation's decision to underwrite the expedition.

Was the second letter connected to the third? *One never knows . . .*

This was how you went crazy, Frank thought. It was

like trying to do a jigsaw puzzle with half the pieces missing.

He sat back and looked at the ceiling. The fan was turning slowly. His eyes fell on the calendar next to the telephone. The days he'd gone running had circles around the date. Maybe he should go running, but . . .

He didn't feel like it. The sky was overcast, and he could tell it was going to pour. The only question was when. Crossing the room, he went to his desk and booted up the computer.

He still had access to Nexis, thanks to the *Post* (or, more accurately, thanks to his ability to hack the password in the Setup file on his office computer). And he was glad that he did because the service was amazingly expensive, and the Internet was anything but a useful substitute. Using the Internet to find out about the Compass Trust, he'd probably have to sort through reams of information about Orienteering.

With Nexis, you went right to the heart of things – and only to the heart.

The database was massive – basically, every newspaper and periodical in the world, from the *Times* to the *Journal of Robotics*, going back twenty or thirty years. All he had to do was select the part of the database that he wanted ('News'), and key in the phrases he was looking for: *Compass Trust* **and** *foundation*. Thirty seconds later he had a list of every article in which those phrases occurred.

There were eleven cites, going back to 1981. Several of the cites were duplicates of one another, or reprints of wire service stories. But the relevant information boiled down to the fact that the Compass Trust had been endowed by J. Kendrick Mellowes, 'a conservative philanthropist.'

Frank smiled at the identification. Mellowes was

unquestionably *that*, but he was also (and in particular) an 'intelligence groupie' who'd paid through the nose for an appointment to PFIAB – the President's Foreign Intelligence Advisory Board.

Frank went back to the main screen and ran another search – this time for 'A. Lloyd Kolp.' Moments later the screen shivered and a list of five articles appeared.

The most recent of these was three years old. It reported that Gen. A. Lloyd Kolp was leaving his post as head of the Army Medical Research Institute of Infectious Diseases (AMRIID). After a holiday with his family, the general was expected to take over as executive director of the Compass Trust.

Frank sat back in his chair and heaved a sigh. He knew who Kolp was. And even without looking at the other stories, he knew what they said. He glanced at the headlines to see if he was right, and saw that he was:

AMRIID CHIEF CLAIMS MONKEY VIRUS NO THREAT
Reston Facility Disinfected: Kolp Visits Site

The general had been famous for a week or two when AMRIID was called in to lock-down and disinfect a privately operated primate research facility in Reston, Virginia. Monkeys had been dying by the dozens, and it was feared that some terrible disease might be loosed.

Kolp and his troops had gone in. They'd behaved heroically. The public's fears had been calmed. And, eventually, a book had been written about the incident.

But Frank knew that AMRIID had a darker history. Behind the polysyllabic institute with its awkward acronym was an older and simpler name: 'Fort

Detrick.' Only a few miles from Camp David, and very close indeed to rows upon rows of newly constructed town houses, Detrick had been action central for the Pentagon's research on biological weapons.

This was, of course, a purely defensive effort – or so the public was told. But the reality was that no nation could develop defenses against these weapons if it failed to understand what the weapons were, how they worked, and what their limitations might be.

Which meant building and testing the weapons themselves.

And so the Pentagon's researchers worked with some of the most dangerous toxins and viruses on earth: botulin, ricin, pulmonary anthrax, pneumonic plague.

Resources had been poured into what was known as the 'weaponization' of biological agents. Teams of scientists explored different methods of 'aerosolization,' trying to identifr the one method that guaranteed maximum dispersal. Others worked on micro-encapsulation techniques, looking for ways to prevent the deterioration of biological agents exposed to water, heat, and air.

Still other researchers applied their talents to increasing the lethality of bacterial and viral agents, searching for MEFs – mortality enhancing factors. Others used recombinant DNA technology to create new and more dangerous germs.

All this in the name of self-defense. Since other countries might be developing biological weapons, the U.S. had been obliged to do so as well, so that it might devise antidotes and be ready in case of attack. Some thought the research was still going on, despite treaties prohibiting it, but who could tell?

Frank drummed his fingers on his desk. Detrick.

Kolp. And Mellowes. The Compass Trust. It didn't take a genius to figure out that the Kopervik expedition was spooked up. And Annie – what about her? Did she know? How could she not? The expedition was *her* baby. It was *her* idea in the first place.

He clicked on the Print button and waited for the stories to kick out.

It was just a hunch – he couldn't prove anything, really – but he knew enough about this *kind* of thing to suspect that the Compass Trust was a conduit, a funding mechanism for projects that the Pentagon and the CIA wanted to run 'off the books.'

The question was: why *this* expedition? And why now? Why would the Pentagon *secretly* fund a project to recover a long lost – and very dangerous – virus from under the permafrost? The answer seemed obvious: because the project was illegal, or in violation of a treaty, like the one that prohibited germ-warfare research.

As he shut down the computer he noticed for the first time that it had begun to rain, and that he was sitting in what amounted to near darkness. Sitting back in his chair, he heaved a sigh and reflected that the darkness suited the mood that was upon him.

Jesus, he thought. Annie! How couldja, babe?

13

He was sitting on her stoop when she came up the walk.

She wore a blue suit with the skirt to the knee, red shoes, and a matching red purse. She was holding a folded-up copy of the *Post* and taking small, shuffling steps so that she wouldn't have to look where she was going.

He'd seen her in one of these outfits before, the first day they'd met, at her office at the NIH. She'd taken off her lab coat to reveal an outfit much like this one – a suburban matron's getup, anonymous and boring. Professional and at ease in her white lab clothes, her attempts at power-dressing failed her. The truth was, she gave the touching but unmistakable impression of a little girl playing dress-up.

'Frank!' she said when she finally noticed him. Big wide smile. 'Hiiiiii.'

He stood up. 'Hey . . .'

His voice told her something was wrong. 'What's the matter?' she asked.

He thought about it. 'Well,' he said, 'it's complicated.'

They sat down together on the stoop, surrounded by the spring. Annie folded the paper in her lap and looked at him.

'I filed some FOIA requests,' Frank said. 'About the expedition.'

Annie groaned and rolled her eyes. 'I thought we weren't going to talk about that.'

'I got some stuff back. I think you ought to take a look at it.'

She looked away, annoyed by his breach of their agreement.

'I know what you're going to say,' Frank said, 'but I really think you oughta hear me out. I really do.'

With a sigh and a look of exasperated indulgence, she turned back to him. 'Go ahead,' she said, her voice as even as it was empty.

He showed her the letter with the B(l) exemption (*So what? I don't know what that's about*), and the next one, from the Compass Trust. *(Let me see that . . . who's Lloyd Kolp?)* He told her who Kolp was, and explained about Mellowes. She was interested now – upset, even. *Doctor K said we had funding from the NSF – he didn't say anything about this Compass thing.*

When Frank was done, he put the papers back in his briefcase. 'You didn't know about any of this, did you?'

Her lips were pressed together, as if she might cry. She shook her head no.

'So . . .' He reached for her hand, but she snatched it away and sat with her elbows on her knees, and her face buried in her hands. 'I was hoping we could talk – about what happened in Kopervik. About Neal Gleason. All that.'

She kept the heels of her palms pressed into her eyes and wagged her head back and forth. He saw dark splotches on her skirt and knew that she was crying. Finally, she said, 'Who's Neal Gleason?'

'He took you off the boat in Hammerfest. He shoved you in the car. He's an FBI agent.'

167

She took a deep breath and started to get up. 'I have to go in,' she said.

Frank reached out to stop her, but she pulled away. 'Annie –'

'I can't talk about it.'

'Look, Annie, this is a news story – and it's a *big* story. The kind of story people need to know about. It won't go away.'

She paused in front of the door. 'I know,' she said.

'Then why –'

'It isn't what you think it is.'

'*What?*'

'I have to go in.'

'No, wait a minute. What are you talking about? The expedition was spooked up. Anyone can see that. It's obvious. And it isn't hard to figure out. When the NSF turned down your application –'

Annie was shaking her head.

' – Kicklighter went to the spooks.'

'No. He didn't. It didn't happen that way.'

'Okay, so the spooks came to *you*! What's the difference? The point is: it's bioweapons research – and it's illegal. I can't believe you'd be a party to it.'

'I'm not. And it isn't. It isn't what you *think*.'

'Oh c'mon, Annie – they *used* you. *I* know that – but that's not the way it's going to look. *Talk* to me!'

She wagged her head sadly and swiped at her eyes with the back of her hand. 'I can't . . .' Taking a key from her handbag, she opened the door and started to go inside. Suddenly, her shoulders sagged and she turned to look at him. 'I really had a great time at dinner the other night,' she said. Then she burst into tears, stepped inside and closed the door behind her.

He sat at his desk, drumming his fingers on the wood,

and tried to think about it logically, but the mystery that lay behind Annie's reticence had no shape for him. What else could he do? After half an hour he looked up at the to-do list on the screen in front of him. It was a very short list:

1. Call Kolp
2. Check manifests

The first task was an exercise in defensive journalism. Calling Kolp wouldn't get him anywhere. The guy almost certainly wouldn't talk. But he had to ask, or the lawyers would be all over him when the time came to publish. *You didn't call the guy? You just assumed he wouldn't talk?*

So he put in the call to Kolp, and it went about as he'd expected. *The general is away from his desk just now. Can you tell me what it's about?*

Like any good gatekeeper, Kolp's secretary pumped him for information even as she shielded her boss. It's *Frank Daly. From the* Post. *Well, actually: I'm on leave to a foundation . . . Right, I know, it's complicated, so – just tell him it's about Kopervik.*

Then he hung up, and turned to the second task on his list:

Check manifests.

He wanted to know what happened to the miners' bodies – where they went, and how they got there. The NSF had turned down Kicklighter's grant because it was concerned about appearances, and in particular, the appearance of risk. Because Frank had been interested in the precautions that Annie had taken, he recalled her description of what was to happen on Kopervik.

To begin with, the cadavers were to be handled by scientists wearing Level-4 biocontainment suits.

169

Removed from their coffins, the bodies would be wrapped in formalin-soaked sheets and placed in hermetically sealed, body-transfer cases. A helicopter would carry the transfer cases to science freezers in the hold of the *Rex Mundi*, specifically to the Cold Room, where the temperature was maintained at four degrees Fahrenheit. On arrival in Hammerfest, the transfer cases would be taken by helicopter to the Tromso military airfield. There, the expedition would be met by a C-131 military transport, deadheading back to the U.S. from Bosnia. Equipped with a science freezer of its own, the C-131 was to take Annie, Kicklighter, and the transfer cases to Dover Air Force Base, Once the bodies had been escorted through Customs, the Graves Registration Unit at Dover would drive the bodies to the NIH in a freezer-equipped truck.

That's what was supposed to happen, or what Frank was told would happen. But had it? Or had the bodies been taken elsewhere – to Fort Detrick, for example?

Frank went into his address book and came up with the number for the Public Information Office at the Pentagon. The officer he spoke with – Captain Marcia Devlin – was crisp and efficient. She said she'd call back within an hour, and she did.

'I have the information you're looking for,' she said.

'Great.'

'C-131 . . . took off from Tuzla at 0600, March twenty-eight, landed Tromso, 1425, same day. Took five passengers on board, March twenty-nine. Departed Tromso at 0500, arrived Andrews eight hours later. That's March twenty-nine.'

'You said Andrews. You mean Dover, right?'

'No, sir. I mean just what I said. They got into Andrews at 1300 hours.'

Frank thought about it. 'So they changed their

minds,' he said.

'Excuse me?'

'I said, they must have changed their minds. They were going to Dover,'

'I wouldn't know. All I can tell you is: they landed at Andrews.'

Frank sighed. 'Well, I appreciate this. Now, if you'll just give me the passengers' names –'

'Can't do that.'

Frank pretended surprise. 'Oh? And why not?'

'There's a Privacy Act.'

'You mean the information's secret.'

'No, sir. I mean it's *private*.'

Frank thanked her for her help, hung up, and thought about what he'd been told. There were five passengers – Kicklighter, Adair, Gleason, and . . . who?

He pulled the telephone directory out of his desk drawer and called the number for Andrews Air Force Base. The switchboard routed him to the press officer, Sergeant Raymond Garcia.

Frank told him who he was and said, 'Captain Devlin said I should give you a call. She's in the PIO office at the Pentagon?'

'Yessir.'

'Well, I'm doing this story for the *Post,*' he lied, 'and . . . uh, Marcia – I mean, Captain Devlin – thought you could help.'

'Well, if I can –'

'It's about the way Customs works with the military. . . .'

'And you're interested in Andrews Air Force Base?' Garcia's voice was wary.

'Not really. I mean, it's close to home – so it's a lot easier for me to work with you than someplace in Alaska.'

171

'And what is it you want to do?'

'Look at some manifests.'

'Which manifests?'

'Oh, I don't know – it doesn't matter, really. Last month's would be okay. So long as it's typical. Was last month pretty typical?'

'You mean, for overseas flights?'

'Yeah.'

'I don't know. I guess so. Probably.'

'Well, then, March would be great.'

'But . . . what is it you're looking for?' It occurred to Frank that Sergeant Garcia's voice seemed to have only two tones: puzzlement and wariness.

'I just want to see the level of traffic, and maybe get some idea of the *kinds* of things that military people bring through Customs – and how it's handled. I mean, there's going to be weapons and medical supplies – but there's bound to be personal things, too.'

'And that's the story?' The sergeant sounded skeptical.

'Yeah,' Frank said. 'That's it.'

'Huh! Sounds kind of dull.'

Great, Frank thought. I've got a journalism critic on the line. 'I'll use a lot of quotes.'

'Well . . .'

'But what I need to know is: does every military aircraft maintain a cargo manifest?'

'Absolutely.'

'And are these available to Customs?'

'Of course.

'And what about the public? For instance: if I wanted to look at the March manifests, could I do that?'

'I suppose so.'

'Interesting,' Frank said.

'Unless it's a classified flight. We get a few of those.'

'But you could separate those from the rest, right?'

'Sure.'

'Then I guess what I'd like to do is set something up. All I need to look at is a single month. March would be fine.'

It took three days, but in the end Sergeant Garcia could find no reason to deny him, and so he made the arrangements. In the meantime, Frank was sure that the PIO had gone through the month's manifests, looking for anything that might cause embarrassment: a congressman returning from Peru with pre-Columbian art, a general with a taste for Danish pornography, a CIA flight that didn't go through Customs at all.

As he drove out to Andrews on Allentown Road, Frank considered the possibilities of what he'd find: if the manifest was there, he'd see who brought the bodies through Customs and where they were going. He'd also learn the identities of Passenger Four and Passenger Five. And if the manifest wasn't there . . . well, that, too, would tell him something. It would mean it had been segregated from the others because the flight was classified, or otherwise sensitive.

At the Andrews main gate, a uniformed man handed him a pass, a parking tag, and a map, then waved him through in the direction of the headquarters building.

Sergeant Raymond Garcia turned out to be a short man with a portfolio of facial expressions so studied that Daly was sure he'd practiced them in front of a mirror. Seeing Frank, he put his hands behind his back, compressed his lips, and made his pitch, rocking back and forth on the heels of his well-polished shoes. 'I'm sure you understand that the army is cognizant of the possibility of abuse of the military transport system. But I can assure you that the incidence of such abuse is minimal. We cooperate completely with the Customs Service.' Head tilt. Meaningful glance.

This was so well-rehearsed that under different circumstances Frank might have looked for the story that had prompted the disclaimer. But at the moment he just wanted to put Garcia's mind at ease.

'I'm not looking for any skeletons, Sergeant. This is a very general piece – and it's not so much about the Army as it is about Customs, and the magnitude of their task.'

In the end he was escorted to a small, fluorescent-lit room where a table and chair awaited him. There was a sheaf of manifests on the table, and a jar of Coffee-mate with a plastic spoon.

'Coffee?' Garcia asked.

Frank signaled his assent, and soon afterward the sergeant returned to the room with a plastic cup. 'Happy hunting,' he said as he handed him the cup. Then, turning on his heel, he closed the door behind him.

Frank spent the next five minutes pretending to go through the manifests. But he knew what he wanted. The files were arranged in chronological order, and it didn't even take him a minute to find what he was looking for.

Flight 1251, out of Tuzla, bound for Tromso on March 28. Then Tromso to Andrews the next day. A notation indicated that the flight had touched down at 1313.

Frank's eyes went to the column under Passengers.

There were five names, and they were in alphabetical order:

Adair, Anne
Fitch, Taylor
Gleason, Neal
Karalekis, Dr. George
Kicklighter, Dr. Benton

He wrote down the names he didn't recognize. Karalekis was probably a doctor at NIH. Fitch could be anyone. FBI. CIA . . .

He turned to the second page of the manifest, where the cargo was listed, and for a moment he thought there had been a mistake.

The hold was empty, except for some computer equipment and the personal belongings of the crew and their passengers.

Frank took a long sip of coffee and looked again. There was nothing about body-transfer cases, or the remains of miners. *Page 2 of 2*, it said.

He checked the other manifests to see if there was another flight from Tromso, either that day or the next, or the one after that. But there was nothing. No body-transfer cases anywhere.

He loved the way the Saab held the road (when it wasn't in the repair shop). It cornered beautifully, and if he hadn't had eight points on his license, he'd have opened it up on the way back to Washington.

But he didn't. He kept the speedometer smack on sixty, which was just as well, because he was in a daze. No bodies. What did *that* mean?

Almost anything, really. Maybe the transfer cases were on a different flight. Maybe they'd been delayed by Norwegian Customs and hadn't left for the States until April. Maybe the bodies had decomposed in some great, unheard-of thaw. Maybe there'd been an

Eskimo Summer on Edgeoya.

Or bears. Annie had told him about the bears, and how the mining community used dynamite to excavate burial sites, making them deep enough to keep the bears from getting at them. Maybe they hadn't gone deep enough. And there was a kind of frost-heave peculiar to the Arctic, where objects worked their way to the surface. He remembered Annie telling him about it, and how, when the objects were bodies, the bodies were called 'floaters.'

He passed RFK Stadium, and headed into the mess around the Capitol.

It was one of the things Annie had said they'd test for in situ – melt-and-thaw cycles in the permafrost. If the bodies had thawed at any time during the past eighty years, the virus would be unrecoverable, and there would be no point in bringing the bodies to the U.S. But if that was what had happened, why hadn't Annie said as much? Why all the secrecy?

And there was another possibility as well. Instead of taking the cadavers in their entirety, Annie and Kicklighter might have settled for core samples. She'd even told him how it could be done, using what amounted to a hole saw to obtain cylindrical sections from the lungs and the major organs.

The trouble with this explanation was that there was nothing on the passenger manifest about 'tissues' or medical supplies or anything like it. And the trouble with all the other explanations was that they did not explain Neal Gleason's presence, the Compass Trust's involvement, or the way they'd stonewalled him in Hammerfest and after.

He had a soccer match that night – indoors at the Sportsplex in Springfield. All the usual suspects were there, and, as ever, no one on his team had exactly the same shirt. They were playing a team of Hispanics, most of whom worked at the World Bank. All of them were kitted out in a blaze of identical colors – actual uniforms, with knee-high socks! – while Frank's side stood around in T-shirts that were . . . kind of dark. Mostly.

'Whattaya mean it's not blue! It's got blue *in* it!'

'C'mon, ref! Es *gris!* Make him change it.'

'It's not *gree*, you fuck. What the fuck is *gree?*'

When the game ended in a draw, the two teams went upstairs to drink beer and heckle the other sides, playing below. It was a good time, as it always was, because it was the only time that he didn't have to think – or think about anything important. There was no Washington *Post,* no thoughts about his father, no Fletcher Harrison Coe, Neal Gleason, or body-transfer cases. Just a dozen guys doing something they liked and were kind of good at. It didn't *mean* anything, and that's what made it so important.

He left around ten o'clock, walking out into the parking lot. He was feeling good, which surprised him, because as soon as he left the building, he remembered that he was at a dead end. He didn't have a clue about what to do next. About Kopervik. Or Annie. Or any of that. And all of a sudden, that mattered again.

But it was a beautiful night, and he stood for a moment beside the Saab, taking it in. An airplane crawled across Orion, moving impossibly slow. Frank watched it for a while and decided it wasn't an airplane. It must be a comet, he thought. Or . . .

The Panoptikon Satellite Corporation was located in Herndon, only a couple of miles from Dulles Airport. It was a publicly traded company whose product was reconnaissance – satellite imagery with a resolution matrix of one meter. Its clientele was a mix of third world countries that couldn't afford their own satellites, minerals' exploration companies, environmental groups, agribusiness, commercial fisheries, and the media. Among other things, it gave great weather.

And it wasn't cheap. Frank felt guilty about spending the foundation's money on a story he'd been told to drop, but he wasn't going to pay for it himself – and it was something that had to be done.

He told the clerk what he wanted, gave her the coordinates for Kopervik and the date he'd worked out for the *Rex Mundi*'s arrival on Edgeoya. The clerk keyed the information into her computer, waited a few moments, and announced, 'No problem. We photograph the Svalbard archipelago twice a day, and it looks like we've got archival footage going back three years.'

Twenty minutes later she returned with a 36 × 48 photograph, black and white, and still a little damp. Along its upper right edge ran a continuous band of print, repeating the date/time stamp and the positional coordinates. She laid the picture on a viewing table and dropped a felt-covered weight on each corner.

They looked at it together.

After a moment she laughed and said, 'Look.' Her forefinger pointed to an oblong puff near the right-hand corner of the sheet.

Frank squinted. 'What?'

'That.' She laid one long, curved, and elaborately painted fingernail next to an oval shape that looked, at first, like a flaw in the paper. 'Polar bear,' she said. 'I've seen 'em before.' She plunked a photo loupe onto the picture and told him to take a look.

She was right. It was a bear. But he was more

interested in Kopervik itself – the clutch of buildings, the church, and the helicopter. With the loupe, you could see that the chopper was sitting in a fog of snow kicked up by its own rotors. They must have been turning when the picture was taken from space.

He swung his eyes back to the village and was able to pick out, from among the other buildings, the shape of the little chapel, with its truncated but recognizable steeple. And near the chapel, a scatter of black dots. Annie, he supposed, and Kicklighter, and the boys from NOAA.

They were gathered in a little group near a dark area, where the snow cover had been disturbed. Now that his eyes had adjusted to the bird's-eye view, he realized that this was the graveyard next to the chapel. He could make out the stone wall that surrounded it, its square geometrical shape clear, even under the snow. Using the magnifying device, he picked out the regularly spaced smudges that must be the headstones and, nearby, a dark area that seemed to be smeared. There were boxes or logs, a jumble of lumber or –

Coffins. A jumble of coffins.

He frowned. It was exactly what he'd expected to see, and yet . . . There was something about the scene that nagged at him. He tapped his fingers on the table and spent several more minutes staring at the satellite shot, sliding the loupe here and there to take a closer look, but it refused to yield any more information to him. He looked at the date band running across the top, and once again he shook his head. He'd chosen the date by working backward from the arrival of the *Rex* in Hammerfest.

It was a three-day trip, so . . . it looked like the expedition was ahead of schedule. Apparently, the exhumation hadn't taken as long as they'd expected.

This was clearly their last day on Edgeoya. It had to be for them to make it back to Hammerfest when they did. Also: there were no work tents at the site, so they must have been returned to the *Rex* by the time the picture was taken. And the other equipment, too, because there was none of that to be seen, either.

He slid the magnifying device over to the helicopter, looking for the body-transfer cases, but the whole area was fuzzy with blowing snow. And besides, he thought, the crew wouldn't have stored the equipment first and then come back for the transfer cases. They'd have been the first things taken to the Cold Room in the hold.

He removed the felt-covered weights from the corners and watched the photo sheet curl up into a cylinder. The clerk expertly tightened it until its diameter was small enough to fit into the cardboard tube with the Panoptikon logo on the side. She pushed a plastic cap into the open end and wrote out a bill for $289.46.

He was halfway back to his apartment when it hit him. Somewhere in Bandarland, just before he got to the Chain Bridge Road, he thought, *Wait a minute* – and hit the brakes. The guy behind him went ballistic, but Frank was already in the middle of a U-turn, heading back to Herndon.

'I want to go again,' he told the clerk

'Excuse me?'

'Same coordinates, make it a month earlier. February twenty-eighth, or whatever . . .'

She looked at him, shrugged, and tapped on her keyboard.

Half an hour later he was looking at the second photograph – which was exactly the same as the first, minus the helicopter, Annie, and her friends.

He slid the loupe over the graveyard. The dark eruptions were there, the jumble of coffins. He looked up at the date band, just to double check and to make sure that the clerk had not misunderstood. But there it was: 1147 February 28, 1998. When Annie and Kicklighter were still in the United States. And yet – the bodies were already gone, and the coffins piled up in a heap.

It was the realization of this possibility that had sent him into a U-turn near the Chain Bridge. Until then, he'd tried to explain everything away. Back too soon in Hammerfest? Well, things must have gone swimmingly at the site.

What had gotten to him, finally, was the coffins. Laying like that in the snow, in a jumble. Annie had explained to him the efforts she had gone to in order to obtain permission for the exhumations. First, she'd had to identify the miners, trace their families, contact them for permission to dig up their kin, then get the Lutheran church to agree that tearing up its graveyard was in the public interest. He knew that once NIH was done with the miners, the remains would be reinterred on the mainland.

It was all so very proper, and almost self-consciously respectful. He just couldn't imagine that Annie would go to all that trouble and then toss the coffins into a heap, as if they were so much scrap lumber.

So someone else had gotten to Kopervik first. And taken the miners. He thought about that for moment, then returned to the counter.

'Hit me again,' he said. 'A month earlier. January twentieth would be good.'

She gave him a look. 'You know – most people don't find this *addictive*.' She tapped and clacked on her computer and then shook her head. 'And anyway: I wouldn't do January – not at that latitude. Unless you're interested in infrared.'

'Why?'

'It's *dark*, all day long. If there were lights, you could pick them out, but –'

Frank shook his head. 'No, it's a ghost town.'

'So . . . ?'

'Try November twentieth, 'ninety-seven.'

It took three more hours, and by the time he was done, the bill came to almost $2,800.

He'd worked his way back a month at a time until he found what he knew must be there: the snow cover pristine, the graves undisturbed. The date was August 20, 1997.

Which meant that the bodies had been taken between then and September 20, when the graveyard was as it appeared in the subsequent months until Annie's arrival by helicopter.

Once he had the time frame, it was just a matter of homing in on the actual date of the exhumation, which turned out to be September 9.

There was a small crane in the graveyard, a Bobcat, and the pegged rectangle of a tent. A helicopter sat behind the church; there were half a dozen people in the graveyard. No matter how much, or how intently, he gazed through the loupe, there was no way that he could identify any of the blurred and grainy figures standing beside the graves.

He moved the loupe to the helicopter, whose size afforded a modicum of resolution. Shaped like a dragonfly, the chopper rested on the snow, maybe twenty yards from the church. Frank stared at the machine's fuselage, searching for identifying markers, but finding none. The resolution just wasn't good enough. Tiring of the process, he sat back in his chair and rubbed his eyes.

When he opened them a moment later, he saw – or imagined – something that he hadn't seen before: a grid. Or, more accurately, *a sort* of grid – there, at the rear of the helicopter's fuselage. Raising the magnifying loupe, he held it above the photograph, raising and lowering it in search of the ideal magnification.

Which, as it happened, didn't exist. Whatever he'd seen, or thought he'd seen, exploded beneath the loupe's thick lens, its lines and edges flying apart as if the magnifying glass were a centrifuge. Frustrated, he pulled back in his chair and went to the counter. Half-dazed, and trying to make sense of what he'd found, he charged the bill to his Visa card and walked outside to his car, carrying a thick tube of satellite photos.

Now, at least, he knew *what, when,* and *where.* Someone had gotten to Kopervik before Annie and the *Rex.* That's why Gleason was there to meet the boat. That's why they'd returned empty-handed. And that's why a wall had gone up around the story.

Only two questions remained.

Who? And *why?*

14

Somebody had beaten them to it. When the expedition arrived at the graveyard, the bodies were gone.

He sat in his car on Chain Bridge, going nowhere, not really listening to the CD that was playing – a Cape Verde blues. He was staring ahead at a long string of taillights whose reflections covered the wet asphalt like pools of blood. Traffic was at a standstill. His wipers ticked back and forth. Every now and then lightning flashed through sheets of rain.

He thought there must be an accident up ahead. He thought that he ought to get some new wiper blades. He thought: the rear window is fogging up. But what he couldn't seem to think about were the implications of what he'd learned at Panoptikon. Instead, he just kept seeing the images themselves: the cluster of rectangular shapes that were the jumble of coffins, the dark smears of the excavated graves.

He didn't *want* to think, that was part of it. He'd been chasing the usual kind of story, a gotcha piece in which the intrepid reporter unearths an unholy alliance between science and the military. He'd thought he *knew* what the story was, but all of a sudden his frame of reference was gone, and now he had no idea. Also, it was beginning to scare him.

He tapped his fingertips on the steering wheel. *Who? Why?*

On the one hand, the pictures explained a lot:

Kicklighter's defeated shuffle as he walked down the gangway from the *Rex,* Annie's deer-in-the-headlights look and her refusal to talk about Kopervik, Neal Gleason's presence in Hammerfest. It explained the connection to the Pentagon, the funding from the Compass Trust. On the other hand . . . *no, it didn't.* It didn't explain anything, really.

The line of cars ahead of him wasn't moving, and in the distance he could hear the *whoop whoop whoop* of sirens. He tried to organize his thoughts about the Panoptikon photographs. Mostly, they weren't thoughts but questions, the same questions: who dug up the graves, and *why?*

Digging in permafrost was as hard as digging in rock – it took days to get anywhere, even with special tools. And Kopervik was so remote that it might as well be on another planet. Which meant that what happened there was a lot more than grave-robbing. Somebody – and somebody with very deep pockets – wanted the bodies for themselves. And the only reason to want those particular bodies was to get the virus they harbored. And that could only mean that the people who took the bodies wanted to culture the virus, just as Kicklighter and Adair had hoped to do.

But *why?*

Not to study the protein coats. Any on-the-level expedition to Kopervik – Annie would have known about it. Since she'd done all the groundwork, she would have been consulted as a matter of professional courtesy and maybe even invited along. And if not Annie, the National Science Foundation would have known about it. So would the mining company representatives, and the families who'd given permission to have the bodies exhumed.

So, what was going on?

He toyed with the notion that a pharmaceutical company might have gone after the virus, hoping to make a vaccine. But why would anyone create a vaccine for a bug that didn't exist, or only existed under the permafrost above the Arctic Circle? They wouldn't. No one would.

Who, then? And *why*?

Why acquire a strain of influenza that was legendary for its virulence? Well, that wasn't so hard, he thought. If you weren't going to study it, and you weren't going to make a vaccine, then the only reason to go after the bodies would be to extract the virus to make a biological weapon.

And what a weapon. As an airborne infection, it was spectacularly contagious, and what was more –

A honk from behind pulled Frank from his reverie, and he saw that twenty yards separated him from the faint red eyes of the car ahead. The traffic had finally started to move. He hunched forward in his seat, the windshield pearly and barely translucent from the pounding rain. Crossing the bridge, he turned up Arizona and swung down Nebraska. At Ward Circle, American U. students splashed across the complicated intersection, giddy and sodden.

Who? The military was the most obvious candidate, but as he'd discovered, it was the military – or at least the intelligence community – that had secretly sponsored the expedition. Which was not something they would do if they had already exhumed the bodies.

Terrorists, then. That would certainly explain Neal Gleason's presence. But, no. Given the resources needed to mount an expedition to Kopervik – an expedition that might well result in nothing but frostbite – one of the bad-boy nations seemed a lot more likely. Iran, Iraq, Libya. The usual suspects.

But he didn't think so. There was something wrong with his analysis, something he was forgetting. But what?

Two blocks from his apartment he stopped at Mixtec, and left ten minutes later with a container of rice and *bistec al pasilla*. Returning home, he tossed the satellite photos on the coffee table and sat down in front of the TV, flicking through the channels until he found the Bullets' game. Or the Wizards'. Or whatever they were calling themselves that week. He watched Strickland dish a no-look pass to Webber, who went up for a reverse jam. Good-looking play, but then the score flashed across the screen and he saw that it was Indiana by sixteen.

He flicked it off. His head wasn't into it anyway. He was still preoccupied with the satellite photos and the sense that something about them didn't add up. But what?

He had the idea that maybe he could spring it loose by looking over his notes and files about influenza. While he finished eating, why not listen to some of his interview tapes? Maybe something would jog his memory. He rummaged through the box of cassettes in the back of his file drawer until he found what he was looking for – *influenza/Adairintvw//3/8/98* – and stuck the tape in the cassette player. He got a beer and a bottle of Yucateco sauce, and listened to the tape.

'It's unintentional. They use host cells to reproduce, and in the process, kill the cells. The fact that they make you sick is a side effect. The ideal virus wouldn't make you sick at all.'

'No? I thought that was their raison d'être.'

(Laughter) *'No. They have the same raison d'être as we do – biologically speaking. They want*

*to make more of themselves . . . So if they kill off
the host, they aren't being efficient.'*

He shook his head. How could he find what he was
after without knowing what it was? He pushed the
fast-forward button. Annie was saying:

*'Now, smallpox is so stable you could put it on
a piece of paper and stick it in a filing cabinet and
it might survive for decades. Centuries. It's a
worry for anthropologists, you know, digging up
mummies.'*
'But influenza –'
'Is a different story.'

He snapped off the machine and got to his feet. He
wasn't getting anywhere with the tape. Better to see the
source herself.

Annie's town house was a few feet above street level.
He sat on the stoop for half an hour waiting for her.
Finally, she came up the steps, laughing, talking with a
small dark-haired woman, both of them lugging
plastic bags full of groceries. This time she wore
sandals, a faded red Hoyas T-shirt, and a pair of Levi's
with shredded knees. Somehow, he could tell that the
knees were frayed by genuine wear and tear and not
for the sake of fashion. The small woman saw him first
and put a hand on Annie's arm. Annie stopped
walking, her laugh died away, and her expression
flickered through some interesting changes – for a
nanosecond she looked really happy to see him –
before settling into a kind of wary smile.

'Is this going to be a regular thing – because if it is,
maybe you could have dinner waiting,' she said.

'I wanted to show you something,' Frank said,

tapping the tube of satellite photos.

'Okaaay,' Annie said.

The other woman stood at the door, indulging her curiosity. Finally, Annie introduced them. 'Frank – Indu. Indu's my roommate.'

'And Frank?' Indu asked coyly.

'Frank's a journalist,' Annie replied.

Indu gave Frank a crinkled smile and, with an amused glance at Annie, went inside.

Annie turned to Frank. 'What did you want to show me?'

'Satellite pix.'

'What?'

'Satellite pictures. A bird's-eye view . . .'

'Of what?'

'Kopervik. March twenty-sixth, about 1300 hours. You look like a dot.'

'You're serious?'

Frank nodded. 'I know what you found.'

Annie regarded him coolly, wondering if this was a trick, and if it was, wondering how he could underestimate her so completely. 'Really!?' she said, her voice thick with sarcasm.

'Yeah.'

'And what did we find?'

'*Bupkis.*'

'What?'

'The bodies were gone. Someone got there ahead of you.'

She looked at him for a long moment, and then she invited him inside. 'I don't think we should talk about this on the street.'

And even inside, with the photographs spread out on the kitchen table, their corners weighted with books, she was still hesitant to talk about it.

'I'm sure Gleason made you sign something,' Frank said. 'But that's gotta be irrelevant now – unless you're holding something back.' He tapped the satellite photo. 'Or is this pretty much it?'

She inclined her head. 'Pretty much,' she said. 'I was in shock. I guess I still am.'

He tapped out the second photo from the tube and put it on top of the first, re-anchoring the corners with the books.

'This is four or five months earlier,' Frank said. 'September seventh.' The snow was pristine and undisturbed. 'And this,' he went on, unrolling a third photograph, 'this is September ninth.' He put the third picture on top of the other two and weighted them down. 'That's when it happened,' he said.

They stared at the photograph for a long while. The ground was torn up, the coffins in a pile. A helicopter sat on the snow, not far from the church. Finally, Annie said, 'So they'd been gone for *months* by the time we got there.'

He nodded.

'Who was it?' she asked.

Frank looked at her as if to say, *If I knew the answer to that one . . .*

The telephone chirped, and chirped again. Neither of them moved until Indu shouted down to Annie that her mother was on the line. Annie grimaced and rolled her eyes, but once she picked up the phone, it was clear that her mother was also her best friend. The talk between them was conspiratorial and animated, girlish and sweet.

'*Oh noooooo,*' Annie was saying. 'You're kidding.'

As they talked, Frank was thinking, Maybe I should do the story now, just write it – instead of trying to *solve* it. Even if he didn't have all the answers, it was

190

still a front-page story. A big story. And if he published it, the spooks would have to respond. Gleason & Company might be able to dodge him, but they couldn't dodge the whole press corps.

On the other hand, once he wrote the story, it wouldn't be his anymore. Better, then, to wait until he was certain he'd gone as far as he could go. And he wasn't certain of that – not at all. There were still things he could do, questions he could imagine answering. Like: what kind of weapon could you make with the Spanish flu? There were people who could tell him the answer to that – in fact, he knew a guy who could tell him that. He'd met him at a conference on terrorism. Two years ago, in Baltimore. He could still see his face. *Broad* face, high cheekbones, black hair. Funny name. Some kind of funny name. Who *was* that guy?

Annie wandered out of the room, then came back, carrying her contact lens container. Still talking to her mother, she removed a lens from each of her eyes. When she looked up at Frank, he saw that she had the mad, unfocused gaze of the very nearsighted.

He gave her a little wave, as if to say, *I'm over here* – and saw her smile.

'I have to go,' she said at the phone. Then, 'Love you! Love you, too.' She actually kissed the telephone before she replaced it in its cradle. Returning to the table, she rubbed her eye with a knuckle and stood staring myopically at the satellite photo.

'I better go,' Frank said. 'There's a lot to do.' He began to remove the books from the corners of the pictures when Annie put a hand on his sleeve.

'Wait wait wait,' she said. 'Wait.'

Frank looked at her, then at the photo. Finally, he said, 'What?'

She pointed at the helicopter. Shot from above, its fuselage showed as a kind of elongated teardrop, its dark rotor blades delineated against the snow. 'Look at that,' she said.

Frank cocked his head and squinted. 'What? You mean the helicopter?'

'The stripes,' she said.

Frank stared harder at the photo. 'What stripes?'

'On the fuselage.'

He looked and shook his head. 'I don't see any stripes.'

'There.' She pointed at a slurry of dots near the rear of the fuselage.

He looked hard. 'I still don't see it,' he said.

'It's an American flag.'

'Get out!'

'You have to squint!'

He squinted. Tilted back on his heels.

'I spend half my life like this, sitting in the dark, looking through an electron microscope, trying to pick out images from pictures that are a lot blurrier than this one. It's a flag,' she repeated 'An American flag.' She took his hand in hers and, with his forefinger, traced a tiny rectangle in the air above the photograph. 'The stripes run like this,' she said, sketching parallel lines over the fuselage. 'See?'

She was right. It was the 'grid' he'd seen, or imagined he'd seen, at Panoptikon. The parallel lines were stripes and, once you looked for them, they were hard to miss – but impossible to see through a magnifying loupe.

'Now I'm really confused,' Frank said. 'It doesn't compute. I mean, not at all.'

'Do you think it's a military helicopter?'

He shook his head. 'Could be. Or maybe not. It

might just be from a ship that's flying an American flag.'

Annie perched on a stool. 'I don't get it,' she said, stifling a yawn.

'Tell me something,' he asked, nodding toward the picture. 'If Kopervik was over here, where was your ship – the *Rex Mundi*?'

She thought about it for a moment, then pointed to a spot on the counter, a couple of feet to the left of the photo. 'Way over here somewhere. We had to get there on snowmobiles. It took a long time.'

He squinted at the dots for a while longer, satisfying himself that they did indeed coalesce into stripes. Then he pushed the books from the edges of the pictures and let them curl up. Finally, he tapped them back into the tube. He was thinking that he might go back to Panoptikon, and see if he could find some coverage of the ship's anchorage. 'Was there a name for the harbor?' he asked.

Annie shook her head. 'It wasn't a harbor, really. And I'm sure it didn't have a name. We just anchored – offshore.'

So much for that idea, he thought, secretly relieved. His Visa card was on fire, and he had serious doubts that the foundation would approve the money he'd already spent – much less finance a second go-round.

Annie walked him to the door, still yawning, and apologizing. 'I got up at six.'

'There's a cure for that, you know.' Suddenly, he wanted to kiss her. But just as he leaned toward her, she jumped back, talking fast and telling him she was glad he knew everything *she* did – at least now there wasn't this wall *of secrecy* between them, so *please* call her and tell her anything he found out. Then she yanked him toward the door and more or less shoved

193

him outside. It reminded him of junior high.

The guy with the funny name was Thomas R. Deer, and what was funny about it was that the middle initial stood for 'Running.' He was a broad-shouldered Sioux from eastern Montana, and an expert on chemical and biological weapons. His office was on the seventh floor of the National Security Studies Institute, across the street from the Bethesda Metro stop.

Frank gave his name to the receptionist and sat down in the elegantly appointed anteroom to wait, leafing through a copy of the *Economist*.

He'd met Deer at a conference sponsored by the Army War College. The topic was something like 'Urban Protection Against Bioterrorism: Crisis Management and Consequences.' Most of the time was taken up with speeches by muscular nerds from the Pentagon and earnest scientists from private consultancies. There were suits from the White House, Agriculture, Justice, and Defense, and others from Lockheed, Cal Tech, and Brookings. There was a woman from the FBI Laboratory, and someone else from the Academy of Emergency Physicians. But the ones who'd interested Frank the most were a lot less smooth, and a lot more endangered. They were the 'first-responders' – the fire chief from Arlington, the nurse from Fairfax, the worried-looking man from NewYork's Office of Emergency Services.

They were the ones who'd be mise-en-scène, and they were not optimistic. The first-responders to a chemical attack would probably fall victim to it themselves. And what could they do, in any case? There were only so many ambulances, so many hospital rooms, so much space in the morgue. Once an ambulance had been used, it would have to be decontaminated – which meant it would be taken out of commission. So, too, with the emergency rooms themselves, and with the people who staffed them: how efficient could they be, wearing biohazard suits? The truth was: a gas attack on a single high-rise would paralyze the New York health-care system within an hour.

And a biological attack would be even worse, because the holocaust would not become apparent for days. It would appear, gradually and then as a flood, in one emergency room after another – until it was too late to do anything but bury the dead. Or burn them. And by then, depending on the pathogen that was used, the hospital workers themselves would be dying.

It was the kind of conference that stuck in your mind.

'Frank?' Deer leaned through the doorway, resplendent in what looked like an Armani. 'I thought that's who you were! Come on back.'

They padded down a carpeted hallway, exchanging small talk about the Washington *Post* and a funky little restaurant in the Eastern Market, where the city's best crab cakes could be found. When they reached his office, Deer gestured to a leather wing chair and settled himself behind a broad, mahogany desk. At his back, a windowed wall looked out upon the capital.

The small talk continued for another minute or two as they caught up with each other's careers, talking about the places their jobs had taken them during the last two years. Deer was first to come to the point. 'What's up?' he asked.

Frank shrugged. 'I'm working on a story that's kind of unusual,' he said. 'I thought you could help.' The tale took about ten minutes to tell, and Frank told it in a way that was almost amusing, beginning with the flight to Murmansk and his stay at the Chernomorskaya. Deer laughed at Frank's description of the hotel, but as the story continued, his brow began to furrow.

'You're sure the FBI knows about this?' Deer asked.

Frank nodded. 'Yeah, they know. So does the Pentagon.'

The consultant grunted. 'Okay, so who took the bodies?'

'I don't know,' Frank said. 'For a while I was thinking –'

'The Iraqis.'

Frank look surprised. 'How'd you know?'

'Because that's what everybody thinks. They always think the Iraqis did it, no matter what it is.'

'But you don't.'

'No. Why would they want something like this?'

Frank shrugged. 'I don't know. Because it's so lethal . . .'

Deer didn't look convinced. '"Lethal" is relative,' he said. 'And with a pathogen like influenza, you'd be looking at a lot of preliminary work, just weaponizing the stuff. You'd be going to a lot of trouble –'

'What do you mean, 'weaponizing' it?'

'Different bugs have different characteristics. Some are virtually indestructible, others die out right away. If you want to turn a pathogen into a weapon, you'll probably want to cultivate a particularly virulent strain. Punch up what we call the "mortality-enhancing factors." Figure out the optimal dispersal method. That's what we mean by "weaponizing" it. And there are a dozen bugs and toxins that have been researched from here to Sunday – and they aren't hard to get. You wouldn't have to go the Arctic.'

'What kind of bugs and toxins?'

'Anthrax. Botulin.'

Frank made a note. 'You can buy them?'

It was Deer's turn to shrug. 'If you work in a university lab, or a commercial one, or even if you've got some phony letterhead that *says* you're a scientist – yeah, you can get what you want through the mail. Q-fever, tularemia, plague – they'll send it to you, FedEx. But the point I'm making is: if you're looking for a biological weapon, why reinvent the wheel? The open literature is full of stuff – including stuff about delivery systems.'

'Such as what?' Frank was writing rapidly in his notebook.

'Aerosols. Ticks. Bats. Bombs –'

'Bats?'

'Absolutely, bats! Pigeons, too. And dolphins!'

'How do you –'

'Strap 'em up.'

'With what?'

'Little porcelain bombs.'

'You're kidding.'

Deer held his eyes with a level gaze. 'Do I look like I'm kidding?'

Frank shifted in his seat. 'But what were you saying? About influenza . . . ?'

'It wouldn't make much of a weapon. No.'

'Why not?'

'Well,' Deer said, 'for one reason: if you're fighting a war, you're facing military units in the field. So you'd want something that has an immediate effect – something that'll knock people down. Like gas.'

'And if you wanted to attack a civilian population?'

'You mean, like Saddam and the Kurds?'

'Yeah,' Frank said. 'Like that. Or a terrorist scenario.'

Deer swiveled around in his chair and looked out at Washington. 'You'd still want something you could control – something you could demonstrate without taking out the planet.'

'Like what?'

'Pulmonary anthrax. With pulmonary anthrax, you could make some pretty strong demands.'

'Why? What's so special about it?'

'Well, it's a terrific germ – I mean, literally. It scares the wits out of people. And it's a pathogen you could work with. You could show people what you could do, and what you could *stop* doing, which is just as important.'

'So you'd stage a demonstration by taking out a city –'

'Or a town. Or even a building. You wouldn't have to do a lot to get people's attention. With pulmonary anthrax, you can't even *bury* the dead. You have to *burn* them.'

'Why?'

'Because the infective agent is about as fragile as a boulder. It's a spore. You could boil it and it wouldn't make any difference.'

Frank nodded. 'All right. And with influenza . . . ?'

'You couldn't *threaten* anyone with it. All you could do is use it. And then the birds would take it. You get a herald wave going in a place like Peking, and bam! – the next thing you know, it's all over the map. It's a pandemic. And that's where we get into what I said about 'relative lethality.' Something like Ebola's got a lot higher mortality rate than the Spanish flu. In fact, it pretty much kills almost everyone who gets it. But *getting* it is kinda hard to do – so it really doesn't kill that many people. On the other hand, with influenza you have a fairly low mortality rate, but it's supercontagious. Of course, if you played with it . . .'

'What do you mean "played with it"?'

'Well, with gene-splicing. Theoretically, you could combine it with something else, another pathogen that was a lot more lethal.'

'Like what?' Frank asked.

The scientist rocked from side to side in his chair, considering the possibilities. 'Cobra venom.'

'What?!'

'Sure. That way, you wouldn't just catch the flu, you'd catch a snakebite to the lungs.'

'Jesus Christ!' Frank exclaimed.

Deer nodded. 'Oh, yeah,' he said. 'It's a scary business. But I don't think that's what *your* people are doing – I mean, the people who took the bodies up north.'

'Why not?'

'Well, because if they wanted to do something like that, splicing one pathogen to another, they wouldn't need a particularly dangerous strain of the flu – or one that was so hard to get. They could use whatever was going around. They could use the common cold. But that's not the point,' Deer went on. 'The point is: everyone gets the flu. That's the thing about it. And you can't control it. So if you used it as a weapon, you might wind up killing millions of people – tens of millions.'

'That's what I'm saying,' Frank said. 'That's what I'm worried about.'

'But why would anyone want to *do* that?' Deer asked.

Frank thought about it. 'I don't know,' he said.

Deer clasped his hands to the nape of his neck and leaned back in his chair. 'My guess is, whoever took the bodies, wanted them for research. It was probably a pharmaceutical company – one of the smaller ones. A start-up with more balls than brains.'

'You think?' Frank asked.

'Yeah. I do.'

'And Gleason?'

'I don't know – the FBI gets into everything. What happened to the expedition – the British have a word for it. *Gazumped*. The expedition was gazumped, so . . . the *federales* show up to see what happened.'

Frank thought about it. Finally, he said, 'You're probably right.'

Deer nodded, then swiveled a quarter turn in his chair. 'On the other hand,' he mused, 'if someone wanted revenge . . . if they were mad at the world . . .'

Frank frowned, and leaned forward. 'Like who?'

Deer shrugged. 'Oh, I don't know. What about . . . what about the Sioux?'

'The *Sioux*,' Frank repeated, uncertain if he was kidding.

'We don't know a lot about icebreakers,' Deer went on, 'but . . some of us are pretty pissed off.'

All Frank could do was stare at him.

Then Running Deer's inscrutability cracked and his cheeks were lifted by a grin. '*Psych* . . .'

15

ALEXANDRIA, VIRGINIA

They'd been waiting six days in the safe house, and Tommy was missing Susannah. He was used to having sex with her, and the lack of it was making him antsy. Despite the yoga and the mindfulness exercises, and the relaxation techniques drummed into them during training, he just couldn't seem to kick his case of nerves. The worst of it was there was nothing at all to be nervous *about*. That was a stone fact. It was just a test, is all. Just a boat ride.

Maybe it was the on-again, off-again part that was getting to him. When they were on a go basis, as they were now, he got real wound up. Useless worries, all of them, but he couldn't seem to keep them from crawling into his head. What if the engine didn't start? What if there was trouble at the marina? What if the Coast Guard showed up? He was the one responsible for the boat. Test or no test, he didn't want it to be his fault if the whole thing blew up in their faces. So, he'd get keyed up, and then, when the decision was made to abort – which had already happened *three times now* – he'd go back to being bored. But nervous-bored, with all this energy jamming him up. He was also getting pretty damn sick of the Weather Channel, which Belinda and Vaughn wanted to watch, like all the time. One more pulsing mass of green surging toward the

Mid-Atlantic and he'd puke.

The dry run, of course, had gone off without a hitch. Didn't miss a step. Despite his secret worry that it might gum up, there was no trouble with the nozzle on the aerosolizer, which was something he'd made in the workshop. Basically, it was just a heavy-duty pressure pump attached to a standard pesticide dispersal unit. Chemlawn meets a snowmaking machine. It looked like a water cannon, and it worked like a bandit. During the tests at the compound in Placid, Tommy's homemade gizmo outperformed the custom-made device Solange had ordered, a thing designed by someone called an aerosol engineer, whatever the hell *that* was. *Kicked its ass.* He could still hear the pride in Susannah's voice: 'Tommy can make anything.' Solange had favored him with a beaming smile and the ultimate praise: 'Well done.'

The dry run had gone off without a hitch, but ever since, they couldn't seem to get past the drive to the marina without the wind shifting, or a scatter of raindrops appearing on the windshield. And then it was back to the television and the Weather Channel, and he was so fucking bored, he was practically crying.

'Would you stop that?' Belinda said, shooting him an annoyed look.

'What?'

'Tapping your foot.'

'Now I can't tap my foot? I *got to* tap my feet.' He stood up and did a little tap-dancing routine, his legs loose and rhythmic. He finished with an exaggerated bow toward her. 'It's in my *blood.*'

Belinda smiled; she had a kind of mother thing about him. She called him Tommy-O. She couldn't really get mad.

'Just cut it out,' Vaughn said in his flat New England

voice. But not like it was really bothering him or anything. Nothing bothered Vaughn. It was like he was pretending to be bothered, so he could line up next to Belinda. 'We're trying to concentrate.'

'*Sor-ry*'.'

It was all right for them. They weren't bored. They were *working*. Belinda was deputy chief of the Special Projects unit, and she was busy as hell. Just communicating with headquarters was a pain. Every message she sent had to be triply encrypted – an encryption of an encryption of an encryption – using three different algorithms, each of which ran to 128 bits.

Tommy didn't actually know what an algorithm was, nor why the number of bits was important. But 128 was a lot. He knew that much.

Anyway, Belinda was a control freak. Which meant that she had a finger in every pie, and had to keep track of it all, all the time. Except when she was sleeping or exercising, she was either talking on her cell phone or hunched over her laptop.

And Vaughn was just as wired as she was. He sat on the bed all day long, clacking away on his laptop. What was he doing? He didn't talk like a normal human being, so it wasn't always so easy to tell. But Tommy liked to ask him, just to hear him talk.

'Hey, Vaughn, what're you doing?'

'I'm working up projections on dispersal rates.'

And then, half an hour later: 'Hey, Vaughn . . .'

'Toxin pattern studies.'

'For what?'

'Wheat-stem rust.'

And five minutes after that, he'd look over his shoulder at the laptop: 'What's that?' he'd ask.

'Flare-droplet nuclei drift.'

Sometimes Belinda and Vaughn would jabber back and forth about things that made no sense at all. Susannah called it 'word soup' when the techies got talking. It didn't seem to bother her, but it made *him* feel left out. And being here all this time, cooped up, he was like a fish out of water. Missing his workshop. Missing Susannah. Missing everybody at the compound. Missing the out-of-doors. Whereas Belinda and Vaughn, they hardly noticed where they were at all. They could work in a closet.

Vaughn was a strange one, all right. So remote, it was almost like he wasn't a real person. Susannah once told him she'd put her hand on Vaughn's arm to see if he was cold to the touch.

Belinda got up and stretched, picked up the remote and punched the button for the Weather Channel. The weather guy was still running the numbers for the Midwest, but Belinda had already come to some kind of decision based on whatever she was getting off her computer. 'Numbers look good,' she said. 'We go at noon.'

'You're the boss,' Tommy replied.

He filled the time with push-ups, sit-ups, lunges, a whole yoga series. He did his affirmations. He did the self-examination ritual and found that he was chock-full of negative thoughts! Putting down Vaughn. Feeling superior. Pride in his aerosol gizmo. Whining about being bored. Sucking his thumb about sex. He did the blue-water meditation exercise, which almost always worked, but even though he was really focused, he couldn't help but hear Vaughn say: 'Oh man! Check it out!' Must be something practically earthshaking to get that out of him, Tommy thought, but then he caught himself. Blue water! Focus! On task! He let the blue water fill up his mind, the level rising slowly until there wasn't any space left, not even for a single thought. It was all blue. Just an ocean of no-think.

Tommy had grown up around boats, that's why he was on the team. He was at home in any kind of marina, comfortable with knots and lines, engines, docking and mooring. The others just followed his lead, and since he was at ease, and the two of them were decked out like tourists, nobody at the Belle Haven Marina paid them any mind. The boat had been leased for three weeks and towed up from Virginia Beach. Tommy himself had made the removable mounts for the water cannons two weeks ago. He and Vaughn had lugged the gear – concealed in coolers and canvas tote bags – on board. Belinda sat on deck, applying sunscreen. In nothing flat he had the *Sundancer* out of her slip and was picking his way through the congested area around the marina. A minute later they were out on the open river.

The sky was overcast, and there were only a few boats on the water, which was not surprising, since it was Tuesday. The operation was timed for midday, when people would be leaving their offices, walking to restaurants, and strolling or jogging on the Mall.

Jets rumbled overhead, heading into National Airport. In the middle of the river, with the airport on one side and East Potomac Park on the other, he cut the engines and let the *Sundancer* drift. Then he set up the portable mounts while Vaughn and Belinda pretended to fish. When everything was squared away, he restarted the engines and headed upriver, moving closer and closer to the District shore.

There were lots of people out, he could see that. There were joggers and bladers, bikers and golfers, tourists and mommies with their strollers. A little motorboat passed to starboard. Some kids in life vests waved. He waved back.

Belinda had done a gazillion calculations, but the truth was, the operation wasn't all that complicated. The main variables were humidity and wind direction, and the boat's proximity to shore. The force of the water cannon was fixed, and so was its arc – which was optimal for droplet dispersion. But the closer they got to shore, the deeper their penetration would be. And the deeper their penetration, the more people would be hit. The wind was the biggest variable, though, because it had to be steady, and it had to come from one of two directions: northeast or southwest. Anything else and they'd have to abort.

The boat was heading up the Potomac in a more or less northerly direction. This meant that if the wind was coming out of the northeast, they'd run as close to the Virginia shore as they could, and dump their load on the Pentagon. But if the wind was blowing from the southwest, as it was today, they'd run next to the District shoreline, shooting their payload into the air between the Washington Monument and the Lincoln Memorial.

If they got enough penetration, the mist would reach the White House, and the President would start wheezing, just like everyone else. Which was funny as hell except, if he had his druthers, he'd have the wind coming the other way, so they could gas the Pentagon. It was only a test, after all, and he liked the idea of fucking up the military.

Still, they had some good targets, even with a southwesterly wind. They'd begin spraying at the 14th Street Bridge, which would give them coverage from the Jefferson Memorial all the way up to the Kennedy Center – and everything in between. Like the Vietnam

Veterans Memorial, and the athletic fields behind the Tidal Basin.

It would be a helluva hit, if it weren't just a test.

When they reached the 14th Street Bridge, which was bumper-to-bumper with traffic, Tommy went aft to ready the aerosolizer. As Belinda piloted the boat, he showed Vaughn exactly what to do, then went below and switched everything on.

And it worked perfectly. You could barely see the plume, the mist was so fine. It arced into the sky and disappeared, trailing a rainbow. 'We got liftoff, man!'

Belinda laughed, and Vaughn said what he always said when he was excited: 'Oh boy.'

'Gimme five!'

Vaughn held up his hand next to his face, like he was swearing on the *Bible,* and when Tommy smacked it, the hand bent back, limp as a glove.

Talk about a killer nerd, Tommy thought, this guy did not have *a clue.*

16

Running on the Mall was Annie's idea.

Usually, he ran along the towpath, or else through Rock Creek Park, but the Mall's broad paths were a nice change – if a little crowded. And it was easy to talk because there weren't any hills to take your breath away.

He liked the way Annie ran. Walking, she seemed a little awkward, like a self-conscious schoolgirl dragged to the front of the class. But running was different. She moved in an easy, graceful way, her long legs gliding over the ground.

Reaching the Lincoln Memorial, they pounded up the steps, side by side, then turned at the top to catch their breath and look at the view they'd run through.

'It's like Seurat,' Annie said.

'The guy with the dots.'

'Afternoon –'

'On the Grande Jatte.'

People were everywhere: in cars, on bikes and Roller-blades. Jogging and picnicking. Strolling along the Potomac. Planes rumbled overhead on their way in and out of National Airport. Motorboats plied the river's broad expanse. And everywhere, there were monuments: Washington, Lincoln, Jefferson, and Einstein. The Vietnam Veterans Memorial. The Reflecting Pool. The Capitol.

Halfway back, they found themselves running

beside a makeshift playing field on which a hotly contested game of touch football was being played. As they ran, a badly shanked punt sent the ball out of bounds, where it took a couple of long and crazy bounces, rolling toward the street.

'Little help!' someone called.

Instinctively, Frank retrieved the ball, turned and threw a perfect spiral to the punter, a clothesline pass that covered forty yards in the air.

'Whooaa!' the man exclaimed as the ball thudded into his chest. 'You wanta play?' Frank shook his head, gave a little wave and continued jogging.

'We could play,' Annie said. 'If you want to.'

'Nah . . . I don't play football.'

'You coulda fooled me. That was like . . . the Redskins or something.'

He shrugged. 'I used to play,' he said.

'But you could really *throw* that thing.'

He picked up the pace a little, forcing her to catch up. She was trying to be nice, but . . . he didn't want to get into it. Football made him think of his father, and . . . *I wonder if he's still alive*. The thought was almost an idle one.

They ran in silence for a while, with Annie wondering at his mood. Finally, she changed the subject, whatever the subject was and however unspoken it had been: 'So!' she blurted. 'Is it over?'

'What?'

'The Kopervik story. You're at a dead end, right?'

'No!' he replied, offended. 'I'm not at a dead end.'

'But what can you do?'

'Lots of things,' he said.

'Like what?'

'Follow out the leads.'

'What leads?' she asked.

He glanced at her. *Good question.* 'I don't know. There are lots of leads.'

Annie laughed. Then she dodged a kid on a bicycle and, returning to his side, repeated the question. 'What leads?' she asked, looking up at him.

'What are you, Torquemada?' Frank asked.

'I'm just curious,' she said.

'Okay . . . the flag!' Frank suggested. 'The flag's a lead.'

'You mean on the helicopter?'

'Yeah.'

She thought about that as they ran, and then: 'How's that going to help?'

Frank rolled his eyes, a remarkably ineffective gesture for a man on the run. 'It's an American flag,' he said, 'so I figure it's probably an American ship. So maybe the bodies came to an American port.'

'Yeaaah?'

'Well, there'd have to be a record of it,' Frank said.

'Unless they smuggled them in.'

'Except, maybe it's not so easy to smuggle them in. I mean, not if you had to keep them cold.'

'And you would!' Annie exclaimed, her voice so clear and emphatic that a couple passing the other way stared at her. She blushed and lowered her voice. 'I mean you would if you wanted the virus. It wouldn't survive above freezing.'

'And once they got into the States –'

'They'd need a lab to work with the virus.'

'What kind of lab?' Frank asked.

He didn't get an answer right away. She was thinking, and as she thought, she slowed down. Frank adjusted his pace.

'If they had a Cold Room, like a big commercial freezer?' She was walking now, and so was he. 'They could take core samples from the bodies – starting with the lungs – and work with a little bit of tissue at a time. That way, they wouldn't need spacesuits. They could work with glove boxes.' She frowned.

'What?' he asked.

She shook her head and chuckled ruefully. 'God! I can't believe it!'

'What?'

'I'm actually *worrying* about them. I'm thinking – like – "I hope they realize that, even in the Cold Room, you have to be careful when you take samples. Some of the instruments can get hot, and if that happens, you could aerosolize the virus."' She shook her head. 'I'm sorry. I'm babbling. I'm thinking, "I hope they know what they're doing." But *do* I?'

'Tom Deer thinks it's a pharmaceutical company,' Frank said.

Annie looked skeptical.

When they reached the steps to the Capitol, they ran to the top, arriving completely out of breath – though Annie had enough strength left to raise her fists into the air, bouncing triumphantly from one leg to another, acting like Rocky.

In the car, on the way back to her place, she picked up the conversation where they'd left it.

'So!' she said. 'The flag. What do you do with it?'

'Well,' Frank replied, turning onto the parkway, 'the first thing I did was call the State Department. Told them I'm doing a story about Americans who die abroad. How do their bodies get back to the States?'

'But these were Norwegians,' Annie said.

'Yeah, but if they *said* they were Americans . . . I mean –'

'Okay. Then what?'

211

'Well, it turns out there are all kinds of regulations, rules about mortuary certificates, various kinds of containers, how they're sealed . . . God knows what else. Anyway, then I called Customs, which oversees human remains coming into the States.'

'And?'

'We danced around for a while, and then I just asked them.'

'Asked them *what*?'

'If anybody brought five bodies into the country, how could I find them?' A cop car hurtled past, going dangerously fast. 'Jesus! You see that guy?' Frank made the turn off Beach Drive and stopped at the light. The Saab stalled, and it took him half a dozen cranks and quite a bit of revving to get it going again.

'So what did they say?' Annie asked.

'Who?'

'Customs.'

'About what?'

She punched his arm lightly. '*The bodies*!'

'Oh yeah. They said I should call the port authorities.'

'Which port authorities?'

'All of 'em,' he replied.

'"All of them"?'

'Yeah. Until I find the bodies.'

'Wow.'

'They faxed me a list.'

'And you're just going to call them? Every one of them?'

'Yeah,' Frank said. 'I'll ask them if any bodies came through in the fall.'

'God! I couldn't do that. I hate calling people I don't know.'

Frank shrugged. 'It's what reporters do.'

'I know, but . . . talk about *tenacious*!'

He laughed. 'Oh yeah, I'm a regular bulldog.'

There were two messages on his voice mail, and they came from opposite ends of the too-real world.

The first voice was Fletcher Harrison Coe's. In his Long Island lock-jaw, he managed to turn Frank's name into a mutisyllabic term of quiet approbation: '*Fraa-ann-nnk. Fletcher Coe here. Reason I called: we're still looking for that* Sin Nombre *piece you promised. Promised for this round, or . . . so I thought. 'Course, understand you're busy, but I'm a little concerned about this rather startling run of expenses and . . . well, without some evidence* of product, *it puts everyone in a bit of an awkward position. A where's-the-beef sort of thing. Give us a jingle, won't you?*'

Christ, now he was going to have to bang out the New Mexico piece. He couldn't call Jennifer or Coe with a lot of excuses; he just had to do it. And he would. If he worked the rest of the night and got an early start tomorrow, maybe he could get it done by tomorrow afternoon.

He deleted the message and played the next one.

Uncle Sid lived on a different planet from Fletcher Harrison Coe, and followed different conversational rules. For one thing, he didn't identify himself. Nor did he have to. There was something about talking to an answering machine that made Sid want to deliver the message in a single breathless shout: '*Frankie? Is that you? Where are you? Now, listen! I know all about this shit with your father you got a legitimate beef I understand that but I thought you oughta know – he's a tough old cob, but this is his second coronary fachrissake and it don't look good Frankie it's the heart muscle you got major damage I don't know if*' *he's gonna make it. He finds out I called ya he'll knock the hell outta me but I thought you'd want to be there for him, y'know? It's been ten years fachrissake! You gonna carry a grudge into the next century? Anyway, they got him in intensive care, over to St. Mary's.'* There was a pause, papers rustling, a fist banged on a hard surface. *'Hell, I can't find the damn thing, Infermation'll give ya the number. St. Mary's!'* And then the phone beeped and he was gone.

Just what I need. Talk about timing . . . A wave of annoyance washed over him, and for a moment he indulged it. Then he felt ashamed. *Talk about self-involved. I'm as bad as the Old Man himself*

Getting a beer from the kitchen, he returned to the living room and sat down at his computer. Switching it on, he sipped his beer and waited for Windows to go through its routine.

He didn't think about his family much. In fact, he didn't think about them at all. They were a part of his childhood, and his childhood had been over for a long time.

A lone piano note, followed by a harp's flourish, told him that the computer was ready to work. Switching into his word processor, he called up his notes on the *Sin Nombre* bug.

What was it Sid had said? *I thought you'd want to be there for him!* Right, Frank thought. Like he was there for us.

Us being him and his mother, the former Sigrid Leverkuhn, one-time prom queen and high school sweetheart of the hardest-hitting linebacker Kerwick High had ever known. (Ta-daaa!)

Frank peered at his notes, looking for a quote from one of the Indians he'd met at the Taos pueblo.

What a mistake that marriage had been. Forged in a

kiln of adolescent glamour, the marriage had faded with the Old Man's glory years. After two 'seasons' at Penn State, and twice as many knee operations, Big Frank returned to Kerwick, looking and feeling like 'the man who lost the war.'

His bride came with him,

And then Frankie was born, and that was that. The future was past – or seemed to be – and all the Old Man's dreams were like so many vanities. He quit, Frank thought. He just got scared, and quit. Christ, he was only twenty.

And he was almost never around. When he wasn't at work at the generating plant, where he had a job as a steamfitter, he was drinking with the boys at Ryan's Bar & Grill – or chasing waitresses, one town over.

Which meant, among other things, that Frank was raised by his mother. They lived in a run-down, clapboard house in a working-class neighborhood. Each of the houses on the block was fronted by a room-sized patch of lawn (or, more often, a square of hardpan) – except the Dalys', and one or two others, which had gardens. This, in fact, was Sigrid's pride and joy, and as a boy, Frankie liked to help her with it.

Not that there was much time. Even when he was a little kid, Frank worked – shoveling snow, mowing lawns, running errands. And then, when he was old enough, he began working weekends at the Safeway, bagging groceries and stocking shelves from nine to nine. In the summers he worked a forty-hour week at the generating plant, feeding the boiler. Every Friday he brought his check home to his mother, and even the Old Man had to admit, *Frankie pretty much pays his own way*.

And so he did, though it must be said that he had a pretty good inheritance. From his mother, he'd acquired a love of reading and a near-photographic memory that, taken together, made him an outstanding student. His aunts liked to brag that he was Sigrid's 'mirror image,' but that was wishful thinking. She'd given him her sea-green eyes and high, raked cheekbones, but it was his smile that reminded people of her. This bashful lifting of the cheeks had a mischievous quality that sparkled in his eyes, drawing those who saw it into a conspiracy of mutual affection.

The rest of him was his father – all gristle and bone, with a shock of dark brown hair lying across his forehead. He was six-one and 160 pounds – a string bean with a right arm that the local papers compared to a shotgun.

The only freshman to make the Kerwick High School football team, he was the starting quarterback by the middle of his sophomore year. His stats were impressive, and they got better, game after game. Before long, the Old Man and his pals were showing up at home and away games, passing flasks back and forth, bellowing the school song. His father's pride was palpable – and never more so than when the kid threw a 'Hail Mary' that traveled sixty-five yards in the air, setting a Pennsylvania high school record even as it won the homecoming game. Everyone knew Frank was destined for a big-time college program – when, suddenly, he stopped playing.

Now, Frank leaned back in his chair and stared at the monitor. It was night, and he hadn't written a word. Car lights slid up the wall, fanned out across the ceiling, then raced down the opposite wall, disappearing into the carpet.

Quitting football, he thought, was really fucked up.

Not that he regretted it. After all, it broke the Old Man's heart – and that was the whole idea.

It happened at the end of his sophomore year, when his mother contracted a respiratory infection that turned into pneumonia. Returning home from school, Frank found her on the kitchen floor, where she'd collapsed. Only fifteen, he carried her out to the car, then searched for the keys and, finding them, raced through traffic to the emergency room – where the nurse sent him home to get the insurance information they needed.

And so it went. After returning to the hospital with the insurance numbers, he was sent back home yet again, this time to fetch his mother's toothbrush, nightgown, and robe. Returning with these, he telephoned Ryan's to see if his father was there, telling them that it was a life-or-death emergency – lest the bartender lie, as he often did.

I'm sorry, Frankie, I haven't seen him for days. But I'll put the word out. Tell your mother to hang in there.

He spent the night in an uncomfortable chair in the brightly lit lobby outside the emergency room. Overhead, a poorly tuned television crackled with bad jokes and frantic music. His mother was in intensive care, and the doctors looked worried. *She's a very sick woman, son. Is there any way we can reach your father?*

All the time, Frank was thinking she'd get better because nobody died of pneumonia anymore. Or did they? No. Of course not. Except for the ones who did.

He stayed with his mother for three days, holding her hand, waiting for his aunts to come. And when they arrived, it was almost worse. All they did was fume over his father's absence and scheme about what they'd do when Sigrid got better. Only . . . she didn't.

The Old Man wandered in during the middle of the

wake. *I was on business,* he mumbled, stinking of breath mints. Frank lunged at him, but Uncle Sid got in the way. *Don't ever raise your hand against your father,* he said.

That fall, Frank didn't go out for the team. He didn't make a big deal about it: he just didn't show up for practice. At the time, the local paper was hyping the football team as Kerwick's 'best ever,' and college coaches were calling twice a week. Frank told them, politely, that he wasn't playing football.

What's the matter, son? Are you hurt?

No. I'm fine.

Then . . . I don't get it.

I'm just not playing. I'm sort of. . . doing other things.

What 'other things'?

Reading. Working at the Safeway.

This is a joke, right?

No.

Then you're going to need counseling – the sooner the better. Get some help.

His high school coach came by – again and again – but eventually even he gave up. He had a team to put on the field, and by then Kerwick was 3-0. Somewhere along the line, it dawned on everyone that Kerwick High School didn't really need Frank. They had a terrific team even without him.

But that wasn't the point. The point, of course, was to break his father's heart, to punish him for quitting on his own life so many years before, and for abandoning his wife to the waiting room of their marriage.

Playing football had been the best part of the Old Man's life, the source of every hope and expectation. Watching his son play had been a reawakening.

218

Watching him walk away was a reinterment.

They never really talked about it, though Frank could see that his father was desperate to do so. The truth was, after his mother's death, they never really spoke at all – except to say, *You seen the snow shovel? You want the car? I'll be gone a couple of days.*

By his senior year he'd resolved to get out of Kerwick. Ironically, he was able to do this by winning a competitive scholarship open to children whose parents were members of the steamfitters Union.

The University of California at Berkeley was as far away as he could get without setting sail. He spent a halcyon four years there, pursuing a liberal arts degree that included lots of creative writing classes. It was there, too, that he fell in love with biology and considered, for a while, going to med school. But growing up the way he did, so close to the poverty line, he recoiled at the enormous debts that med school would have necessitated. Graduating in '89, he returned East to look for work.

And he found it in New York City, as the English copy editor on the *Alliance,* a Russian-English newspaper in Brighton Beach. Soon, he was publishing stories about 'Little Odessa' in the *Village Voice* and *Boston Globe Magazine.* By 1992 he'd won statewide journalism awards for feature writing and investigative reporting. The latter was a series about gasoline-bootlegging operations masterminded by émigré Russian hoodlums. And that was when he applied, successfully, for a job on the Washington *Post.* His work on the Metro desk, covering the police and the courts, earned him a promotion to the more exotic National Security beat. He'd done well there, too, and was beginning to develop a good network of sources when he was transferred to the National desk to cover the presidential election. This, too, was a promotion, but not a happy one. He didn't like political reporting. It was all about positioning and spin, gossip and leaks.

What drove him to the Johnson Foundation was the prospect of yet another promotion, this one to the White House, where his job would be to cover the First Family 'from a feature perspective.' Aghast at the idea, he applied for one of the Johnson grants, proposing to explore 'the brave new world' of emerging viruses.

It was an acceptable way to take a year off from the *Post* without 'losing ground.' Meanwhile, it would give him time to think about who he was and what he wanted to do – while writing about a subject that genuinely interested him.

In fact, as Frank watched the car lights slide across the ceiling, he was thinking about who he was right now. Was he the kind of guy who would, as his uncle Sid put it, 'carry a grudge into the next century'? Maybe. Probably. It sure looked like it.

But then, he figured, what the hell, maybe it's time. Lifting the telephone from its receiver, he dialed the information number in Kerwick and waited.

There was a tone, and then a woman's voice. 'The area code you have dialed has been changed. The new number . . .'

Christ, he thought, it *had* been a long time. They'd changed the area code on his childhood.

17

The next morning, he made coffee and read the *Post* at the kitchen table, feeling groggy.

He'd stayed up until three, working on the *Sin Nombre* piece, and it still wasn't done. Which was a problem. Today was the second Friday of the month, and that was deadline for the foundation's newsletter. So, too, if he didn't canvass the port authorities today, he'd have to wait until Monday.

For an instant it occurred to him that he might be able to buy a postponement by calling the foundation to say the piece would be late; his father was in the intensive care unit at St. Mary's and . . .

No. He wouldn't use his father's illness as an excuse to get around a deadline. He wasn't completely corrupt. Instead, he'd work on the *Sin Nombre* story until noon – make that, *until he finished it* – and then begin to call the ports. As for his father . . . he'd call later.

By two o'clock the story was on its way to Jennifer Hartwig, stuffed into the backpack of a spandex-clad bicycle courier who looked and acted like an outtake from *Road Warrior*. Accompanying the story was an abject plea for reimbursement of his expenses.

I never thought my fairy godmother would be a five-foot-ten-inch California girl, Frank thought.

Taste of Thai delivered an order of pad thai, which he ate straight from the carton while working his way through the list of port authorities.

It was tedious work, and probably a waste of time, But it was also the only lead he had. So he dove into it, and after half a dozen calls, he had his rap down pat.

How quickly he got an answer depended on the intelligence and cooperation of the person at the other end. Sometimes, he got an answer in a minute or two. Sometimes, it took him ten minutes just to get past the automated switchboards, drumming his fingers on the desk as he listened to their moronic catalog of unwanted alternatives.

Then, too, an amazing number of people were 'away from desks,' 'on another line,' 'at lunch,' or 'out'. Still, he'd reached nineteen ports by four P.M., and eleven of them could be ruled out. Either they hadn't received repatriated remains in the past year or they'd done so prior to September of '97. That left dozens of ports still to go.

He stood up and stretched. This could definitely suck up some serious time.

And then he got lucky.

The phone rang, and it was a woman named Phyllis or 'just-Phyllis-if-you-don't-mind,' who worked out of the Port of Boston. In a clipped New England accent she reported that the port had processed eight sets of remains in the past year – five of which had come all at the same time.

Frank sat in his chair, rattling his coffee cup. 'You're sure?' he asked.

'Oh, yes, de-ah! I'm not likely to make a mistake about that. It was so unusual.'

'How so?'

'Well, the number of people – that was one thing. And they came in by ship. Usually, they're brought home by air – but this was an accident at sea.'

'Do you have the name of the ship?'

'The *Crystal Dragon*. I thought at the time, what a pretty name!'

Frank started to thank her, but she cut him off.

'Just doing my job, deah. It's all public record. Now if you'll give me your fax number, I'll send you the particulars.

Five minutes later eight pages of documents rolled out of the machine. These gave the names of the dead, and included death certificates signed by the ship's doctor, one Peter Guidry, M.D. The cause of death in each case was drowning.

A signed and impressively stamped letter from a foreign service officer at the American embassy in Reykjavik, Iceland, made reference to an 'accident at sea,' and authorized the remains to clear Customs 'absent the usual consular mortuary certificate.' This same document indicated that on arrival in Boston, the remains should be consigned to a certified mortician in the employ of the J.S. Bell's Funeral Home in Saugus, Massachusetts.

Since the deaths had occurred at sea, it was the mortician's responsibility to inspect and certify the 'containment of remains' – after which they would be released into his care.

There was a document to the effect that this had occurred, signed by a mortician whose name Frank could not read, and checked off by a Customs official, who supplied only his initials. Frank knew from talking to the guy at the State Department that this was more or less the normal procedure. Maybe, he thought, J.S. Bell's had some kind of steady arrangement with the Port of Boston to receive repatriated bodies.

He looked at the list of names, which were arrayed in alphabetical order:

Leonard Bergman, 22
Arturo Garcia, 26
Thomas O'Reilly 39
Ross D. Stevens, 52
Christopher Yates, 27

None of them meant anything to him. But what did jump out at him was the fact that each of the dead men had the same hometown: Lake Placid, New York.

How could *that* be? And then he thought about it. Maybe they were volunteer firemen who'd won a trip, or salesmen for a mail order outlet, or . . .

I don't think so, he thought. Unless we're in the presence of an astounding coincidence, this is it. The satellite photos proved that the miners' bodies were exhumed from the Kopervik graveyard on September 9. The date on the death certificates in front of him was September 12, with the remains coming into Boston four days later.

He thought about what to do, and the answer was obvious: *Easy does it. Don't jump. You don't even know what the game is.*

He got the number for J.S. Bell's Funeral Home in Saugus and dialed it.

According to Annie, the miners' bodies would have gone through a lot of changes. After eighty years in the ground, there'd be some dessication. *You mean they'd look like mummies?*

No, she'd replied. *More like what happens to food in your freezer. After a while, a chicken breast changes texture because it's losing moisture. Ice cream changes, too, and so do cadavers. After a month or so, even ice cubes are only half their size.*

It was good copy. The sunken eyes, the prominent ribs, the lips drawn back in rictus. *It was zizzery-zoo.*

The bodies would have lost about half their weight – which wasn't something you could hide. A mortician would see it immediately.

A woman answered the phone on the third ring and, hearing that Frank was a reporter, told him they didn't have anything 'new for him.'

'I'm sorry?' Frank said, bewildered.

'You're on the obit desk, right?'

'No,' Frank replied. 'I'm not writing obits, I'm . . . I'm with the *Post*.'

'The **Washington** *Post*?'

'Yeah.'

'Oh. Oh! Usually, it's just the local paper, but – if you'll hold?'

In fact, it was nearly six minutes before a man's voice came on the line, and during that time, Frank put the call on speakerphone. Then: 'This is Malcolm Bell.'

Frank lunged for the receiver.

'Hello! Yes, it's Frank Daly, Washington *Post*.'

A pause. 'Well . . . How can I help you, Mr. Daly?'

'Frank,' he corrected, sounding a little weaselly to himself. 'I'm working on a story that's . . . well, it's pretty unusual in that it . . . well, it involves some deaths that occurred, uh – quite a while ago . . . and some people who drowned and . . . I guess the *remains* were . . . *handled* by . . . you.'

'Yes?'

Frank hesitated, trying to figure out how to put his question in a tasteful way. 'Well, as I said, these were drowning victims.'

'I see.'

'Right, and . . . as I said, there was an accident . . . at least, we think it was an accident . . . at sea. And this was on a ship called the *Crystal Dragon,* which is –'

'I know what the *Crystal Dragon* is, Mr. Daly.

225

What's your question?'

'Well, what I'd like to ask – and I know this sounds strange, but – did the *deceased* . . . Let me put it this way: was there anything unusual about the appearance of the bodies you handled?'

After a long pause, Bell replied in an apologetic tone. 'I'm sorry, Mr. Daly, but there are privacy concerns. Industry regulations and – well, as you can understand, we aren't in a position to discuss the *appearance* of the deceased – not with the press, in any case. There are sensitivities. . . .'

'I understand what you're saying, but –'

'If you could explain your *interest,* perhaps I could help. You said you're working on a story?'

'Right . . .' It was obvious to Frank that the tables had been turned. He wasn't going to get anything from Bell.

'But you said you're with the *Post* . . .'

'Yes, well –'

'I'm curious why the *Post* would be interested in something that happened – well, so long ago and far away. If you see what I mean?'

'I do.' Frank was beginning to get the uneasy feeling that *he* was the one being interviewed. 'But, uh . . . well, look, sorry I bothered you.'

'It's not a bother! I'm happy to help. If you'll give me your number –'

Frank tapped the Flash button on his phone. 'Can you hang on for a second?' he asked. 'Let me just see who this is. . . .' He pressed Hold and counted to ten. Finally, he returned to Bell. 'Listen, I'm going to have to take this. Why don't I get back to you tomorrow?'

'Yes, of course, but – it was 'Daly,' right?'

Somewhere in the middle of his chat with the

mortician, Frank had begun to feel uneasy. Very uneasy. And it was his own fault. He'd been impatient. He was always impatient! When he was on a story that interested him, and the leads were panning out, he had a tendency to just *wade* in – when what he ought to do, of course, was sit back and think it through. Make a game plan. Prioritize the calls. Otherwise, you wound up telling people more than they were telling you. And sometimes you were talking to the wrong people – and that was what he had just done.

Because, when you thought about it, if someone was going to bring five dead Norwegians into the States, pretending they'd been killed in an accident at sea, they'd want a mortician they could trust when the bodies came through Customs. And that, obviously, was Mr. Bell, whose curiosity was at least as great as Frank's own. *Yes, of course, but it was 'Daly,' right?*

Irritated with himself, he turned on his computer and logged onto Nexis – which, he knew, was what he should have done before calling the funeral home. If five Americans died at sea, it was a *news* story.

At the prompt, he keyed in his User ID and password, and clicked on the All News button. A new page flashed on the screen, and he filled in the Topic:

crystal dragon and drowning and five

It took about ten seconds before another page replaced the last, reporting that twenty-seven hits had been found. He scrolled through the list. The first story was a Boston *Globe* piece, dated September 16. The most recent one ran in the Albany *Times Union* on March 5. He called up the first story, which was headlined:

In the story, the captain of the *Crystal Dragon* said that the ship was making a transatlantic crossing, east to west, when one of the crewmen was swept overboard in high seas. Four others put to sea to rescue him, but their boat was quickly overturned. Though each of the men was equipped with a life vest, all of them drowned. The fact that the men were wearing vests, and that the ship was equipped with a helicopter, enabled them to recover the bodies.

The last paragraph reported that the *Crystal Dragon* was a 'missionary vessel' owned by the Temple of Light, a 'new religion' headquartered in Lake Placid. Led by a charismatic healer named Luc Solange, the Temple operated 'wellness centers' in Big Sur and Cabo San Lucas. Each of the crewmen was said to be a member of the church, and a collective service was planned.

Frank was intrigued, but Nexis was expensive, and he wasn't actually supposed to be using it. Not while he was at home, and not while he was on a leave of absence. With a practiced eye he scanned the stories as quickly as he could, and saved them to his hard disk. Then he signed off the service and printed them out.

As the printer did its work, he called St. Mary's. His father was still in critical condition, the nurse told him.

'May I speak to him?' Frank asked.

'No!' she barked, 'you can't speak with him. We have a very sick man. He's under sedation. He's intubated.'

'I see.'

'You said you're family?'

'His son. Could you tell him I called?'

'Tell him you *called*? That's the message?' Her tone spoke volumes about what she thought of his filial devotion. 'Just tell him his *son* called?'

'Yeah. Tell him I'm on the way.'

18

MADISON, WISCONSIN

Ah, Madison, Madison in the spring!

Under a brilliant blue sky, Andrew trudged up Bascom Hill, thrilled by the thaw after months of freezing cold. Although it wasn't quite warm enough for shorts, the hillside was littered with young women, prone and supine, their white legs pale against the bright green grass.

Like a lot of the students he knew, Andrew had a part-time job that helped to pay for his tuition and books. Students did anything and everything to earn money. He knew girls – serious students – who made extra money dancing at the topless place, and others who dressed up as clowns for little kids' birthday parties. He knew a guy who had a summer job driving the Wienermobile for Oscar Mayer. Now, that was cool.

Andrew's own job was a work-study assignment: as part of his financial-aid package, the university required him to work fifteen hours a week. Whenever possible, the school tried to match the work-study assignments to the student's own interests (assuming those interests could be ascertained, which in fact was not always the case). In general, though, Library Science majors worked in the stacks. Theater Arts majors sold tickets in the box office at the Student

Union. And Ag students worked in the university's legendary ice cream shop.

As an Engineering student, Andrew had been given a work-study assignment at the steam-generating plant, where he added chemicals to the boiler feed pump and made drawings to facilitate pipe runs or the replacement of old equipment on the plant floor. Like many large institutions, including hospitals and military bases, the university found that it was a lot more economical to heat with steam than electricity.

Andrew came down the hill, heading toward the West Campus where the Walnut Street generating plant was located. The sidewalks were packed with students, coming and going to classes, and his progress was slow. But it didn't matter: he had lots of time.

Still, he was nervous. Even if it was just a test, if he got caught putting anything other than Amertrol in the boiler feed pump, his boss would crucify him. And what if a lot of people got sick, really sick – could they trace it back to him?

He thought about it. No, he decided. No way. That was the beauty of it.

The other reason he was nervous was that he wanted to do a good job. Solange was counting on him. That's what the woman from Special Affairs had said, and he believed it. She'd shown up at his apartment two weeks ago, unannounced, holding a Walkman. 'There's something you need to hear,' she said, and handed him the earphones.

And then Solange's voice was deep in his head, saying, *Andrew . . . her name is Belinda, and I want you to do exactly what she tells you to do.* There was no question it was him. Andrew had listened to his voice a hundred times – on radio, TV, and motivational tapes. His voice was unmistakable, as unique as a hurricane. And hearing Solange address him by his own name, speaking directly to him as if they were friends, made his heart climb the walls of his chest. *We need your help in the secret war. Everything is at stake, and you're the only one who can do this thing. Don't fail me, Andrew. Don't fail me, old friend.*

Until that moment he'd had no idea that anyone at the compound – much less Solange – even knew that he existed. He'd sent checks, of course, and subscribed to all the necessary publications. He'd attended seminars, and healed his chakras at the wellness lodge in Big Sur. But he'd never visited the compound itself, or met anyone who was really high up in the Temple. Until now.

And yet, Belinda had known everything about him, including things about himself that he himself hadn't known – until she revealed them. *Solange says you were brothers in another life. Is it possible, Andrew? Have you sensed that?*

Of course he had.

He passed the football stadium, with the Bucky Badger billboard and the message:

WISCONSIN ATHLETICS:
SEE BUCKY RUN SEE BUCKY PASS   SEE BUCKY DRIBBLE
SEE BUCKY KICK SEE BUCKY SWIM SEE BUCKY PLAY!

See Bucky puke, he thought, going through the security gate and heading for the lockers. He hung up his backpack and jacket and took out a pair of red coveralls, pulling them on over his jeans and shirt. The coveralls were loose, with a large cargo pocket that held the thermos easily.

The thermos looked a lot like one of those fancy, brushed-chrome jobs that Starbucks sells. And if anybody asked, that's what he'd tell them it was.

The generating plant was kind of neat, though not many people knew how it worked or what it really did. Most people – even engineers – thought it was a closed system that was only used to produce heat in winter. But that wasn't true. The steam, which was super-heated to 750 degrees, was used throughout the year. Delivered by miles of pipes, it heated buildings in winter and helped to air-condition them in summer. It provided hot water year-round. And far from being a closed system, the excess steam it generated was vented into the open air through underground traps all over campus.

The vent traps were critical to the system's operation, because they prevented 'water hammer.' People with radiators in their homes were acquainted with the phenomenon. Essentially an imbalance of pressure caused by condensation, water hammer surged through the pipes, causing them to rattle and knock. To fix it in a house, you bled the pipes, removing the bubbles of air and equalizing the pressure. But what was only an annoyance in a home-heating system was a problem of a whole other magnitude when it occurred in an industrial system that used superheated steam. If left unchecked, water hammer could build up sufficient pressure to rupture the pipes, sending a geyser of steam into the air, where in an instant it would expand to 1,700 times its original volume. In other words, it would explode. And it would take your head off if you were anywhere near it.

The vent traps prevented this by continually and

automatically releasing steam in tiny amounts, so that uniform pressure was maintained in the pipes. Called 'flash steam,' it was vented into the storm sewers beneath the university, and then escaped to street level through manhole chimneys in the streets.

'Hey, Drew, how's it shakin'?' Steve Belinsky, one of the electrical engineers, rattled open his locker and began to remove his coveralls.

'Can't complain,' Andrew said. 'Nice day.'

'A beaut. I was thinkin' of goin' fishin' – over to Monona.'

'Hope they're biting.'

'I don't even care. Out on the lake . . . coupla brewskis . . . who needs the fish?'

'Meanwhile, you're leaving me here in the belly of the beast.'

'Sucks to be you,' Belinsky said, shutting his locker door with a clang. 'Catch you later, man.'

Andrew shut his locker door, twirled the dial on the combination lock, and stopped at the office to pick up the day's checklist. He headed first for the feed pump, where one of his jobs was to oversee the addition of Amertrol into the water supply. This was a demineralizing chelant that formed a resinous mass, overcoming the valent attraction of the pipes, and capturing impurities like calcium and silica. It prevented minerals from forming deposits inside the pipes, which would have impeded the flow of steam.

He'd add the contents of the thermos to the water supply at the same time he added the Amertrol. It would only take a few seconds, and there was very little chance that anyone would notice. There were only five workers in the entire plant.

Solange says you were brothers in another life. Is it possible, Andrew? Have you sensed that?

Of course he had. He could feel it even now.

19

Frank had been down with the flu all week, and so had Annie.

It was a woozy, snuffling, ache-in-the-back kind of thing that hung on and on and *on,* as if it would never go away. It had taken him out of commission for three straight days, and was only now beginning to get better. The *Post* said there was a lot of it going around: half a dozen schools were closed, K Street was almost empty, and Congress was having trouble getting a quorum.

All this, despite the fact that the flu season had been over for weeks. And it wasn't just in Washington. L.A. had its own outbreak. They called it the 'Beverly Hills flu,' because that area had been hardest hit. Frank had seen a story about it on the evening news. The reporter sat in the Polo Lounge, surrounded by empty tables. At the end of the piece he ordered a bowl of chicken noodle soup and winked at the camera. Cute, Frank thought, and blew his nose for the umpteenth time.

He shook his head to clear it and began to go through the take from Nexis. Mostly, it was the same story – an AP dispatch that ran in scores of newspapers, a concise version of the *Globe*'s piece.

He read it over and over, but there wasn't much to it. If anything, the piece was curiously bland. There were no 'I was there' interviews, and no quotes from fellow seamen describing the storm, the size of the waves, or the moment when the lifeboat overturned.

There was only the captain's account, a concise and seemingly straightforward one, of what had happened.

Even stranger, to Frank's way of thinking (which is to say, from a journalist's point of view), was the absence *of local* stories. The *Lake Placid Sentinel* – which might have been expected to put the story above the page one fold – did the opposite. It ran an abbreviated report on an inside page in a column dedicated to 'World News,' treating the incident more like a tidal wave in Bangladesh than what it was: a disaster at home.

The exception to this was a series of stories by a guy named Eric Overbeck, writing in the *Rhinebeck Times-Journal*. The stories reported the travails of Martha and Harry Bergman, parents of one of the sailors.

FAMILY BARRED FROM FUNERAL SERVICE
Parents Press Inquiry
Rhinebeck Couple Sues
Cult for Son's Remains

According to the articles, the Bergmans were outraged by what they felt was a perfunctory investigation of their son's death. 'Everyone seems to just take these people's word for it,' the father said. 'Except me. I'm not satisfied. I'm not at all satisfied! And I won't shut up about it.' The paper ran a photo of the couple's son, a handsome young man who had 'dropped out of SUNY New Paltz in his senior year to join the Temple of Light.' Finally, the story noted that the Bergmans had hired a private detective to investigate the matter. They had also engaged an attorney and were pressuring the Dutchess County district attorney to investigate the Lake Placid-based 'church.'

Obviously, the Bergmans were the ones he needed to talk to. Then he turned to the last story in the pile.

MYSTERY TORSO LINKED TO RHINEBECK WOMAN

ALBANY – A torso found in the Adirondack wilderness last week may be that of Rhinebeck resident Martha Bergman, who disappeared with her husband, Harold, nearly six months ago.

Police confirmed reports that the torso is that of a woman of approximately Mrs. Bergman's age and weight.

Dutchess County officials cautioned that while distinguishing marks on the body were consistent with those found on a dermatological 'mole map' obtained from the Bergmans' medical records, deterioration of the body made positive identification impossible.

'Without the head or the hands, it's very difficult to make a positive identification,' Dutchess County police spokeswoman Marilyn Savarese said. 'Obviously, we can't make dental or fingerprint comparisons. We are proceeding, however, with DNA testing, using materials recovered from the Bergmans' residence.' The results of the tests will not be known for several weeks.

Mrs. Bergman and her husband, Harold, mysteriously disappeared in November. Authorities say they are baffled by the case, particularly since the Bergman residence showed no signs of foul play.

The Bergmans are said to have been depressed by the recent death of their son, a votary of the Temple of Light.

A ruminative grunt rumbled in his throat.

It was at once the sound of realization and a warning to himself – a whispered mixture *of Eureka* and *uh-oh*.

Now that things were beginning to make sense, he regretted his bull-in-the-china-shop way of investigating things. He should have been more patient. The mortician's voice came back to him: *It was 'Daly,' right?*

Indeed, it was. And would you like my address? Or should I just shoot myself? You can cut off my head when I'm dead – whatever's convenient for you!

He made the sound again, a little louder, and a little longer. *Mmmnnnn.*

It was a curious sound when you listened to it: a sort of moo. But a worried moo.

He couldn't prove anything, really, but he thought he knew what had happened. For whatever reason, the Temple of Light had gone after the bodies at Kopervik, and faked an accident at sea. The miners' bodies were then put in body bags and tagged with the names of the drowned crewmen – who were still aboard the ship, in hiding, or . . . dead. Unless they'd never been aboard in the first place. Enter the mortician, Bell . . .

The ruse worked fine until the Bergmans began to press for an investigation. *Everyone seems to take these people's word for it. Except me!* Indeed. A certificate of death hadn't been enough for Harry Bergman. He'd wanted an autopsy.

And it seemed as if he'd found a sympathetic ear in the DA's office – when Bergman disappeared.

Frank searched through the printout for the *Times-Journal* stories.

What was the reporter's name? Overbeck. He was the only one who'd written more than a single article.

He called directory assistance in the 914 area code, and found an E. Overbeck just across the Hudson, in a town called Port Ewen. He dialed the number.

A little girl answered on the second ring. 'Hello?'

'Is Eric there?'

'One sec! Oh! May I say who's calling?'

'Frank Daly.'

There was a clunk as she put the receiver down, and he heard her walking away from the telephone, her voice receding. 'Daddy! *Daddy!* Telephone call!'

Frank could hear the end of the exchange between the two as they came back within range. 'I don't know,' the little girl said petulantly. 'Ask him your own self.'

'Hello?'

'Eric Overbeck?'

'Yes?' Tentative.

'This is Frank Daly. I'm a reporter with the *Post*?' (Well, sort of. It sounded so much more impressive than *I'm on leave from the* Post.)

'*Oh*, yeah, sure! How can I help you?'

Frank could hear it in the man's voice. He was impressed. Nice to know the paper still had éclat. 'Well, I don't know, really. I'm working on a piece that connects with some of your stories. I guess I was hoping to pick your brain.'

'You're talking about the power plant, right?' His voice was excited. Happy, even.

'Well, no,' Frank replied. 'No, I was actually calling about the Bergmans. You wrote a couple of stories –'

'Yeah.'

One hundred eighty degrees.

Overbeck's voice was no longer that of an eager reporter anxious to get his name in the *Post*. It was more like someone's who'd just received a subpoena to testify against Hezbollah. 'Look,' Overbeck said, 'I'd like to help you, but I'm pretty busy right now.'

'It'll only take a minute.'

'I'm sorry. I really don't have the time.'

'But –'

'Don't try to convince me,' Overbeck said. 'I just don't need the aggravation, okay? The paper I work for has a circulation of two thousand. We get sued by the Temple, and I'm out of a job. It's that simple.'

'Did the Temple threaten to sue you?'

'I'm not getting into this.'

'Did they threaten –'

'I gotta go,' Overbeck said.

And then he was gone.

Frank tried to call him back, but the line was busy. And it stayed busy in a way that made it clear the phone was off the hook.

He went into the kitchen and found a bottle of Negra Modelo in the refrigerator. Returning to the living room, he called Annie and filled her in on what he'd done and heard and imagined.

'So you think they killed her,' she said. It wasn't a question.

'Yeah,' he said. 'I'm pretty sure they did.' There was a long silence on the line. 'Why don't I come over?' he asked. The line remained quiet.

'Maybe not tonight,' she said. 'I'm still a little woozy. Maybe tomorrow.'

They stayed on the line together, not talking.

Finally, she asked, 'What next?'

He shrugged. Literally. Then he laughed at himself, because she couldn't see it. 'I've got a couple of calls in. The D.A. in Dutchess County. A P.I. in Poughkeepsie.'

'A what?'

'A private investigator. He worked for the Bergmans. His name's Kramer. Martin Kramer.' He paused. 'And the other thing is . . . my father's sick, so –'

'Oh, no!'

'I'm probably gonna have to see him.'

The next afternoon, he stood in the lobby of St. Mary's Hospital waiting to make eye contact with a human being. The security guard's mind seemed to be on Pluto; various orderlies and nurses rushed in and out without looking at him. The admissions clerk, who under the dreary fluorescent lighting looked as if she ought to be admitted herself, finally completed her lengthy telephone call and looked up at him.

'May I help you?'

'I'm counting on it,' he said, with a warmth that brought a smile to her face. He explained that his father was on the intensive care ward, and that he himself had just come in from out of town. 'I'd like to see him. See how he's doing.' She made a phone call and, with a smile, sent him up to the nurses' station.

The hospital corridors reminded him of his mother, and the memory intensified when the nurse directed him to a waiting room at the end of the hall. There were two other people in the room – a fiftyish blonde wearing bright pink sweatpants and a sweatshirt with spangles that spelled: *Atlantic $ity!*

The other person was a tired-looking man, dressed in greasy overalls. On his chest was an elliptical blue ring and, inside it, the man's name: RAYMOND. Their heads snapped up when Frank came through the door, and he saw the apprehension flash across their faces, then fade to relief. One look at him and they knew he wasn't delivering any kind of news, good or bad.

It was the same room he'd sat in when his mother was dying, fourteen years before.

And the feeling was the same. The air was dense with dread and hope, while canned laughter pulsed from the television set on the wall. Together, the three of them watched without seeing, lost within themselves.

Finally, a nurse came in.

'Here for Mr. Daly?'

For the first time, Frank realized that the woman in the pink pants was somehow connected to his father, because they both stood up at the same time, surprising each other. For a moment they regarded one another warily, then turned to the nurse.

'The doctor will be here in a moment,' she said, 'but I wanted you to know that the arrhythmia has been stabilized.' A little pat on the woman's arm, and a buck-up smile. 'He's doing good.' At this the woman grabbed Frank's hand and squeezed it so fiercely that it hurt.

'I'm Daphne,' she said, and then revealed that she was his father's *wife*.

'Well,' Frank said, nonplussed. 'I'm Frankie.'

'Oh.' She frowned, then recovered, touching his sleeve. 'Are you okay?'

He wondered if the frown had to do with the way he looked, or with his identity. There wasn't any way to tell, so he said, 'Yeah, I'm fine. I'm just getting over the flu.'

'It's going around,' she supposed.

There wasn't much to say, and both of them were relieved when the doctor came in to say that 'Francis' seemed to be getting better, but that he was nevertheless a very sick man. 'He hasn't taken care of himself,' the doctor said. 'But even so, he's strong as an ox. Maybe this will be a lesson to him. We can hope.'

He would only allow one of them in to see him at a time, and Frank deferred at once to Daphne. But she refused. 'It's been a long time for you,' she said. 'I think it's better that *you* go in.'

'No, that's okay –'

She turned her back on him and picked up a dog-eared copy *of People*. 'It's none of my business,' she said, 'but I think it's time you saw him.' Then she sat down, and he had no recourse but to go in.

And so he did.

The Old Man was lying on his back, with his face to the ceiling. There were tubes coming out of his nose, and a catheter lead trailing from under his nightgown. There was an IV in his left arm, and a thick stubble on his cheeks. His eyes were dark, and his breath came in wheezes.

Jeez, Frank thought.

He found a chair and pulled it up next to the bed. The minutes passed. Though his father's eyes were open, he couldn't be sure if the Old Man was actually conscious. There was no emotion on his face, and his eyes were like glass. Then his head lolled to the side and the Old Man's eyes locked with Frank's.

'Hi,' Frank said.

The Old Man blinked.

They sat together like this for what seemed like a long time. It was clear the Old Man couldn't speak, and just as clear that Frank himself didn't know what to say. Finally, he reached out and took his father's hand in his own. He was surprised at how rough it was, but he knew he shouldn't have been: after all these years in the boiler room, the Old Man's hands were like asbestos gloves. Holding the hand in both of his own, he gave it a gentle squeeze and heard himself speak for the two of them: 'I'm sorry,' he said. 'I'm just sorry there was so much . . . unhappiness.'

The Old Man blinked for the second time. Then his hand tightened in the grasp of his son and he pulled the young man closer. His head tilted in what was meant to be a shrug, and a *what can ya do?* smile lifted the corners of his mouth.

For a moment Frank could have sworn there were tears in the Old Man's eyes, but then it occurred to him it was the other way around. Like a mountain getting to its feet, his heart surged in his chest, and for a moment it felt as if he'd swallowed a razor blade.

The Old Man looked away, and soon it was all right again. They sat together for a long time, hand in hand, saying nothing, holding on. Frank's childhood flickered across the backs of his eyelids, and he saw his mother, and the boiler room, the schoolyard, the grocery, the garden, the football field – *Christ!*

And then the Old Man wheezed and *chuffed,* and then he was gone.

Daphne invited him to stay at the house – 'You can have your own bed, your dad would never let me touch it' – but Frank declined, saying he'd already paid for his room at the Red Roof Inn. Still, there was no avoiding the wake, which turned out to be a kind of open house for cheerful mourners. Arriving at what he still thought of as 'home,' Frank was saddened to find the garden gone to seed, the roses unpruned, last year's flowers left on their stalks. Stepping inside, he saw immediately that Daphne had worked her magic on the living room, where an almond-eyed waif gazed tearfully at the projection TV and leather BarcaLounger.

This inauspicious beginning soon gave way to something else, however, when his father's friends invited him to join them for a drink in the kitchen.

'Pull up a chair, Frankie!'

'I hope you aren't payin' for the casket, son! Didja ever see such a thing?'

'I'm tellin' ya, Frankie, I thought it was the QE-2!'

'Get young Frank a beer – he looks a little green around the gills!'

'Every bell and whistle,' someone said. 'A mahogany Lexus – your father would have loved it!'

'Sit down, Frankie – fachrissake, you're makin' me tired. Did you see him there? Lying in state like J. Edgar fuckin' Hoover –'

And Uncle Sid: 'I'm not sure it was him! He never looked so good!'

'The man's right! Since when did your father have rosy cheeks?'

'Never,' Frank said.

'Not to mention a shave!'

And so it went, with the women standing in the living room, talking respectfully among themselves, while the conversation ebbed and flowed in the kitchen. A yarn spun out, a burst of laughter, hands slapping the table. Another round of drinks. Another story, more laughter. The women looking in from time to time, appearing stern, or rolling their eyes, bemused.

He stayed till ten P.M., and by then he'd learned more about the Old Man than he'd ever known before. Listening to his father's friends, he began to understand, for the first time, how someone might have loved this deeply flawed man. And loving him, might even have forgiven him.

The next morning, he rode beside the bawling Daphne in the cortege to Holy Cross Cemetery. There, Father Morales said a few words. Frank threw a handful of dirt on the casket. And it was time to go home.

But you have to look through his things,' Daphne said. 'There might be something you'll want – I mean, you know, *to keep.*'

It seemed easier to ride back with her to the house than to argue with her, and so he did.

'It's in the bedroom,' she said. 'There isn't a lot. He wasn't much for collecting things.'

Frank went into the bedroom, where the Old Man's clothes had been gathered into a pile and laid neatly on the bed. There were a couple of tired sport jackets, half a dozen pairs of slacks on wire hangers, two boxes of dress shirts, fresh from the cleaners, and a dark blue overcoat. Uncomfortable with what he was doing, Frank tried on the overcoat, and was surprised to find that it was tight in the shoulders. He'd always thought of his father as a bigger man. But apparently not.

He put the overcoat back on the bed and went over to the dresser. Pulling open the drawers one by one, he found the usual things – T-shirts and underwear, socks and polo shirts, a couple of sweaters and sweatshirts. There was an old Timex on top of the dresser, lying next to a battered wallet.

Feeling like a burglar, he opened the wallet and looked inside. There was twelve dollars in cash, a driver's license, Visa and Exxon cards, insurance information, and an ATM card. His union card was there as well. And tucked away in the back, where Daphne would be unlikely to see it, was a black and white photo of Frank's mother.

He took the picture out and put it in his own wallet, then glanced around for the last time. There was nothing else.

'I've got to get back to work,' he said.

'Of course, but –'

'Let me know if there's anything . . . you know, just anything I can do.'

'But isn't there anything you want to take back?' she asked.

247

Frank shook his head. 'No, I don't think so. You should probably give it to Goodwill.' He was standing beside the door.

'Well, you'll have to take the books,' she said. 'It wouldn't be right to just throw them away.'

'What books?' he asked.

She left the room, and returned a moment later with three oversized scrapbooks – the kind that people use to keep photographs. Each of them was bound in fake burgundy leather with a double gold line embossed a quarter inch from the edge. She handed them to him and, curious, he opened the top one.

On the first page was his first byline, a long piece in the *Alliance* about Orthodox Jews proselytizing among the émigrés in Brighton Beach. Deeper in the scrapbook were the stories that he'd done for the *Village Voice,* and then the first byline he'd ever gotten at the *Post.* It sat atop a carefully scissored, yellowing rectangle of newsprint held in place by strips of transparent tape. To the right of the story was the date, written in blue ballpoint:

July 16, 1992

Frank was dumbfounded. Among the three books, there must have been hundreds of articles – indeed, every article he'd ever written. He looked at Daphne, who gave him a hapless shrug. 'How?' he asked.

'He just . . . *subscribed,'* she said. 'He always subscribed.'

He'd called Annie from Kerwick on the night of the wake, so she already knew about his father when he got back to Washington.

'You okay?' she asked.

248

'Yeah, I'm fine. It was good I went. How about you?'

'You mean, with the flu?'

'Yeah.'

'I think it's finally on its way out,' Annie said. 'Anyway, I'm back at work. What's up?'

'I was looking over some of the stories I found about these people who drowned, or who were supposed to have drowned, and it's interesting.'

'How so?' she asked.

'Well for one thing, all of the obits are the same. Like they were churned out by the same person, which I suspect they were. And the families – I finally got around to calling them.'

'And what did they say?'

'Well, the first one I called was O'Reilly's sister, Megan, who – it turns out – is a member of the Temple of Light. Just like her brother.'

'Huh!' Annie said.

'And then there's Mr. and Mrs. Garcia, the parents of Arturo. They're members, too.'

'Really!?'

'Yeah, except I didn't find this out until *after* I'd talked to them. The Dutchess County D.A., he's the one who told me they were beamed up.'

'What do you mean, "beamed up"?' Annie asked.

'*You* know,' Frank said. 'Like "mobbed up." Or "spooked up." Except it's a cult thing, so –'

'I get it.'

'Okay. So, anyway, the way these two reacted, it was really awkward. I mean, they were hostile. They didn't like the questions I was asking, and they had a lot of questions of their own. "No, they didn't think there was anything *strange* about the accident on the *Crystal Dragon*. And, *no,* they had no reason to believe Arturo or Thomas was alive! What did you say your name was? What's your telephone number? Who's your supervisor?" They said that my calling them was religious harassment. Do you *believe* that? I mean, is that the way *you'd* react if someone called you?'

'Of course not,' Annie replied. 'But what about the others?'

'Well, that's the flip side of the coin. I talked to Ross Stevens's daughter – and by the way, this guy was no kid, he was fifty-two years old – and Chris Yates's mother. I talked to her, too. And it was totally different.'

'How?'

'Well . . . they wouldn't talk to me. I mean, not at all.'

'Because it was . . . too painful?'

'No. Because they were scared to death.'

Annie was silent.

'And I know it's jumping to conclusions,' Frank went on, 'but – the parents who complained, the ones who pressed for an investigation – the Bergmans – well, they fell off the edge of the earth, didn't they? I mean, if the D.A.'s right, they disappeared completely until . . . well, until they found the –'

'Torso,' Annie said. 'The newspapers called it a "torso." '

The line was quiet for a while, and then Frank said, 'I'm thinking of going up there.'

'I really don't think –'

'I'm going.'

A long silence, and then: 'Frank?'

'What?'

'What *is* this Temple thing? Who *are* these people?'

He thought about it for a moment, listening to her

250

breathing at the other end of the line. 'I don't know,' he said. 'Maybe they're just folks. But I don't think so.'

20

He took the New Jersey Turnpike to Interstate 287 and into the New York Thruway, crossed the Hudson River to Poughkeepsie, and followed the main street into town, looking for a restaurant called Fernacci's. Finding it, he parked in the lot next door, turned off the ignition, and sat back. It was 6:35, and he was supposed to meet Martin Kramer at seven.

Rather than waiting in the restaurant, he opened the *Post* to the sports page and started to read.

Twenty minutes later a new black Jag pulled into the lot. It was an XJ-12 with a burled walnut dashboard and, Frank supposed, seats made with the skins of Chinese felons. A stocky man stepped out and gave him a quizzical look.

'You Daly?' he asked.

'Yeah,' Frank said.

'Marty Kramer. Nice ta meecha.'

They shook hands and walked into the restaurant, which was surprisingly nice, and air-conditioned to about sixty degrees. Lots of tile and wood, and *Turandot* playing softly in the eaves. The maitre d' showed them to a table in the corner, where they sat down.

'Nice ride,' Frank said with a glance toward the parking lot.

Kramer shrugged. 'It gets me where I'm goin'.'

He was a short, pigeon-chested man with a beaklike

nose, crooked teeth, and glittering black eyes. His dark hair was short and spiky, and glistened with goop. 'Hey, Mario!' he called out. 'What do you have to do to get a drink around here?'

With a smile, a waiter sauntered over with the wine list and told them about the specials. Then he took their order for drinks and went back the way he'd come.

In the course of the next hour, they worked their way through a couple of drinks (Knicks versus Wizards); two orders of carpaccio (Clinton versus Starr); what must have been a loaf of bread dribbled with olive oil (10K training regimens); and their entrées: osso buco for Kramer, and tortellini for Frank.

Kramer proved himself an engaging raconteur and a good listener, but a reluctant source. After fifty-five minutes of schmoozing, Frank had learned next to nothing about Kramer's work for the Bergmans – and he remarked upon it.

'Y'know,' he said, 'you haven't told me anything.'

Kramer smiled. 'What do you want to know?'

'Well,' Frank said, pouring each of them a glass of Montepulciano, 'to begin with, were the Bergmans murdered? What do you think?'

Kramer screwed up his face, seesawed his head back and forth and winced. 'Look,' he said, 'I got a problem here. My name gets into print – I lose clients. It's as simple as that. And, hey. Why not? You look at the card I gave you? What does it say?'

'It says you're a private investigator.'

'Exactly. A *private* investigator.'

'Trust me, we're off the record.'

Kramer scoffed. '"Trust me . . ."'

Frank smiled.

'I'm serious.'

Kramer cocked an eye at him. 'You sure?'

By way of an answer, Frank folded his hands in front of him. 'Absolutely.'

Kramer sighed, seemingly worn out by Frank's insistence. 'Okay,' he said, putting his napkin aside. 'I'll give it a shot. What do you want to know?'

'Whatever you can tell me about the Bergmans,' Frank replied.

The P.I. sat back in his seat, thinking about it. Finally, he said, 'Coupla squirrels.'

Frank laughed, then let the smile fade. 'What do you mean?'

'I mean: what happened, really? Their kid ran away and joined the circus. *Wah wah wah!* Gimme a break.'

'Yeah, but . . . his parents hired you after he was dead, right? So it wasn't like it was a missing person thing.'

Kramer twisted his lips into a knot of fleshy skepticism. 'That's not exactly right,' he said. 'They came to me about six months after the kid joined the Temple. This was two years ago.'

'What did they want you to do?' Frank asked.

'Kidnap him. That's not what they called it, but that's what they meant. They had a 'deprogrammer' standing by.'

'And what happened?' Frank asked.

Kramer shrugged. 'I looked around. Asked some questions. Near as I could tell, the kid was fine. Happy. So I backed off. Told them it couldn't be done.'

'And after he drowned? They hired you again?'

Kramer looked uncomfortable for a moment, then leaned forward: 'What I don't understand is, what's your interest? I mean, this isn't exactly a national story, and it isn't in the *Post*'s circulation area – so I don't get it. What are you looking for?'

'The truth.'

Kramer sneered. 'Then I think you should try Krishnamurti.'

'That's funny,' Frank said.

'I'm serious. Are you a police reporter, or what?'

'No,' Frank said.

'Then, what?'

'I'm working a medical story. But it's complicated. And I guess, to answer your question, what I'm trying to find out is whether or not the people on the ship –'

'The *Crystal Dragon*?'

'Yeah' Frank said. 'I'm trying to find out whether or not they actually drowned. Because in my opinion, maybe they didn't. Maybe they faked it. And if I'm wrong, and they *did* drown, maybe it was murder.'

Kramer stared at him for a long time, took a sip of Montepulciano, then said, 'Where were we?'

Frank thought about it for a moment. 'You were telling me how you worked for the Kramers twice. Once when their son joined the cult –'

'And after he drowned,' the detective said. 'That was pro bono.' Frank's eyebrows must have lifted, because Kramer hurried on with his explanation. 'I felt sorry for them. And, I guess I was feeling a little guilty. I don't know . . . maybe I shoulda gone after the kid in the first place.' He looked regretful. 'Anyway,' he went on, 'it wasn't a lot of work. I talked to some of the people on the ship –'

'And what were *they* like?'

'Cooperative. Didn't act like they had anything to hide.'

Once again Frank must have looked skeptical, because Kramer leaned toward him and said, 'Look, here's the deal. The Bergmans were crazy when it came to the Temple. You couldn't talk to them about it. The way they saw it, they had "religious beliefs," but *the kid* was "brainwashed," the kid was in a "cult." So what does that tell you?'

'I don't know,' Frank said.

'They were *bigots*,' Kramer went on. 'And *paranoid*. My God, it was like they were lookin' under the rugs for land mines. All the phones were tapped. There were people watchin' the house . . . Christ almighty, they went out and bought a gun! Kept it in the vestibule, in case someone broke in on 'em.' Kramer laughed.

'What kind of gun?' Frank asked.

He shrugged again. 'I don't know. I think it was a .38.'

Frank frowned. 'So –'

'Look: what it came down to? They wanted someone to blame. They *needed* someone to blame. Otherwise, they gotta blame themselves – y'know what I mean?'

'So you don't think the Temple was at fault?'

Kramer shrugged. 'I don't know, maybe they could have made a case. There might have been some liability with the ship – not enough lifeboat practice, something like that. But that's not the point. What I'm trying to say is, in this business, you meet a lot of people chasing rainbows. Half of them? I could say – put your wallet back in your pocket, I know right now I am *not* going to be able to give you what you want. I mean – look at the MIA people. You ask them: no one's missing. There's no such a thing as *missing*. There's just a bunch of "secret prisoners." Same thing with the TWA crash. Was it an *accident*? Fuck, no. It was a missile, a bomb, a maintenance error – *something*. Because when you're dealing with families, there's no such thing as an *accident*. The loss has to be for a reason, there has to be someone to blame. You've gotta get *payback* – money, revenge, whatever. Otherwise, there's no meaning to it. It's random. And that's when the *quest* takes over. The investigation stops being about what happened, and becomes something else. And, like it or not, that's where I make a lot of my money.'

'And you think this is what happened with the Bergmans?'

'I *know* it.'

'And the body they found?'

'You mean, in the Adirondacks?'

Frank nodded.

Kramer shrugged. 'They don't know it's her.'

Frank agreed. 'But . . . if it is?'

Kramer frowned, and thought about it. 'I don't know, maybe you're right. Maybe the Temple chopped them up. I don't see any *evidence* of it, but –'

'If it wasn't the Temple . . .'

'Let's put it this way: I think the D.A. should be lookin' for *Mister* Bergman.'

The suggestion took him aback. 'You mean –'

The detective leaned forward and lowered his voice. 'The Bergmans were having some pretty serious problems.'

'What kind of problems?' Frank asked.

'Problems that didn't have anything to do with Junior,' the detective replied. Frank started to say something, but Kramer shook him off. 'I don't want to get into it,' he said, 'but – what *I* hear? Bergman moved a lotta money to the Cayman Islands, right before he and his wife turned up missing.'

'I had no idea,' Frank said.

Kramer shrugged. 'You talked to Tuttle yet?'

'You mean the guy in the D.A.'s office? Up in Placid?'

257

'Yeah.'

'Well . . . just by phone,' Frank said.

'I guess you could ask him about it, but I don't think he'll tell ya anything. It's a big lead they're working.'

Frank sipped his wine and thought about what Kramer was saying. Then he tried another tack. 'What about the exhumation? Did they ever get –'

The detective shook his head. 'No, it got all hung up in the courts. The county was ready to exhume, but the Temple won it on appeal. I mean, they had the kid's documents. Signed and sealed. Notarized. There was a will. *His* signature, no question. He wanted to be buried up there, and he didn't want his remains 'violated.' Said so, right in the will. The next thing you know, Mom and Pop pull a vanishing act, and – boom – the issue's *moot.*'

The waiter arrived with the check, and Frank gave him his Visa card, wondering if it was still any good. 'Listen,' he said, 'you think you could get me the names of the people you talked to on the ship?'

'The *Crystal Dragon.*'

'Yeah, I was thinking, maybe I could talk to them.'

Kramer pursed his lips. 'I guess I could,' he said. 'Gimme your fax number and I'll send you the memos I wrote.'

Frank told him the number and asked, 'So what's it like up there? In Placid.'

Kramer shook his head. 'I don't know. It's . . . well-kept. Pretty well-organized. They've obviously got some dough. Leader's a toon, but – hey, it works for them.'

They parted company in the parking lot, with Kramer thanking Frank for the meal and promising to get in touch if anything came across his 'radar screen.' Then he got into the Jag, which started with a roar, and with a little wave over his shoulder, glided out of the parking lot and into traffic.

Frank watched him leave, then got in the Saab, thinking about the conversation they'd just had. Maybe Kramer was telling the truth, but it seemed to Frank that the P.I. had an agenda, and the agenda was to dismiss the story. Why would he want to do that? Frank wondered. Most P.I.'s were publicity hounds. The more their names got in the paper, the more clients they had.

As he pulled out of the lot and headed north, he regretted what he'd said about the investigation and, in particular, his suspicions about the men who'd drowned. And he regretted it even more when, only a few blocks from the restaurant, he passed a 7-Eleven. Kramer's Jag was sitting in the lot, and the detective was talking animatedly on the pay phone outside.

Frank slowed, making sure it was him, and then drove on. Hope that's not about me, he thought.

21

DAYTONA BEACH, FLORIDA

Like most of his Pine Creek neighbors, Gene Oberdorfer was retired. He'd moved to Florida from Lake Placid some four months earlier, swearing he would never spend another winter in the frozen north.

Built around a golf course, with a gatehouse at each of its two entrances, Pine Creek was like a lot of subdivisions in Florida. But it was actually very special, and what made it so became apparent to anyone riding a golf cart between the seventh and eighth holes. Adjacent to the striped asphalt that marked a crossing over what seemed to be a small road, a wooden sign read:

YIELD TO AIRCRAFT

In Florida, as everywhere else, developers prefer raw land because it spares the expenses of demolition. Accordingly, they'd ignored the Pine Creek messet for years, regarding the World War II airstrip at its center as a liability. With plenty of undeveloped land available, they saw the complex of runways as an extra expense – something that would have to be busted up. Which meant a lot of labor and heavy equipment.

But where others saw a lemon, Pine Creek's

eventual developer saw an opportunity. Dubbing his creation the Pine Creek Fly-In, he created a haven for owners of small aircraft – people like John Travolta and Gene Oberdorfer. The central hangar at the tiny airport and the tie-downs on the adjacent tarmac were nothing special – much, in fact, like the facilities at the little airport where Oberdorfer used to keep his Cessna.

What made Pine Creek unique were networks of taxiways in front of the houses, and the hangars that looked like oversized garages. Owners like Oberdorfer could jump into their planes as easily as some people get into their cars. In a minute or two they could be out of the driveway and onto the taxiway. Five minutes later they could be airborne.

So it was perfect for Oberdorfer, whose mission required both a small plane and a private hangar.

As usual, he got up at five-thirty, did his morning exercises and meditation, then walked to the clubhouse to tee off at seven with his new friends. Most days, he enjoyed golf, though the truth was, he wasn't very good at it. And today he was distracted. None of the forecasts predicted rain, but clouds were piling up on the horizon, and it worried him.

On the other hand, he thought, sending a spray of dirt and grass into the air, if the rain *did* hold off, the meteorological conditions would be just about perfect. Temps in the eighties, high humidity, light winds out of the east. Not that it mattered, really. He could go today, or he could go tomorrow. Which day he went was up to him, so long as the conditions were right. Still, it was distracting. And the distraction hurt his game. Especially his short game. His drives had gone to pot, and as for his putting – forget it.

'Dammit,' he said as his ball sliced into the rough off

the fourteenth tee. 'You guys mind if I take a mulligan?'

The question drew hoots. 'One mulligan isn't going to help you today, Obie,' a man named Johnson joked. 'You need a mulligan stew.'

By noon they were in the clubhouse eating lunch – his treat because of his lousy run on the back nine. By two he was home. The weather was holding. Barometer steady. Wind unchanged. An hour later he was in the hangar, checking over his gear for about the tenth time.

The fact that he had a private hangar made rigging up the plane a snap. Most crop-dusting equipment is simple enough, consisting of lengths of tubing attached to the following edges of the wings. Twenty spray nozzles had been fitted to the tubing, and it worked quite well. Indeed, he'd been able to buy everything he needed at Home Depot.

The canister itself was kind of large, but fit into the passenger seat behind him. It was a Swiss-made device that was apparently used for fogging against some kind of insect in the Bernese Oberland. Headquarters had come up with it, and they'd done good. Its dispersion rate was preset, and there was a built-in air compressor. All he had to do was charge it up, fill the thing with water, and introduce the material. Airborne, one flick of the switch, and a fine aerial spray would fan out behind the plane.

He waited until four-thirty. Like most small airports, Pine Creek had no instruments to control takeoffs and landings. For local trips, there was no need to file a flight plan. Some of the guys – especially the ones with vintage planes – liked to go up and do dipsy-doodles and barrel rolls. But there wasn't anyone else up now, not that he could see. And there was no wait for the runway. (It was only on the weekends, really, that you ever had to line up for takeoff.)

He loaded the canister into the passenger seat and tossed his jacket on top of it. He went through his checklist, stood back and admired his handiwork. Really, the nozzles and tubing were barely visible, even at this distance.

Outside, the wind sock was slack, although every now and then a breath of air lifted it up. Up top, he didn't see another plane in the sky except for a commuter heading south.

From the sky it was clear that this part of Florida was now almost fully developed. Off toward Orlando, a few farms hung on, their green patches bright with new grass. Apart from those, and some golf courses, and a narrow greenway along the creek, subdivisions and shopping centers stretched in every direction for as far as the eye could see. Which was good. They needed pretty good population density for the test.

The oceanfront was only four miles from Pine Creek, and within a matter of minutes he was flying over the north-south condos and hotels that crowded the shore. His plan was to execute 'a line-source laydown' – the technical term for spraying a small amount of material in a continuous line, relying on a favorable wind to carry the inoculant inland.

Not that there was any danger of missing the target.

Directly below, cars crawled along the blond beach, outnumbering the swimmers. The town had curtailed the hours a bit, but it hadn't outlawed the practice – which stuck in his craw. Half the planet was paved, and these idiots had to drive on the beach!

It made him angry.

Dropping lower, he reached behind him and flicked

the toggle switch on the air compressor. *Incoming!* he thought, as the plane cruised above the beach, the compressor thundering away, a fine mist spewing from the edges of the wings.

22

Cal Tuttle sat across the desk from Frank, with the flags of his office behind him. A doughy-faced man in his late forties, District Attorney Tuttle was not much of a talker.

Frank asked him how the torso had been found.

'Campers' dog.'

Was he surprised?

Tuttle cocked his head and looked at him. 'To find a decapitated woman with her hands cut off, layin' in the woods?' He thought about it for a moment and shrugged. 'Not really.'

When the body turned up, did he connect it to the Bergmans?

' No.'

Why not?

'Nothin' to connect it *with.*' He made a little snapping sound with his tongue and gums. 'DNA tests take a while. Then we'll know.'

Could you tell me the names of the campers?

'No I don't think they'd like that. Dog's name was Taz.'

'Thanks. But you're in touch with Dutchess County on the case, right?'

'If you say so.'

'Well, it would be newsworthy if you weren't,' Frank replied, becoming irritated.

Tuttle smiled, pleased to get his goat.

'I'm told Harry Bergman is a suspect in his wife's death,' Frank said, watching Tuttle's reaction. 'Is that true?'

A regretful smile. 'Well,' Tuttle replied, 'it's a novel idea.'

'Is it?'

'Yeah,' the D.A. said. 'I hadn't heard that one.'

Frank frowned. Unless Tuttle was a very good actor, he was telling the truth. 'Well, maybe my source was misinformed.'

'I think he may have been.'

Frank decided to switch tacks. 'What about the Temple?'

'What about it?'

'I don't know. What are they like?'

Tuttle shrugged. 'They stick to themselves. We don't see 'em that much.'

Frank sighed. He'd been trying to have a conversation with this man for almost half an hour, and the effort had worn him down. So he put his pen away and asked if Tuttle could direct him to the Temple's headquarters.

Tuttle sketched a map on a piece of paper and pushed it across the desk. 'Probably won't let you in,' he said, shaking Frank's hand.

'Why not?'

Tuttle shrugged. 'Standoffish.'

And, in fact, they wouldn't let him in – except to the Visitors Center.

This was a dog-and-pony show housed outside the compound in a white clapboard saltbox. A couple of hundred yards farther along the road, Frank could see a set of wrought-iron gates and a small stone guardhouse. The gates appeared closed, so he stopped at the Visitors Center, lifted the pineapple door knocker and let it fall. Once. Twice. Again.

A cheerful young woman appeared and welcomed him inside. He showed her his press pass and told her, 'I was hoping to see the compound, but the gate's closed.'

The woman apologized, explaining that the gate was always closed: no one was allowed inside the compound without an appointment.

'So, who do I call for an appointment?' Frank asked.

'I'm afraid you'll have to write ahead,' she answered.

'You mean, there's no one I can call?'

'Not really.'

'What about him?' Frank asked, nodding toward a photograph on the wall. The picture was of a man in his thirties, standing on a mountaintop, laughing at the camera. Behind, and below him, was the world.

'That's Solange,' she said with a smile. 'I don't think he's available. But since you're with the press, you could call the Public Affairs office – only I don't think they're here today. I think they're at a demonstration in Buffalo.'

'But –'

'We have a Web site – you could e-mail them, if you want. Just go to the site, then click on Public Affairs!' She handed him a brochure printed on stiff, gray stock. 'It's all on here,' she said, 'the snail-mail address and the e-mail one.'

He thanked her for it,

'And if you want to look around, the center has three sections: Inspiration, Information, and the Shoppe. But you'll have to hurry,' she said apologetically, 'we close in half an hour.'

Frank agreed to hurry.

The first thing that hit him when he entered the 'Inspiration' room was the smell of incense and burning candles. Then he saw the striking black and white photograph that occupied the entire back wall.

It was a man's figure – in fact, Solange's – walking on a beach, just where the surf met the sand, his pant legs rolled up, a dog beside him, the sky radiant and golden. Gulls wheeled overhead, and a calligraphic banner read, FOLLOW ME. WALK IN THE LIGHT.

As Frank approached the image, he noticed the music for the first time. A boy's choir, singing a haunting melody in a language he couldn't identify. Romanian. Bulgarian. Something like that. The pure voices washed over him, rippling the air. Helluva sound system, Frank thought.

Displayed along the walls of the room, which were covered in a soft gray fabric, was a series of smaller photographs, each about the size of a large poster. Like the larger picture, they were beautifully framed and artfully lighted. Frank looked at the images, and saw that each of them was different: a spiderweb spangled with dewdrops. A pine forest laced with shafts of sunlight. Children walking hand in hand toward the sunset.

What each of the pictures had in common, he realized, was *light* – brilliantly captured light. Frank moved from one to the next, walking through the waterfall of music. He felt . . . *good*. He actually felt kind of uplifted.

A few of the photographs – those with Solange in them – had an audio feature. Frank picked up a set of earphones and pressed a button.

He was looking at a picture of Solange, standing in a wheat field. With the sun at his back, it seemed, almost, as if he had a halo. And the wheat, too, was sunstruck, the sparking off its tips making stars of light. When he pushed the button, the wheat seemed to move, to bend and sway, as if in the wind. Leaning closer, he could see that the image itself was steady but that behind it, some device made the light coruscate and shimmer. The effect was heightened by a background track of wind soughing through a field. And then a voice spoke, riding on the wind.

'And the Lord said, let the earth bring forth grass, the herb yielding seed, and the fruit tree yielding fruit after his kind, whose seed is in itself upon the earth: and it was so. And the earth brought forth grass, and herb yielding seed after his kind, and tree yielding fruit, whose seed was in itself, after his kind: and God saw that it was good. And the evening and the morning were the third day.'

Frank passed a few more images and picked up the next set of headphones, standing now in front of a campfire scene, with Solange beside the fire and a sky strewn with stars. This time the audio track was the crackling fire – and like the wheat in the previous photograph, the fire seemed to sparkle and move. So, too, did the stars, which became even brighter as the voice-over rang in his ears:

'And God made two great lights, the greater light to rule the day and the lesser light to rule the night . . .'

Ah, Frank thought. Genesis. He made a brief circuit of the room, confirming this, and saw that the various images were meant to recapitulate the Creation story. Pretty slick, he thought.

He ducked into the 'Shoppe.' It seemed to sell vitamins, supplements, soaps, aromatherapy oils, candles, that kind of thing. One entire wall was devoted to inspirational books and tapes. Classical music played – Pachebel's Canon, he thought. The brunette who'd met him at the front door stood behind the counter, wrapping up the purchases of a middle-aged woman with braided hair. 'Do you want to buy anything?' she called out. 'We have to close, you know, in about' – she glanced at her watch – 'gee! Two minutes.'

He demurred and hurried into the Information room. He didn't have time to do much more than take a quick, visual inventory. He saw a lot of graphs and charts and maps, more audio displays, with multiple sets of earphones tethered to a wooden counter. One display showed a map of the U.S. with tiny lights glowing in various sectors. On a central table, under a large banner that read WARMING, sat a fat globe with a thermometer stuck into it. Suspended from the ceiling was a 'population clock' shaped like a bomb. It ticked noisily away, its digital numbers whirling faster than the eye could see. On one wall the rain forest burned in Brazil. On the opposite wall a forest of pines appeared to have been mown to within an inch of the ground.

'We're closed now,' the brunette said in her sweet, friendly voice. 'But you could come back tomorrow. We open at nine.'

She gave him a small plastic bag with 'some free samples. Try the mango-lavender shower gel,' she said as she walked him to the door. 'It's fabulous.' He grabbed a couple of brochures on the way out.

He'd hoped to drive straight back to Washington, but by nine o'clock, on the Jersey Turnpike, he found himself nodding off. A semi's horn jolted him awake, and he decided to look for a motel.

He found one a few miles south of Cherry Hill. It was a Norman Bates kind of place with a bar off the lobby. The bar was reached through a thatched-hut entrance, flanked by signs trumpeting:

VINNIE & THE GEE-GNOMES!
ONLY AT THE LEAKY TIKI!

His room was an off-rust color: orange walls, drapes, bedspread, carpeting. Next to the bed someone had put his fist through the drywall. It was the kind of place where you hook a chair under the doorknob. He did that, and took a shower.

The mango shower gel was terrific.

Revived, he pulled out his laptop and wrote a couple of short memos to himself about his interviews with Kramer and Tuttle, and his half hour at the Visitors Center. Reading over what he'd written, he realized what a bust the trip had been.

If you believed Kramer, he was on a wild-goose chase. And why *not* believe Kramer? Kramer was closer to the story than anyone. He knew the Bergmans, knew the problems they had with their son – and he'd actually interviewed people on the ship. And according to him, there was nothing to any of it. His clients were as flaky as the people in the Temple – maybe more so.

On the other hand . . . Tuttle seemed genuinely surprised when asked about Harry Bergman and whether he was a suspect in his wife's death. What had he said? *That's a novel idea*, his voice heavy with sarcasm. And yet, if you believed Kramer, this was a big lead.

The operative words being, *if you believed Kramer*. Did he? Frank thought about it. Why would he lie? he wondered. And the answer suggested itself: nice car.

None of which meant anything, really. He was back

where he started – stuck in a cheap motel with a lot of expenses and no real story. He might as well be in the Chernomorskaya.

Hunching over the computer, he typed the words: *Temple of Light – Visitors Center*. Then he pulled out the brochure and typed in the Temple's specifics: address, fax, phone, Web site, e-mail. Anything else worth recording? Not really. Except that they obviously had a lot of money. A 'flagship.' And a helicopter. And a 'compound.'

Where did the money come from? he wondered. The shower gel was great, but how much dough could you make from that? It wasn't like they were selling the stuff at Wal-Mart.

Wondering what their Web site was like, he hooked up the laptop to the telephone and jacked into the Matrix (or at least AOL), thinking, Frank Daly, Cyber Sleuth.

It took about thirty seconds for the Web page to fill in, an image of the Earth – as shot from space. But instead of the random scarves of cloud that swirled over the familiar 'blue marble,' the artist had pulled the clouds together into a ghostly stylized image: a prancing white horse with a wild eye. *Temple of Light* pulsed on and off, changing colors. Below the banner were an array of smaller boxes, each of which contained an image. He clicked on the first one: Solange and the dog on the beach. It was the same one he'd seen in the Inspiration room at the Visitors Center.

Not much there. The text identified the Temple's leader, Luc Solange, as 'the reluctant guru of the ecology movement,' and 'an avatar of muscular environmentalism.' The mission statement of the Temple was 'to reestablish harmony between Mother Earth and Childe Man.' Solange was said to be a frequent lecturer at the Temple's 'wellness centers' in Big Sur, Taos, Cabo San Lucas, and other 'vortices of spiritual convergence. There were options to click onto sites offering these lectures, and information about the wellness centers.

Subsequent pages offered options such as 'Envirogeddon,' and 'Revelations Decoded,' the latter Solange's take on the Seven Seals. He took a quick look and found it to be a dense, scholarly, footnoted work, sprinkled with references to numerology, the Qabbala, and more. He moved on to another page, 'Dragon Tales,' and watched the profile of a large ship crashing through heavy seas slowly materialize on his screen. He clicked on the ship, but got a 404 error message, indicating the page couldn't be found. He went back.

A 'Book of Days' showed pictures of smiling Templars at work, at play, and *en famille*. There were order forms for the Temple's 'Eco-Vita' product line (aromatherapy products and nutritional supplements) and its publications. Finally, there were links to other Web sites, including Earth First and PETA, and 'A Letter from Luke,' inviting readers to join the Temple in its fight to save the planet.

Frank looked at his watch and signed off. It was ten-thirty, and he wanted to call Annie before she went to sleep.

'Heyyyy,' she said, sounding happy to hear from him. 'Where are you?'

'I'm in Jersey. My room is orange. I feel like I'm inside a pumpkin.'

She laughed, and made a joke about Cinderella. Then she turned serious. 'So how did it go?'

He told her about Kramer and the Visitors Center, and added that he'd just logged off the Temple's Web site. 'You might want to look at it,' he said 'it's kinda interesting – if you like that stuff'.

'I'll check it out,' she replied. 'It's either that or sleep.'

They talked for a few minutes more about nothing in particular and then hung up, leaving Frank with a choice between going to bed or checking out the Gee-gnomes.

It was way past midnight, almost one when the phone rang, dragging him up from a deep, REM sleep. 'Wha . . . ?'

'Frank, it's Annie!'

'Hullo,' he mumbled, flicking on the light.

'Wake up!'

'I *am* up,' he said, glancing around the room. 'I was just . . . sleeping. Now I'm up.' He paused. 'Why am I up?'

'You have to come home.'

'I am. I will. I'll be there in the morning. I mean, the afternoon. Twoish.'

'No,' she said, 'you have to come back right away. Now!'

There was something in her voice – fear, excitement, a mixture of both. 'Are you okay?' he asked, throwing the covers off and swinging his legs out of the bed.

'Yes,' she said. 'I'm fine. But I checked out the Web site –'

'What Web site?'

'The Temple's.'

'Oh, right.'

'And it's them!' she said. 'It's the Temple.'

'Of course it's the Temple. It's their Web site. What are you talking about?'

'You're a genius,' Annie told him. 'You were right.

It was the Temple that took the bodies!'

'That's on their Web site?'

'No! I mean, yes – in a way. The horse is on the Web site!' Annie said.

'What horse?'

'The white horse – with the crazy look. It's a part of their logo.'

'You mean . . . the one in front of the Earth?' Frank asked. 'With the clouds and everything?'

'Yes!'

He thought about it. 'So what?' he asked. 'It's a horse.'

'It's the *same* horse,' Annie told him.

'As what?'

'The horse in Kopervik. There was a horse painted on the side of the church – a big horse – but it was graffiti. And it spooked us. And now, seeing the horse on their Web site – it's like, their signature. They stole the bodies, and signed the church, "Kilroy was here"!' She fell silent for a moment, and then: 'Frank?'

'What?'

'Why would a . . . a religious group . . . want something like that? A virus. I mean –'.

'I don't know,' he said.

'But we have to tell someone, right?'

'Yeah. Sure.'

'Then . . . who?'

He thought about it, but there wasn't any choice. 'Gleason,' he said. 'We have to tell fucking Gleason.'

23

He checked out of the motel and drove to Washington that same morning, arriving a little after four A.M. Miraculously, he found a parking space just up the street from his apartment.

Letting himself in, he didn't quite know what to do. He'd promised to pick up Annie first thing in the morning – at seven, and go with her to the FBI. Which meant he still had time to catch a couple of hours sleep.

In the alley behind the apartment he could hear the garbagemen knocking the cans around. Better to take a shower, he thought. Type out some notes, get the satellite pictures together. Make some coffee.

Five minutes later he was standing in the shower with the hot water needling the back of his neck. Then it hit him.

This isn't garbage day. Garbage day is Thursday. This is Tuesday. And besides, the garbage guys came early, but not this early. He looked at the clock. Four-thirty.

He stood there a little longer, thinking about it, then shut the shower off. Stepping out, he pulled a towel around his waist and walked to the window in the kitchen – the one that looked out over the alley.

There were two men, and they were tossing garbage bags into the back of a U-Haul. Which is not the way the city did it. While the District's government was in infamous disarray, Frank was sure it hadn't come to this. Not yet, anyway. He peered at the men.

They were pulling the garbage bags out of the Dumpster that serviced his building and slinging them into the back of the truck. The Dumpster across the way remained full, as did others, farther up the alley. I wonder what they're after, he thought, then flashed back to Kramer, standing outside the 7-Eleven, talking on the pay phone.

They're stealing my garbage, he thought, and thought again. Nah. Couldn't be. And yet . . . The other apartments in his building were occupied by a Charlotte Seltzer, a D.C. schoolteacher, and by Carlos Rubini, who worked at HUD. Neither of them seemed likely targets of trash stealers. And yet . . .

He opened the window and leaned out. 'Hey!' he called, 'What are you doing?'

The two men froze, then slowly looked up. They seemed to confer for a moment, then walked calmly to the back of the truck, tossed the bags they were holding inside, and lowered the door with a squeal of metal. Slowly, they walked around to the front of the truck, got in, and drove off

Frank peered at the disappearing license plate, but it was too far away to read. Then the truck turned, and a moment later it was gone.

With a groan, Frank thought about what might be in his trash. Orange peels and Kleenex, drafts of stories, transcripts of interviews, empty milk cartons and moldy bread, to-do lists and tax forms . . . Jesus Christ, he really ought to get a shredder.

Neal Gleason's office was in an area – you wouldn't call it a 'a neighborhood' – known as Buzzard Point. Ever since Frank moved to the city, people had been talking about the area as the next likely spot for a miraculous urban renaissance. With the river as backdrop, and only minutes from the Capitol, the vision was of something like Baltimore's Inner Harbor: a waterfront showcase, with a promenade along the sea, and behind it, apartments, hotels, restaurants, upscale shops.

But despite all the talk and architects' models, Buzzard Point never seemed to change. The streets were full of potholes and so patched up that they had an almost homemade look. Between a handful of ugly concrete office buildings and scruffy vacant lots stood the occasional marginal enterprise. These shared a certain barricaded look that, as they say, 'came with the territory.'

There were mom-and-pop grocery stores with metal gates to protect them at night, liquor stores where the clerks stood behind bulletproof Plexiglas, check-cashing services, bunkerlike barbershops, and hearing aid stores. At the gas stations, kids hustled to clean windshields or fill gas tanks for tips.

Frank was a little uptight about parking his car on the street, but as it turned out, there was no choice. The area didn't get enough visitors to warrant a parking lot.

The building was one of those fifties rectangles with nothing to distinguish it but a banal parade of under-sized windows on each floor. Inside was no better, with stained blue industrial carpeting and acoustic tile ceilings beginning to shred and sag. A duo of armed and uniformed men maintained security. One stood at the door and the other sat behind a fake wooden counter next to a turnstile. You had to walk past the first man and spend some time with the second before you were allowed to proceed to the bank of elevators beyond.

The man behind the counter telephoned Gleason's

office, made them sign their names on a clipboarded list, looked in Annie's purse, examined Frank's briefcase, and pried open the cap on the tube containing the satellite photos. He then laboriously wrote their names and that of Neal Gleason on rectangles of yellow cardboard, slipped those into plastic sleeves, and directed them to pin them to their clothing. A bulky woman got off one of the elevators beyond the turnstile, and they were permitted through. The woman escorted them upstairs, showing them into an anteroom furnished with a row of easy chairs upholstered in apricot plastic. Framed pastel prints of flowers adorned the walls.

They didn't have to wait long. Gleason came out and without a word gestured that they should precede him into his office. The FBI man was in shirtsleeves, a gun in a shoulder rig clearly visible as he made his way around them to his desk. His eyes were a pale and startling blue. Baby blue, you'd have to say. Frank realized that he'd never before seen the man without his aviator shades.

'So,' Gleason said. 'You wanted to talk to me? Talk.'

'I know why you were in Hammerfest,' Frank started, beginning to extract the satellite photos from the tube.

'Hmmm,' Gleason said. 'Visual aids. Nice touch, but I don't really have time for show-and-tell. So why don't we just stick to 'tell' and keep it short, okay?'

Frank had forgotten just how much of a prick Gleason was. 'I wanted to make sure you understood that Dr. Adair told me nothing,' he said. 'I found out about the bodies from other sources.'

Gleason nodded, then made a little circle with the finger of his right hand, meaning that Frank should hurry up. So Frank gave him an abbreviated rap, finishing with the fact that, according to Annie, the horse painted on the side of the church in Kopervik was identical to the image on the Temple's Web site.

Gleason applauded with big, wide, slow claps. 'Fascinating,' he said.

Annie shot Frank a puzzled look.

'You don't sound fascinated,' Frank said.

'Well, to tell you the truth, I'm not sure why you thought I'd be interested in this,' Gleason said. 'Let me make something clear to you. To both of you. The Bureau doesn't have jurisdiction over graveyards in Norway. And even if we did, we're not in the business of investigating religious groups.

'But –' Annie said. 'You were *there*. You –'

'I think what Dr. Adair is trying to say is that we *know* the Bureau is working the case, and we thought you –'

'And I'm telling *Dr. Adair* that discussing this matter is a violation of the national security oath she signed, and I could have her indicted for that.'

'What?' Annie was outraged. Her cheeks were on fire, as if she'd come inside from ice-skating. 'I didn't tell him anything,' she said. But what difference does that make, anyway? Don't you get it? This *group* took the bodies and has the virus and –'

Gleason raised his voice and hardened it at the same time: 'It's none of your concern, Dr. Adair. And as for you, Mr. Daly, I really think it would be in your best interest to walk away from this one – or you'll both wind up in the slammer.'

'I think you're forgetting something, *Neal*. I didn't sign jack-shit.'

'You don't have to sign anything, smart-ass. We've got laws – including laws against treason.'

Gleason was just rattling his cage. He couldn't be

serious, not about treason. But two could play the threat game.

Frank's eyebrows shot up. *'Treason?* Maybe there's a bigger story here than I thought. I didn't know we were at war. Or maybe you just misspoke. In which case, why don't we look at the First Amendment issues? Because it seems to me, *Neal,* that 'prior restraint' hasn't worked all that well. I mean, look at the Pentagon Papers –'

Gleason said, getting to his feet, 'Thanks for your help.' He nodded toward the door. 'The interview's over.'

'Wait a second,' Annie said. 'I don't understand. I mean, this is totally –'

'I *said:* this interview is over.'

Annie got to her feet, her face still red. Frank returned the papers to his attaché case and refastened the cap on the photo tube. Then he stood up and, taking Annie by the arm, walked out.

They didn't actually speak again until they were on the street. 'Can they *do* that?' Annie asked. 'What does it mean?'

Frank looked at the sky. It was overcast, with clouds moving fast overhead. The surface of the river was metallic-gray. 'It means they're on the case, and they don't want us in the middle of their investigation. That's what it means.'

Annie thought about it. 'Well, that's good, isn't it? I mean, that they're on the case?'

Frank shrugged. 'I don't find it all that reassuring.'

'Why not? It's the FBI! They're good at this.'

'I don't think Richard Jewell would agree.'

She frowned. 'Who?'

'The security guard in Atlanta. Remember – the Olympics.'

'Oh! Sure, but –'

'They were so intent on setting the public's mind at ease, that they *wrecked* this guy. Not to mention blowing any chance of finding out who really did it.'

'But –'

'Do you think they would have found the Unabomber if his family hadn't turned him in?'

A fat drop of rain crashed to the sidewalk. Then another. And another.

'I would have thought Mr. Gleason would at least want to know what *we* know,' Annie said.

'Don't call him "Mr. Gleason."'

'Then what *should* I call him?'

Frank cocked an eye at her, then shook his head. 'I'm probably not the best person to ask that question.'

Annie smiled. 'I see your point,' she said.

24

Stern was Annie's idea.

He was a graduate student in the Religious Studies department at Georgetown, writing a doctoral thesis on new religions (or some such thing). They'd gone out together once or twice ('Just for coffee or a movie,' Annie said), and then lost track of each other for about two years. A couple of weeks ago she'd run into him at the Starbucks on Connecticut Avenue, across from the Uptown Bakery. He was still working on his thesis, he said, and publishing 'a more or less quarterly' newsletter called *Armageddon Watch*. It was about cults and new religions, brainwashing, and the millennium. *I'm an expert on wackos,* he joked. Which made her want to say something funny about her own speciality, which was 'bugs' – but then it was her turn in line, and she didn't know whether she wanted a cappuccino or a latte and –

Then he was gone.

'I think he probably knows a lot about the Temple,' Annie said. 'It's right up his alley.'

Frank agreed that they should approach him.

They found Stern in the book. He was living a long way from Georgetown, way out on Reservoir Road. Annie made the call, and Stern invited her to come over.

'Do you mind if I bring a friend? We're kind of working on something together.'

No, he said, he didn't mind. And in fact Stern turned

out to be a perfect host. After meeting them at the door of his shabby apartment house, he made them a pot of black tea, and encouraged Frank's curiosity about the many books he had. These lay in piles, big and small, hunkering on every horizontal surface. They were on the floor, the tables, the windowsill, the radiators – everywhere except on bookshelves (of which there were none).

He was older than Frank had imagined – no kid, but a man in his very late twenties. He had watery blue eyes, and a thinning head of hair that was either too long or too short for whatever it was that it was supposed to be. He wore boots and jeans and a big flannel shirt, and smiled a lot.

Frank and Annie sipped their tea, sitting on the edge of a worn-out couch with a funky green slipcover. From a corner of the room the Five Blind Boys of Alabama sang Jesus' praises through the black mesh of opposing Bose speakers.

'Ben's brilliant,' Annie said, softening him up. 'His thesis is fantastic.'

Stern chuckled. '"Fantastic" is right. It's six hundred pages long, and I'm no closer to the end than I was when I began it, three years ago.'

Frank winced in sympathy. 'I know the problem,' he said. 'I've been working on the same story for months.'

'The thing is: the more you know, the more complicated it gets – so the end keeps receding. It's like Zeno's paradox,' Ben said, 'except it isn't mathematics, it's prose.'

'Annie said you're writing about cults.'

Stern listed from side to side, rolling his shoulders as he weighed the remarks. 'I guess so. Cults, sects, new religions – what you call 'em depends on your point of view.'

'So what's your thesis?'

Stern shrugged. '"The more things change, the more they stay the same."'

'Unh-huh.'

Stern smiled. 'It's a comparative study – the Taborites and Mankind United.'

Frank shook his head. 'Never heard of 'em.'

Stern shifted uncomfortably in his chair, as if he'd been caught reading a UFO magazine. 'Well, it's apples and oranges,' he said. 'I mean, they're very different, but also . . . they're also quite alike. The Taborites were a fifteenth century religious sect in Bohemia. They declared war on the priesthood, and preached a sort of proactive millenarianism.'

'What's that?' Annie asked. 'How do you –'

'They thought it was up to them to usher in the millennium, rather than sitting around, waiting for it to happen.'

'And how do you "usher in the millennium"?' Frank asked.

'You rid the world of sin. And that's what they tried to do, using whatever tools they had at hand – the dagger, the pike, the catapult, the crossbow. Trust me: it's a good thing they didn't have the bomb.'

'So they went around killing people?' Annie asked.

Stern's eyebrows shot up, and he fished a pack of Camels from the pocket of his shirt. Lighting one with a Zippo, he took a long drag, and said, 'They killed *sinners*. Hey! They were agents of the millennium. It was their job, their duty, their *religious* duty, to massacre anyone who wasn't a part of their own movement. Because that's how you could tell if someone was a sinner. They didn't belong. And so you killed them. And that's how you cleansed the earth.'

'Jesus,' Frank said.

'Exactly.'

With a mock frown, Stern leaned across the steamer trunk that served as a coffee table and grabbed Annie by the wrist. Speaking in a malevolent whisper, leavened only by a bizarre attempt to affect a Czech accent, the aging grad student muttered, 'Accursed be he who withholds his sword from shedding the blood of the enemies of Christ. No pity for Satan, No mercy for evil. So sayeth Jan the Pious.'

'Wow,' Annie said, withdrawing her arm and rubbing her wrist.

'And the other guys?' Frank asked.

Stern looked puzzled for a moment, and then said, 'Oh – you mean Mankind United. They were . . . different.'

'You said they were alike.'

'Well, yeah. But they were five hundred years apart, plus – whatever the distance is, psychologically, from medieval Prague to Depression Santa Monica.'

'I should think the distance was quite large,' Frank said.

'Me, too,' Annie added.

'Mankind United sprang up in the early thirties,' Stern said. 'It was run by a guy named Arthur Bell, who spun a conspiracy theory about our secret masters,' the "international bankers" –'

Uh-oh,' Frank joked, 'here come the Jews.'

Stern laughed. 'You're right! He was a big-time anti-Semite. But he was selling the millennium, too, just like the Taborites. Except in his case, utopia had more to do with air-conditioning than land reform.'

Annie giggled.

'But he had the same idea. He said there was going to be a bloodbath, a natural catastrophe followed by an Armageddonlike war that would kill – I don't know how many people – *most* of the people – in the world. And this would be a good thing, he said, because it would usher in the New Age. A.k.a. "the millennium." A.k.a. "heaven on earth." After the war, everyone would have free air-conditioning, a $25,000 house, and a sixteen-hour workweek – unless you wanted to be retired, in which case you'd be given a pension.'

'Works for me,' Frank joked.

'It worked for a lot of people. Bell got rich.'

'So what you're writing about,' Frank said, 'is the fact that these two guys, Jan the Pious and Arthur the Air-Conditioned, shared a dream.'

'Exactly,' Stern said. 'Them and a million others, down through the centuries. They all shared – they all share – the same bloody dream. You want more tea?'

'Sure,' Frank said. 'Please.'

Stern filled his cup, and turned to Annie. 'So,' he said, with a let's-get-down-to-business tone. 'What's up?'

'Up?' she asked.

'Well,' Stern said, 'I know you didn't call to say you love me – and, anyway, you said you were working on something. You said you and Frank were working on something *together*.'

'Oh, *yeah*,' Annie replied, 'we are. We're working on this . . . thing.' Then she turned to Frank and, smiling, came as close to batting her eyes as a microbiologist can come. In this way, the ball was put firmly in his court.

Frank sighed, and cleared his throat. 'We're interested in the Temple of Light,' he said.

For a moment the air seemed to go out of Stern. His body tensed, ever so slightly, and then he leaned back in his armchair and held them with his gaze. He didn't say anything for long time. Finally, he turned to Annie with a look that might have been reserved for someone who'd tried to sell him a fifty-dollar Rolex. 'What *is* this?' he asked.

Annie blinked. Frank frowned. 'What do you mean?' she replied.

'"What do I mean?" Jeez, Annie! I haven't seen you for *what* – two years – and then you call me up out of the blue and say, "Oh! by the way! This is my friend, and we're interested in the Temple of Light?" Is this a joke?'

'No,' Frank said, 'it's not a joke.'

Until now, Stern had been looking at Annie. Abruptly, he turned to Frank. 'Who are you with?' he asked in a matter-of-fact voice.

'Who am I *with*?' Frank repeated. 'I'm not *with* anybody. I'm with Annie.'

'He writes for the *Post*,' Annie said.

'Really!' Stern cocked his head. 'What's your phone number?'

'My phone number?'

'Yeah! At work. What happens if I call you at the *Post*?'

'Well, actually, I'm on a leave of absence.'

Stern rolled his eyes. 'Give me a break,' he said.

'I'm serious! Look.' Frank took out his wallet and showed him his press pass and his Washington *Post* ID.

'Anybody could make one of these,' Stern said. 'It's a piece of shit.'

'Right! That's how you know it's authentic: the *Post*'s cheap,' Frank said.

'This is ridiculous,' Annie declared. 'It's me, Ben! What are you thinking?'

Stern ignored her, looking at Frank. 'So if you're on leave, what are you doing?'

'I have a Sam Johnson fellowship.'

'Which is what?'

'They have a sort of contest every year. Reporters submit proposals, saying what they'd do if they had a year to write about what they're interested in. So I gave them a proposal and . . . they liked it.'

Stern held his gaze. 'And this was about the Temple of Light?'

'No,' Frank said, 'it's about emerging viruses.'

Stern's frown deepened.

'You can call the foundation. They're in the book.'

'And how do I know they aren't a front?' Stern asked.

'The *Johnson* Foundation? For what?'

'For the Temple.'

'*The Temple*?!'

'*Why* not? The Temple gives money to half a dozen foundations – the Institute for Religious Experience, the Gaia Foundation. They spread it around. It's good P.R.'

'Maybe. But they don't give money to *this* foundation. Trust me. Old man Coe would have a heart attack.'

Stern continued looking at him, and then he nodded, as if he'd just made a decision. 'Let me show you something,' he said. Getting to his feet, he crossed the room to a desk beside the window. Pushing aside a pile of papers, he picked up a newsletter and returned with it to his chair. 'Check it out,' he said, and tossed the newsletter onto the steamer trunk between them. Then he sat back down.

It was the spring issue of *Armageddon Watch* – thirty-two pages of heavy stock paper, stapled down the middle. The cover blazed stories about the Church of Scientology and the Internet, a Santería sect in western Louisiana, and a brainwashing spa in the south of India.

Frank turned the pages one after another until he came to page eight. There, embedded in a column under the heading, '**Personalities**,' was a picture of Luc Solange, squinting into the sun as he gripped the wheel of what must have been the *Crystal Dragon*. The cutline read, *Helmsman*.

Frank showed it to Annie. 'He's handsome,' she said, sounding a little surprised.

Beneath the picture was a short paragraph.

A rare glimpse of Temple of Light guru, Luc Solange, at sea aboard the Temple's flagship, the *Crystal Dragon*. After 15 years in the U.S., the Swiss-born Solange is once again on the road, traveling most recently to Tokyo, where he addressed the Chosen Soren organization this past November. *(Photo: Anon.)*

'Nice job,' Frank said.

'I've got 341 subscribers,' Stern told him. 'Mostly academics and parents. A couple of journalists, a few P.I.'s – and, of course, the cults themselves. They're the ones with P.O. boxes for addresses.'

'Have you written a lot about the Temple?' Frank asked.

Stern shook his head. 'This is the first piece in more than a year. I'm sort of testing the waters.'

'What do you mean?' Annie asked.

'I mean it's dangerous,' Stern replied. 'It's a hassle. I don't need it.' He paused for a moment, then went on. 'Remember the last time we got together?'

Annie nodded. 'I was submitting my grant proposal. Two years ago.'

Stern nodded. 'How'd that go, anyway?'

Annie glanced at Frank. 'They turned it down.'

Stern winced in sympathy. 'Bummer. Anyway, that was the last time I wrote anything about the Temple – until this.'

'What did you write about the first time?' Frank asked.

'Some of the same stuff that I've been telling you about. I drew connections between Solange and earlier cult leaders, pointing out the similarities. I called him "a secular apocalyptic" who's substituted the principles of deep ecology for the Ten Commandments. And he's proactive, too. He wants to bring it on.'

'What?'

'The apocalypse. Armageddon. Whatever you want to call it. If you read what he's written, Solange says that he's the last "world historical" figure –'

'What do you mean?'

'Jesus, Buddha –'

'Solange,' Annie suggested.

'Exactly. And his importance lies in precisely that fact: he's the midwife to the End-times. Or so he says.'

'But why would anyone want to be that?' Annie asked.

Stern's eyebrows bounced up and down. 'Solange doesn't see things the way you and I do. His worldview is an ecocentric one.'

'Earth first,' Frank said.

'Exactly. People aren't the most important actors. Nature is. What Solange is after is the restoration of Eden – which, among other things, means the end of industrial civilization.'

'Sounds like a dangerous man,' Frank remarked.

'You bet. That's why they call him "the First Horseman."'

'The First Horseman?' Annie repeated.

Stern nodded. 'Yeah. Of the Apocalypse.'

The three of them fell silent for a while, and sipped their tea. Then Frank said, 'So what happened to you? I mean, between you and them? You said you were "testing the waters" when you published his picture.'

'Well, yeah,' Stern said. 'The piece I wrote back then was pretty straightforward, actually. Mainly, it was a pull-together of things that other people had written – journalists, mostly – and a little historical perspective along the lines I just gave you. The only new material, really, came from a couple of reports I got from a friend in the A.G.'s office in California: his son disappeared into the Children of God about ten years ago, and he's been an activist against new religions ever since. Anyway . . . they came after me.'

'Who came after you?' Annie asked.

'The *Temple*. Or, as they like to call themselves sometimes, "the meek." They put me under surveillance.'

'You're kidding.'

'No,' Stern said. 'It was just like the movies. I had *a tail*. There was a car outside my apartment sixteen hours a day, from six in the morning to ten at night, seven days a week.'

'Sounds expensive,' Frank remarked.

'I was *flattered*. I joked about it with them when I passed the car. Then they killed my dog.'

'*What?*'

'Oh, nooo,' Annie said. 'Not the Lab. Not Brownie!?'

'Someone gave him a steak, marinated in warfarin. You know what he was like! He'd eat anything, as long as it wasn't dog food. Poor guy . . . And then the phone started ringing all night long, no matter how often I changed the number, or had it unlisted – so I pulled the plug. The next thing you know, people are showing up at my office, *screaming* at me. I mean, these were not people you could talk to.'

'What did they look like?' Frank asked,

'They looked like students. They looked *normal*. The only thing *ab*normal about them was that they were yelling at me – and throwing blood all around.'

Annie blanched.

'Once, a woman burst into the library, dragging a little kid behind her, screaming that she'd "caught me" with him! Right after that, a couple of people in the department, including one of my thesis advisers, started getting e-mail.'

'What kind of e-mail?' Frank asked.

'Oh, it was this really jejune stuff. Hate mail. I mean, one of the people in the department's gay – it's no secret – so naturally he receives this homophobic diatribe. And my thesis adviser's African American, so guess what he gets? All this Christian Identity crap!'

'And your name was on it?'

'No, they're much more subtle than that. They signed it the "White Avenger," or something. But that didn't matter, because they routed it through my computer, and the police were able to trace it.'

'How'd they route it through your computer?' Frank asked.

'Easy,' Stern replied. 'They broke into the apartment when I was out, logged on, sent the e-mail, and that was that.'

'That's horrible,' Annie said.

'I was *arrested,*' Stern went on. 'They were going to *charge* me! With a hate crime! Can you imagine?'

'But you beat it,' Frank said.

Stern nodded, then laughed. 'Yeah, they fucked up. I was teaching a seminar when the e-mail went out. It was right there in the header: Thursday, two-fifteen Pee-emm. I couldn't have sent it.'

'So what happened?'

'Nothing. The cops got in touch with the Temple's lawyers, and you know what they said? They said I was so crazy, I'd probably poisoned my own dog. And then they said, "Maybe he changed the clock on his computer" – which, in fact, would be easy. I could have done that, but – *duh!* Why bother, when you could send the letters through an anonymous remailer, and there wouldn't even *be* any headers?'

'So . . . was that the end of it?' Frank asked.

Stern shook his head. 'No. It went on for months. They filled out a change-of-address form at the post office – so my mail disappeared, which was a problem, because somebody started charging things on my Visa and MasterCards.'

'What things?' Annie asked.

'Embarrassing stuff, the kind of stuff that could get you in trouble – just for being on the mailing list. Violent pornography. Grow lights. Precursor chemicals for meth. There were a thousand dollars in calls to 900 numbers, and subscriptions to newsletters from the North American Man-Boy Love Association and the Church of the Mountain.'

'What's the Church of the Mountain?' Annie asked.

'It's a Nazi thing. But the point is, I had a lot of collection agencies on my back – not to mention the DEA and Customs.'

Annie rolled her eyes.

'Then they filed a libel suit –'

'What *for*?' Frank asked.

'Why not? They could afford it. And it cost me an arm and a leg just to get it thrown out of court.'

'And then?'

'Then nothing. They stopped.'

'"They stopped"?' Annie repeated.

'Yeah. They just . . . stopped. Like they'd made their point, and now they were moving on to more important things. I guess it was a warning.'

'Jesus,' Frank whispered.

'So that's why I'm a little paranoid,' Stern added. 'I mean, I put Solange back in the newsletter – and, the next thing I know, *you* show up, asking about the Temple. You can see where I'm coming from.'

Frank nodded. 'Yeah,' he said, 'I can.'

'I'll make some more tea,' Annie said, getting to her feet. Wordlessly, she took the teapot from the top of the trunk and carried it into the kitchen.

Stern looked at Frank. 'You know,' he said, 'the one thing they never did: they never tried to kill me.'

'Yeah, well . . . the night's young.'

'But they would have, you know. I mean, if I'd been anything more than a nuisance.'

'You think so?'

'I know so. And I mention it because – I don't know what you and Annie are doing –'

Frank started to say something, but Stern cut him off.

'– *and I don't want to know*. I just think you ought to be careful. For her sake.'

'I will be,' Frank said. 'I'm kind of fond of her myself.' He paused for a second, then went on. 'But the thing that can help us the most is information.'

Stern shrugged. 'What can I tell you? How much do you know?'

'Solange is Swiss.'

Stern nodded. 'He came to the States in 'eighty-two. They say he was broke.'

'Why'd he leave?'

'I think he wanted a bigger canvas. I think Switzerland was getting a little claustrophobic. He'd run for parliament on the Green ticket, and split the party by insisting on a lot of ultra positions – which got a bunch of people mad at him. And then, about the same time, his business went under.'

'What business was that?'

'He had a homeopathy clinic in Montreux, and a couple of patients died of kidney failure – some kind of herbal remedy that backfired.'

'So he came to the States.'

'Yeah, he came to the States. And he opened a clinic in L.A. Did pretty well. Got involved in environmental politics. Started something called "Verdure," which was a little like Earth First! but a lot more secretive. Got some press, got some followers. Started to give lectures in the U.S. and abroad.'

'Then what?'

Stern's cigarette had been out for a while, so he lit another, and blew a long stream of smoke into the air above Frank's head.

'Well, he got bigger. And bigger. I think it was around 'ninety-two . . . a guy who'd been in the Moonies took over "the recruitment hat."'

'What do you mean – "hat"?'

'They have a "hat" for everything: finance, recruitment, intelligence.'

'Intelligence?'

Stern nodded. 'Yeah. They've got an in-house intel bureau that's as good as it gets. Anyway, this guy from the Moonies – I mean he *used to be* in the Moonies – he comes in, sits down, and reorganizes their recruitment operations. So, now, all of a sudden, they're really aggressive. And *diabolical*. They go after two groups: people in their twenties, because they've got energy; and people in their eighties, because they've got pensions. They set up nonprofits "to help" unwed mothers, "counsel" kids with drug problems, and "care" for the elderly. But what they're really doing, of course, is getting close to a lot of vulnerable people – who turn out to be the easiest people to recruit. They even started lonely hearts clubs in half a dozen cities, just so they could arrange dates between members and people they wanted to recruit.'

'I see why you called it "diabolical,"' Frank said.

'It was amazing. They paid ten thousand dollars for a database composed entirely of deadbeats. I mean, people who were *drowning* in debt. They ran their credit histories, and built up dossiers on every one of them. Then they banged on their doors and promised to show them a way out. "You're a victim," they said. "You're not to blame. It's America that's at fault! Amerika with a K. It's consumerism! Pack a bag, burn your bills, and come with us. We'll give you a job, instant friends, and a place to stay." And that's what they did. Only they forgot to mention that the jobs didn't actually *pay* anything, and the place to stay was a dorm where people were sleeping four to a room. Not that it mattered. By then they'd been love-bombed by every babe or baldwin in the org, and sleeping four hours a night, every other night!' Stern paused and caught his breath. 'It was a helluva recruitment operation,' he said.

'So, what happened?' Frank asked.

Stern shrugged. 'They reached critical mass. One day there's this deep ecology thing called "Verdure," with maybe two hundred members. Two years later there are thousands of people, their eyes are glazed, and they're calling themselves the "Temple of Light."'

'Where's the sugar?' Annie called out from the kitchen.

'I'm all out,' Stern said.

'So how many people are in the Temple?' Frank asked.

'According to them?' Stern replied. 'Thirty thousand. But actually? Maybe a quarter of that. But even that number – there's an inner and outer order.'

'And how does *that* work?'

'Like you'd expect. The ones on the inside are hardcore – round-the-clock staffers. Maybe a thousand people in half a dozen cities. Plus the ones at the compound. They've got about three hundred there.'

'Where?'

'At the compound – outside Lake Placid. They bought a private school, turned it into their headquarters.'

'And the outer order?'

'They send their checks in, subscribe to the newsletter, and buy Solange's vitamins.'

'Tell us about that,' Annie said, coming into the room with a pot of tea on a tray. 'Tell us about the vitamin factory at the compound.' Setting the tray on the steamer trunk, she poured a cup for herself and carried it over to the window.

'It's not that exotic,' Stern went on. 'I mean, they make homeopathic remedies and aromatherapy products. Ginseng. Juniper oil. Plus the vitamins.'

'And this brings in a lot of revenue?'

'It brings in *some*. Plus, they've got patents.'

'On what?' Annie asked, turning away from the window.

'Time-release things. Where you put chemicals in polymers so they'll dissolve at different rates.'

'Like what? What kind of chemicals?' Frank asked.

'All kinds. Painkillers. Insulin. B-12. Whatever you want. It's like those little colored things in Contac, except smaller.'

'He's talking about microencapsulation,' Annie said over her shoulder as she looked out the window.

'Right! That's what I said. Anyway,' he went on, 'I was telling Frank how there's an inner order – and an inner order within that! And this is something you need to know about that, because they're the ones who are gonna come after you – the Office of Special Affairs.'

'What's that?' Frank asked.

'Spooks,' Stern replied. 'They're the Temple's in-house intelligence agency. And they're good, too. Very professional. Lots of firewalls. Lots of money to play with. Also, a lot of outside people on the payroll – private investigators, journalists, cops, academics . . . you name it.'

'Sounds formidable.'

'It *is*. In fact, it's a nightmare. And then they've got the special teams.'

'For what? Punt returns?'

Stern smiled. Thinly. 'No,' he said. 'For grabbing people.'

'You're kidding.'

Stern shook his head. 'Look, what I'm telling you is this: if you piss them, they'll come after you One day you'll wake up and – boom! You'll be gone.'

'That's the part I hate,' Frank said, stirring his tea. 'I always hate it when I disappear.'

'It isn't funny,' Stern said.

Frank nodded. 'I'm not laughing. But getting back to what you were saying, about the money . . . they get most of their money from what? Vitamins? Patents?'

Stern shook his head. 'No.'

'Plus the gifts,' Frank said. 'From the members. And I suppose they tithe –'

'That's not the point,' Stern said. 'That's not where the big bucks are from. The big bucks come from somewhere else.'

Frank looked puzzled. 'Where?' he asked.

Stern stubbed out his cigarette and immediately lit another. 'Chosen Soren,' he said.

Frank thought about it, and then remembered. 'Oh, you mean the Japanese guys,' he said. 'In your newsletter.'

'Right,' Stern replied. 'Except, Chosen Soren isn't Japanese, really. It's for Koreans who *work* in Japan. Mostly *North* Koreans. They do the shit work for the Japanese, and they send a lot of their money home. It's a big foreign-exchange earner.'

'And that's where the Temple gets its money?'

Stern nodded. 'Most of it.'

Frank was dumbfounded. 'But . . . *why*?'

'I don't know,' Stern replied, 'but the Koreans have given them fifty million bucks since 'ninety-five.'

'How do you *know* that?'

'Customs report. I got it from the A.G.'s office in California. They busted this guy who was riding circuit – L.A., Tokyo, Geneva – back to L.A. And like that. I guess they found a lot of cash on him that he wasn't supposed to have. Anyway, they questioned the guy, and he cracked. He told them everything he was doing.'

'Which was what?'

'Moving money, lots of money, in and out of different accounts, so no one could tell where it came from.'

'And this was that . . . Chosen Soren money?'

'Yeah.'

'So where is this guy?'

Stern blew a smoke ring at the ceiling. 'They fucked up. Instead of pursuing the case, Customs had him deported. Next thing you know, he gets off the plane at Narita, and that's it. He never gets out of the Customs hall. His wife is standing there with two kids, right outside Passport Control and – forget about it. All they found were his suitcases, sitting on a cart in the hall. End of story.'

'They never found him?'

'No. It's like I said: end of story.'

'Hey!' The shout was Annie's. She was standing at the window with her teacup in her hand, crouching slightly to yell at someone outside. 'Hey!'

'What's the matter?' Frank said, moving quickly to her side.

'Someone's in your car.'

He pushed the curtain aside and, looking out, saw that she was right. The Saab was at the curb in front of the apartment house, and the driver's door was wide open. A woman in a blue dress was leaning inside, half in and half out of the car.

'Be right back,' Frank said, and without waiting for Annie, went through the front door, past the elevator, and down the stairs, two at a time. A few seconds later he was in the lobby, and then he was in the street. His car door was closed and the woman was about twenty yards away, pushing a stroller toward the corner.

'Wait a second!' he called, and loped after her. 'Hey! *Excuse me?*'

The woman turned, raising a hand to shade the sunlight from her eyes, and he saw that she was young – just a girl, really – with the freckled innocence of a 4-H beauty queen. 'Hi' she said, bathing him in a bright and glittering smile.

He found himself unexpectedly out of breath, more from the excitement than the exercise, so his voice was choppy. 'Sorry I yelled, but – I was looking out the window and – you were – you know – you were in my car.

The smile exploded. 'Was that *your* car?' she asked, rolling the stroller back and forth to keep the baby happy.

'Yeah,' Frank said, feeling a little foolish in the searchlight of her friendliness. 'It was.'

'Oh! Well, I turned out the lights for you. You left them on.'

'I *did*?' He thought about it for a second. 'I don't think so. Why would I have the lights on? It's –'

She shook her head, and he saw that she had green eyes. 'I don't know. Were you, like, in a *tunnel* or something?'

The baby gurgled, and Frank glanced in its direction. He couldn't tell if it was a boy or a girl, but like its mother, it was adorable. 'Cute kid,' he said.

'Thanks!' she replied, cocking her head like a cheer-leader at the end of a routine. Then she turned and gave the stroller a little push. 'I have to go now,' she said. 'Papa's coming home.'

'Well . . . thanks for the help,' Frank said.

As he walked back to Stern's apartment, he saw that the car lights were off – which was good (though, of course, the battery might still be dead). He'd try it in a minute, but first he had to get Annie.

'Who was it?' she asked.

'I don't know. I guess I left the lights on. She turned them off.'

'You *did*?'

'Yeah,' he said.

'I didn't notice any lights.'

Frank shrugged. 'Well, it's good she did. Anyway . . .' Turning to Stern, he offered his hand. 'We better get going,' he said. 'But . . . thanks for the help – really.'

'No problem.'

'If I have to, can I get back to you?'

'Well 'Stern said, thinking about it. 'I guess . . . but . . . if you and the Temple are going at it – don't call me from your house. And for chrissake, don't just drop by. Send smoke signals or something.'

Frank laughed.

As they went out to the car, Annie was shaking her head. 'I'm sure you didn't leave your lights on,' she said.

'Right. I didn't leave my lights on. So what? Did you hear what he was saying? About this Chosen thing? Fifty million dollars? What's *that* all about?'

'I don't know,' Annie said. 'I'm more worried about this vitamin factory, or whatever it is.'

He opened the door to the Saab and slid behind the wheel. Annie was saying something about micro-encapsulation as he put the key in the ignition and switched it on.

The Saab started with a roar, but the sound was almost drowned out by Frank's exclamation: 'What the fuck is that!?'

Annie turned to him and saw that he was looking at his hands – which, like the steering wheel, were wet with a kind of transparent grease.

'What's the matter?' Annie asked.

He was holding his hands in front of him, palms up, like a Catholic saint. 'I don't know,' he said. 'It's like I've been slimed. Get me a towel from the back, okay?'

Annie reached into the backseat, where a roll of paper towels rested on the floor. Grabbing a handful, she helped him get the grease off his fingers and the steering wheel. When they were done, Frank stuffed the towels under the front seat, shifted into gear and pulled out of the parking space, heading toward Annie's house in Mount Pleasant.

'*She* did that,' Annie said.

'Did what?'

'Put that stuff on the steering wheel, what do you think?'

'I don't know what I think. I think it was gross.'

Annie shivered. 'It's not right,' she said.

'She had a *baby*. It's probably just some kinda baby stuff,' Frank said. 'Something that was on her hands.'

They went up Foxhall Road to Nebraska, and cut across to Wisconsin. They sat for a couple of minutes in front of the Sidwell Friends School, which was just letting out, then turned left onto Porter and cut across the park to Mount Pleasant. The trip took about twenty minutes, and by the time they got to her house, he didn't feel well.

'You okay?' she asked.

He nodded. 'Yeah, I'm all right. I'm a little out of it, is all. I haven't eaten anything all day.'

Annie gave him a skeptical look as she eased out of the car. Then she turned and leaned in through the window. 'You're certain?' she asked.

'Yeah. Too much tea, or something.'

And then he was off, nosing through the traffic on his way to Columbia Road, driving past the bodegas and nightclubs and cop cars . . There was so much to pay attention to – like the drunks on the corner, and the dogs, and the 7-Eleven.

When he reached Columbia Road, he realized with surprise that he was sweating, a sour, clammy sweat, like the onset of a fever. And, really, he didn't feel well at all. His heart was racing, and he had this shaky feeling in his stomach and chest – like stage fright, except he wasn't onstage. He was in his car, and the adrenaline was surging through him for no reason at all. It wasn't like he was going *fast*. In fact, he was going – what? Six miles an hour.

No wonder they were all beeping at him.

Something was wrong, and he knew what it was: suddenly, he was intensely aware of every possibility, and saw in every possibility a threat. If for example, he turned the wheel a bit to the left, the car would cross the centerline, and crash. That there was no reason for him to turn the wheel was irrelevant. The point was: he could. And that possibility was a terrifying one because, of course, a lot of people would be hurt. And if before turning the wheel, he sped up, the car might then continue onto the sidewalk, plowing into God knows how many people.

So that there'd be blood everywhere.

The fear he felt was a kind of vertigo, irrational and uncontrollable. Anyone could walk a straight line, but try to do that on the railing of a balcony, a hundred feet above the street, and you'd go over.

And that was how he felt now, as if he were about 'to go over,' as if his mind were pulling him over an invisible ledge. Driving was impossibly complicated – like rubbing your stomach while patting your head. So much could go wrong so easily, and catastrophically. How could anyone do it? How could they pay attention to so many things at the same time? To the speedometer and gearshift, the clutch, brakes, and accelerator – other cars, and traffic lights, people crossing and recrossing the street. The tachometer! The world was a tidal wave of places and events, foaming with consequences.

And I'm drowning in it, Frank thought.

And the other problem was: a crucial part of him was missing – his *stance* toward the world, or his perspective on it. It was as if he'd forgotten not so much *who* he was, but what it was like to *be* who he was. Not the facts of himself, but his interpretation of himself.

Suddenly, he knew what it was: he'd forgotten his point of view. He'd forgotten what it was like to *be* Frank Daly, and having forgotten that, he couldn't imagine ever getting it back. His whole vocabulary of being had vanished, so that to be himself was like trying to speak a language he'd never learned. It was beyond his grasp. *He* was beyond his grasp.

And this realization filled him with a feeling of dread that was all the more profound for the fact that it was inescapable – it came from within, from the place where Frank was supposed to be, and where now there was nothing. A hole.

He knew what had happened, of course. He'd been drugged. By Stern, or by Annie, or else by the girl that he'd caught in his car. The freckled mommy with the bright smile. But knowing this was no consolation at all. Whoever had done it had taken everything from him, so that now there was less than nothing left. There was no *him* left. And he knew that he'd never get better because what he'd lost was about as substantial – and elusive – as Eastern Standard Time.

It was taking an awfully long time to get back to his apartment – which was where he needed to be.

So he floored it. The Saab lurched into the opposite lane and shot forward down the busy street, parting the traffic like a zipper. A man in a business suit dove toward the curb, and horns exploded from every direction. Chief Ike's Mambo Room flashed past, followed in rapid succession by Popeye's, Mixtec, the Crestar Bank, and a knot of bodhisattvas, waiting for the light to change at the corner of Eighteenth and Columbia Road.

He had to get to bed. He'd be safe in bed. But first he had to park the car. And, under the circumstances, there was no way he could do that. Even if he found a spot, parking the Saab would be like docking the space shuttle, maneuvering a ton of steel through three dimensions, using only his hands and feet. Impossible. No one could do it. So he slammed on the brakes with both of his feet, bringing the car to a shivering halt in the middle of the street.

As he got out, he turned on the lights, thinking it would make it easier to find the car later.

He was surprised at how woozy he felt. It was almost as if his head were on roller bearings. A man came toward him from the sidewalk, speaking quietly in Spanish, then backed away, frightened by something in Frank's eyes.

A moment later (or maybe it was longer – maybe it was an hour later), he was standing in his apartment, listening to his telephone messages.

'Frank! It's Jennifer. About these satellite expenses . . . Is this a joke? Give us a call.'

And the next message: *'Hey, Frankie! it's your uncle Sid. Listen, everybody's broke up about your dad, but – hey, it was good to see ya and . . . y'know, don't be such a stranger!'*

And the third message, from a woman who wanted to wish him well: *'Hi there! We met this afternoon? I just wanted to say, have a nice trip – and, oh yeah! If you want to come back? And stay back? Maybe you should work on something else!'*

And then the phone was ringing, and the answering

machine switched on, and it was Annie: 'Frank – it's me. I'm worried about that *stuff* that was on the steering wheel. Call me back, okay? Or maybe . . . maybe I'll just come over . . . Are you there? Pick up!'

Not likely. The phone was pulsing, rising and falling like a termite queen, breathing in the dark. And his hands – *Jesus, his hands! You could do such terrible things with your hands.* . . .

25

THE COMPOUND
MAY 23

The Temple's headquarters were on the campus of what was formerly a private school. About twenty miles from Lake Placid, the old school grounds lay behind an impressive set of rusted iron gates in a long and serpentine valley.

Once past the gates, an asphalt drive twisted through a forest of tigertail spruce, arriving eventually at a small clearing that served as a parking lot. From there a gravel path led through a dark wood, emerging in a tamed meadow, where a black-water pond sat at the foot of a low and gently sloping hill.

At the western edge of the meadow were a cluster of white cottages that had formerly housed the school's teachers but were now reserved for the Temple's senior staff. Nearby, a pair of crumbling dormitories were home to the rank and file of the Temple's inner order.

More impressive were the labs. These were an interconnected complex of hypermodern glass and steel structures that housed the compound's infirmary, food hall, administration offices, research laboratories, and production facilities. It was from here that the Temple ran its international operations, while manufacturing a mix of vitamins, homeopathic remedies, and aromatherapy products.

At the top of the hill, in full surveillance of the dormitories and the labs, was the Headmaster's House, an immaculately restored Tudor mansion with mullioned windows, surrounded by vine-clad pergolas. This, then, was Solange's residence, and the Temple's inner sanctum.

Sitting on the flagstone terrace under a canopy of pink wisteria, Susannah gazed at the surrounding mountains and wished her nervousness would go away. The problem was, she didn't know why she was here. And this made her nervous, because there were stories about the terrace and things that happened there.

But that's all they were, she told herself, *stories*.

The truth was, being summoned to the Temple's headquarters was almost always a good thing. Solange sometimes arranged marriages among the staff and when he did, the announcements were always made on the terrace. So, also, it was on the terrace that rewards were handed out, and special tasks assigned. Which, Susannah thought, was the reason *she* was there – for something good. And, after all, what else could it be? She'd done everything she'd been asked to do – in Rhinebeck, L.A., and Washington – and everything had gone off without a hitch. On the other hand, so had Tommy and Vaughn and everyone else. So why was she the only one who'd been asked to come to the compound? Why was she the only one on the operations team sitting on the terrace?

Shyly, because little Stephen was feeding at her breast, she looked up at Solange, who was questioning Belinda about a defector.

'So how did you find him?'

'The P.I.s found him. He was in a motel somewhere, and I guess he made a mistake.'

'And what was that?'

'He phoned home. They always phone home. Just like E.T.'

Solange nodded, happy with the reply. 'And Kramer had the phones covered?'

Belinda nodded. 'There's a phone-phreak he works with. I think he put something on the line, or maybe he hacked the Caller ID. Anyway, they found him in a Motel 6 on the Jersey shore.'

'And where is he now?' Solange asked, referring to the defector.

Belinda tossed her head in the direction of the labs. 'Infirmary. Doc's got him stoned to the gills on Halcion and Thorazine – so it's not like he's talking to anybody. If you want to talk to him, they'll have to bring him down.'

Solange shook his head. 'No, just keep him that way.'

He's so cool, Susannah thought. He stands there with his head tilted back and his eyes half closed, like a jazz musician listening to someone else's solo. And then, when he moves, it's on the balls of his feet, like a quarterback dropping back into the pocket.

He's like a cat, Susannah thought. But not a tabby.

Solange was just over six feet tall, and lean as a snake. He wore faded jeans and hiking boots, and a white shirt with the sleeves rolled up to the elbows. A dark stubble peppered his cheeks, and his ink-black hair needed cutting. Agate eyes under thick brows, flecked with gray.

The eyes have it, Susannah thought, making a joke (but not really). That's where his power comes from – it's not what he says, but the way he looks at you when he says it, as if to say, *You're the only one who understands, the only one who **really** understands.*

311

And when you heard that, or saw it, or sensed it, well, it was almost like falling in love.

Which wouldn't be hard. Solange was the most attractive man Susannah had ever seen – not that he was handsome, really. Not in the ordinary sense of the word. He was saved from being 'handsome' by his nose, which had long ago been broken, and never reset. The result was an eagle's beak that, with his eyes, gave his face a predatory cast, even when he was laughing.

And there was the Voice. As deep as a mine, it was lightly accented and cadenced in a way that was strangely compelling. Watching him talk, listening to him speak, feeling him with her eyes, Susannah knew that she was in the presence of a great man. Or a swarm of great men. At one time or another, the newspapers had compared him to Hitler and the Pied Piper, John Muir and Koot Houmi (whoever *that* was – she meant to look it up).

And the others shared her feelings. Like her, they were enraptured by Solange (and just a little afraid of him).

There were fifteen of them on the terrace, in addition to little Stephen, Susannah, and their guru. Each of them was 'on staff' which meant that they lived their lives entirely within the orbit of the organization. At one time or another, all of them had sailed on the *Crystal Dragon*, and since then, they'd shared meals and beds, safe houses and codes, secrets and felonies. They were full-time communards, and they were everything to one another – family, lovers, shipmates, friends. They had no one but themselves, and no possessions but those that they held in common. Even their pasts were not their own, for each of them shared the same symbolic birthday – which was the date they'd come 'on staff.'

While her baby sucked at her breast, Susannah's eyes drifted from one person to another. With the exception of herself and one other person, she saw, each of them was a divisional director, or a deputy.

Within the Temple, these people were legends, and Susannah knew almost all of them. The emaciated man with tobacco-stained fingers was Saul, who ran the division in which she herself worked, the Office of Special Affairs. Sitting on either side of him were his deputies – Antonio, Belinda, and Jane – who were in charge of Research, Operations, and Security.

Veroushka, who was said to be Solange's mistress and who was so sexy that Tommy said he could 'smell her across the room,' was responsible for Recruitment.

In addition to Veroushka and the Special Affairs crew, there were the directors and deputy directors of Banking and Communications, as well as the heads of administration, Technical Services, and Litigation. Susannah knew who they were, but not their names, or not all of them, anyway.

And there was one person she didn't know at all, a Jap or something, who clearly didn't belong. Dressed in a dark suit, white shirt and tie, he stood apart from the others, silently observing.

'What about the parents?' Solange asked.

Belinda turned to a weedy young man who was sitting nearby with his back against the wall, looking bored. 'Fred?'

'They know he's here,' the lawyer said, 'but there's nothing they can do about it. He doesn't have to see them, he doesn't have to talk to them. He's twenty-three. Besides, I've got an affidavit from him, saying everything's fine – or I will, anyway, as soon as I can get it typed up.'

'And you think he'll sign that?'

'He *signed* it five years ago, when he came on staff. Everybody signed one. More than one! Now, we just have to fill in the date and decide what it *says*.'

'Okay!' Solange said, clapping his hands together and turning on his heel. 'Who's next? Avram! What can you tell us?'

The chief of the Temple's Technical Services division was a wall-eyed Russian refugee with a bad case of psoriasis. Cleaning his bifocals with the hem of his shirt, he cleared his throat and glanced myopically in Solange's direction. Then he smiled. 'We're ready to go,' he said.

Solange regarded him with surprise. 'You're kidding.'

'No. Though, if you don't mind, I must tell you: this was not an easy thing. We've worked around the clock for nearly eight months – on this and nothing else. We've had temperature problems. We've had problems of competence and discipline with one or two of the staff. And the vaccine!' He paused and peered at each of the people on the terrace. 'Do you have any idea how hard it is to buy twenty thousand fertilized eggs without attracting attention from the FDA?'

Solange and the others laughed, and Avram smiled.

'But . . . yes!' he concluded. 'We can begin vaccinating tomorrow. Whenever you like.'

Solange closed his eyes for a moment. 'And the Lady?' he asked.

Avram returned the glasses to his nose and blinked twice as his eyes snapped into focus. 'The Lady is stronger than ever,' he said. 'And replicating nicely.'

'You say she's "stronger than ever." This is a *theory* you have.'

Avram shook his head. 'No. This is a fact.'

'But how can you know that?'

'Because we've run tests – not in the field, but in the lab. And they're consistent. We've amplified the mortality rate by a factor of five.'

'How?'

Avram cocked his head and peered at Solange. 'You want a technical explanation?'

'Just tell me,' Solange ordered.

Avram shrugged. 'We mapped the genome in October. Ever since then, we've been trying to find a way to – how should I say it? – a way to *stealth* the virus so it's invisible, or almost invisible, to the immune system.'

'And?'

'We succeeded.'

'But how?'

Avram sighed, proud of his accomplishment but resenting the need to explain it to laymen. 'Trial and error,' he said. 'We found that by removing a particular segment of DNA, we could make the virus secrete a material that masks its immunogens, hiding it from the body's B-cells. It's like the virus is coated in Teflon. The sialic acid receptors can't bond to it, and without that happening, there's no immune response. So half the time, the virus proceeds unchecked.'

'Which makes the mortality rate –'

'About fifty-five percent.'

No one said anything for a long moment. Finally, Solange exclaimed, 'Okay! So we begin vaccinating tomorrow. Everyone in the compound, eh?'

Avram nodded. 'I'll arrange it,' he said.

Solange tossed his head, flicking the hair out of his eyes. 'And Mr. Kim?' he asked, putting his hands together in a prayerful gesture and bowing toward the Asian man with exaggerated ceremony.

'I can have a package for him in two days,' Avram replied, scratching his neck.

'Okay,' Solange said with a wild grin. 'Is that okay with you, Mr. Kim?'

The Korean looked at him blankly, not understanding a word.

'Two days,' Solange said, speaking slowly and holding two fingers in the air. 'Then . . .' His hand dipped, and soared. *'Pyongyang.'*

Kim smiled his understanding and nodded happily.

Veroushka raised a hand, and Solange acknowledged her. 'What about the people we have abroad?' she asked. 'I've got recruiters in Russia, Israel, France – one or two other places. I'm talking about staff people. What do we do? Do we bring them home?'

Before Solange could say anything, Belinda answered her. 'It's cheaper if we go to them. If you'll get me a list of who's where, I can have a courier in the air – same day. We can get them all vaccinated within a week.'

Veroushka frowned. 'I was thinking . . . maybe we should bring them home. I mean, how will you get through Customs?'

'We'll get a notarized letter for the courier, saying she has diabetes,' Belinda replied. 'We'll put the vaccine in insulin ampoules. I don't think anyone will bother her.'

'Okay,' Solange said, 'let's go to the next item on the agenda.' With a smile, he turned toward Susannah and held out his hand for her to get up. 'Susannah?'

She thought her heart would stop. Little Stephen pulled his head away from her breast and, for a moment, it seemed as if he were about to cry. Handing him to Belinda, she got to her feet and adjusted her blouse.

'My God, you're something!' Solange said. 'Look at you! You're *beautiful.*'

Susannah's cheeks burned and she lowered her eyes.

'Saul – why didn't you tell me she looked like this, eh? What do I have an intelligence service for, if you keep secrets like this from me?' He put his left arm around her shoulders and pulled her to him.

'I sent you the reports,' Saul said with a smile. 'Belinda signed off on them.'

'Okay,' Solange said. 'But *reports* – next time, I want a picture, too. But listen: I've read the reports, and I know what she's done. And I tell you, I'm going to change this girl's name to "Bond." Okay?! Susannah Bond. Is that okay with you, *cher*?'

Susannah nodded, embarrassed by all the eyes that were on her, and thrilled to have Solange's arm around her.

'I'm telling you,' he went on, with his soft accent, 'this girl has no holdback. If I told you what she's done, I'd have to kill you!' He laughed, and the others joined in. 'I'm not kidding. It scares even me!'

More laughter.

'*But* . . .' He threw the word into the air like a grenade. 'There is a problem.'

Susannah's heart stopped for the second time in as many minutes. 'Wh-What problem?' she asked, looking up at Solange.

He shook his head regretfully. 'The little boy,' he said.

Suddenly, Susannah knew why she was there, knew what was wrong, knew what she'd done. When you joined the Temple, you gave up having children because people were . . . what was the word Solange used? *Meta-sizing!* They were *metasizing* all over the world. Like roaches. And this was the biggest problem, but . . . 'But –'

'Sshhhh!' Solange whispered, and pulled her to him even more tightly. She hadn't realized how strong he was. 'No excuses. I told you, *cher*: you're a hero! You'll always be a hero – so don't fuck it up with a lot of bullshit. Okay?'

She nodded.

Removing his arm from around her shoulders, he walked over to a sort of wood box that Susannah hadn't noticed before. Lifting its lid, he reached inside and withdrew a handful of transparent, plastic garbage bags. One by one he passed them out to the people sitting on the terrace.

Without thinking, Susannah reached for a bag, but Solange shook his head. 'Not for you, *cher*. For them.'

Crossing the flagstones to Belinda, he lifted Stephen by the arm, shook out one of the bags, and put the baby inside. Then he spun the bag in his hand and knotted it off at the top. 'Take it,' he said, and gave it to Belinda.

Susannah couldn't believe it. She was speechless as Stephen's muffled cries seeped through the bag. She could see him in there, thrashing around, raising the temperature, turning the bag's transparent skin opaque. Her knees buckled, but Solange caught her by the arm and steadied her.

'You have to be strong,' he said. 'For the little boy – it's important, *cher*.' Then he turned to the others. 'Okay,' Solange said. 'Everyone except Susannah and Mr. Kim.'

One by one her friends put their heads into the plastic bags and tied them off at the throat. Horrified, Susannah watched the bags puff in and out, contracting around their cheeks and noses, then pushing out again.

Solange returned to the wood box and reached inside a second time, returning with two pairs of boxing gloves. Tossing a pair to Susannah, he gestured for her to put them on, and did the same himself.

'It's a complicated problem,' Solange said as he worked his hands into the gloves. 'Earth, she is the mother – sacred. Just as life is. This is our religion. This is what we know. But we know, too, that we're killing her – you and me – we're killing her, and we're killing her children – the millions of species she generates. (Don't worry about making a knot, *cher*. Just get your hands in them.) We've punched holes in the atmosphere, poisoned the groundwater, fouled the soil, laid waste to the forests. Now, with these bags, maybe you can understand how the earth feels, what it's like to be smothered in plastic, choking on your own gases. Now, when I tell you civilization is murder, maybe you will remember this.' Solange clapped his hands together and shuffled his feet.

'Is it okay to let Stephen out?' Susannah asked. 'I don't think this is so good for him.'

'But, *cher,* that's just the point. I don't think he's so good for *us,* do you? Hey – you know as well as I do, what is the problem? It's population, eh? We're too many. And yet, you give us another predator to feed. What were you thinking about? What were you thinking *with?*'

Susannah shook her head. Solange was between her and Stephen now, and she couldn't see him.

'If it were anyone else, *cher,* I'd drown him like a baby cat. As an example. But he's yours, so I tell you what we'll do: we'll box for him! One round. Three minutes. And if you're standing at the end of that, you can rescue him, *cher,* okay? But if you are not, well, then, I think he stays where he is.'

'But – I can't. I don't know *how*!' The panic was surging in her chest.

'I'll teach you. The important thing is to get going, you know? Because until then it's just a waste of time, eh?'

Susannah nodded.

'Okay, so now we start. A little punch. C'mon, *cher*, it's like you said. I don't think this is so good for him.'

She jabbed at him, and Solange stepped gracefully to the side, eyeing his wristwatch. 'Okay, the liftoff. But maybe not so good. Punch *through* me, *cher* not at me! C'mon!'

She knew how to fight. She'd grown up with three brothers, and one of them had been a bully. But she couldn't concentrate on Solange. It was taking all her strength not to rush over to Belinda and –

Stars! Suddenly, she saw stars. Solange snapped her head back with a left jab, then rocked her with a right cross that sent a stream of little lights across her eye. She staggered backward, disbelieving. Her brother had never hit her like that.

'Keep your hands up, *cher,* and close on me. I have too much reach for you. C'mon! You have to think. Get inside my arms.'

She could taste the blood in her mouth, and her eyes stung with tears. *What did he say? About standing? About being on her feet? About Stephen?*

Solange threw a left that she took on the shoulder, and then a right that she avoided, jumping back. 'Good! Two minutes now!'

He said he'd leave him where he was. He said he'd leave him in the bag.

'Not bad,' Solange said, 'but you have to get inside, *cher,* or you'll get hurt. I'm too big for you.'

She was moving in a circle around him, trying to

stay away from his arms but not really succeeding. He kept closing her off, hitting her with a succession of jabs, pounding her upper arms.

'Don't ever run when you're attacked, *cher*. It's an important lesson. When someone comes after you, go after him. Otherwise . . .' He set her up in mid-sentence, popping her with three quick jabs that loosened her teeth and filled her mouth with blood. Then he pivoted at the hips, stepped in and hit her so hard in the stomach that it felt like the butt end of a telephone pole had been driven through her.

Suddenly, she was on her hands and knees, unable to breathe, choking on the pain she felt.

'A minute twenty!' Solange said, standing over her. 'C'mon, Susannah! Get up, or I'll add injury time!'

She still couldn't breathe, but she did what he told her to do: she pushed herself up from the flagstones and, ducking her head, rushed into his arms, tying him up. The move surprised him, and she took advantage of the surprise to hit him twice, catching his jaw the second time.

She held him as tightly as she could, locking her arms around his back. Together, they turned in a circle, and she saw the faces of her friends, pulsing inside the bags, watching her. But something was missing, and as she struggled to hold on to the much stronger Solange, she realized what it was, and it panicked her: little Stephen wasn't crying anymore.

'Thirty seconds, *cher*! Don't let me down!' She clung to him as hard as she could, but he twisted suddenly, rolling away from her. And then he began to head-hunt, popping her in the mouth, the nose, the chin, the cheeks, one jab after another, turning her in a circle around the terrace, showering her eyes with stars, heating her face with punches.

She was barely standing, shocked and swaying on trembling knees. Slowly, she raised a glove to her face and touched her cheek, as if to make sure that her face was still there. And, dazedly, she saw him windmilling his right arm like he was a fast-pitch softball player, or a cartoon boxer getting ready to deliver a punch that would send her into outer space.

Then he laughed and stepped forward, and like a groom at a wedding, he pulled her into his arms and lifted her off the ground. 'Not bad, *cher,* not bad at all.' Then he turned to the others and with a wicked grin shouted, 'What are you doing with bags on your heads? Are you so ugly? Take them off! What silly people!'

And so the bags came off, and everyone was laughing and gasping at the same time, while Mr. Kim applauded and Susannah fell to her knees at little Stephen's side and, frantic and bleeding, tore at the bag with her fingers.

A moment later the boy was in her arms, crying with life, and she was so happy, she burst into tears and, with an adoring look at Solange, thought *Thank you thank you thank you . . .*

26

'I'll be back at five,' Annie said. 'You call me if you start feeling funny – you promise?'

Frank sat in the easy chair in Annie's living room, in front of the television set, which was tuned to the *Today* show. At first it seemed to him that Katie Couric was speaking with Annie's voice, although he knew that wasn't true.

'Frank?'

He frowned and leaned toward the television. Katie spoke but it seemed to take a long time for her words to reach his brain. He felt as if he were watching a foreign movie, with subpar lip-synching.

'Are you all right?'

He turned to Annie. Her words seemed also to arrive in his brain after a small but significant delay, as if she were on the phone from Tokyo.

'Tip-top,' he said, swiveling back toward the television. Katie Couric said something that sounded like 'poppadom crocodile.'

'Maybe I should skip work again. I mean *really*.'

'I'm all right,' Frank said.

And miraculously, he was, having slipped into one of those bubbles of clarity, into the state that he recognized as 'normal.' The doctors assured him that in the next few days the lingering effects of the drugs would fade, 'episodes' would occur with diminishing frequency, and he would find himself feeling better for longer and longer periods. In a few more days he should be fully recovered – although the occasional flashback was possible.

'You're sure?' Annie asked. She was dressed for work in one of her kindergarten-teacher outfits. 'I don't know.' She leaned down to kiss him, and he pulled her into the chair, wincing slightly as he received the weight of her body.

'Don't go,' he said weakly. 'I *do* feel funny.'

She giggled. 'Frank . . .'

'Okay. Get outta here.'

After Frank's doping, he'd ended up in the psych ward at Georgetown. It was a setting where they were equipped to deal with a person in the throes of violent hallucinations. He'd assaulted the paramedics who responded to Annie's panicked call – an incident he remembered as a desperate attempt to get away from men who were holding him down so they could dismember him. When a black-and-white arrived to sort things out, he'd attacked the cops as well, raving all the while. The Saab was towed from the middle of Columbia Road, where it had become the focal point of a memorable traffic jam.

It had taken all day, and all the stubborn insistence Annie could muster, to persuade the authorities that Frank was in fact the *victim* of a crime and not a druggie who ought to be charged with assaulting a police officer. The Saab was impounded, dusted for prints, the leather steering wheel wrap removed and sent in for testing.

The theory was that the drug – which was identified as a military grade psychotropic called BZ – had been administered through the use of DMSO. This was an industrial solvent – sometimes used by athletes as a kind of super liniment – that penetrated directly into the bloodstream and deep tissues. It functioned as a transdermal delivery system for medication – or poison.

After four days on the psych ward, Frank had been moved to a regular room. Two more days, and they let him go, albeit doped up with tranquilizers to take the edge off the lingering effects of what, for the record, was called 'involuntary acute indeterminate drug poisoning.'

His body had suffered the inevitable effects of forcible restraint by four adult men. But at least he wasn't still pissing blood. He shuffled to the bathroom, feeling like an old man, splashed water on his face and took a look. The first day after 'the incident,' his face had resembled meat loaf. Now, the swelling was down – except for the area around one eye, which was still surrounded by puffy tissue that had turned a sort of chartreuse color. With indigo streaks. In the indentation above his chin were the sutures where he'd bitten through his lower lip.

Apart from the face, he had two cracked ribs where one of his rescuers had weighed in with a little too much force. Also, the thumb and middle finger of his right hand – which he'd put through the kitchen window while trying to get away from the paramedics – were stitched, splinted, and bandaged.

As long as he was in one of his 'lucid' periods, he thought, he ought to work. He headed, slowly, up the stairs to Annie's room. Typing or even operating a mouse with his hand like this was slow going, but at least he could do it. His laptop, which Annie had brought over from his apartment, was impossible.

Yesterday, he'd printed out his interview with Tom Deer, and he scanned it as he waited for Annie's computer to boot up.

Deer: You couldn't **threaten** anyone with it. All you could do is use it. And then the birds would take it. You start a herald wave in some place like Peking, and bam! It's all over the map.

Frank drummed his fingers on the table.

Deer: Everyone gets the flu. That's the thing about it. You can't control it. So if you used it as a weapon . . . you'd kill millions.
Deer: Why would anyone want to **do** that?
Deer: You couldn't **stop** it.

Frank remembered Deer joking around at the end of their interview, kidding about the Sioux. Vhat did he say? He frowned, looked through the pages.

Deer: On the other hand, if someone wanted revenge . . . if they were mad at the world . . .

Mad at the world. The more he learned about the Temple of Light or at least its leader – the more apparent it became that the group was definitely 'mad at the world.' And Frank knew that killing 'tens of millions of people' would be grand as far as Solange was concerned. In fact, it would go a long way toward redressing what the Temple's leader called an 'infestation of a species gone amuck.' That species, of course, being humankind.

Annie's computer played the corny little Windows fanfare and Frank logged into Editor, a directory he'd created to hold the word processor he liked to use: XyWrite.

Yesterday he'd spent a couple of hours on the Net, exploring sites related to the Temple of Light. And he'd summarized what he found in a file called *Overview*.

Temple/Solange

Le Monde: Temple of Light founded Lausanne in early seventies. Original name: Académie des Recherches et de la Connaissance des Hautes Sciences – ARCH. 1979: two of its members firebombed the cathedral at Einsiedeln, protesting the pope's opposition to birth control. 1980: member indicted for murder in drive-by shooting of the director of the Swiss nuclear authority. Other incidents included violent attacks on environmental organizations that Solange said were 'insufficiently militant.' Following suspicious death of a liberal politician who'd pronounced Solange 'a bacillus of hatred within the Green movement,' ARCH and its leader disappeared from public view.

Two years later the organization reemerged in San Francisco as the Temple of Light, a newly incorporated 'religion' guided by Luc Solange.

According to *U.S. News & World Report:* Solange 'served up a weird mix of mysticism and "deep ecology" to a following that was remarkably well-educated.' Temple recruiters were 'particularly active on the science and engineering campuses of some of America's best universities.'

Under the heading 'Temple Money,' he detailed how the Temple's recruitment of scientists had paid off, both through its line of Eco-Vita products and through the substantial royalties derived from Temple patents. He noted that the Temple's most lucrative patents, worth about $10 million a year, were micro-encapsulation techniques leased to pharmaceutical concerns. He quoted Annie:

Adair (5-12-98): 'Basically, microencapsulation encloses very small particles in self-decaying protective sheaths, enabling biological agents to survive in conditions – such as stomach acid or high temperatures – that would otherwise kill them.'

He yawned, and frowned. His concentration was for shit; it faded in and out like a weak cellular telephone signal. *Stern*, he thought. He ought to get in touch with Stern.

And, in fact, he'd tried. He'd called him three times, but so far Stern had not returned the calls. He ought to check him. After all, it had been outside the grad student's apartment that he'd been drugged, so the girl who did it must have known who he was talking to.

But he didn't want to drive over there now. He was too tired, and he was finding it impossible to concentrate. He'd check on Stern tomorrow, or the day after, and make sure he was okay.

The police had been finished with the car for three or four days now, and yesterday he'd been called and told to retrieve it from the impoundment lot. Starting Monday, the clerk told him, he'd be charged twenty bucks a day for storage. There was also the towing fee. He couldn't believe it. It was like being raped a second time.

On Thursday his eye was almost normal-looking, and the stitches in his lip were out. No longer a danger to himself or others, he'd bailed the Saab out.

When Annie went to Atlanta for an annual

gathering of influenza specialists, which she called 'the flu powwow,' it seemed awkward – staying in her apartment without her – so he moved back to his own place. Indu had never really warmed up to him. In Annie's opinion, this was probably because the second night Frank had stayed at the apartment, just back from the hospital, he'd wandered into Indu's room by mistake and climbed into bed with her.

How he ended up in *Annie's* bed, how they had become lovers – this event was lost somewhere in the fog bank of his memory, where it might well remain forever. Sometimes he caught a glimpse of it, a shudder of memory. Once or twice he had a flash of her concerned face, leaning over him, and when he spoke her name, 'Annie,' her face lighting up in a sudden flare of joy. And then he could see her bending over, tenderly pressing a damp towel to his forehead, and remember her sliding into bed next to him, her warm body stretched out along the length of him. And then the memory would turn gauzy and dissolve. Twice she'd referred to their 'first time,' once with a happy, starry look in her eyes, the second time with a lascivious giggle. He just smiled, because it clearly wouldn't do to *ask*. Besides, it was kind of fun – if distracting – to imagine . . . In bed, Annie was surprisingly uninhibited and passionate, or at least as passionate as his injuries allowed.

Stern still hadn't returned his messages, so on his way back from the impoundment lot, Frank drove to the grad student's apartment.

And though he wasn't to be found at home, neither was there any evidence that he was missing. No piles of newspapers or mail. He knocked on a neighbor's door.

A skinny black man wearing wire-rimmed glasses answered. No, he said, he hadn't seen Stern. 'Must be outta town, because I don't hear any music. He *likes* his music, I can tell you. Likes it *too* much, in my opinion.'

Frank pressed him. 'Does he ever, I don't know, ask you to water his plants, take in his mail or anything?'

Stern's neighbor stared at him. 'Ben doesn't have any plants. He's not the plant type. I told you: he's the music type. I don't know about the mail. I think he has a post office box somewhere.' He peered at Frank. 'How well are you knowing Ben?'

'Not well at all,' Frank conceded.

The slender man made a spiral motion by his temple. 'Ben's a little *unusual,*' he said.

When he got home, he found a message from Annie waiting for him on his voice mail.

'Hi, Frank, I'm down here in Atlanta.' Pause. 'I'm calling you because . . . something weird is happening,' she continued in an urgent voice. 'And I think it might . . . Anyway, there've been these strange outbreaks of flu in different parts of the country – strange because it's the wrong time of the year for it, you know? I didn't think too much about it until I got down here. But it's an* archival *flu –*' She hesitated. '*What I mean by that is . . ., oh, I wish you were* there, *I hate talking to machines. Anyway, the thing is, what's happened* can't *be a natural occurrence, because –*' And here the machine cut her off.

The second message began: '*The thing is, there's no way this flu could occur in four separate places! And there's something else . . .*' She took a deep breath, and sighed. '*This is too frustrating. I'll be back tomorrow. We can talk then.*'

Frank played the messages again, and frowned. what the hell was an 'archival flu'?

He found her at home at one o'clock the next afternoon. 'I'm on the phone,' she said, rushing back to the kitchen. He followed her. 'Take a look at those,' she said with her hand over the telephone, gesturing toward some papers on the kitchen table. 'Not yet,' she said, speaking into the receiver again. 'I'm heading over to the lab as soon as I catch my breath.'

The papers turned out to be two issues of something called *MMWR*, which was put out by the Centers for Disease Control. The acronym, Frank saw, stood for *Morbidity and Mortality Weekly Report*.

The headline of the lead segment, under the banner 'Epidemiologic Notes and Reports,' read:

INFLUENZA A OUTBREAKS

CALIFORNIA – On April 18, the California Department of Health (CDH) initiated an investigation of an outbreak of acute respiratory illness reported by area sentinel physicians, urgent care facilities, and hospital emergency rooms in the Los Angeles metropolitan area. During April 4-11, 1,395 cases were reported, of which 1,011 had a documented temperature of >100 F. (37.8C) and cough. Patients ranged in age from 34 to 99 years. 67 were hospitalized; 9 had radiographic signs of pneumonia. Onset of similar symptoms was reported by 27 of 142 reporting medical care facility staff members. Unusual prolongation of acute phase noted in many patients, along with attenuated recovery phase.

Testing by CDC-supplied reagents of 1997/98 circulating influenza strains failed to produce conclusive identificahon. Amantadine was administered for treatment.

Annie was scribbling on a pad of paper. 'Maybe tonight,' she said. 'If I'm lucky. *Sure,* day or night.'

Frank continued leafing through the *MMWRs,* concentrating on the sections reporting influenza outbreaks. Apart from the outbreak in California, there were similar reports of infection from Washington, D.C.; Madison, Wisconsin; and Daytona Beach, Florida.

'Thanks, Ozzie. Yeah,' Annie said. She hung up and dropped into the chair opposite him, looking very tired. 'What are we going to do?' she asked. 'There's no *medical* solution to this. There's not enough amantadine to protect the population of *Washington,* let alone –'

'What are you talking about?' Frank asked. 'This just looks like a bunch of people who got the flu. And it can't be *our* flu, because they didn't get sick enough. No one *died.* So . . . what's the big deal?'

'You're right. It's not *our* flu. Not yet. But these people that got sick – they didn't just get the *flu,* Frank. First of all, flu cases in April are rare, and in May – the Wisconsin and Florida outbreaks – exceedingly rare. It's the only reason we're even aware of it, frankly. The first outbreak, in L.A. – initially, they didn't even test for flu. If it had occurred a month or two earlier, we wouldn't have a *clue* that this weird flu bug was even out there.'

'What do you mean that they didn't just get the flu?'

'They got an *archival* flu, that's what I was trying to tell you on the telephone.'

'What –'

She was up and pacing. 'I just talked to a friend from CDC. Most of us have access to a genomic database that stores the nucleotide sequences of flu strains – it's how we track what's out there, how we do comparative studies, how we spot new variants. Well, the results from Wisconsin and Florida are in now, and they match what we found out about the bugs in L.A. and D.C. All these people who got sick, Frank – people in four different geographical locations – they got a flu that is genetically identical to a strain called . . .' She paused, to look at the white pad next to the telephone. 'A/Beijing/2/82.' She threw her hands out to the side. 'Well, that just doesn't happen.'

'Why not? What's "A/Beijing –"'

'It's a strain of influenza that was first identified in China. In February, 'eighty-two. And here it is again. But that can't happen, Frank. Influenza is in a constant state of mutation. That's what influenza *does*. It's unstable. It mutates. You don't get *exact replicas* of sixteen-year-old strains.'

'But we did.'

'Down at CDC – this is the mystery du jour. When it was just the outbreak out in L.A., they thought it was an accidental lab release and the epidemiologists were giving all the labs hell, trying to track down the source.'

'What do you mean?'

'Virologists, pharmaceutical labs, epidemiologists, people in the vaccine industry – we all work with old strains of flu sometimes, to study them. Occasionally, there's an accidental release. It's happened. That was the logical explanation for the L.A. outbreak – until the same strain popped up in Washington. And then in Wisconsin. And then in Florida.'

'But what if people infected with the strain in L.A. got on a plane? Wouldn't that explain it?'

'No because the pattern's wrong. If that happened, you'd get little clusters of infection here and there. That probably *has* happened, in fact. But no one's going to notice it because people are not getting terribly sick. And it's not the flu season, so most of the cases will just go down as respiratory infections. But these outbreaks –' She picked up the *MMWRs*. 'None of these was caused by an infected carrier, or even a jumbo jet full of carriers, Look at the numbers from Madison, Wisconsin. You have over twenty-eight hundred cases in a single week. And the onset isn't staggered, it doesn't start with a case or two and build, it's *boom* – all at once. And in Florida there's almost as many and it's the same thing. And then look at these numbers right here, in D.C. There are almost *four thousand cases reported*! My God, it's probably what we had!'

'Is that a lot?'

'Yes it's a lot! It's a hell of a lot. Because it's just the tip of the iceberg. Most people with a mild flu don't even go to the doctor.'

'So what are we talking about?'

'*Tests*!'

'What tests? What do you mean?'

'They're dispersion tests.'

'*What?!*'

She pointed to the *MMWRs*. 'And this is how they found out which method was the most successful. CDC puts this out on the Web, every week. The Temple – they didn't even have to tabulate results. All they had to do was check out the *MMWRs* to see how it went, and which method produced the greatest infection.' She picked up the papers, held them up and rattled them in the air. 'And the winner is: your nation's capital. Washington, D.C.!'

'How would they do that? Disseminate the virus, I mean.'

'There are lots of ways. All you have to do is put it

in the air. You could use a plane, a car – you could throw it off a rooftop.' She sighed. 'All you have to do is get the virus in the air where it will be inhaled.' She took a breath. 'I don't know what to do. Maybe if we go see Gleason –'

'Right. Why does that not inspire confidence? If I remember correctly, the last time we knocked on Mr. Gleason's door, he more or less threatened to charge us with treason.'

'But if we take all the work you've done since then, and these *MMWRs,* and maybe if I talk to Doctor K – and get him to come with us.' She looked at the ceiling. 'I'll show Doctor K the Temple's logo – the horse! He'll remember that from Kopervik. And he was in Atlanta, too. He's as puzzled by these outbreaks as everyone else. If Gleason won't listen to me, maybe he'll listen to Doctor K. Maybe even Benny Stern – he could help explain about the Temple.'

'Stern seems to be out of town.'

'Well, I still think we have to try. With Gleason, I mean.' She looked at her watch. 'I'm going to the lab and look at this sample I brought back.'

'What for?'

'Because there's something funny about it.'

'What do you mean?'

She picked up the *MMWR.* 'Where is it? Here it is.' She read:

'"Unusual prolongation of acute phase noted in many patients, along with attenuated recovery." What they're saying is that a lot of people aren't getting better as fast as they should. The symptoms just *drag on.* So something is making the infection persist, or somehow preventing the immune system from kicking in. It's as if the virus had been camouflaged somehow.'

'Is that possible?'

She squeezed her eyes shut, then opened them again. 'I'm worried that whoever did this has tinkered with the genome in a way that inhibits the immune response. With A/Beijing/2/82, it's no big deal. It was a mild strain. But if they did this to the 1918 flu . .'

'What?'

She stared at him.

'Annie. *What*?'

'Well, you'd kill almost everybody who got it. The only recourse would be global immunization.' There was a beat, and then Annie smiled and waved her hand crazily in the air and started talking too fast. 'I'm probably just a lunatic. Maybe the Beijing strain was a particularly long-lasting flu, and we just don't have enough data about it because it was so mild.' She stopped. 'But I want to take a look – because one thing's for sure.' She slapped the MMWRs. 'These were *tests*!'

'I'll call Gleason,' Frank said.

On the way back to his apartment from Annie's, he stopped at Mixtec and grabbed some lunch. While Annie was at the lab, he'd print out his notes about the Temple. He intended to fashion some concise document about the chain of events and evidence – something even Gleason couldn't ignore.

And if they got nowhere with him, he was thinking maybe they'd go to FEMA. Call Tom Deer. Whatever.

His door was open.

At first he thought maybe he'd forgotten to lock it. And then he went into the room that was both his bedroom and his study. Even then it took him a second to register what was wrong. His keyboard was there, his monitor was there, his printer was there – but the CPU was gone. And so was his laptop. His filing cabinets were empty. His zip drive was gone. There were no diskettes at all, not anywhere – his entire archive was missing.

'Fuck,' he said, and just stood there for several moments, thinking about how much of his *life* was now missing. It wasn't his current work he was worried about – or not much – because most of that would be on the backup diskettes he kept in the refrigerator. It was everything else. His personal letters. His running log. His address book. Tax records.

The rage rose in his chest. It was a primitive, powerful feeling, akin to the way a dog or a wolf might feel on returning to its lair and finding the scent of an interloper. If he were a dog, his hackles would have been up.

Instead, he followed the conditioned response of a citizen of the late twentieth century: he headed for the telephone to complain to the police. Not that it would do any good. It was just what you did, a routine he knew personally because two years ago, his stereo and TV had been ripped off. The call was made, not because the police would find his stolen stuff and punish those who took it. It was made because the insurance company required a police report or it wouldn't pay.

It was only then, as he was reaching for the telephone, that it dawned on him that this wasn't a garden-variety robbery, that the theft had been a theft of *information,* that his television, monitor, stereo, and speakers – none of those had been touched. And in the instant he composed that thought, he knew who was responsible.

It was just then, as he lifted the receiver to call the police, that something slammed into the back of his head, driving him toward the floor. On the way down, his head hit the telephone table and a spray of sparks fanned across his eyes.

A second later the man was on him, and Frank could feel his breath. An arm went around his neck, and there was a whiff of something sickly sweet, a hospital smell that could only be chloroform. A hand went over his mouth, clamping a damp rag to his face.

Frank thrashed. Rolled. Struggled. And, finally, went limp, holding his breath.

He lay that way for what seemed a long time but could only have been a relatively few seconds. His lungs were in a panic, his heart pounding, but he could feel his attacker relaxing, just a little, just enough.

Frank exploded beneath him, driving his head into the man's face, sending him sprawling. Then he lurched to his feet, intending to kick the guy while he was still on the ground. But the man was too quick, and Frank too woozy. The intruder spun away from the kick, rolled and scrambled to his feet.

Frank got a look: black jeans and T-shirt, gingery hair, and a round white face with a bright stain of blood around the mouth and nose. Frank lurched after him, but was slowed by the pain in his ribs, which didn't allow him to straighten up. The man got to the door before him and yanked it open. 'Claude!' he shouted then stepped outside and slammed the door shut.

Frank reached for the doorknob, but it wouldn't turn. His assailant was pulling from the other side and the door wouldn't open, until, an instant later, it exploded inward, driving its sharp edge into Frank's forehead. He reeled backward, and in the wide-open doorway, caught sight of his assailant's bloody face, and behind him, another man, dark and scowling. The stink of chloroform filled the air.

It was fear that drove him forward, but it was football that saved him. He knew how to hit. He saw that round face in the doorway, and the other man's behind it, saw the chloroform rag in his hand – and he put his head down and *drove* into them.

The attack took them by surprise; they were off balance and stumbling backward near the top of the stairs. He kept driving until, in the end, the three of them were tumbling down the stairs in a pained tangle of knocked heads and flailing limbs.

Then a quavering voice threaded itself into the din: 'Hey! What the hell is going on here?'

Frank's assailants were on their feet by the time they hit the ground floor. They launched themselves at the front door, bouncing Carlos – his neighbor – out of the way and sending his groceries flying. 'Hey!' he squeaked.

Frank pulled himself up by the banister and rushed out into the street, but it was too late. He watched the men jump into a black van, double-parked halfway up the block. He started after them, hoping he could get close enough to catch the license number, when the truck pulled out and accelerated.

'Jesus Christ,' he moaned. This was getting painful.

Carlos came up alongside, holding a head of lettuce and breathing hard. 'Frank,' he said in a beseeching tone, 'what is going *on?*'

27

Ozzie Vilas had done most of the prep work at CDC, and Annie was glad he had.

An electron microscope scans a field of approximately one millionth of a millimeter. Viruses are exceedingly small – several million virions could fit inside a comma. But in tissue or blood, they were dispersed, and moreover, the number present depended on the status of the infection. In order to be able to find virus to look at, without a frustrating and lengthy search, viral samples were cultured, often in layers of green monkey kidney cells and then concentrated through the use of high-speed centrifuges. Sometimes, virus was replicated through a technology called PCR.

The viral sample Ozzie provided to herself and Dr. Kicklighter had already been concentrated and then pelletized, the viral material dispersed within a resin. The resulting tiny, hard pellets were put in tubes, the tubes packed in cotton, and encased inside a metal container with the biohazard flower imprinted on the exterior.

NIH had any number of electron microscopists who were skilled at preparing grids and searching for pathogens. Annie used them extensively, because she was not fond of spending time with the electron microscope looking for viral footprints. The microscope itself was a clunky affair, about the size of an old-fashioned telephone booth, and always housed in its own separate room – which was usually in the basement.

Because of the need for absolute steadiness, the room was heavily insulated and balanced on struts. That's what Annie disliked about it. It was a dead room with the ambience of a bell jar. Spending time in it was like being buried alive.

She stashed her belongings in her office and went through the laborious procedure of dressing to deal with an infectious agent. That done, she put a pellet into place and rotated the diamond blade of the resin machine toward it, shaving off a number of tiny, angstrom-thick slices of the viral pellet. The machine dispensed these onto a pool of liquid. Then came the tricky part – picking up the tiny round 'grid' that would be inserted into the microscope and trying to get one of the viral samples onto it. The 'grid' itself was a tiny disk, an eighth of an inch in diameter, the size of a very small button or pill. It was scored with a viewing matrix. The trick was to grasp the curved lip of this disk with micro-dissection tweezers and 'catch' or 'scoop' one of the floating slices of viral material off the liquid so that the slice adhered properly to the surface of the viewing grid. She stared at the floating slices of virus and looked for one with the glint of gold. The gold ones were the thinnest slices, and therefore the best. The thinner the slice, the more likely you were to isolate a recognizable viral sample from what was always a distracting mess of visual material.

Two samples draped over the lip of the disk and had to be discarded. A third tore when she tried to float it onto the grid. And then, on the brink of success, she started to cough at the worst possible moment, just as she maneuvered the grid under a perfect gold slice. She lost it, of course, and it took three more tries before she got one. God, she was sick of this flu.

And now, she was going to see what it actually looked like. She placed the grid into place in the 'box,' and snapped the box into the microscope and turned it on. It took almost an hour to find what she was looking for and, of course, when she did, and ratcheted up the magnification, she couldn't find it for a while. When she finally located it again, she frowned.

Influenza virus resembles a round ball with a large number of spikes and knobs protruding from its surface. The spikes are the antigens, hemagglutinin and neuraminidase, and they grab onto the mucous membranes of the respiratory tract. In each strain of virus, the spikes are shaped differently. When the immune system is alert to a particular strain through previous infection or vaccination, the body's immuno-globulin recognizes the spikes, and responds to their presence by locking onto them and neutralizing them. But in the case of the viral sample she was looking at, the spikes looked . . . strange. They were unlike any influenza sample she'd ever seen. They seemed almost *slimy* – sort of gooey and indistinct, as if the surface proteins were covered by a viscous gel.

She frowned. Often, you couldn't really be sure of what you were looking at when on the microscope itself. Things tended to become clearer when you made a print. She went through the process of producing a micrograph. Some of the newer machines were hooked up to computers, allowing the operator to simply store a series of images – which could then be colorized and put through various visual manipulations that clarified the images. Time on those machines was strictly rationed, apportioned like viewing time on a famous telescope. Annie was working with an old machine. It was fitted out so that it made a glass plate negative, which could be exposed through an enlarger just like any other photographic negative. She made several positive prints – certain the CDC would want a copy – hung most of them to dry, and took one of the wet prints out to her office. She wanted to compare it with existing micrographs of A/Beijing/2/82 – which were on a computer database.

She logged onto the central NIH database and maneuvered her way into the visual archive of influenza virus samples. She tapped in the search term, then waited for the graphic display to fill in. This took a maddening amount of time because her computer was old and poky. When A/Beijing/2/82 was there on the screen in front her, she shook her head. It was identical to the image on her micrograph and yet – it was not the same. The image on the screen was sharp and clear, without the indistinct look of its counterpart. Yet their *structure* was the same. She didn't get it. She tapped a few keys and made a print of the computer sample.

Ozzie had also given her slides from immuno-fluorescence tests on the virus. This was the way most strains of influenza were identified. Samples were subjected to antibodies from known strains that had been tagged with radioactive markers that made them fluorescent. Under a fluorescent microscope, when the antibodies from a particular strain encountered antigens of the same strain, the virus lit up brilliantly, bright as neon.

In this case, what she saw was very strange. A few viral particles lit up, but with a dim glow, not the bright radiance that was normal. There should also have been many, many more viral particles than she was seeing in the faint scatter of light. It was as if some of the virus was invisible to the antibodies, and even when it was visible, the marker effect was tremendously diminished.

She practically ran to Doctor K's office, where they talked, and then took turns peering at Ozzie's samples under the fluorescent microscope. Doctor K wanted to make sure that the initial slide wasn't anomalous. But there they were again – not a dense cloud of bright stars, but a scattering of dim ones.

'I'll be damned,' he said. 'It's as if the receptors are somehow inhibited from locking onto the antigens.'

It was the known antibodies that were tagged; the visible fluorescent reaction occurred when they found the viral antigens they were specific for and locked onto them. In this case, the antigens were there, all right, but the antibodies were not finding them.

'Right,' Annie said, 'and you know, I think it's that . . . goo. It repels the B-cells.'

'No wonder people are staying sick for so long. And you think someone's spliced it to repress immune response?'

'Well, if not to repress, at least to delay the response. I mean we are seeing those dim reactions, so maybe the B-cells eventually get the picture.'

'Right.'

'It reminds me of measles,' Annie said suddenly. Measles was another RNA virus structurally similar to influenza. And like the influenza strain they were looking at, the measles virus interfered with B lymphocyte production of immunoglobulin.

By the time she and Doctor K finished a conference call with Ozzie and others at CDC, Annie was exhausted. She couldn't stop yawning. Now she understood why this flu was dragging on like it was. With her own immune response repressed, she was like an AIDS patient.

344

Dr. Kicklighter was still on the phone when Annie finally packed up her briefcase. She knocked on his doorjamb and gave him a little wave before she headed out. He returned the wave without looking at her. The two of them had talked about the possibility that he might be needed to speak to the FBI, and he had agreed – if somewhat reluctantly. He was more excited about the scientific implications of the altered virus than he was concerned about what it might mean vis-à-vis the cult's plans for the Spanish flu.

'It's amazing,' she heard him say into the receiver. 'It's as if the virus is exuding Teflon, you know? I'd love to know how it was done, because if you could turn this inside out, and *enhance* the immune response . . .'

Annie was very tired as she walked to her car, and despite the warm night, she shivered with cold. Cones of light shone down from the mercury vapor lamps. She could hear the surf sounds of traffic from Wisconsin Avenue and the Beltway. Whatever energy she'd had, she'd expended in the lab, and it seemed like a very long trudge through the immense and largely deserted NIH lot. She was relieved when she finally got to her Honda. She just wanted to go home and go to bed.

She was waiting to turn into the main exit lane that would put her on Wisconsin Avenue when the car hit her. Her body jolted forward at the sharp impact. Metal crumpled against metal. The seat belt had a kind of slingshot effect, and when she reached its restraining limit, her body bounced back hard against the seat.

Rear-ended.

Oh . . . *no*, she thought, just what I need. She blew her nose and wearily unfastened her seat belt to get out and take a look. She already knew there was enough damage that she'd have to go through that whole tiresome routine of getting insurance numbers and maybe even waiting for the police.

The young man who'd run into her was already out of his car, looking at her crumpled fender with a heartbroken expression on his face. He had a baseball cap on backward. 'Oh man,' he said, shaking his head sadly. 'My dad's gonna *kill* me.' The fender was tilted and bent. The license plate hung by one corner. Pieces of the shattered taillight lay on the asphalt. 'I'm so sorry, ma'am. I just –' She stood at the juncture of the cars – his big black van looming above her little Civic. The left rear wheel looked to be pinned by the crumpled fender.

He stepped up next to her. 'You reckon we should call the police?'

'I guess,' Annie said.

A U-Haul truck pulled up next to them. A red-haired man leaned out the window. 'You need help out there?'

He didn't wait for a reply, but got out and joined them. 'Whoa,' he said to the kid. 'You really nailed her.'

'Yeah, I –'

And then the van guy threw his arm around her shoulders, crumpling her against his body, and shoved a damp, sweet-smelling rag against her mouth and nose. Wild-eyed, she saw and heard the back door of the U-Haul fly open. Panicked now, she struggled and writhed, but it only took a second and then she was inside the van. And so was someone else. And then the door closed and the lights went off inside her head.

There was a tall cop and a short cop – a Mutt and Jeff combination that made Frank wonder who played the

346

good cop and who played the bad cop when it came time to play those games.

'You got insurance?' Mutt asked. He was looking at the doorjamb, studying the dead bolt.

Frank said that he did.

'In that case, I'd recommend you change the locks. You're gonna be way over the deductible anyway, and most times they cover that. You could do better than this lock.'

He handed Frank a slip of paper with the number of the police report. 'You got any way to find out your serial numbers – I'm talking about the computers – phone 'em on in. Although chances are, you never going to see those babies again. They chop 'em up, just like cars. This time next week, your motherboard's in Hong Kong, your hard drive's in Mexico.' He nodded to his partner and they headed for the door.

'That's *it*?' Carlos said. 'That's all you going to do? You take the fingerprints. You talk to Frank. You ask him what happened. What about me? I want to give a statement. In fact, when these men are ever apprehended, I want to press charges for assault.'

Frank was bored, the cops were bored, but Carlos remained in a state of high excitement.

The tall cop – whom Frank thought of as 'Jeff' – gave Carlos a look. 'Excuse me?'

'I want a police artist involved. I want the description of these men circulated. I, personally, would like to view the lineup when that time comes. I am a corroborative witness.'

Mutt looked at Carlos. 'You watch a lot of television, Mister . . . ?'

'Carlos,' Frank interrupted, 'I think the officers have –'

'*Rubini*,' Carlos said emphatically, ignoring Frank.

'My name is Carlos Rubini. And as far as your resources are concerned, you act like this was a simple burglary, and it was not. It was a *kidnap* attempt. A very serious crime. A *capital* crime, if I'm not mistaken. You have to *do* something. As a citizen, I am not satisfied with your response. Look at this man.'

Carlos jabbed a finger toward Frank. He'd cleaned up, but he looked like he'd been in a brawl. His right eye was fading to black and, on the way down the stairs, he'd ripped open the recently healed stitches in his finger and thumb. That was the biggest problem. He couldn't seem to get it to stop bleeding. The hand was wrapped in a towel, and although this was the third one, it was still soaking through.

The tall cop tossed Frank a 'this guy's a real prize' look. 'Seems to me,' he said, 'Mr. Daly disturbed these dirt-bags in the middle of a burglary. I didn't hear anything about any weapons. So, the way I see it,' the cop continued, 'one man was carrying stolen objects down to the vee-hicle – which, this being Adams-Morgan, and there being a whole line of *other* double-parked vehicles in the way – was half a block away instead of right out front. So, we got Burglar B toting stuff to the car, Burglar A still in here scoping out what else to take – when Mr. Daly comes home. The inside man steps into the closet. I think that's the likely scenario. When Mr. Daly reaches for the telephone to call 911, the guy comes out of the closet. So to speak. Mr. Daly?'

Frank shrugged. 'Sounds about right.'

Carlos frowned and expanded his chest. 'This is *not* right. Why, then, do they take Frank's *papers*?'

The short cop had been talking into a cellular telephone, and when he was finished, he had a suspicious look on his face. 'Desk sergeant says we were out here a few days ago. Something about drugs. That have anything to do with this?'

'"Something about drugs,"' Carlos said indignantly. 'This man is poisoned, he could have been killed, and now I'm hearing *innuendo*.'

Mutt shrugged and said he didn't mean to imply anything.

'I hope not,' Carlos said sharply.

'They take your papers, your computer,' Mutt said. 'You said you're a reporter, right?'

Frank nodded.

'So . . . you working on something . . . might get someone *upset*?'

Frank wanted them to leave. The cops, Carlos, everyone. He wanted to call and see how Annie had made out at the lab, and then he wanted to go to her place and work on the thing he was writing for Gleason. He shook his head. 'No,' he said, 'I'm just working on a story about the flu.'

When the police were gone, Carlos expressed his disappointment in his squeaky, officious voice. 'Really, Frank – you *know* this was not a burglary. I will tell you this: a citizenry gets the government it demands.' He wagged his finger. 'You should not let them get away with their slipshod ways. How will they ever do better?'

Frank tried not to smile. 'I'm sorry, Carlos. And I really appreciate your help. If you hadn't come in just when you did . . . Anyway, I'm just kind of wrecked.'

'I am going to speak to the super about installing a new exterior lock downstairs. Will you support me in this?'

'Absolutely.'

'I don't like it,' Carlos said, 'that someone can just waltz in here,' He gestured to Frank's hand, 'You want me to drive you to the emergency room? I think you should have stitches.'

'That's all right. My girlfriend can take me there later.'

Annie's phone was busy. Frank threw some water on his face and carefully cleaned off the blood with a washcloth. Then he poured half a bottle of hydrogen peroxide over his hand and watched it fizz up into pink froth around the cuts in his finger and thumb. He wrapped them up in gauze and fastened it with adhesive tape.

Annie's phone was still busy, so he headed down the stairs and drove to her place. If she wasn't home, Indu would let him in, and he could wait for her. And when he knocked, it was Indu who answered. She pulled aside the curtain and peered out at him, then quickly unlocked the door.

'Annie's not here, Frank,' she said, her forehead creased into a frown. 'In fact, I'm a little worried. Please,' she added, stepping to the side and pulling the door open. 'Come in.'

'Worried,' he said. 'Why?'

In the hall light, she got a good look at him. 'Oh my goodness, what *happened* to you?'

He ignored that. 'Why are you worried about Annie?'

Indu's smooth brown face knotted up into a puzzled frown. 'The police called about her car.'

'What about her car?'

'They found it in the NIH lot – *abandoned.*'

Frank felt as if the air had gone out of the room. 'Abandoned,' he said.

'Well, they said it had been in a fender bender of some sort. But – Annie – why would she not call a tow

350

truck? She's not going to just leave her car there, Frank. I'm worried that she was hurt, that maybe she's in the hospital.'

'When was this?'

'They called, oh, just half an hour ago.'

He spent the next hour on the phone. First he hit all the hospitals. Annie was not in any emergency room. Then he called the police – D.C., Bethesda, Park Police, Maryland cops. No one had called 911 or the alternative 'nonemergency' number to report the accident. NIH security had spotted the car and reported it to the police.

'I'm really worried, Frank. What if she's – I don't know, wandering around, dazed or something.' She hesitated and brightened. 'Maybe she's at *your* house – you think it's possible?'

He called. No, she wasn't there, but maybe she'd left a message. The phone had been knocked off the hook in the struggle. If she'd called while it was off the hook, she'd have gotten his voice mail. He called it, tapping in the number for his mailbox. The neutral female voice informed him that he had three messages. The first two were from Annie – her flipped-out calls from Atlanta, raving about archival flu and tests. He'd forgotten to delete them.

The third call was only half an hour old, and it made the hair stand up on the back of his neck when he heard it. The voice was mechanically altered, an electronic drone that surged through the phone with an inhuman timbre.

Missing something?' There was a rat-a-tat-tat laugh. And then, a hideous, mock version of part of Annie's message from the night before: '*Oh, Frank, I wish you were there. I* **hate** *talking to machines.'* The rat-a-tat-tat laugh again. '*So here's the deal. You want to see*

351

your girlfriend again? Take a walk in the light, buddy.'

'What?' Indu said, when he hung up the telephone. 'Did she call? What is it?'

' I think she's been kidnapped.'

'What?' Her big brown eyes were wild under the knotted eyebrows. But he was up and on his way out the door. *'Frank!* Where are you going?'

He stopped long enough to ask the terrified Indu to file a missing person's report and ran out to his car. He jumped into the Saab and cranked and cranked, but the engine wouldn't catch. Fuck! In frustration, and forgetting the two injured fingers, he slammed his hand hard against the dashboard, A stab of pain shot through his hand, followed by a deep ache that seemed to pin him against the seat for a second.

And then he was out, and running. The streets of Mount Pleasant and Adams-Morgan were crowded, as always, and he was weaving in and out of alarmed yuppies and puzzled kids and worried-looking women, making deft cuts and swerves and dangerous slashes between moving cars. A panhandler stationed outside the McDonald's put his hand up like a traffic cop. 'Hey!'

He was obsessed with the idea that he had to get to his phone before anyone else called to leave a message. The thing was, he knew the fuckhead who'd left the message would certainly have blocked Caller ID using *67. But Frank had a voice-mail system called Omnipoint, which circumvented the blocking device and displayed the number of the last caller. Thank God he'd hung up before the system answered when he'd called from Annie's. He pounded up his stairs, and there it was. A 914 exchange.

He headed for his computer, hoping to check the number on his reverse directory. And then he remembered that he didn't *have* a computer.

Carlos hesitated before letting Frank in, but then grudgingly opened the door. The thing was, Carlos was the ultimate computer geek, with the newest and best of everything, and within two minutes he'd chased down the number for Frank. 'It is a Poughkeepsie number,' Carlos said in his high-pitched voice. 'In New York. For Martin Kramer Associates. Do you know these people?'

'Yeah,' Frank said. 'I know him.' Frank flashed back to their lunch at Fernacci's. *Coupla squirrels*, Kramer said. *Bigots. Paranoid. Looking under the rugs for land mines.*

'You want the address?' Carlos asked.

'No thanks,' Frank said. 'I know where he lives.'

28

He thought about calling the feds, but after Waco and Ruby Ridge, the Bureau did not inspire confidence where hostage-rescue operations were involved. He'd try a different tack.

Half an hour later he stapled the JetPak closed. It contained the diskette from his refrigerator, with all the information that he'd compiled about the Temple, the Spanish flu, and Luc Solange. It also held a memo, hastily composed on Carlos's computer, which sketched out the information *not* on the diskette – up to and including what Annie had said about the *MMWR*s, her guess that the recent outbreaks were dispersal tests, her kidnapping, and his own plans. Knowing Gleason's relentless skepticism, he included his voice-mail codes so the FBI agent could listen to the threatening message from the Temple, which he had not deleted.

Carlos (the Citizen) Rubini solemnly promised to deliver the package to Gleason's office at Buzzard Point the following morning. Carlos was starry-eyed with excitement at Frank's insistence that the less he knew, the safer he would be. Carlos was to insist that Gleason himself should come down to fetch the JetPak. If Gleason was not there, Carlos would say that it was a matter of urgency, a national security matter, and that the JetPak must be delivered to Gleason instantly.

'Don't worry, Frank,' Carlos said, eyes gleaming. 'I will make certain this reaches Mr. Gleason. I *knew* that was not a simple burglary. I was not fooled.'

With his fallback position taken care of, Frank thought about going across the border to Virginia and buying a gun. But then he discarded the idea. A gun might be useful, but only if he had a functioning right hand. Just driving was going to be enough of a challenge.

And as for driving, he decided not to screw around with the Saab. What if it crapped out on him somewhere along the way? Besides, an automatic would be easier to handle. So he grabbed a taxi to National, rented a car from Budget, put his head down and drove. North.

By the time he hit Delaware, a hard rain was pounding the windshield. The side windows kept fogging up. The car was hydroplaning. He was propelled by an irrational sense that as long as he pursued Annie, as long as he was intent on her rescue, she'd be okay. It was magical thinking, but it was what kept him going, speeding steadily north in the rain.

He fought off images of what might be happening to her. He fought off Benny Stern's voice in his head. *You know the one thing they never did: they never tried to kill me. But they would have if I'd been anything more than a nuisance.* He played music – loud – and concentrated on driving. Every now and then a big semi rocked by, smashing the windshield with water, obliterating his vision. Because it was a distraction and took him away from his worries, he almost enjoyed his own terror at these moments: he was sightless, in a tunnel of noise, hurtling through the rain.

He pulled into Lake Placid at about four A.M. It had

finally stopped raining. Then he was on the other side of town, driving through the country, passing only a few houses. The older ones stood close to the road; the newer ones were set back at the end of long driveways. Once his headlights caught a clutch of deer in a field, just by the edge of the road. They stood motionless as he approached, and then they bolted into the darkness. There were no lights, anywhere, in any of the houses. Not a porch light, not the blue shimmer of a television, nothing. The rain had stopped and the landscape glowed under a fat moon that cast a ghostly radiance on the rolling terrain. Once out of town, he didn't pass a single car. The emptiness pressed down on him. I'm alone in the world, he thought. Everyone else is dead.

He passed the white clapboard house that he remembered from his visit to the Temple. Behind it he saw the gates to the compound. He pulled the car off the road, humping it up on a grassy shoulder. He knew that gates and a guardhouse controlled the road leading into the compound – so that vehicular traffic in and out was clearly monitored – but he hadn't noticed any kind of wall.

He didn't have even a rudimentary plan. Somewhere, away from the gates, he'd walk into the woods. And then? He didn't know. He'd look for Annie. Find her. Take her home.

He ran alongside the road, moving at a jog, so jazzed on adrenaline and nerves that he could hear the blood thrumming in his ears. He left the road and angled in through the trees. The moonlight was dazzling, the trees silver and black.

It was an old forest, a *groomed* forest, so that given the ambient light and the space between the trees, walking was easy. The ground was carpeted with needles, spongy and soft underfoot. It was so quiet he could hear the whirs and chirps of insects, or maybe they were birds, and every now and then the skitter of an animal.

After a while the woods got thicker and darker. It was slow going, moving by touch, and the branches of the trees slapped at him, reaching out through the dark, grabbing at his face with stiff fingers. And then, suddenly, he was in a clearing, and not just a clearing, but a parking lot. Gravel crunched under his feet. The moon was down, but in the afterglow he saw cars, drained of color by the thin light, neatly arrayed against the sides of the square. They had a malevolent, hard-shelled look, like ranks of black beetles. He looked at his watch. The luminous dial read 5:10. Beyond the parking lot he saw a gravel path, which disappeared into the trees.

He took the path and emerged a little while later in another clearing. This time, a meadow. Off to the right he could detect a slight brightening in the sky, the faintest apricot glow that must be either the first glimmer of dawn or the wash of light pollution from a settlement of some sort. He passed a pond and tennis courts. Then buildings – a cluster of white cottages, and past them, some larger shapes which, when he got closer, turned out to be old brick dormitories.

A campus. He almost said the word aloud, he was so relieved to get a fix on what in the dark had seemed so mysterious. *A campus:* that snapped it into focus, that brought it down to size. Now he remembered Stern talking about it. An old private school, something like that. He was walking uphill now, where the path widened into a service road. When he crested the hill, he almost gasped at the sight of a complex of modern glass and steel structures: a factory, a warehouse, office-type buildings. It was so sleek, so *big*, so clean and expensive-looking, a little industrial park hidden away in the woods. And from the complex came a set of noises different from the sounds in the woods: an automated hum, a faint mechanical chatter. Parts of the complex were lighted, operating – the whole area exuded a kind of cool, fluorescent glow. Roads ran between the buildings. A couple of large trucks were backed up to the bay of the warehouse, their white sides emblazoned with a setting sun and the words ECO-VITA.

So far he had not seen a single human being, but he sensed that they were present, working inside this complex. *Making virus?* Despite Tom Deer's assertion that making virus was about as difficult as whipping up a vat of home brew, he found that he'd been harboring a secret hope that the Temple would not be up to the task, that they'd screw it up. Seeing the size and scope of the operation here, that hope died.

Beyond the steel and glass buildings, Frank could see another stand of trees. And beyond that, perched high on the hill, with old-fashioned globe lights marking the winding drive that led up to it, stood a large house. A mansion.

Chez Solange.

He wanted to skirt the buildings, and to do that he was forced to sidetrack, back into the woods. By the time he'd angled around, the sky had brightened considerably. He was able to move faster, so that he was soon next to the woods that stood between the factory complex and the mansion. This was an old forest of tiger-tail spruce, each tree trunk as straight as a pencil. Here, close to the mansion, the lower branches of the trees had been pruned away so it was possible to walk beneath the canopy. There was no deadwood anywhere; it was maintained like parkland.

Frank leaned against a tree to catch his breath.

A whirring sound made him look up. It was a sound he'd heard often as he made his way through the compound, a bird, a bug, one of the night sounds. So his glance was instinctual. He didn't really expect to see anything. But he did.

And what he saw almost made his heart stop. It was a tiny red light attached to a surveillance camera. The camera swiveled as he looked at it, a mechanical adjustment of angle. It swept right with a tiny whir and then stopped, adjusted, swept left.

His heart sank.

He wasn't sure if the machines were infrared sensors or surveillance cameras, but he knew that the whirring sound had been with him all along. He'd been monitored ever since he entered the compound.

Still, surveillance cameras didn't mean a thing if no one was paying attention. Besides, he sure as hell wasn't going back to the car. He was going to find Annie and get her out of this. There had to be a way.

He'd planned to stay clear of the mansion's manicured grounds, its carefully lighted and landscaped drive. He'd planned to keep to the edge of the woods, where the light was better, and make his way just inside the perimeter of the trees. Loop up behind the mansion. Have a look-see.

Instead, he found himself standing in a floodlight, bathed in its hard brilliance, blinded. A woman's voice said, 'Step into the clearing, please, and keep your hands visible.'

He was shackled, hands and feet, and dumped into a small room that had nothing in it save a recessed light in the ceiling and a toilet bowl in the corner. He was allowed that glimpse and then the light was turned off.

It was impossible to say *how* long he was in the room, because he had no way to gauge the passing of time. He thought it was at least twenty-four hours, but who knew? The faint rim of light around the door never varied in its intensity. Certainly, he was in the room long enough to get very hungry and thirsty. Long enough so he dozed off several times, each time waking in a sort of disoriented stupor that began to seem preferable to full consciousness. Long enough so he began to worry that either he'd been forgotten or, worse, left in the room to die.

And then the door opened and out of the dazzle stepped two armed men. They gave him water, and then took him to another room, this one far different.

'Can I offer you some refreshment?' Solange asked. 'You look as if you could use a little something.'

They sat across from one another, at an oak library table set atop a fine old Bokhara, in a room that was a masterpiece of burnished woodwork. It had an elaborate coffered ceiling, floor-to-ceiling bookcases, rolling library ladders, one wall of low cabinets topped by a bank of mullioned windows. Beneath an intricately carved mantel, a fire snapped cheerfully. There were two doors into the room, fan-shaped windows above, mullioned side windows in amber glass. Flanking each door were a man and a woman, each dressed in blue jeans and a white shirt. They held what looked to Frank like Ingram submachine guns. These were small weapons, black, compact, efficient-looking. None of the guards had so much as looked at him. They were as impassive as the Beefeaters stationed in front of Buckingham Palace.

Frank had been in the room for more than an hour, trussed to a chair. Finally, Solange had arrived, and sat down.

'Where's Annie?' he asked.

Solange leaned back in his chair, tilting on two legs, something Frank was unable to do. His hands were free, but his legs were bent back at the knee, secured to the chair legs with industrial fasteners – thick-ridged plastic strips that had self-locking buckles. He was tied to the chair in such a way that his quadriceps were pulled as tight as iron bands. The result was that he leaned forward slightly all the time, trying to ease the pressure. Before Solange's arrival, the chair had been in the middle of the room and Frank had been compelled to perform a continual, delicate balancing act. On the one hand, if he didn't lean forward, the pain in his thighs became agonizing. On the other hand, if he leaned too far forward, the chair would clearly become unbalanced and he would fall on his face.

At Solange's arrival, the chair was carried to the table – a tremendous relief to Frank because he could lean forward to ease the strain on his legs without worrying about balance.

Between the two men, on the table, sat a tray of cheese and fruit, a decanter of wine, and two empty glasses. Solange poured wine into one glass, swirled it around, sniffed, then finally took a small sip, rolling it around in his mouth. He looked at Frank, a fake frown of concern curling his heavy eyebrows. 'You're sure?' he said. 'This is a really excellent claret.'

'Where is she?' he said.

'I wouldn't turn it down if I were you, Frank,' Solange said. 'Why not enjoy, while you can?'

'Why not go fuck yourself?'

Solange winced, then wagged his head indulgently, as if Frank were a willful toddler. A sip of wine, a sigh.

361

Then he sprang to his feet and strode to the fireplace. He had a predatory, feline walk, way up on the balls of his feet. He removed the fire screen and knelt, expertly rearranging the wood with wrought-iron tools. After a moment, a shower of sparks shot up, and the fire, which had been smoldering, leapt into flames. Solange replaced the tools and the screen and regarded his handiwork. Without turning his head, he raised a summoning hand and one of the guards, a freckle-faced kid so young the Ingram looked like a toy in his hand, approached. Solange said something and the kid left the room.

Solange returned to his place across from Frank and sat down again. He put his wine aside, made a steeple with his hands and rested his chin on them, regarding Frank with a curious gaze.

'You interest me, Frank. Why did you come here? I mean – what were you thinking of? Not that we aren't *grateful,* but . . . really!' His eyes glittered like a predator's.

Frank said nothing.

'Sure about that wine? You might find it relaxing.'

The door opened and Frank turned, hoping to see Annie. But it was a thin, almost cadaverous man who stood in the doorway. Solange went to him and the two men spoke briefly. The thin man left, and Solange returned to his seat. He sat motionless for a few moments, then seemed to make a decision. He drummed his fingers on the table, picked up his wine and tossed it back. 'Now, Frank,' he said, 'I have some questions that I know you don't want to answer, but . . . as you can imagine, there are things I really need to know. For instance, how much of what you've learned have you shared with the FBI? Hmmmm? How much?'

Solange was on his feet now, and pacing, his

extraordinary voice rising. 'Does Gleason know about the dispersal tests? Does he know you're here, you and Dr. Adair?'

Frank looked up.

'Now, if Dr. Adair is to be believed –'

'I'll fucking kill you,' Frank said. 'What did you do with her?'

'*Do with her?* Well, we questioned her, of course. And I have to admit, she had *every* incentive to be truthful. Still, you just never know.' He made a signal with his hand, and the guards came over to Frank. Seconds later he was on his feet, his legs freed, his hands secured behind his back.

Solange popped a grape in his mouth, and stood up. 'Let's go,' he said. 'That's a ten thousand dollar rug, and I don't want to make a mess on it.'

An elevator took them down three floors and then they were walking along a corridor, rough concrete on either side, the floor made of some rubbery, resilient material. Frank's legs had recovered, although they still felt watery and weak. 'This floor is made entirely out of recycled tires,' Solange said. 'It's very durable, and as you can see, pleasant underfoot. Do you realize how many tires there *are* out there? Just mountains of them.'

Out of his fucking mind, Frank thought, trying not to think about what Solange meant about 'making a mess' or what might be at the end of this long corridor. He didn't want to go into a little room with these people.

'As far as recycling is concerned,' Solange went on, 'you can't simply reimburse people for a deposit that they pay at point of purchase – because a certain percentage won't give a damn about that deposit.

Then again, make the deposit high enough to motivate everyone and it becomes punitive to the poor. Nor can you make it expensive for people to *discard* things, like tires. Because they'll just dump *illegally,* won't they?'

'So . . . what?' Frank heard himself asking. 'You make this stuff?' I must be going nuts, Frank thought. What next? A lecture about catalytic converters?

'Oh yes,' Solange replied. 'We pioneered the technique – made the prototype right here. Sold the rights to PetroChem.' He paused. 'I wish we had time for the tour,' he said. 'I'd love to show you the facilities.'

They entered another corridor, and Solange opened a door on the left. A moment later they were in a small room, concrete, with a drain on the floor. Incongruously, in the middle of the room was a black metal-mesh garden table, surrounded by four matching armchairs of the same material. In the corner, a double sink. A garden hose lay coiled on the floor. There was a closed door next to the sink.

The guards pushed Frank into one of the chairs. Solange ran a hand through his hair. Then he gave a sharp nod and one of the guards spoke into a round grill embedded in the wall near the door. A moment later the far door opened and two burly men came in, supporting Annie between them.

'Annie!' Her name came involuntarily out of his mouth.

The figure drooping between the men did not even look up. She was heavily drugged, he saw, as the men led her closer. Her eyes were glassy and unfocused, her feet barely shuffling. They lowered her into the chair and her head lolled onto her chest.

'You drugged her,' Frank said, sounding stupid to himself.

Solange bounced his eyebrows. 'Yes, well. You know how it is.' He tilted his head and pasted a crazy, cartoon smile on his face. 'Sometimes you feel like a fuss,' he sang, in the tune of a candy commercial. 'Sometimes you don't.'

'Should we get the plastic sheeting?' one of the men asked. He set two bottles of Pepsi, a church key, and a cookie tin on the table. Frank stared at the bottles, thinking that Solange was intent on playing the host again, and how very weird that was. They were heavy glass bottles, slightly opaque with the scuff of tiny scratches. Returnable bottles.

'No,' Solange said, leaning against the wall. 'We'll just hose it down when we're done.'

Suddenly, Frank found himself tilted backward in his chair. Then a wet rag was stuffed into his mouth. One of the guards put his finger over the top of the bottle and shook it up. Solange, Frank noticed, was smiling.

The man came up to him and held the bottle under his nose. A moment later a jet of supercarbonated foam slammed through his nostrils and into his sinuses. Frank thrashed uncontrollably as the pain shot through his head and every cell in his body panicked. He was drowning. He was dying. He was suffocating in a rush.

And then the chair was vertical again, and the soda was running out of his nose. He felt drained. Annie was weeping.

'Right to the switchboard!' Solange exclaimed, laughing. 'Pow!' He began to pace, talking in an amiable tone. 'What I like about it, Frank, is –' He pulled on his fingers, each in turn. '– first, it's low tech. Secondly, it doesn't use any resources. Third, its not detectable. Four, inflicts no permanent damage. Five?

You can do it over and over, and it never loses its punch.' His hands fell to his sides and he took a deep breath. 'Now, tell me about Gleason. Does he know you're here? Does he know about the dispersal tests?'

Frank just looked at him.

Solange shrugged, and Frank's chair was tilted back for the second time. The rag went back in his mouth and, once again, his head exploded. Then he was upright again, snuffling, tremors running through the odd body part. He watched his leg spasm – as if it were a frog's leg laying on a lab tray. Galvanic response. Annie's head lolled on her chest, her eyes closed.

'So,' Solange said. 'I was asking about Gleason.'

One of the guards pulled the rag out of his mouth, but Frank said nothing.

'You're a hard case, Frank.' Solange sighed, and nodded to the guards. Frank watched the man shake up the bottle.

Solange held up a hand and inclined his head toward Annie. 'No,' he said. 'Her turn.'

Blood rushed to Frank's head. 'Leave her alone.'

'Ah . . . the gift of speech.' Solange came over to the table and opened the cookie tin. Removing a small, translucent plastic bag, he shook it open. Frank saw the word Safeway.

'A secondary use of the bag,' Solange said. 'This is actually considered better than recycling.'

Out of his fucking mind, Frank thought, watching in horror as one of the guards picked up a small aerosol can. In a single choreographed moment, he sprayed it into Annie's face – as if he were spraying an insect – while Solange pulled the plastic bag over her head, looping the handles around her neck and pulling them tight.

Frank surged to his feet, but was pulled down from

behind and restrained in his chair –

While Annie exploded from her torpor. But with her hands cuffed behind her, she had no way to remove the bag, which deflated and inflated horribly with each frantic sucking breath. She lurched, thrashing her head from one side to another, trying to get the bag off, biting at it, her face flushed with whatever it was that they'd sprayed.

'*Hello,*' Solange said with a chuckle. 'Pepper gas.'

How long this went on – the Pepsi jetting into his sinus cavities, Annie, the bags, the pepper spray – Frank could not have said – although at the end, both of the bottles stood on the table, empty. It could have been ten minutes; it could have been a couple of hours. Pain, as it turned out, was a landscape with its own dimensions, where ordinary rules of duration didn't apply.

He 'talked,' of course, and later wondered why it had taken him so long to do so. But it didn't make any difference. There was always another question, and if Solange was skeptical of an answer, the rag went back in his mouth and the Pepsi shot through his nose.

And then, when Frank had given up hope that this would ever end, Solange stopped it. 'They've had enough,' he said sharply, as if to rebuke the others. He approached Frank and gave his shoulder a squeeze. 'It's over,' he said. 'No more pain. That's it. It's over.'

Frank knew he should have felt revulsion at Solange's touch, but instead he felt *gratitude*. He knew better. But that's what he felt.

'Bring them some clean clothes,' Solange ordered. 'And ask the doc to give them some Xanax or something, just to take the edge off.' And then he was gone.

Half an hour later they were escorted through the halls like two oddly subdued houseguests, to the mansion's former ballroom, a large chamber with a gleaming wooden floor and barrel-vaulted ceiling. The room had been converted into a large office. The walls were arrayed with pie charts, maps, bar graphs, satellite photos. There were desks, computers, telephones, ranks of filing cabinets. The horse logo was on virtually everything.

Frank and Annie, hands secured behind them, were led toward a desk where Solange sat, working on a computer. He did not glance up at their approach. They stood and waited. Above Frank, on the cork-boarded walls, were a series of false-color photographs of what seemed to be wheat fields, shot from above. In each case, a circle had been inscribed on the photograph, a wedge shape marked into the circle. In each case, the wheat seemed afflicted – either diseased or else suffering from drought. The severity of the affliction varied, from a few speckles of brown on a healthy-looking crop to, in another case, a field of wheat that seemed to have collapsed into a dark smudge, as if it had melted. Each bore a date and information scrawled in grease pencil in the photograph's margin. Frank looked at the notations.

Puccina Graminus 272 – 4017/9
Puccina Graminus 181 – 2022/7
Puccina Graminus 101 – 1097/3
Puccina Graminus 56 – 6340/7

Solange finished whatever he was working on and turned off his computer. He glanced up at Frank and Annie, and smiled warmly. 'Ah. Here you are. Looking much better.'

368

'What is Puccina Graminus?' Annie asked. Her voice sounded odd to Frank, somehow robotized. That was the effect of the tranquilizers; he assumed he would sound the same way. Certainly he felt odd, not exactly tranquil, but weirdly disconnected, as if he were pretending to be himself.

'Wheat-stem rust,' Solange said. He gestured at the photographs. 'Those are some early field trials. We're like horse breeders, looking to create the fastest and bestest Puccina Graminus. So far – fifty-six is our Secretariat, but it's early days yet. Apart from the wheat rust, we're also working with various corn blights and rice blast. Those are the major food crops.'

Annie frowned. She tossed a quick look at Frank. Despite her dead voice, despite the clear evidence of her ordeal, he was heartened by the lively awareness in her eyes. Otherwise, she looked as if she'd been stranded on a life raft for several days. Her skin was chapped and reddened, her lips blistered, her eyes limned in red. 'But why?' she said. 'Why are you doing this?'

'To redress the balance,' Solange replied. 'To weigh in on Mother Nature's behalf against a species which has tipped the balance against every other. You're a scientist. You ought to understand. The "green revolution," with its hybrid wheat and disease-resistant corn and rice, supports a population that's laying waste to the planet. We don't need it. And nature doesn't want it.'

'So,' Annie said, 'you create plague and famine.'

Solange didn't answer her. Instead, he looked at his watch and sprang up. 'Time to go,' he said, and the whole strange parade – the shackled Annie and Frank, the silent and ever-present phalanx of guards, followed the ebullient Solange toward the elevator.

'You mentioned famines and plagues?' Solange said. 'But why not? If one man can create a vaccine against influenza, and that's natural, why is it unnatural for another to create a superflu? If we had time, I would love to show you why it's necessary. I could show you the numbers, the projections, the damage that the earth will sustain. Then you'd see that it is necessary to interfere with a species that is metastisizing out of control. You'd see, and you'd join us. And you'd be useful in the labs, I don't doubt that – although,' he frowned, 'I can't really envision a role for Frank. But –' He clapped his hands together. '– we don't have that time.'

Frank's heart started beating faster when they got into an elevator and he saw one of the kids press 3B. It was the floor where they'd been tortured. Indeed, they walked down the same corridor. Annie's footsteps picked up pace as they passed the room, and Frank found himself holding his breath. But Solange kept going past it. They went through two sets of green safety doors with wire mesh in the glass windows before Solange turned and walked down a short corridor. One of the guards pulled a key ring out of his pocket, unlocked two separate dead bolts, and held open the heavy door. Solange stepped in and they followed.

Soon, they found themselves in a square room with cinder-block walls and a raked gravel floor – like a Zen garden's. There were two rattan chairs and, between them, a small rattan table, upon which stood a bud vase holding a single sprig of lilac. One entire wall of the room consisted of a set of white enameled doors, each of which bore a decal of the white horse against the big blue marble of the earth.

'Sit down, please,' Solange said, gesturing at the

chairs. They sat down. At a nod from Solange, the guards unshouldered their weapons and aimed them at Frank and Annie.

'I apologize for the drama,' Solange said, 'but folks do get *upset*. We've learned to anticipate that.'

Annie shot Frank a terrified look, and both of them stared at the guns until Solange noted their focus and rushed to reassure them. 'Oh, don't worry, we'll give you a few hours to meditate, and cleanse your minds, before we put you in Bertha here,' he said, patting the enameled door as if it were the hide of a prized steer. 'She's solved one of our most persistent people problems. I only wish we'd had her for the Bergmans.' He pulled open the doors. The room itself was so spotless and austere that Frank was surprised to see that the interior of the refrigerator, or whatever it was, was quite dirty – streaked with soot and dirt, clumps of what appeared to be ashes on the floor.

Frank struggled to make sense of what Solange had just said. What did he mean, 'for the Bergmans'?

'It's a microwave chamber,' Solange said. 'Basically, it boils away the liquid, and then it's a form of rapid dessication. You end up as a little pile of soot.' He reached up behind him, rubbed his finger against the interior wall, and then showed them a dark and oily smudge. 'Well, this is your friend Ben Stern.'

Even though he felt the drug pressing him down in his seat, even though moving through the air was like moving through water, even with the guns pointed his way, Frank surged to his feet and lunged toward Solange. 'You psycho fuck,' he said.

Solange ducked to the side and swung at him, hard. And again. His blows were powerful, and Frank was helpless, his feet rooted, his hands shackled behind him. Finally, he took a punch in the stomach, which doubled him over. The guards shoved him back into the chair.

Solange was laughing, a rolling chortle, laughing in genuine shoulder-shaking amusement. Finally, he stopped and shook his head. 'I give him enough drugs to stop an *ox* and he comes at me.' He sighed. 'Very impressive.'

'Why are you doing this?' Annie asked. She spoke in the labored cadence of a stroke victim, each word emerging separately.

Solange looked nonplussed. 'I told you. It's a disposal problem.'

'No!' Annie said. 'I mean the Spanish flu. Wheat-stem rust.'

Once again Solange looked startled. 'Because I am the First Horseman. Aren't you paying attention?'

'What are you talking about?' Frank demanded.

Solange looked at him. 'Revelation.' And then he began to speak, but in a different voice, a voice that was powerful and nuanced. A preacher's voice.

'And I saw the Lamb open one of the seals, and I heard the noise of thunder, and one of the four beasts saying, Come and see.

And I saw and beheld a white horse: and he that sat upon him had a bow; and a crown was given unto him: and he went forth conquering.'

The guards were starry-eyed.

'God sends me forth to conquer, to conquer, yes to conquer a species gone amok, spiraling out of control, a species destroying its earthly paradise.'

Frank couldn't help himself. He turned to the

guards. 'You *believe* this shit?' Then he turned back to Solange. 'You're the craziest motherfucker I've ever heard in my life!' And then he started laughing. He couldn't help himself. He was so scared, it was either that or cry.

Solange stared at him, and for a moment Frank thought he was going to kill him, there and then. But just as Solange took a step toward him, a cell phone chirped in his pocket. It was such an unexpected, incongruous sound, it seemed to go straight to the middle of Frank's head. Solange plucked the phone out of his pocket with an annoyed look.

'Yes,' he said impatiently. 'What is it?'

He listened, for perhaps an entire minute, and during that minute Frank could sense Solange losing interest in the room, in him, in Annie. It was as if his awareness were palpable and its sudden absence made Frank feel oddly abandoned. Solange frowned, removed the phone from his ear, pushed down the antenna, and strode to the door without another glance at them. 'Let's go,' he said.

'What about *them*?'

Solange shrugged. 'Let them think about it,' he replied.

Frank heard the dead bolts shoot home, first one, then the other.

Because the floor was gravel, it took a long time to smash the bud vase, which was quite thick. When they finally succeeded, it was a relatively simple matter to cut themselves loose. But as they soon found out, there was no way out of the room – which was locked from the outside.

There was nothing else they could do, really, except hold each other. Frank told Annie that when the door opened, he'd take out the first person who came through it. They'd have surprise on their side, and maybe he could grab the guy's gun. Or something. It wasn't much, but in fact it was the only thing, the only thing they could do.

Then they slept, lying on the floor next to each other.

Annie dreamed of Stern and whimpered in her sleep.

Frank dreamed of Carlos.

And he was still dreaming when he heard a noise like distant thunder, a series of concussive shocks that made the fluorescent light rattle and the door shudder. He thought at first that it was part of his dream. Either that or he was starting to hallucinate. But Annie heard it, too, and woke up and stared at him. They wondered if the pharmaceutical labs were exploding.

And then the noise stopped, and soon they were dozing again.

Suddenly, an amplified voice exploded around them. 'STAND CLEAR OF THE DOOR.'

The men who came in were in flak jackets with FBI imprinted in huge letters on their backs. They wore helmets and gas masks and were heavily armed. They were not friendly, either, and did not understand that Frank and Annie were victims, not Temple followers hiding out in some inner sanctum.

It took quite a long time, really, to make that point.

Nor was Neal Gleason, when they were finally face-to-face with him, happy to see them, or even pleased that they'd survived.

Gleason's blue eyes were bloodshot and he looked like a man who hadn't slept in several days.

'I guess you got the message,' Frank said.

'Somebody tipped them,' Gleason said. 'They must have someone in the Lake Placid P.D. Because they were the only ones who knew about the raid.'

'Who got away?' Frank asked.

'Solange,' Gleason said. 'Solange and his Special Affairs team.'

29

He sat in the great room of the Headmaster's House, watching over Annie as she slept through the sleeping pills she'd been given. He wanted to work on the story, of course, but writing was impossible. He wasn't Victor Hugo. He needed a computer, or at least a typewriter. Even a telephone. He could *dictate* the story.

But the phone in the great room was dead, and the one in the hall was off-limits. An ATF agent sat outside the great room with a wire in his ear and an Uzi in his lap, making sure no one came or went without Neal Gleason's approval.

It took a while, but Frank finally got an explanation – of sorts. 'I'm supposed to protect you,' the agent said in a peeved tone. *'Okay?'*

'No,' Frank told him. 'It's not okay. I don't want protection. I want a fucking ThinkPad.'

But that, of course, was precisely the point. Gleason didn't want him to write a story – not, at least, while Solange was on the loose. So he was left to browse, to pace, and to stand at the windows, watching the scene outside.

Which was strangely sinister, a surreal tableau that, if painted by Bosch, might have been called, 'Eden Invaded.' A helicopter sat in the meadow next to the pond, its rotors turning slowly, while German shepherds towed ATF gunmen up one path and down another. Marines in biohazard suits wandered in and out of the labs, looking like advertisements for Intel, while FBI agents in matching windbreakers piled computers and filing cabinets into the back of a large white van. Otherwise, the campus seemed deserted, with the Templars confined to dormitories, waiting to be questioned.

Eventually, Frank tired of the view and sat down at an elaborately carved desk in an alcove off the great room. Its four clawed feet rested on a vintage Kilim beneath a portrait of Edward Abbey. A nineteen-inch Toshiba monitor sat on the desk's surface with its cables dangling toward the floor.

There was no CPU.

It would have been nice to have gotten a look at Solange's hard disk, Frank thought. But maybe there was something else . . . a notepad, a floppy, a calendar – anything.

One by one he opened the drawers of the desk and looked inside. But there was nothing. A couple of pens, some pencils and paper clips, an empty notebook, and a ream of Iroquois laser bond. A map of New York City, a pair of scissors, some thumbtacks, and empty note cards.

He unfolded the map and looked at it. Nothing, he thought. No marks or pinpricks. No hand-drawn lines. It's just a map. With a sigh, he leaned back in the chair and closed his eyes.

He sat that way for a long while, and then, suddenly energized or just impatient, he sat up straight. Sweeping the map from the desk, he took out a piece of paper and began to write. Who *says* I'm not Victor Hugo?

He passed about fifteen minutes in this way, and then looked over what he'd written – half a dozen variations on the same lead paragraph. Okay, so I'm not Victor

Hugo, Frank thought. I'm the writer in *The Shining,* the one Jack Nicholson played. Crumpling the pages into a ball, he tossed them into the wastebasket.

Solange's wastebasket. Which was half full.

Was the FBI really so sloppy? Could they have possibly overlooked the wastebasket?

Apparently.

Getting to his feet, he dumped the contents of the basket on the desk and began to sort through it. There wasn't much. A laser-printed copy of last week's *Morbidity and Mortality Weekly Report.* The first two pages of an essay entitled 'The Politics of Dystopia.' Crumpled Post-its with messages like 'Call Nikki,' 'Tues. intvw. w/*Futurist*,' and 'Query Belinda @ recruitment tables.' There was an empty bottle of Evian water, a crumpled box of Lakrits mentholated lozenges, and fragments of what turned out to be a four-by-five, black-and-white snapshot.

The picture had been torn in half three times. Reassembled on the desk, the eight pieces combined to form a photo of a little house. Or not quite a house – a construction shack. Or something *like* a construction shack. Whatever it was, it sat in the middle of an industrial urban nowhere, as anonymous as a slab of cement. Its blasted surroundings might have belonged to parts of Yonkers or Anacostia, East L.A. or South-side Chicago. Hard to tell. Harder still to guess what it meant to Solange (if, indeed, it meant anything).

He was still puzzling over the picture when an FBI agent came through the door with a bag full of chicken salad sandwiches and cans of Mountain Dew. 'If I could just get a statement from you and your friend,' he said, 'we might be able to move things along.'

'You mean, we could leave?'

'That's up to Neal,' the FBI agent said, 'but until we

get your statement, I don't think anything's going to change real quick.'

And so he woke up Annie – it was mid-afternoon, after all – and when she was ready, they told the Bureau's man what they knew. Or most of what they knew. When Frank mentioned the Chosen Soren organization, the agent suddenly stopped taking notes. With a sigh, he recapped his pen and got to his feet, saying he'd be right back.

In fact, it was two hours before anyone came, and when someone did, it was a large and fashionably dressed woman with a Hermes attaché case and a gravelly voice. 'Janine Wasserman,' she offered, shaking hands with Frank and Annie. 'I'm helping the FBI.'

'That's nice of you,' Frank replied, 'but I was hoping to see Gleason. We'd like to leave.'

'Oh, you'll be on your way in a little while,' she said. 'But so long as we're waiting, I was hoping you'd tell me about the North Koreans.' With a smile, she found her way to a green leather wing chair and sat down. 'Do you mind filling me in? I can promise it's for a good cause.'

Frank and Annie looked at each other. Finally, Frank said, 'There's not that much to say. We think they're bankrolling Solange.'

'You *do*? Well, I suppose they *might* be, but . . . why do you think so?'

'There's a Customs report about Korean money coming out of Japan. And it makes sense. I mean, that the North Koreans would –'

'Does it?' Wasserman asked. 'I wonder. Do you have the report? I'd love to see it.'

'No.'

She frowned. 'No, you don't have it? Or –

'No, we don't have it,' Annie said.

'But you've *seen* it,' Wasserman supposed.

Frank shook his head.

The woman's eyebrows lifted. 'Then . . . ? I guess I just don't understand.'

'We were told about it,' Frank said.

A swish of nylon as Wasserman crossed her legs. 'I see,' she said. 'So it's a rumor.'

'Right.'

'Well,' Wasserman remarked, 'some rumors are true. I suppose it depends on the source. Who are we talking about?'

'Actually, I think the source is dead,' Frank said. 'A Georgetown grad student named Ben Stern. Solange killed him.'

'Okaa-aay,' Wasserman replied. 'Okay *for now*. But . . . I don't get it, really. Why would the North Koreans "bankroll" Solange? They don't have a lot of foreign exchange to play with.'

'You're asking my *opinion*?' Frank asked.

'Mmmm.'

Frank shrugged. 'Well, in my *opinion*, there's a convergence of interests.'

Wasserman frowned, 'I don't see how that could be,' she said. 'I mean, they're worlds apart. What could they ever have in common?'

Frank thought about it for a moment, but it was Annie who spoke: 'Are you asking that because you want to know the answer, or because you want to know if we know the answer?'

'Oooh!' Wasserman said. 'What a good question. I wonder.'

'Do you have a *card*?' Annie asked.

The heavy woman shifted in her chair. 'No,' she said, with just a trace of regret in her voice. 'I'm afraid I don't.'

380

Frank made an exasperated sound.

'Look,' Wasserman said, leaning toward them. 'Here's the deal. If you want to get out of here tonight, you'll try to be helpful.'

'"If I want to get out of here tonight" – who the fuck *are* you?' Frank asked. 'And what's going on here, anyway? Are we under arrest?'

Wasserman weighed the question. Finally, she said, 'No. As I understand it, you're not actually "under arrest." It's more like preventive detention.'

'Preventive detention!' Annie exclaimed.

'What *is* this?' Frank asked.

'Actually,' Wasserman said, smoothing the creases in her dress, 'it's a national emergency. The President made it official at three-seventeen this morning.'

Frank fell back into the cushions of the couch and sighed exasperatedly. 'And why is it we're being held?'

'That's something you'll have to take up with Neal. He's the one who's calling the shots on the domestic side.'

'But we haven't done anything wrong,' Annie said, suddenly teary-eyed.

'I'm sure that's true,' Wasserman replied. 'And I'm sure that Neal will straighten everything out. But as you can appreciate, we're very short of time – so if we could just get back to the subject, I'm sure that would help immensely. Okay?'

Annie nodded.

'We were talking about "a convergence of interests,"' Wasserman said, looking at Frank.

'Right,' Frank replied. 'And here's what I think: I think Solange and the North Koreans would love it – *both* of them would love it – if America came apart at the seams.'

'Okaaay . . . for argument's sake . . .'

'And Solange can make that happen. And he's deniable!'

Wasserman looked genuinely puzzled. 'Why do you say that?' she asked.

'Because he's a "kook." They're all kooks. So no matter what happens, no matter what they say or do, it happens out of context. It *has* no context. Once you say a "cult" did it, you strip the event of any political significance it might ever have.'

'Why?'

'Because a cult is basically a convention of lone nuts,' Frank replied. 'I mean, that's what people think. And because they're nuts, what they do isn't seen as rational. So their actions don't have any coherent meaning. Which is just another way of saying they're *beyond investigation*. "Deniable."'

Wasserman nodded, thinking about it. 'Let's say you're right. Why do you think North Korea would want to jumpstart an epidemic that might kill half the people in the country?'

'Because if that many people died, the country would fall apart. Our highest priority – our only priority – would be to bury the dead. Or burn them. And even if we still had a government that worked, I don't see it sending people off to fight a foreign war. I think we'd stay right where we are. Cut wood, and build crematoriums.'

Wasserman was silent for a while. Then she asked, 'You mentioned "a foreign war."'

'I was thinking about North Korea invading the South.'

'And is this something you intend to write about?'

Frank rubbed the stubble on his jaw. 'I don't know,' he said. 'Maybe.'

Wasserman nodded. 'Or maybe not. You can't prove it.'

'Right,' Frank said. 'I can't prove it.'

'And it really doesn't matter, anyway,' Wasserman added, getting to her feet.

Annie looked shocked. 'It doesn't *matter*? How can you say that?'

'Because Mr. Daly's right. Solange *is* deniable. And look at the possibilities. If Solange succeeds, the question of responsibility is moot. Half the people in the country will be dead, and you're right – I'm not at all sure that, under the circumstances, we *would* have a government interested in foreign affairs.'

'Okay. And what if he fails?' Frank asked.

'Well, then he's just a nut. Even if you could trace the money that he was given – and I don't think you could – what would it show? That it came from North Korea? I don't think so. The most you'd be able to prove is that it came from Korean workers living in Japan. To which a lot of people would say, so what? Maybe Solange has a lot of Korean followers. Maybe they're crazy, too.'

'And the point is, what?' Frank asked.

Wasserman shrugged. 'Only that you should be careful. In the end, what's really at stake is Frank Daly's credibility. And let's face it, I don't think you want to look like a conspiracy theorist – even if you're right. Now, do you?'

Before he could answer, she turned on her heel and left.

Soon afterward, Gleason came to the Headmaster's House to ask Frank and Annie if they'd like to accompany him to New York. 'Do we have a choice?' Frank asked.

'Sure,' Gleason replied. 'You can stay here if you'd

rather. Or there's a Motel 6, just up the road. I could put someone outside the door. But I don't think you'd like it there, and this way, I can keep an eye on you – and you'll be closer to the action. That's what you want, isn't it?'

The helicopter was noisy, the flight interminable. And when they landed, it seemed as if they'd traveled as much through time as through space.

A turn-of-the-century Coast Guard station, closed the year before, Governors Island lies off the coast of Brooklyn in New York's Upper Bay, where the Hudson and East Rivers converge. Less than a mile from lower Manhattan, the island has little in common with the crowded, noisy, neon-lit city that the public knows, but is instead an oasis of clapboard buildings, wheeling gulls, and salty breezes.

Frank and Annie spent the night, unguarded, in a guesthouse about a hundred yards from the docks. There was no phone, but the view from the porch was spectacular, a panorama that included the Statue of Liberty, the Brooklyn Bridge, and Manhattan in between.

The next morning, they joined Gleason on the bridge of the *Chinquateague,* a 110-foot Coast Guard cutter with a 25mm machine gun mounted to its deck.

'The thing is,' Gleason said, gazing through a pair of high-powered binoculars at a queue of freighters waiting to enter the bay, 'we know what he's going to do. Or what he thinks he's going to do.' He paused for a moment. 'Then again, if you look at it from the other side, he *knows* that we know. So why should he do it?' Passing the binoculars to Annie, he pinched the lids of his eyes between his thumb and forefinger and yawned.

A soft breeze played with the flag at the stern of the ship, but otherwise it was a perfect day for 'a biological incident' – humid, warm, and overcast.

'He'll do it,' Frank said, 'because he's a megalomaniac. They aren't known for their flexibility.'

Gleason nodded. 'That's what I think, too. I think he'll do it to prove that he can do it.'

Annie wasn't so sure. 'And what if he goes to Plan B?' she asked.

Gleason looked blank. 'What's Plan B?'

Annie shook her head. 'I don't know. But I'll bet he has one. He ran tests in California and Wisconsin, and other places, too – and he always used the same archival flu.'

'And what does that tell you?' Gleason asked.

'That he was testing dispersal methods – and not the virus itself.'

Gleason looked worried for a moment, but the moment quickly passed. 'Yeah, well, we're way ahead of him. We ran our own tests – in the fifties. And I can tell you what the results were: if you're after maximum infectivity, you've got three choices. Boat, plane, or subway.'

'And you've got 'em covered, right?' Frank asked.

The FBI agent nodded. 'Yeah,' he said. 'They're covered.'

Frank looked skeptical.

'FEMA's given us all the powers we need,' Gleason said.

'FEMA?' Annie said.

'The Federal Emergency Management Agency,' Frank replied.

'We've shut down the New York and Washington air corridors to small planes. Same thing with the rivers. You won't see any motorboats on the Hudson or East Rivers – or the Potomac, either. Not until this is over, and maybe never again.'

'What about the big ships?' Annie asked, nodding toward the queue of freighters.

'They don't get in the harbor until they've been searched and we've put a team on board.'

'And the subways?' Frank asked.

'We've got people on every train.'

'What about a car?' Annie asked. 'Or a truck. If they've micro-encapsulated the virus, it could pass through the catalytic converter and right out the exhaust. All they'd have to do is drive around. No one would notice a thing.'

Gleason thought about it.

'Jesus,' Frank said, looking at Annie. 'You could be dangerous.'

'I don't think so,' Gleason decided. 'You wouldn't get the kind of penetration that you want. Not with a car. You'd need a boat or a plane. Something that goes all over the place. A subway system would be good.'

'And the water supply?' Frank asked.

Gleason shook his head. 'No. It's a myth about dumping something into the water supply. You wouldn't get the kind of dispersion that you'd need. And I'm told that you might not be infected anyway, if you drank it. It's a respiratory virus.'

'What I don't understand,' Frank said, 'is why you think you can handle this without anyone noticing. I mean, just the pilots –'

'Oh, they'll notice, all right. People will *notice*. But you won't see anything about it in the press.'

'Why not?'

'Because every media outlet in the country got a fax or a phone call this morning.'

'So now we have censorship?'

Gleason made a moue. 'No more than we had during Desert Storm. Anyway, it's just this, and it's only temporary,' he said. 'You can still read the box scores.' Seeing Frank's frown, the FBI agent elaborated. 'Look, it's the twentieth century. Which is another way of saying we're living in a crowded theater. People start running around, yelling "Fire" –'

'What if there *is* a fire?' Frank asked.

'We'll *handle* it,' Gleason replied.

'Okay,' Frank said. 'So handle it. What do you need *us* for? I mean, if I can't publish the story –'

'It's not that simple,' Gleason said.

'Why *not*?'

'Because of the Internet,' Annie suggested, her voice disconsolate.

Gleason inclined his head in a way that was half nod, half bow. 'It's a big problem,' he said.

Frank watched a seagull turn in a gyre above the gun on the bow. 'So what's next?' he asked. 'How long do we sit here?'

Gleason shrugged. 'That's up to Solange,' he said.

30

STATEN ISLAND

Susannah wasn't used to driving trucks, but the U-Haul was really easy. It had an automatic shift, and terrific visibility. Which was good, because ever since the boxing match, she was having trouble with her eyes. Behind the heart-shaped sunglasses she wore, her right eye was almost completely closed, and her left was filled with blood and kind of blurry. The doctor said it would be all right, but not right away. It would probably take a while.

Meanwhile, Stephen sat in his car seat, gurgling.

Talk about the 'butterflies.' She was scared. Not so much by what they were about to do, and what might happen if it went wrong – but of *getting it* wrong. She had special instructions from Solange, and God help her if she fucked up. . . .

She'd gotten to the dock almost an hour before, arriving about a minute after the ferry left. This looked like bad luck, but it was actually intentional. *First on, first off,* Solange had said, like it was important.

So she'd sat there for fifty-nine minutes, and then, when the gate lifted, she drove slowly forward until the truck was deep inside the ferry. In the rearview mirror she could see the Frenchman's car, with Vaughn and Belinda in the backseat.

She was really nervous. But she shouldn't have been.

In most ways, her job was the easiest. In fact, she didn't really have anything to do unless they got into trouble. *Which is where you come in,* cher, *You're Plan B.*

Cool, she thought. I'm Plan B. No one else is Plan-anything, except, I guess, for Plan A. That's what they are. But I'm Plan B. She squinched her eyes together because they were tearing up, which they'd been doing a lot lately. Outside, she could hear the ferrymen shouting to one another, and the boat's horn – a deep, howling *tooooot*. Then the floor began to tremble, and the walls, too, and suddenly they were rumbling ahead. Smoother now, gathering speed. Lots of speed. She could feel it.

As if on cue, Vaughn and Belinda climbed out of the car behind, then went around to its trunk, where the Ingrams were stashed. They were wearing the matching T-shirts Solange had designed – so everyone could recognize each other, right off, no matter how confusing it got. The T-shirts were cool – bloodred, with a mudman's head on the front, and above it:

the meek

She wished she had one . . . but not really. Because this way it was even better. She was special. She was Plan B. Ordinarily, she might have felt left out, but this time, she didn't. Because Solange wasn't wearing a T-shirt either. So he was Plan B, too.

Behind her, the door to the U-Haul shrieked as someone, probably Saul, rolled it up into the roof. Then the truck rocked and, a moment later, she could hear them dragging out the aerosolizer.

She eased herself out of the truck and went around to the other side. Opening the door, she unhooked

Stephen from his car seat, boosted him up to her shoulder, and headed for the deck. 'Rotsa ruck,' she said, walking past a grinning Solange.

And then she was outside, and it was kind of glorious, the air fresh and damp and breezy. There were lots of people on deck, mostly smiling, and inside, too. 'Look at that,' she said to Stephen, pointing, 'that's a *big* city! Can you *see* the big city? Where is the big city? Oh! *There* it is!'

An old black man with a shoe-shine kit gave her a smile, then turned to a guy who looked like a banker and, nodding at his wing tips, said, 'You need help, my man! You kinda scruffy!' A blues band started to play in the main salon. Someone threw a Nerf ball to someone else. Kids ran shouting up and down the deck.

She was standing at the railing, showing Stephen the Statue of Liberty, when she heard a soft burst of submachine-gun fire from somewhere in the middle of the boat. A woman screamed as a second gun came into play, and people started running this way and that, as if there was somewhere to go. Then the screaming stopped and the ferry slowed almost to a halt, and her friends appeared out of nowhere, looking so cool you couldn't believe it.

Saul and the Frenchman, Vaughn and Belinda, Veroushka and Avram. Maybe four or five others – all of them carrying Ingrams. Except Saul, who was lugging the aerosolizer to the bow, and the Frenchman, who carried an electric drill.

'Everybody inside,' Veroushka ordered.

'Let's go!' Antonio shouted, pointing his Ingram at a fat woman and her family.

'Move it!' Jane yelled. 'Are you stupid?'

One by one, and then by twos and threes and tens,

the passengers surged into the main salon.

It was neat being in charge, Susannah thought. Neat to be part of something that everyone else was afraid of. She laughed as the Frenchman went past her and, turning, fired the battery-operated drill at her, pretending it was an Ingram, then looked wide-eyed and shocked when the drill went *whir whir* instead of *brrrt-brtt.*

Talk about funny . . .

And then, just for a second, while Saul and the Frenchman anchored the aerosolizer to the deck, things got wobbly. This kid with a buzz cut grabbed Jane by the hair, jerked her back and threw her to the ground – all in one motion, coming up fast and cold with the gun in his hand. Jesus, Susannah thought, this guy knows what he's doing.

But then, as it turned out, he didn't. Veroushka threw her gun to the ground and her hands in the air – 'Don't shoot!' she screamed. Which made the guy turn, and just as he did, Antonio came out of the main salon, firing his Ingram in a left to right sweep that almost cut the kid's head off.

He stood there for what seemed like a long time, with his hands at his side and his head on his chest, swaying, while a woman a few feet away slid to the deck with a hole in her throat. Then Veroushka gave the guy a little push and he fell like a tree.

People were screaming and crying as Veroushka blew a kiss to Antonio and picked up her gun. 'Shut the fuck up!' she yelled, as if she were trying to watch television. And the amazing thing was, they did. They shut the fuck up.

Solange was on the deck above, watching it all with a little smile, totally in control. Susannah sidestepped a rivulet of blood and pulled Stephen closer to her.

'Yuck-a-puck!' she whispered, feeling the stickiness on the soles of her shoes.

'Look at that,' Annie said, pointing.

Frank squinted. 'What?'

'The ferry. It's stopped.'

Frank stared. 'You're right,' he said, then changed his mind. 'No, it's not. It's moving again.' He lifted a pair of binoculars to his eyes and trained them on the boat. For a moment he was puzzled. You'd think there'd be a lot of people outside, but there were only a dozen or so on deck. He turned the focal ring on the binoculars, trying to get a better look, but it was too far away to see much. All he could do was make out shapes and colors. Red, mostly.

'Do they wear uniforms on the ferry?' he asked.

'Who?'

'The people who work on the ferry?'

'I don't think so,' she said.

'Because –'

Suddenly, Gleason came running up the stairs with the ship's commander, a young lieutenant named Horvath. 'We've got a problem,' Gleason said.

'With what?' Frank asked.

'The ferry,' Horvath replied, picking up a phone and shouting orders to the crew. Somewhere below them, a bell began to ring, and a horn sounded three quick blasts.

'What's the matter with it?' Annie asked, as the ship's engines began to turn and sailors cast off from the dock. 'What's happening?'

'They've hijacked it.'

Annie stared at him. 'You can't let them go up the Hudson,' she said. 'I mean, you absolutely can't.'

The *Chinquateague* slipped away from the dock,

turned, and began to gather speed, heading into the Upper Bay. Frank leaned on the bridge's console, steadying the binoculars. 'They've got a gun or something on the bow,' he said. 'Like a water cannon.'

'It's the aerosolizer,' Gleason said, dialing a number on his cell phone. Turning away, he spoke urgently into the phone, saying, *Now, right now,* then flipped it closed and put it away.

'How do you stop it?' Frank asked as the Coast Guard cutter pounded over the waves.

'If I have to,' Gleason said, 'I'll sink them.'

'You can't *sink* them,' Annie said. 'There's a couple of hundred people on the boat!'

The FBI agent ignored her and turned to the Coast Guard lieutenant. 'I'll have a combat helicopter here in twenty minutes. Can you stop them?'

The lieutenant looked unsure. 'I don't know,' he said. 'I guess I could ram them, if I had to, but . . . I'll tell you what I *can* do: I can keep them away from the aerosolizer. I can make sure they don't have a chance to use it.'

'Do it!' Gleason said, and got on the phone as the lieutenant ordered the cover removed from the 25mm gun.

Saul was the one who really *caught* it, Susannah thought. He was getting the aerosolizer primed when the Coast Guard ship did a sort of brodie in the water, maybe a hundred yards away. Then the fed started talking to them through the bullhorn, acting like he was their father, all reasonable and calm –

Until Vaughn and Veroushka came to the railing and emptied their clips in his face. God, that was cool, Susannah thought, the way the glass exploded on the bridge, with the megaphone going *urrrrrrp* and the feds or Marines or whatever they were diving every which way.

Except it wasn't so cool, because that's when Saul caught it, really *caught* it – and it wasn't like he was doing anything. He was just standing there next to the aerosolizer, watching the show, and the cops opened up with this cannon or whatever it was, and, Jesus, they just about sawed him in half. *I mean, really!* And the other kid, too, the kid who was with him – except he wasn't dead, just bleeding.

And now the ferry was stopped, so it rolled a lot, and the passengers were getting seasick, sitting on the floor of the main salon, all quiet and pukey.

Why were *they* scared? Susannah wondered. All the pressure was on her and her friends. If you looked outside, there were a couple of police boats, two fireboats, and a Coast Guard cutter. And that wasn't all. They had a matte-black helicopter dead ahead, swaying like a dragonfly, its gun sights pointed right at the bow. She wondered how long it could sit there like that, just hanging in the air, before it ran out of fuel and dropped to the water. Not that it would matter: they probably had frogmen, too.

She was standing on the bridge with Veroushka and Solange, listening to the Frenchman. He was pacing back and forth with a cell phone clapped to his cheek, arguing with the guy from the FBI, the negotiator.

'Listen,' Gleason said, talking into the phone. 'What you've got to understand is, that boat is not going up the Hudson. I'll sink it before I let that happen. In fact, maybe you noticed the helicopter. That's what it's *for*. Now, once you understand that, everything else is negotiable. So talk to me.'

The FBI agent paced as he listened, his eyes on Annie

and Frank.

'I'm glad you brought that up,' Gleason said. 'And I'll tell ya what I can do. You don't need that many hostages. You don't even want them. They're a logistical problem.' He listened for a moment, then cut back in. 'So we can make a deal. You let the women and children go, I'll see you get some food – how's that? Pizzas. Whatever!'

Gleason listened for a moment, then flipped the cell phone closed.

'What did he say?' Annie asked.

'He's thinking about it.'

'Let's go, *cher.*'

Susannah hesitated. 'Stephen, too?' she asked.

'Absolutely, Stephen,' Solange said. 'Would I leave Stephen? Do I look crazy?' Then he picked up the book bag, the one with the virus ampoules, and slung it over his shoulder. 'Étienne,' he said, turning to the Frenchman, 'when you talk to him – be a pain in the ass, eh? Don't make it too easy, or he'll be suspicious. And tell him! Only an ambulance on the dock. Insist on it. Nothing else.'

The Frenchman – she'd never known his name – nodded. 'Eh, *bien,* but . . . what if they won't let us dock?' he asked, pronouncing the last word *duck*.

Solange scoffed. 'He *wants* you to dock. It's more dangerous for you there. So negotiate with him. Tell him you'll trade the aerosolizer for a plane to Cuba. You give him that, and he'll give you anything you want.'

'And afterward?'

Solange shrugged. 'You've been vaccinated. Go to Cuba.' The Frenchman looked doubtful. 'Don't you get it?' Solange laughed, slapping the words on the

Frenchman's T-shirt. 'You've inherited the earth, you idiot! It's *yours,* man!'

'No hard feelings,' Gleason said as Frank and Annie got into the motor launch. 'I did what I had to do.'

'You really think this is over?' Frank asked.

Gleason gestured to the ferry, which was tying up at the dock. 'Yeah. Except for the shouting, I do. I think it's over. Otherwise, you wouldn't be going ashore.'

'Right,' Frank said, trying not to look too skeptical.

'We're trading pizzas for people,' Gleason insisted. 'I'll take that deal every time.'

'Who wouldn't?' Annie asked.

'You watch: ten minutes from now, there's going to be a lot of women and kids coming off that boat. And after that? We're gonna deal for the aerosolizer. So, yeah, I can hear the Fat Lady, loud and clear.'

You *are* the Fat Lady, Frank thought, then waved as the motor launch turned and nosed through the water toward shore.

Annie looked at him. 'This is too easy,' she said.

'I know.'

'So . . . what do you think they'll try to do? Spray from the dock?' Frank shook his head. 'Gleason won't let him get near the aerosolizer. He'll cut him in half.'

'Then . . . what?'

'I don't know. Something.' Lights were winking on in the Financial District. In the east, the Brooklyn Bridge stretched across the river like a monochrome rainbow. On Gleason's orders, the motor launch left them at a pier near the Old Slip, about a block behind the police line that began at the corner of South and Broad streets.

'Where do you want to go?' Annie asked.

'Nowhere. I just want to watch the ferry.'

Susannah made sure that Stephen was safely in his car seat, then put the U-Haul into gear and rolled forward. First on, first off, she thought, understanding for the first time why it was so important that the U-Haul should be the first vehicle on the ferry. Solange had thought of everything.

As the truck trundled off the ferry and into the street, she could see the other women and children streaming onto the dock. The area around the terminal was deserted, except for a paramedic who stood next to an ambulance, directing everyone to a first-aid tent in nearby Battery Park.

Susannah turned onto State Street, saw the roadblock up ahead, and swung right on Water. The street was empty, but she could see the lights of police cars on the next block, and she instinctively avoided them. Turning left onto Whitehall, she found herself with nowhere to go. Up ahead, a trio of squad cars sat in the intersection, blue lights whirling. On the sidewalks behind them, a crowd jostled with a television crew to get a glimpse of the ferry.

Susannah slowed. Stopped. Rolled down her window as a cop came up to her.

'You okay?' he asked.

'Uh-huh.'

The cop looked in the window at little Stephen. 'How's the little guy?'

'Oh, he's fine,' Susannah said. 'We just want to get home. It's been scary.' She rubbed Stephen's hair. 'And it's been a long day, y'know – moving and all.'

'Can I see some ID?'

'Sure,' Susannah replied, fumbling in her handbag until she found her wallet. Taking out her driver's license, she handed it to the cop. He glanced at it and returned it.

'You mind if I look in the back?' he asked.

Susannah shook her head. 'Whatever,' she said. She watched him in the rearview mirror as he walked along the side of the truck. Reaching the back, he disappeared from view and, a moment later, she heard the shriek of the aluminum door as the cop shoved it up into the roof. There were a dozen other cops in the intersection, and all of them looked tense. But then they relaxed as the door came clattering back down again.

The cop returned. 'We didn't know there were any vehicles coming off the ferry,' he said.

Susannah made a helpless gesture. 'They said I could leave. So I got in the truck. Was that wrong?'

The cop chuckled. 'No. It wasn't wrong. It was just a surprise.' Then he looked concerned. 'Is your husband on the ferry?'

Susannah shook her head. 'No. I'm supposed to meet him at the truck place.'

'Well, they're gonna want to debrief you. So, what I want you to do is this: hang a left on Bridge Street, right up there, and follow it over to the park. There's a first-aid tent behind the memorial – you can't miss it. Tell the officer why you're there – tell him you came off the ferry. Otherwise, you'll get a ticket.'

Susannah nodded, quick little jerks of her head. Her heart was beating against her chest like a woodpecker on a dead tree.

Frank and Annie were standing behind the police line at Whitehall and Pearl, looking toward the ferry, when the U-Haul drove up. They watched the cop as he talked to the driver, then walked around to the back of the truck and looked inside.

Annie's hand tightened on Frank's arm.

'What?' he asked, sounding distracted.

'It's like the one *I* was in,' she said.

Frank didn't know what she meant at first, and then he understood. She was talking about the truck they'd used to kidnap her. 'Well,' he said 'it's the same size, anyway.' He wanted to get a look at the driver, who was talking to the cop again.

'That's not what I mean,' Annie insisted. 'I mean it's *really* like the one I was in.'

He heard the urgency in her voice, and turned to her. 'What do you mean?'

'It's got that southwestern motif – just like the other one.'

Frank glanced at the U-Haul, which the cop was beginning to wave through the intersection. He wanted to see the driver's face, but he was on the wrong side of the street for that.

But Annie was right about the 'motif'. A Flamenco dancer, or something like that, was painted on the side of the truck. She held a fan in front of her face, and the way her eyes were, you could tell that she was laughing.

Then the truck was past him, and he saw that it had New York plates – which, when you thought about it, didn't make sense, not when you saw the logo. If the truck was from New York, it should have had skyscrapers on it. Or a giant apple, or something. But not a señorita. Instinctively, he started walking after the truck, then jogging, pulling Annie along behind him. The U-Haul was signaling left, but it didn't turn. When it got to Bridge Street, it accelerated and kept on going.

'*Putz!*' the cop yelled, throwing his hands in the air.

And that's when it hit Frank. He didn't know why, but suddenly he got the joke and knew that he had to catch the truck.

'It's the Spanish Lady,' he said. 'It's a señorita, but –'

'I *get* it,' Annie shot back, hurrying to keep up with him.

When they reached the next corner, Frank glanced left and right, looking for a car or a cab, then spotted a black limo waiting outside a restaurant on Stone Street. The chauffeur was sitting on the front fender, reading a newspaper. Frank walked past the car and, seeing the keys in the ignition, told Annie to get in the passenger's seat and lock the door.

'But –'

'Just do it,' he said, and watched as she complied, her reluctance almost palpable. The door slammed shut.

'Hey!' the chauffeur exclaimed, surprised to hear the car door slam. 'Hey, lady! Whattaya doin'? This ain't your car!' Irritated, he slid off the fender and came around to the passenger's side, just as Annie locked the door. 'Get outta there!' he ordered, knocking on the window. 'You can't be in there!'

'Sorry about that,' Frank said, going around to the driver's side and pulling open the door. 'Let me talk to her.' Then he climbed in, pulled the door shut behind him, and turned the key in the ignition. The limo started with a roar. The chauffeur yelled 'Muh-thuh-*fuhhh*?!' And the car leapt from the curb.

In his rearview mirror Frank could see the chauffeur running down the street, screaming for the police. And then they turned a corner and he was gone.

The whole thing had taken less than a minute, but even so, it was sheer luck that they caught sight of the U-Haul – and that it was the right U-Haul. Maybe the driver had gotten lost in the maze of streets around the World Trade Center, or maybe she was just slow. But after a minute or so they spotted it about a block ahead of them, rumbling down Fulton toward the FDR.

The lights were all wrong, turning red just as Frank hit the intersections, but it didn't matter. He'd have welcomed a police car's lights but, naturally, there wasn't a cop in sight.

There was, however, a car phone, and Frank told Annie to call Gleason.

'How?' she asked. 'I don't know his number.'

'Just call him,' he said. 'Call the FBI's Washington field office. Tell them it's an emergency. Tell them it's about Solange. That'll get their attention. Do the same with FEMA and the Coast Guard. One of them will put you through.'

'But how do I get their numbers?' she asked.

Frank groaned. 'Five-five-five, one-two –'

'But how will they call us back? We're in a stolen car.'

He took a deep breath, exhaled, and said, 'You don't like making phone calls, do you?'

'I mean it!' Annie said defensively. 'How do I tell them to get back to us?'

'It's the FBI,' Frank replied. 'They *probably* have Caller ID. In fact, they could probably sequence your DNA over the phone, if you hung on long enough.'

With a deep, mistrustful frown, she picked up the phone and began dialing, regarding the instrument as if it were a snake.

Meanwhile, Frank drove, or tried to. He kept the U-Haul in sight beneath the elevated highway, then followed it up the ramp, with numerous cars now between them. Traffic on the FDR was bumper-to-bumper, surging from fifteen to twenty-five miles per hour and back again. Even so, he could see the U-Haul, maybe a hundred yards ahead.

'Where is it going?' Annie asked, putting her hand over the receiver.

Frank shook his head. 'Uptown . . .' he replied, leaning forward to turn on the radio. He found a news station right away, but there was nothing about the Staten Island Ferry, the Temple, or anything else. They passed the Williamsburg Bridge.

'That's Gleason,' Frank remarked, gesturing at the radio. 'Gleason and FEMA. If it was up to them, you'd need a Q-clearance to get a weather report.'

The Lower East Side rolled by, and then the Midtown Tunnel. When they came abreast of the U.N., Frank thought he had a chance to close the gap, but a motorcyclist cut him off, and that was that. Soon they were on the Upper East Side, and the U-Haul's turn signal began to blink. At Ninety-sixth Street it exited the highway, and so did Frank and Annie.

But once again the lights betrayed them. The U-Haul rumbled through an intersection on yellow, but there wasn't any way Frank and Annie could make it. A wall of traffic surged across their path and –

'Goddammit!' Frank cried out, slamming his palm against the steering wheel and falling back against the seat.

When the light finally changed – and it seemed to Frank as if it took an hour – he floored the limo without a thought as to where he would go. A block later he turned right and began driving toward Harlem.

'Why Harlem?' Annie asked.

'Why not?' Frank replied, looking left and right, hoping to see the U-Haul.

Three or four minutes passed that way, and then, with a triumphal look, Annie handed him the telephone. 'I got him,' she said.

'Gleason?" Frank asked.

'This better be important,' the FBI agent replied. 'We're kinda busy here!'

'I think someone got off the ferry who wasn't supposed to.'

There was a silence on the other end of the line, and then: 'What do you mean?'

Frank told him about the U-Haul.

'And you're following it?' Gleason asked. 'Where are you?'

'I lost it in Harlem,' Frank said. 'But it's somewhere around here. Or it was. Anyway, I'm at 122nd and . . . what? Third Avenue.'

'I'll get the NYPD to help.'

'What I'm worried about is whether or not there's virus on the truck.'

'I know.'

'What do you mean, you know?'

'We ran a voiceprint on the guy I'm negotiating with.'

'And?'

'It's not Solange.'

Frank blinked. 'What? Then who is it?' he asked.

'What's the difference, who it is? It's some *frog*! Or Rich Little. Or – Who cares who it is? The point is, it ain't Solange.'

'Give me your number,' Frank said. 'In case we find the truck.' Gleason did, and they hung up.

'Solange is loose,' he said. 'They've been "negotiating" with the wrong guy.'

Annie rolled her eyes in despair.

Five minutes later they saw it. The truck was parked near the corner of Madison Avenue and 132nd Street, just off the FDR. Frank pulled up behind it and stopped. He told Annie to call Gleason and tell him where they found the truck. Then he got out of the car and, cautiously, walked around to the front of the U-Haul.

The woman was sitting behind the wheel, nursing her baby. He recognized her right away. It was the same bitch-madonna who'd jangled his *chakras* two weeks before, smearing the steering wheel of his car with the shit that sent him through the Looking Glass. 'How sweet,' he said, yanking the door open, reaching in to take the keys.

'You're too late,' she replied, her eyes on the baby, uninterested in Frank.

'Where'd he go?'

'Fuck you.'

He almost pulled her out of the truck, but his sense of priorities got the better of him, and he slammed the door instead. Then he walked around to the back, where Annie was waiting.

'The cops are on their way,' she said.

Frank nodded, then grabbed the handle of the truck's rear door and, yanking it upward, sent it clattering into the roof. Looking inside, he found what he'd expected: a false wall, about two feet deep, between the truck's cab and the cargo area. A part of the wall gaped open, just as Solange had left it.

'That's where he was when they came off the ferry,' Frank said.

'Who's the driver?' Annie asked.

'Remember the bitch who said I left my lights on?'

'Really!?'

Frank nodded. 'She's feeding Junior.'

'But . . . where's Solange? What's he going to do?'

'The same thing he tried to do on the ferry.'

'But how? How *can* he?'

'I don't know,' Frank said, shaking his head and

looking around. They were in the midst of a blasted urban landscape. There was a burnt-out building. A few high-rise buildings and some redbrick projects, filigreed with graffiti. Some tenements. A vacant lot. Every hundred feet or so a column of steam rose from the street, swirling out of the manholes.

Steam.

Frank turned back to Annie. 'Where was it the students got sick?'

'What students?'

'When they ran the dispersion tests.'

She tried to remember. 'Madison. The University of Wisconsin. Why?'

'Because we never figured out the methods they were using.'

'Well, they definitely used a boat, somewhere. And a plane.'

Frank shook his head. 'But in Madison – how come only students got sick?'

'It wasn't just students, really,' Annie said, correcting him. 'Teachers got sick, too.'

'But it was pretty much confined to campus. Right?'

Annie nodded.

'So how come?'

'I don't know,' Annie said.

'Well, I think I do,' Frank mused. 'It was because of the method they used.'

'And what method was that?' Annie asked.

Frank nodded at the fog rising from a nearby manhole.

'Steam?' she asked.

'Count on it,' Frank replied. 'Hospitals and universities use it. They use it to heat, but also for air-conditioning. Cities, too. Half the buildings in this city are heated by steam. Maybe more.'

'But . . . it's a closed system,' Annie said. 'The steam doesn't get into the building's ventilation system. It just heats the radiators –'

'It's vented *everywhere*,' Frank insisted. 'Not in the buildings, but on the way to the buildings. It's vented through traps on every street corner in the city. Look around you.'

She did. Little wisps of steam were everywhere. Finally, she asked, 'Where'd you learn about this?'

'My father worked in a generating plant,' Frank told her. 'In Kerwick. I helped him a couple of summers.'

'But . . .' Annie looked confused. 'How can Solange get the virus into the pipes?'

'If he gets into the plant, there's a place where they add chemicals – polishers and demineralizers. It goes right into the system.'

'But aren't the plants guarded?'

Frank nodded. 'Yeah,' he said, 'they're guarded.' Suddenly, he looked doubtful. 'It's just a theory. And, anyway, I don't see any generating plants in the neighborhood, do you?'

They looked around them. There was nothing like that. Just slums.

Annie nodded toward the front of the truck. 'What does *she* say?' she asked.

'"Fuck you,"' he replied, then seeing the startled look on her face, added, 'I'm quoting. It wasn't a suggestion.' His eyes returned to the street, searching for Solange. He knew he was nearby. He had to be.

But there was nothing. Some bodegas. A vacant lot, this one with a chain-link fence, and some kind of shack or blockhouse. A storefront church. The redbrick housing project, its grassy public areas worn down to hardpan dirt. Kids jumping rope.

Solange's wastepaper basket. The shack was the

same one whose picture he'd fished out of Solange's wastebasket. The picture he'd torn into pieces.

'He's in there,' Frank said, pointing to the building.

Annie frowned. 'How do you know?' she asked.

Frank shook off the question. 'Just keep an eye on Mother Teresa,' he replied, and broke into a run.

The shack was a cinder-block cube that rested on a carpet of glass in the center of a vacant lot, surrounded by a chain-link fence that was topped with razor wire. Frank walked along the fence, looking for the opening he knew would be there. And, finding it, he slipped inside.

He approached the shack as if he were walking through a mine field, expecting at any moment to be shot. But there was nothing. A broken lock lay on the ground, and the door was ajar. Stepping inside, he found the shack empty.

But now he knew where he was, and he knew what the shack was. It was a 'headhouse,' an unheated building that enclosed a vertical shaft, whose ladder carried utility crews into the city's underground. This would be a spectacular, if unseen, maze of catacombs and tunnels, vaults and chimneys, sewers and water-courses, that gave access to utility lines of every kind – electric and gas, water and steam, cable and telephone. Frank knew this because all steam systems were set up more or less the same way. Also, one of the steamfitters in Kerwick had previously worked for Con Ed in New York. Just like the city it served, the system was famously huge and complex and the guy never shut up about it. He could almost hear the guy's voice now. 'In New York . . .'

The entrance to the shaft was under a metal plate in the floor. Frank lifted the plate, recoiling from the sewery smell that welled up at him, sat down and put his feet into the shaft. And then, with all the care that fear could muster, he began his descent, hating every rung.

For him, it was the worst of possible worlds – a fusion of vertigo and claustrophobia. The shaft was barely as wide as his shoulders, dimly lit and evil-smelling. He had no way of knowing how far it descended – whether thirty feet or a hundred – but it was a long way to fall, in any case. And the ladder was slick, slimy to his hands, greasy to his feet. Twice he slipped. Twice he hung on.

And then he was on the ground, listening to his heart race as he stood at the end of a low, dank tunnel that reminded him – ludicrously – of an old horror movie. *The Thing.* Where the bad guy turns out to be a carrot.

Pay attention, he told himself. You don't want to get killed in here. You don't even want to get lost in here.

Slowly, he began to move forward. And then, as his eyes adjusted to the twilight around him, his pace quickened, a rush of urgency overtaking his fear. He had to get Solange before Solange got to the plant.

Fortunately, he didn't have to decide which way to go. The tunnel was a straight shot. There were a handful of galleries on either side, but he quickly saw that each was a dead end – so there were no decisions to make.

He was jogging now, slapping through pools of water, fearful that he was already too late. But it was noisy going, and it occurred to him that if Solange heard him, he'd be dead.

And, for a moment, he thought he was. A burst of submachine-gun fire exploded through the tunnel, obliterating the watery drip that was all around him. He froze, waiting for the pain to hit, then realized he wasn't hurt. Either Solange had missed, or he was firing at something else.

Frank squinted into the darkness. He could hear Solange, and a few steps farther on, he could see him. His back was to Frank as he yanked at the iron door to the generating plant, whose lock he'd just riddled. The Ingram was on the floor beside him, leaning against Solange's backpack, and Frank could hear him, swearing in French as he jerked at the door.

There wasn't time to think. All Solange had to do was get to the boiler feed pump, and that would be the end of it. However many guards there might be outside the plant, there wouldn't be more than one or two workers inside. That was all it took to keep a generating plant running for a single shift.

Which meant there wasn't anything to decide. It was a straight shot, for him *and* for Solange. So he took off, running on his toes, wishing he had the 4.8 speed he'd had in high school, but knowing that he didn't. There were twenty yards between them when Solange heard his footsteps and, turning, saw Frank bearing down on him like someone who should have had *Peterbilt* written on his forehead.

It's too far, Frank thought. I'm too late.

Solange lunged for the Ingram, and came up fast, fingers splayed on the barrel. It only took a second, *less than a second,* to shift the gun from one hand to the other, fumble for the trigger, raise the barrel, fire –

There was a flash of pain, and two loud pops as Frank slammed into him. The gun jumped out of Solange's hands and the air burst from his mouth as he backpedaled into the wall, the back of his head thudding against the concrete. Frank stepped back, then rolled forward with a looping overhead right that swept a row of teeth out of Solange's mouth.

Then he hit him again, and again, until, tiring of

that, he drove his forehead into the bridge of Solange's nose.

The guru was out on his feet when Frank drove a forearm into the red pulp at the center of his face, sending a spray of blood flying through the air. Then he spun him around and, taking him by the hair, slammed Solange's face into the edge of the door. Once, twice, again. Solange staggered away, as if he were looking for somewhere to fall. Frank helped him, driving the edge of his hand as hard as he could into the knob at the back of Solange's neck. There was a crack like a popsicle stick snapping, and Solange sprawled.

Frank could hear the police now. They were running down the tunnel. And a couple of steamfitters were standing in the doorway, gaping. Frank took a step back, looking for a bit of room so he could put his foot through Solange's chest – when he realized that something was wrong. He was weaker than he should have been and, for some reason, he couldn't seem to get his breath. And his chest was wet. *Soaking* wet. He looked down.

Jesus Christ, he thought. *I'm dying . . .*

EPILOGUE

And, in fact, he almost bled to death.

He'd been shot twice in the chest, and one of the bullets had tumbled, tearing through a tangle of blood vessels and soft tissues to lodge about a quarter of an inch from his spine. For nearly a week, then, he'd lain in the intensive care unit at Columbia Presbyterian Hospital, breathing bottled oxygen and taking nourishment through a tube. After two operations, a doctor had finally pronounced him on the mend, and ordered him moved to a private room on the VIP ward.

Which was good and bad. Good, because the room was large, bright, and well-appointed, with a couch and sitting area next to a broad expanse of windows. Which would be perfect for Annie, if he was ever allowed visitors. But it was bad, too, because the room didn't have a telephone. And it was strange, because he knew his insurance would never pay for a room like this – never in a million years – and knew that the hospital knew. Also, and not incidentally, he wasn't a Very Important Person – except, perhaps, to Annie.

And yet . . . here he was.

He asked his doctor what was going on, but all the doctor would say is, 'Don't worry about it. Call it an upgrade.'

'Okay,' Frank replied, 'but do I get a phone with my upgrade?'

411

This made the surgeon hesitate, 'Well,' he said, 'not just yet.'

'And visitors?'

'Of course. Very soon. When you're stronger.'

This was fine with him, at first, because he was so zonked out on painkillers he didn't know where he was half the time. But after four or five days he began to realize that something was wrong, or if not wrong, *up*. And he would probably have tried a wheelchair escape if the doctor hadn't opened the door one morning and said, 'There's someone here to see you.'

Frank smiled and, still tender from the stitches in his chest, pushed himself up against the pillows. But his smile faded when he saw that it wasn't Annie who'd come to see him. It was an Air Force colonel named Fitch. 'Taylor Fitch,' he said, extending his hand.

'Hi,' Frank replied, suddenly wary. They shook hands, and Frank asked, 'What's up?'

'Well,' the colonel said, taking a piece of paper from his attaché case, 'before we have our little talk, I was hoping you'd sign this. It's just a technicality.' He handed the paper to Frank and, with a hopeful look, took a pen from his pocket.

Frank glanced at the page. It was a 'nondisclosure' agreement. 'Not for me,' he said. 'Thanks,' and handed it back.

The colonel returned the agreement to his attaché case. Then he sighed, but not heavily. 'It doesn't matter.'

Frank shrugged. 'I'm a journalist. I get paid to write. And it's a good story.'

Fitch nodded. 'Hey – it's a helluva story. No question.' Then he frowned. 'But you can't publish it.'

Frank squinted at him. 'Do I *know* you?' he asked.

Fitch shook his head. 'No.'

412

'But I've seen your name.'

It was the colonel's turn to feel uncomfortable. 'Maybe,' he suggested. 'I'm pretty active in Scouting.'

Frank shook his head. 'I don't think that was it.'

'Well,' Fitch said, signaling a change in subject. 'That's neither here nor there. I –'

Frank turned his head toward the window, his brow furrowing. 'It was on a manifest,' he said.

'What was?'

'Your name.' He thought about it some more, and then it hit him. 'Now I remember! You flew back from Hammerfest with Annie and Gleason.'

'Who?' Fitch asked.

'Neal Gleason.'

'I don't think I know him,' he said.

'Yeah, right,' Frank replied, suppressing the little laugh that threatened to move through his chest like a razor blade. 'I don't think any of us really *knows* Mr. Gleason. I don't think any of us really *wants* to. But that's who your seatmate was.' He paused and cocked an eye at his visitor. 'I was gonna look you up, but – I got busy. Is that *really* your uniform, or is it just a costume?'

Fitch grinned. 'I'm in a Reserve unit.'

Frank looked away again. 'CIA, huh?'

Fitch shrugged. 'Let me show you something,' he said, removing a kind of plain-paper newsletter from his attaché case. He handed it to Frank. 'I turned the page down,' he said.

Frank looked at the cover: *The Federal Register*. He opened it to page thirteen. 'You want me to read this?' he asked.

'Just so you get the drift,' Fitch replied.

Under the heading 'Declaration of National Emergency' was a letter to Congress from the

President of the United States.

> **Because the actions and policies of the Government of the Democratic People's Republic of Korea (DPRK) continue to threaten the national security, foreign policy, and economy of the United States, a national emergency is declared, pursuant to the National Emergencies Act {50 U.S.C. 1622(d)} . . .**

Frank looked up at his visitor. 'So?'

'I'm trying to save you a lot of trouble.'

'How's that?'

'Well, before I get into that, I want you to understand that everyone's very grateful for what you did. I *mean* that.'

'Thanks.'

'But the other thing you need to understand is that a declaration of this kind gives the President, and by extension, me, some extraordinary powers.

'Such as what?'

'Well, basically, it lets us do pretty much what we want to do. Where matters relative to North Korea are concerned, the Constitution is pretty much suspended. If the need arose – and we'd be the ones to decide that – we could seize property and commodities, send troops abroad, institute martial law. The whole doctrine of habeas corpus goes out the window, which means we can hold anyone we want for as long as we want – without charging them with a crime.' He paused, and looked around. 'You like your room?'

'Yeah,' Frank said. 'It's nice.'

Fitch smiled. 'Good. I'm glad you like it. But that's not all. If we have to, we can restrict travel, too, and if necessary, we can impose censorship.'

'Who's "we"?'

'The federal government.'

Frank looked skeptical.

'I know what you're thinkin', but you can look it up. The Constitution provides for national emergencies – and it defers to them. Article Nine, section one. You want me to write that down?'

'No,' Frank said. 'I don't think that's gonna be necessary.'

'The funny thing is, we got half a dozen of them going at any given time. Iran, Iraq, Angola, Libya – you name it, its an emergency. Hell, Roosevelt declared a national emergency that lasted forty-three years – no kiddin'! From 'thirty-three to 'seventy-six. So no one really pays much attention to it unless – like you – some poor sonofabitch gets his tit in a ringer. And then he's got problems.' Fitch paused, and sighed. 'How you feeling?'

'I'm okay,' Frank said.

Fitch nodded. 'Good. Anyway,' he concluded, 'it's the same everywhere. Every country's got a provison for this kind of thing. In France they call it a "state of siege." In England –'

'What's your point?'

'Just this: if you try to sell this story, it's gonna cause you a lot of trouble. No one's gonna believe it, and even if they do, they aren't going to publish it. I guarantee it.'

Frank looked at him. 'Are you, like, an editor at *Writer's Digest*, or something? I mean –'

Fitch chuckled. 'That's funny,' he said. And then the smile disappeared. 'Look, I know what you're thinking. You're thinking we can't stop you –'

'Uh-oh,' Frank interjected. 'Is this where you tell me you're gonna kill me?'

415

Fitch looked shocked. 'Of course not! You're an American citizen.'

'Then, what?'

'This is where I tell you that you can't prove it.'

'Bullshit,' Frank said. 'People got killed. They were killed on the ferry –'

Fitch shook his head. 'Some nuts tried to hijack the ferry. So what?'

'I was *shot*. Solange –'

'Was in custody when you were shot.'

Frank stared at him.

'It happens all the time' Fitch said. 'You were in Harlem, for chris423

sake.' With a smile, he removed a newspaper clipping from his attaché' case. 'This is a week old,' he said, 'but I thought you'd want to see it . . .'

POST REPORTER, DALY, WOUNDED IN NEW YORK

May 23 (New York) – Washington *Post* reporter Frank Daly was shot in East Harlem last night, the victim of an apparent robbery.

A national-desk reporter on leave of absence from the *Post,* Daly is in critical condition at Columbia Presbyterian Hospital. A police departmeun spokesperson said there are no suspects in the robbery.

Frank looked up from the clip. 'Amazing,' he said.

Fitch smiled sheepishly. 'We're pretty good, when you get down to it.' Then he got serious again. 'The problem, Frank – from our point of view – is that North Korea is a psychopathic state. It's like Hannibal Lecter on bok choy. And it sits there, desperate, with the wind at its back, and nothing to lose. If they should ever decide to take out Japan with anthrax or smallpox, they could do it in a heartbeat – using weather balloons, or just the people they have on the ground in Tokyo. Plus we've got a couple of battalions of our own standing in harm's way, just below the DMZ. So the point is: we don't want to set them off, understood?'

'I hear you,' Frank said.

'And from *your* point of view, the situation isn't much better. You don't have a sample of the virus, or anything like it. And you don't have any witnesses, either. So if you start running around, talking about dead Norwegians and the Spanish flu, you won't get anywhere – unless we decide to *put* you somewhere. Which, of course, we can do.'

'There's Annie,' Frank said.

'What about her?'

'She's a witness.'

Fitch slapped himself on the side of the head. 'Oh, that's right,' he said. 'She saw everything, didn't she? So I guess you could put the story on the Internet, or publish it abroad – and you *would* have a witness. I hadn't thought of that! Except . . . oh, now I remember: she signed a Secrecy agreement! So I guess *that* won't work.' He sat down on the side of the bed. 'Because, I'll tell you something: you put her in a story, and I know for a fact Neal Gleason will send her *away*. Through space *and* time.'

Speak of the devil. Annie was admitted about thirty seconds after Fitch left. And she was angry.

'I've been waiting for days out there,' she complained, 'and this *general* comes in –'

'He's not a general. He's a colonel.'

'I don't think he's even a colonel. When I met him, he was a CIA agent.'

'I know. He was on the plane from Hammerfest.'

She kissed him softly on the lips and sat down at his side.

That evening, a telephone was installed in the room, and Annie brought him a newspaper from the gift shop.

JAILED CULTISTS IN EXTRADITION FIGHT

June 7 (Havana) – Two weeks after arriving in Cuba, eight Amencan cultists are fighting extradition on kidnapping and murder charges stemming from the bizarre hijacking of the Staten Island ferry last month.

In an interview with Agence France Press, a spokesperson for the jailed Temple of Light members, Belinda Barron, said she and her group fled to Cuba to escape 'religious persecution.'

'What happened aboard the ferry,' Barron told reporters, 'was the fault of the police and the FBI. They overreacted. What we were doing was 'guerrilla theater,' pure and simple. It was a nonviolent demonstration against water pollution – and the cops turned it into a bloodbath . . .'

In the weeks that followed, Frank spent hours each morning in therapy for what the doctors said was a bruised spine. The rest of the time he spent reading the newspapers, looking for traces of the story.

US, NORTH KOREA SIGN WEAPONS PACT
Inspections Tied to Food Aid

July 2 (Pyongyang) – After more than a month of meetings with North Korean leaders, United Nations officials announced today that an agreement has been reached, tying humanitarian aid to weapons' inspections in this impoverished country.

George Karalekis, American head of the first U.N.

inspection team to arrive in the North Korean capital, said that his unit would begin immediately to look for biological weapons labs in the Diamond Mountains.

'We've had some unconfirmed reports that the North Koreans may be looking at these kinds of weapons,' Karalekis told reporters. 'Naturally, it's something we're concerned about . . .'

A second story came out the day Frank went home. It was on page three of the *Times*, under a photograph of the young woman who'd driven the U-Haul off the ferry:

THREE CULTISTS, PRIVATE EYE
CHARGED IN COUPLE'S DEATHS

July 20 (Albany) – Three Cultists and a Poughkeepsie-based private investigator listened impassively this afternoon as prosecutors told a gruesome tale of murder and mutilation.

An emotional Susannah Demjanuk, 23, told the court that she and the others were 'acting on orders' when they dismembered Rhinebeck residents Harold and Martha Bergman earlier this year.

'Luc told us what to do,' Demjanuk testified, 'and we did it.' Asked to identify 'Luc,' she pointed tearfully to Temple of Light guru Luc Solange and said, 'That's him at the defendant's table. The one with the neck brace and body cast.'

The defendants' attorneys dismissed Demjanuk's testimony as 'the ravings of a mentally unstable woman who has no right to throw the first stone.'

The reference was apparently to Demjanuk's recent plea in the microwave murder of Georgetown University student Benjamin Stern, 28. A critic of the Temple, Stern wrote about the organization in a self-published news-

419

letter, *Armageddon Watch*. He disappeared in April.

In her testimony this afternoon, Demjanuk told the court that the Bergmans were taken from their home in Rhinebeck, N.Y., and killed in the back of a U-Haul van. At the time of their deaths, the couple was seeking a court order for the disinterment of their son, Leonard, who drowned at sea while a member of the Temple of Light.

In addition to Solange, the accused include Martin Kramer, 44, of Poughkeepsie; Thomas Reckmeyer, 26; and Vaughn Abelard, 25. A fourth cultist indicted in the case, Étienne 'the Frenchman' Moussin, 29, is believed to be in Cuba. All except Kramer are from the Lake Placid area.

There were no other stories that month, unless you counted the one in the *Post*:

DALY, ADAIR SET TO WED

By then he'd already written two hundred pages of the book.

'What's it about?' Annie asked over his shoulder as he typed.

'I told you,' he said, looking up at her. 'It's a novel. A thriller.'

'But what's it about?'

'Well,' he said, 'it's about . . . this journalist . . .' He paused for a moment to type a few words, then turned back to her. 'This *ruthlessly handsome* journalist . . .'

'Yeah?' She looked skeptical.

'And a girl.'

'And what's she like?'

'She's tall.'

'Just "tall"?!'

'No. She's also . . . brilliant . . . and ravishing. Very ravishing.'

'And what happens?'

'Well,' he said, 'there's this icebreaker.'

She gave him a suspicious look. 'Yeah?'

'And she's on it, because – well, because she's a scientist. And he's stuck in this cheap hotel, somewhere in Russia . . .'

THE GENESIS CODE

John Case

'Superb . . . I felt propelled by the incredible pacing, the lure of the scientific secret at its core, and Case's sheer storytelling power. The pages of this terrific thriller practically turn themselves.' John Saul

ITALY: a dying doctor makes a chilling confession to the priest in a remote hillside village.

WASHINGTON, D.C.: A mother and her young son are savagely murdered. Their house is then burned down.

JOE LASSITER, the woman's brother, discovers a chain of similar killings around the world.

What is the link? Who are the shadowy, merciless killers? And what is the Genesis Code, the secret so unthinkable that powerful men will do anything to make sure it remains in the grave?

'*The Genesis Code* rattles you to the bone . . . I woke up at three in the morning wondering: What if . . . ?' Stanley Pottinger, author of *The Fourth Procedure*

Other Bestselling Titles Available

☐ The Genesis Code	John Case	£5.99
☐ The Street Lawyer	John Grisham	£5.99
☐ The Pelican Brief	John Grisham	£5.99
☐ The Chamber	John Grisham	£6.99
☐ The Firm	John Grisham	£6.99
☐ Nimitz Class	Patrick Robinson	£5.99
☐ Kilo Class	Patrick Robinson	£5.99
☐ Java Spider	Geoffrey Archer	£5.99
☐ Scorpion Trail	Geoffrey Archer	£5.99
☐ Fire Hawk	Geoffrey Archer	£5.99

ALL ARROW BOOKS ARE AVAILABLE THROUGH MAIL ORDER OR FROM YOUR LOCAL BOOKSHOP AND NEWSAGENT.
PLEASE SEND CHEQUE, EUROCHEQUE, POSTAL ORDER (STERLING ONLY), ACCESS, VISA, MASTERCARD, DINERS CARD, SWITCH OR AMEX.

☐☐☐☐☐☐☐☐☐☐☐☐☐☐☐☐☐☐☐

EXPIRY DATE .... SIGNATURE ....
PLEASE ALLOW 75 PENCE PER BOOK FOR POST AND PACKING U.K.

OVERSEAS CUSTOMERS PLEASE ALLOW £1.00 PER COPY FOR POST AND PACKING.

ALL ORDERS TO:

ARROW BOOKS, BOOKS BY POST, TBS LIMITED, THE BOOK SERVICE, COLCHESTER ROAD, FRATING GREEN, COLCHESTER, ESSEX CO7 7 DW.

TELEPHONE: (01206) 256000
FAX: (01206) 255914

NAME ....

ADDRESS..

....

Please allow 28 days for delivery. Please tick box if you do not wish to receive any additional information
Prices and availability subject to change without notice.